T

Virginia wasted no time ~~~~~~~~

'I have spoken to your brother about you, Miss Martins, and to my husband. You are older than most nursery-maids, but that may be an advantage. Some of them are *so* irresponsible. I don't see why you shouldn't be suitable. Nanny Webster, as you have probably gathered, has a very sharp tongue and is a keen disciplinarian, but you would be working under her and her word is law.'

Grace, remembering Fanny's advice, searched for a way to answer which would sound neither scared nor smart.

'I'd do my very best,' was the rather unsatisfactory result.

'I certainly hope so. Nanny Webster has been with us ever since George was born and she came with the highest recommendations.' Virgina hesitated. 'So far we have not found a nursery-maid who could work with her, but they were all so young. I think that a more mature person might be able to cope.'

'To *survive*,' amended Grace silently.

PAMELA OLDFIELD

Turn of the Tide

WARNER BOOKS

A *Warner* Book

First published in Great Britain in 1988 by Century
This edition published in 1994 by Warner Books
Reprinted 1998

Copyright © 1988 by Pamela Oldfield

The moral right of the author has been asserted.

A CIP catalogue record for this book is
available from the British Library.

ISBN 0 7515 0868 3

Printed in England by Clays Ltd, St Ives plc

Warner Books
A Division of
Little, Brown and Company (UK)
Brettenham House
Lancaster Place
London WC2E 7EN

For my sister Barbara, with love

Chapter One

While a nation mourned the passing of its beloved monarch, Grace Martins fell in love. She fell in love without knowing how or why and afterwards when she tried to understand what had happened, she could only remember that Alexander Latimer was fair and gentle, that he spoke quietly, almost hesitantly, and that his lips were only occasionally surprised into a smile. He was not particularly tall, perhaps about five foot ten, nor particularly handsome, although his face was pleasant enough. His eyes were grey. She remembered his eyes. While, in London, a grieving people filed slowly past the body of King Edward VII, Grace was miles away in the stables of Berwick House where her brother John was head groom. The house stood about a mile from Beaulieu with the New Forest to west, north and south and Beaulieu Heath to the east. The river flowed past the house and beyond that the land stretched away towards Southampton Water and the town itself. Grace was talking to John when suddenly his expression changed and he muttered, 'Oh Lord, Grace, here comes the guv'nor. Just you watch your tongue.' Then in quite a different voice he said, 'Good evening, Mr Latimer, sir.'

'Good evening, Martins.'

'I hope you don't mind, sir. This is my sister, Grace.'

Cool grey eyes inspected Grace courteously as their owner gave her a slight nod. 'Good evening, Miss Martins.'

'Good evening, sir.'

She was surprised that her voice sounded so normal for her heart was racing.

'I didn't know you had a sister, Martins.'

'Oh yes, sir.'

Grace thought her brother's tone a fraction too affable.

'Did have two sisters,' John went on, 'but one died a

7

few years back. Grace here lives at Lyndhurst. She's just walked over to see me; it's her day off.' He gave her a quick look which was meant to convey a warning that she should say as little as possible. That way he thought she was less likely to speak out of turn. He had no illusions where Grace was concerned and had always considered her name most inappropriate. As a small girl she had been a source of great embarrassment to him and he found it hard to believe that she had grown out of her wilful ways.

Alex Latimer smiled at Grace. 'That's a very long walk.'

'I don't mind it, sir. It didn't rain but – ', she held up a large umbrella, 'I brought this just in case and I reckon that's what kept the rain away. If I hadn't had it, we would most likely have had a downpour. The way I see it – '

John coughed warningly and she stopped and coloured faintly.

Alex said, 'Such a long walk must have given you an appetite, Miss Martins. Have you had anything to eat?'

'Yes, thank you, sir,' said Grace. 'Cook gave me a bit of – ' She broke off again and looked guiltily at John.

'I hope you didn't mind, sir,' said John, cursing her indiscretion, 'but Cook said she could have a bite of something.'

'Of course I don't mind. We can't have your sister fainting away for lack of nourishment.' He looked at Grace. 'Do you get enough to eat? You don't look very robust.'

Grace said, 'Oh yes I do, sir. I'm just not made to be plump. I never have been, have I?' She appealed again to her brother.

'Never,' John agreed. 'Skinny as a rake when she was little; legs like twigs.'

Alex looked at her curiously for a moment, then he asked, 'What do you do, Miss Martins?'

'I'm a companion, sir, to a Miss Ivy Cummings. I've been there nearly a year and before that I was nursing my mother up to her death. Miss Cummings has been up to London these last two days to see poor King Edward that was, so I had a bit of spare time and decided to come – '

The head of a horse appeared over the stable door behind them and she broke off in alarm.

John took the chance to steer the conversation away from his sister. 'Caradox heard you, sir. He's sharp, that horse; he recognized your voice. He knows you'll most likely have some sugar-lumps.'

Grace edged away from the horse but Alexander, seeing her nervousness, said, 'Caradox won't hurt you, Miss Martins. His looks are deceptive but he's a very gentle giant. Here, you feed him.' He pulled three lumps of sugar from his pocket and dropped them into Grace's hand. 'Keep your fingers quite flat and then he won't nip you.'

Grace longed to refuse and would most certainly have done so had John suggested it, but his employer's grey eyes were on her and reluctantly, she held out her hand, fingers flat as she had been told. As the horse's velvety muzzle brushed her palm she shivered slightly but then watched in fascination as the sugar disappeared noisily behind the animal's large teeth.

'And you like it, Miss Martins?' Alex asked.

'The horse, d'you mean?'

He smiled. 'No, the work you do. Do you like being a companion? Are you happy?'

Grace opened her lips to say 'No', but the sudden pressure of John's boot against her ankle caused her to say instead, 'Oh yes, sir. I'm very happy.'

'That's good.'

His eyes were still on hers and she felt sure he had read the lie. Later, she promised herself, she would recall his every word and look.

Alexander laid his hand affectionately on the horse's smooth brown neck.

'Don't you like horses?' he asked her.

'They do scare me a bit, sir,' she confessed, but then, sensing his disappointment, went on hurriedly, 'They're so big, but I'm sure I *could* like them if I got used to them. I rather like the way they smell, sort of warm and musky.' To her surprise he laughed with obvious delight at this comment and, encouraged, she continued, ignoring John's expression.

'Miss Cummings had a pony and trap when I first went there, but when the pony died she wouldn't get another. Course she's getting on a bit.' John coughed again, but Grace was just getting into her stride. 'She's well over seventy and she didn't like the groom. At least, she says she didn't trust him.' She lowered her voice a little. 'She thought he was cheating on the feed bills. Now her married sister, Florrie, takes her into Southampton if she wants to shop. Florrie lives in the village too. It's Florrie who has taken her up to London, but they went on the – ouch!'

Grace bent to rub her ankle, cursing her runaway tongue. She had talked too much and now John was annoyed with her. Glancing up at Alex, with relief she saw only amusement in his eyes. She knew that she would enjoy the long walk back to Lyndhurst because she would think about John's 'guv'nor'.

Alex smiled suddenly. 'No one would take you for brother and sister,' he said.

'No, sir,' said John quickly before she could start again. 'We're chalk and cheese, me and Grace. That's what they used to say when we were younger. I'm a Martins, a real chip off the old block. Grace here's a throw-back!' The remark was meant as a joke and Grace smiled obligingly.

'And what will you do, Miss Martins, when your employer is no longer alive?' Alex asked as though he really wanted to know, and Grace was touched.

'Well, sir, I – '

'She might be getting wed, sir,' John put in. 'She's promised to – ' Grace hissed furiously, 'I am *not!*' but he went on as though she had not spoken. 'A certain Mr Harris has shown an interest, sir – a strong interest – and I have advised her to consider it very seriously.'

Pompous idiot, thought Grace and bit back an angry retort. It would never do to squabble with John in front of his employer.

'Aren't you willing then, Miss Martins?'

Aware of John's eyes, Grace picked her words carefully. 'It's Miss Cummings' nephew, sir,' she explained. 'I am *not* promised; he's hinted once or twice, that's all. I haven't given him any encouragement although he swears I have, because I don't think I could marry him.' She drew her brows together earnestly. 'I just don't think I could love him, that's the trouble.'

'But love isn't everything, is it, sir?' John appealed to his employer. 'I have told Grace that love and romance are luxuries. A good husband and a secure home are not to be turned down lightly. At least give it some proper thought, I told her.'

Mr Latimer raised his shoulders in a slight shrug.

'Love should never be underestimated,' he said, looking at Grace. 'Have you known the young man long?'

'Ever since I went to work for Miss Cummings.'

'Is he an honest man?'

'I think so, sir.'

'And kind?'

Grace nodded reluctantly. 'But he's not the sort of man I really *admire*,' she told him. 'He will make somebody a very good husband, I'm sure, but I don't think he's for me. Least, I hope not.'

'Beggars can't be choosers,' cried John, mortified by her rebellious attitude. Goodness knows what the guv'nor thought of her – he shuddered to think. 'When Miss Cummings goes, she'll have nothing.'

'I'll manage,' said Grace. 'I'll find another job.'

There was an awkward silence, broken by the whinnying of another horse further along. At once John forgot about Grace and became the head groom again.

'That's Firefly, sir,' he began. 'I'm not happy about him at all and I would like to call Smithers in again. He's not eating and the sweats persist.' For a moment Mr Latimer did not answer, for his eyes were still on Grace's flushed face. Then he smiled at her politely, said, 'Please excuse us, Miss Martins,' and turned his attention to the matter of the ailing horse.

Grace was left alone as the two men moved off towards

Firefly. She bit her lip, annoyed with herself for allowing John to goad her into such unseemly behaviour, and wished she had never confided in him about Alfred's unwelcome attentions. Digging the point of her umbrella into a crack in the tiled courtyard, she twirled it aimlessly and thought about Alfred. He was nice enough, but in her eyes he was a bit of a wet fish with a rather mournful expression and large hands. Poor Alfred! She tried to imagine sharing a bed with him and could not resist a smile. The prospect was impossible. Beside her Caradox tossed his head, rolled large brown eyes at her and blew softly through his nostrils. Timidly she put up a hand to stroke him.

'Alfred Harris won't really do for me,' she told him. 'I just couldn't bear it. I could never love him.' He seemed to nod in agreement and she grinned suddenly. 'I knew you'd understand,' she told him. 'What was it Mr Latimer called you – a gentle giant? You're certainly a beautiful animal. No, I've no more sugar, I'm afraid, but if ever I come again I promise I'll bring you some.'

What was it Mr Latimer had said – love should never be underestimated? A rather odd comment, she thought, and wondered what had prompted it. Presumably he was married. She sighed heavily. Earlier, she had seen a small pony, so there must be a child or children in the family. How wonderful to have such a man as a father, she thought, and there must be a wife, too. She felt a flash of envy at the thought of the woman who shared his life.

Five minutes later John came back alone and she plied him with questions. From his answers she learned that Mr Latimer's name was Alexander and he was the elder of two sons of Guy Latimer who owned Berwick House. Alexander was married to Virginia and they had two children – George aged six, the owner of the pony, and Victoria who was only four.

'Is Virginia nice?' Grace asked, dreading the answer. John shrugged as he peered into an empty stall and shouted irritably for the stable lad.

'Well, she's a bit older than him,' he said. 'She was a widow when they married. She's a real looker if you like

12

that type, but I don't have much to do with her. Now hadn't you better get a move on? You won't get home before dark if you don't go soon.' He shouted again for the stable lad and a young boy ran up breathlessly from the paddock at the end of the yard. But Grace persisted in spite of John's waning interest.

'Are they happy, do you think?' she asked.

'God knows,' said John. 'I suppose they are; they say he adores her. Now do get along, Grace, I have got work to do.'

'You want to get rid of me,' she grinned and he gave her a half-hearted peck on the cheek. 'Maybe I do,' he agreed. 'Thanks for walking over. Mind how you go.'

'I will.'

As she left and set off in the direction of Brockenhurst, she heard him scold Ben the stable-boy for sloppy work. As she walked she thought about the man she had met. It began to rain before she was half-way home, but a friendly farmer gave her a lift for the last two miles and she arrived at Salter's Cottage bedraggled but in good spirits. The house was built of grey stone, surrounded by a small garden which was laid out symmetrically with standard roses, square lawn and brick paths. It was situated at the upper end of the town where the Bournemouth Road passed the top of Shrubs Hill. Ivy Cummings had been born in the house and had never lived anywhere else for her two sisters had married, leaving her to nurse her elderly parents until they died. It was Ivy's boast that Lyndhurst possessed all that she needed and she had never had the slightest desire to live anywhere else. Salter's Cottage suited her, too, having a garden that was easily maintained with minimal help from a jobbing gardener and only one flight of stairs.

Grace let herself in at the front door and was pleased to find that the cook had not returned from her day out. It was a rare treat to have the house to herself and she went straight to the kitchen, cut three slices of bread and spread them with butter and jam. 'Alexander,' she said aloud, for the pleasure of hearing his name. 'I shall call you Alex. Alex Latimer, I love you!'

13

The ancient tabby cat heaved himself out of his basket by the back door and mewed hopefully. Grace filled a saucer with milk for him. 'Alex,' she said again, 'you have nice eyes and you seem to care about people. I hope Virginia appreciates you.'

As she devoured the bread and jam she recalled with pleasure the cold ham and pickles she had eaten in the bustling kitchen at Berwick House. Abruptly, she got up and crossed to the mirror which hung behind the door. Intent grey eyes stared back at her from the mirror; the mouth was full, the skin pale and clear except for a sprinkling of freckles which were the bane of her life. Brown, fly-away hair framed a square-shaped face and Grace regarded it critically. In her opinion her jaw was too heavy and she pursed her lips in disapproval. She had always longed for fair hair, blue eyes and a heart-shaped face – that was her ideal. She wondered what Virginia looked like. No doubt a ravishing beauty, she thought, if Alexander adored her. In her limited experience rich women were usually beautiful and frequently adored, even worshipped.

'And you, Grace, are supposed to marry Alfred Harris,' she told herself. 'Well, I shan't! No, I shall never love and obey Alfred Harris. Not now I have met Alex.'

She pushed the last mouthful of bread and jam into her mouth and had just swallowed it when she heard the front door open and guessed that 'Cookie' had also returned. The staff of Salter's Cottage consisted of Grace, Cookie and a daily girl who did the heavy scrubbing. Only Grace lived in.

'Is that you, Grace?' called Cookie.

'Yes, it's me. Who else would it be?'

Cookie waddled into the kitchen, expertly balancing her huge body on feet that looked as though they belonged to another, much smaller person. She collapsed panting into a chair.

'Had a good day?' Grace asked her.

Cookie nodded and said, 'You look very cheerful.'

Grace hesitated. She wanted to shout out to the whole world that she had met Alexander Latimer and fallen in

14

love with him, but since the man in question was already married and to a woman whom he adored, there really did not seem much point in mentioning it. She nodded and said only, 'I walked to Beaulieu to see John.'

That night she took out from beneath her mattress the small notebook which served her as a diary and to which she confided her most private thoughts, hopes and fears. On the blue cover she had written ACCOUNTS and this word was to deceive Ivy Cummings who, Grace was convinced, occasionally entered the room in order to satisfy her curiosity about any private life her young companion might manage. Inside the cover of the book Grace had written, 'This does NOT concern you,' and had boxed in the words in red. She doubted if this would deter Ivy from reading on, but at least she hoped it would prick at her conscience.

Now she waited, pencil poised, in a fever to record the world-shattering event – her meeting with Alexander Latimer – but for a while no suitable phrases presented themselves. 'I met Alex Latimer' simply would not do. It was not the meeting so much as the effect the encounter had had on her heart. On her whole life, in fact. For now she knew she could never marry Alfred. With a deep sigh she turned the page to read the last entry.

The King is dead. It was very sudden. His body is going to lie in state in Westminster Hall in London and Ivy and Florrie are going to London to see it. Why do people want to look at a dead body? I think I shall walk over to Beaulieu to see John. Last time the cook gave me a huge slice of mutton pie. I live in hopes . . .

She smiled. A slice of mutton pie! That was all she had expected. Instead she had met Alex.

Carefully she wrote, '10th May 1910' and underlined it. After a little more thought she began to write in earnest: 'Today I met the man I shall love to the end of my days . . .'

*

Alex stood looking down at the frail old man in the

makeshift bed. His eyes were closed, his breathing stertorous and his lips moved from time to time but soundlessly. Annie, large and angular, shook her head
despairingly.

'He does that,' she told her employer. 'He's trying to
say summat, but Lord knows what. Sometimes I make
out I hear him. "Yes," I say to him, "that's right, dearie,"
but he doesn't hear. Leastways, I don't reckon so. But
just in case, you see, sir. If he's trying to tell me summat,
I want him to think I know what it is even if I don't. Set
his mind at ease, if you see what I mean.'

'I do see,' said Alex. 'I'm sure it's for the best.'

She nodded. 'I always thought I'd go first. Funny, isn't
it. I worried about what he'd do without me. Now it'll
be me without him.'

In the protracted silence Alex glanced round the small
room. Charlie had been brought down to the kitchen and
laid on a low trestle with an assortment of blankets and
a well-patched pillow. The room was sparsely furnished
and reasonably tidy, but there were dead flowers in a
brown pitcher on the window sill dropping their curling
petals on to the fading paintwork.

'Will you take a cup of tea, sir?'

He accepted gratefully. Any excuse to turn away from
the pathetic figure on the bed, he thought guiltily, as the
old woman busied herself with hot water and tea-caddy.
Shortly they were sitting either side of the kitchen range
which glowed comfortingly below the newly-filled kettle.

'Course they never wanted me to marry him,' Annie
confided, her faded eyes large above the cup of tea she
held in both hands. She sipped noisily, blew across the
surface of the tea and sipped again. 'No, they were dead
against it, all of them. Cast me out like a leper, but I
expected it. He's a gorgio, you see, not a Romany. My
folks wanted me to marry decently. Least, that's how
they put it to me, but I was so stuck on Charlie I wouldn't
listen. Charlie Abrahams. I used to whisper his name like
a chant, over and over. I knew I was heading for trouble
but I would have him, you see, sir. Headstrong, that was
me. Seventeen and thought I knew it all.'

'And they cast you out?' Alex repeated. 'Just because – '

'Because I married a gorgio.' She nodded and cackled suddenly at the memory. 'Sod 'em! That's what Charlie said when I told him. "Sod the lot of 'em!" ' Her laughter trailed off and became a sigh. 'Course, I did miss it all and I can't pretend I didn't. It's not a life you can give up easy. Oh dear me no! I've gipsy blood in me veins and I wanted to wander. It was very hard at first. This cottage seemed like a prison at times – no disrespect, sir!' she added quickly, afraid of offending him.

'None taken,' Alex smiled reassuringly.

'It was just that I'd been brought up to wander. Always on the move – except when we was at places like Norley Wood. That's how I come to meet Charlie. He was collecting wood to sell for firewood. We stayed there for months at a time, Norley Wood. Winter time mostly. Summer time we were off – up north for the big horse fairs and east to Kent for the hops. Always moving on, we was, but it's a way of life and you don't think anything of it. You pity the gorgios, stuck in one place all the time – begging your pardon, Mr Latimer – but we did. We pitied them. We despised them in a way, I suppose, because our life was tougher.'

'So you were the first in your family to marry out of your tribe?'

'As far as I know. See, they never kept in touch after. I made my bed and I had to lie on it. Brought shame on them, I had, so they had to disown me.' She shook her head again. 'We was a proud family, you see. We had our own vardi – that's a caravan to you, sir. Lovely, it was, with coloured pictures painted on the ceiling. I used to look up at them when I was young and think it was heaven. All white fluffy clouds and plump little people and flowers and such like. Oh, I loved that ceiling. I can see it now. And there was a window with curved glass and outside we always had a finch in a wicker cage. Real pretty little birds, finches.'

'What did your father do?' Alex asked.

To his surprise, she tossed her head. 'What did he do?'

she asked. 'What *didn't* he do, my father! That's more to the point. He could turn his hand to most things. A bit of tinkering – he'd mend a hole in a kettle in ten minutes flat. No one could better him. And he could sharpen knives. Course he made pegs, too; all the menfolk did, but he could make 'em faster than most. Oh yes, I was very proud of my father. I used to boast to the other kids. Broke my heart to leave him and that's the truth, but when you're seventeen and madly in love . . .' She shrugged. 'Head over heels I was, sir, with poor old Charlie. Course, he wasn't poor old Charlie then, he was young and handsome Charlie. Devil-may-care Charlie. He'd fight anyone – and did! He *had* to because my brothers, they tried to give him a hiding – to scare him off me – but he showed them a trick or two. He lost a tooth and got two black eyes, but he said it was worth it. He fought for me, Charlie did, and to me he was a hero.'

She looked up at Alex and her lips trembled. 'He may not look much of a hero now, but . . .' Choked, she stopped and sucked tea noisily into her mouth to hide her emotion.

Alex said, 'I've always admired him.'

Her eyes widened.

'I've always thought,' Alex invented, 'that he had a quality most men lack. Integrity, that's the word.'

She regarded him doubtfully. 'Integrity,' she repeated. 'Is that so?'

She did not understand the word, but recognized from her employer's tone of voice that it was complimentary.

'Integrity?' she said again.

He nodded.

'Yes,' she agreed. 'He had that all right, did Charlie.' They finished their tea in silence.

'There was glass knobs,' she said suddenly, her face breaking into a smile. 'Beautiful glass knobs. A sort of gold colour, they were. Oh, I loved them knobs. On the window shutters, they were, and on the door. I liked the feel of them in my hands. They was round with little flat bits all over them, if you know what I mean. Our vardi

18

was one of the best and my mother kept it spotless. She had a lamp too, that was coloured glass and so pretty. There was a sort of fringe all round the mantelpiece. Funny how you remember those things. Bobbles, they were. I cut one off once, to keep, and I hid it. Lordy! What a to-do that was. A right hiding I got for that. It really spoilt it, you see — one bobble missing right in the middle where it showed. Still, when you're young you do these funny things.'

As he nodded gently, Charlie moaned and they both turned towards him.

'He won't last long, sir,' Annie whispered. 'Will you stay with him to the end? He'd like to think you stayed and I . . . well, I'd be glad . . .'

Tears spilled suddenly down her pale cheeks and Alex moved instinctively to comfort her, putting an arm round her quivering shoulders.

'Of course I'll stay,' he told her. 'I'd be proud to.'

An hour passed as Annie rambled on and then Charlie moaned again. They moved to his bedside and waited while Annie held his hand and murmured words of encouragement. Alex stood silently beside her. Five minutes passed and Charlie suddenly opened his eyes.

'Annie!' he exclaimed.

'I'm here, Charlie.'

He smiled up at the ceiling then slowly turned his head towards her.

'Oh, Charlie,' she said tremulously.

He gave a deep sigh and for a moment Annie and Alex watched waiting and hoping for another breath. But it was all over and now it was Annie's turn to sigh.

'That's it, then,' she said. 'Will you close his eyes, sir?'

While he did so, the old women went to a cupboard and produced a new candle which she set in a brass candlestick. She lit it and placed it on the rickety cane table that stood beside the head of the bed.

'That will keep his ghost away,' she said. 'Now, if you'll keep watch over him for a minute or two I'll fetch old Mrs Bray to lay him out.'

'I could help you do that,' Alex suggested, but Annie drew her brows together.

'Oh no, sir, thank you kindly but we Romanies don't like to handle our dead. Not that Charlie was a Romany, but he's mine and — well — I'd rather Mrs Bray done it if truth be told. She's done it before for other folks and she knows what she's about. Proper reverent, too. No, thank you for the offer, Mr Latimer, but she'll do nicely for Charlie.'

Alex waited until Mrs Bray arrived and then left the cottage. He was sorry that the old man had gone but now he had the problem of his widow. Charlie would have to be replaced and the new man would need the cottage which went with the job. Annie was too old to qualify for one of the newly introduced pensions and it was obvious from what she had told him that none of her relations would give her a home. The Workhouse was a terrible alternative.

*

Guy Latimer rustled *The Times* impatiently and Virginia smiled to herself as she waited for the inevitable comment from her father-in-law.

'Eight kings and an emperor. Incredible!' he declared. 'Quite incredible. That shows you the strength of our monarchy. Spain, Greece, Norway, Russia — not to mention archdukes and the like. I wish I'd been there. This damned foot!' He snorted irritably.

He was in his early sixties but looked much older. His still thick hair was snow-white, as was his moustache, and a pockmarked skin and hooked nose coarsened his appearance. His voice was as loud as it had been all his life, possibly louder, for now he was growing deaf. Guy Latimer was a man used to being heard and he expected his opinions to be sought and respected. Too much port had undermined his health and weakened his eyesight so that he now read with difficulty and only with the aid of a magnifying glass.

'Princess May is a handsome woman,' he said.

20

'She's not Princess May any longer,' Virginia reminded him. 'She's Queen Mary now.'

'Queen,' he agreed with a heavy sigh, 'and a new King. It doesn't seem possible. A couple of weeks ago King Edward was at Covent Garden for *Siegfried* and now he's on his way to the grave. Two hundred and fifty thousand, that's how many people visited the catafalque. Two hundred and fifty! A quarter of a million people. That's how much the British public thinks of King Edward.'

'Ex-King,' said Virginia, greatly daring. 'George is King now.'

Her father-in-law chose to ignore this second correction. He allowed Virginia a greater latitude than the rest of the family, for he had always found her attractive. She had dark brown eyes, a pale olive skin and a mass of black hair which waved naturally and made a perfect frame for her face. She was tall and she moved well. She was too good for Alexander in his opinion, but he kept that to himself. Too good for him and too old.

Virginia had married Alexander in 1901 when she was twenty-five and he only twenty – and a young twenty at that. Guy had been all set to resist the match until he actually met Virginia and then he capitulated instantly and from then onwards allowed himself to be twisted around her little finger. His own wife was still alive at the time or he would have done his utmost to steal her from Alexander. Virginia knew this intuitively, as women do, and because of this their relationship had always been most harmonious.

'There's a picture here of the King's dog, Caeser, following the coffin,' he continued. 'Did you see it? Straining on the lead to follow his dead master. That's loyalty, that is.' He shook his head. 'He'll most likely pine and die without him. Dogs do that, you see. They won't transfer their attention to a new master. Poor old Caeser! Damned shame.'

'Poor little thing,' agreed Virginia. She put down the tapestry she was working on and crossed the room to stand beside her father-in-law. Looking down at the photograph in his newspaper, she repeated, 'Poor little thing. He looks so lost, doesn't he?' She moved away again to stand at one of the tall windows overlooking the lawn, knowing as she stood looking out that Guy's eyes would follow her and that her slim figure silhouetted against the light would be properly appreciated.

'So Lucien will be coming home soon,' she said casually. The old man snorted as she had known he would.

'He's always on leave, that boy,' he remarked. 'When do they do any work in this modern Army, that's what I'd like to know. It's a far cry from the Ashanti business, I can tell you. A damned far cry. There was no home leave for us. It was, "Put down the Ashanti in two months flat." That was all we had. Two months before the rains came, you see. What a place that was. The Gold Coast. Huh! Nothing golden about it if you happened to be a soldier. If the Ashantis' spears didn't get you, the fever did. We lived on quinine, lived on the stuff.'

'Well, he won't be staying with us long this time,' said Virginia. 'Just a few days and then he's off to darkest Berkshire for a weekend and then on to Edinburgh.'

She made an effort to keep her tone noncommittal but in fact she was secretly dismayed by Lucien's itinerary. Alexander's younger brother was lively and stimulating and she always enjoyed his visits home. Less sensitive than Alexander, he could on occasions be positively tactless but he was never dull. Although only twenty, he was blessed with striking good looks and flirted outrageously with her whenever he had the chance.

'It seems,' she said, 'that he's met a young lady – '

'Oh?' The old man's head came up sharply and *The Times* went down. 'When did this happen? It's news to me.'

'She's the friend of the daughter of his colonel,' Virginia told him, turning from the window. 'They met while she was visiting the regiment and she has invited him to visit their home – '

'In Berkshire?'

'Yes. Her name's Eleanor Sharp and he does rather go on about her in his letter.'

'Does he now? Well, let's hope something comes of it,' said the old man. 'That boy ought to settle down. He needs a sensible young woman to keep his feet on the ground. Eleanor Sharp? Hm. We'll have to hope for the best.'

'I expect we shall hear all about her from Lucien when he arrives,' said Virginia.

But she was thinking wistfully of the outings she and Lucien had shared together and the trips to London for shopping or a matinee. He made Virginia feel younger than her thirty years and when they were alone together away from Berwick House she could forget the cares of motherhood and recapture, albeit briefly, the carefree days which she had surrendered so foolishly at the age of eighteen to her first husband. Alex was a good husband and she had no complaints on that score, but life at Berwick House lacked the excitement for which she secretly craved. If anyone had bothered to enquire whether or not she still loved her husband she would have answered in the affirmative with a proper show of indignation, but in truth married life bored her and she was full of regrets for her lost youth.

Guy glanced at the ormolu clock which occupied the centre of the marble mantelpiece and his face brightened.

'Ah, nearly time for the children,' he observed.

Victoria and George saw their parents twice a day – once, briefly, during the morning and for a longer period in the late afternoon. Apart from these visits – which varied in duration depending upon the whim of the adults – the children remained out of sight, tucked away in the nursery wing with Nanny Webster who reigned supreme and brooked no interference. Sometimes both parents were present when they visited, at other times only one of them was available, but Guy was always there. Their visits broke the monotony of his day, for rheumatism had recently compounded an old leg injury he had sustained during the war; he could no longer walk any distance without pain and even riding caused him great discomfort.

23

'Two more minutes,' he said and began carefully to fold up his newspaper. 'Is Alex coming?'

Virginia shrugged elegantly. 'It doesn't look like it,' she said. 'He's probably down at the cottages. Old Abrahams hasn't long to go, apparently. The doctor has given up on him, poor old boy. I know I ought to go instead of Alex, but it *does* depress me to see him like that and his poor little wife so tearful. I know it's understandable, but I can't bear all that wringing of hands when there's nothing anyone can do. I can only take so much and then I have to make my excuses and leave.' She spoke defensively, although her father-in-law had not uttered a word of criticism. 'Anyway,' she went on, 'Alex is so much better at comforting than I am. I am quite desperately sorry for the poor old things, but the words simply stick in my throat. I'm no good with them and never have been. Those poky cottages and the terrible smell of stale cabbage or whatever it is they eat, is quite ghastly, but they don't seem to see it that way. They are just grateful for a roof over their heads, a steady job and a master who cares about them. Alex will say and do all the right things when the old man dies.'

'What about the wife?' asked Guy. 'She must be getting on now. Amazing, isn't it, how the time has gone? I can remember Abrahams marrying her. Gipsy stock, she was. Caused quite a fuss as you can imagine, her marrying outside the gipsy tribe. What was her name now? Annie, yes, that was it. Annie Abrahams. Mother took me down with her to give them a wedding present. A gold sovereign, I remember, and a side of bacon. Yes, Annie, that was it. She must have been about seventeen then. We all thought Abrahams a confirmed bachelor, but he surprised us; he was older than her.'

Virginia shrugged again. 'I suppose it will have to be the Union for her,' she said. 'These pensions, or whatever they are, start at seventy and she has a few years still to go. She can't be much more than sixty.'

There was a knock at the door and Guy called out cheerfully, 'Come on in you little terrors, the door's open.'

The nanny came in pushing the two children in front of her. They both took after Alexander with fair hair and grey eyes, but while six-year-old George had straight hair, his sister's curled. Both children clutched a toy and appeared very subdued. Nanny Webster was very erect and her plain face was set in stern lines. She wore a dark grey uniform and the brown leather belt at her waist emphasized her thin body, while the stiff white collar fastened at the front with a single stud accentuated her long neck. Grey hair was scraped up under a white lace cap.

'Here we are,' she announced and this phrase was the recognized signal for the children to move towards their mother and grandfather.

'Good afternoon, Mama,' piped George tremulously. 'Good afternoon, Grandfather.' Suddenly, he dropped the wooden ark he had been holding and hurled himself into Guy's outstretched arms. Nanny Webster's lips were instantly compressed at the sight of the wooden animals spilling out on to the floor, but she satisfied herself with a barely stifled exclamation of disapproval.

After hugging his grandfather, George moved to his mother who kissed the top of his head and said, 'Pick up the animals, George dear.'

Victoria hung back beside the nanny, a rag doll clutched tightly to her chest with both hands. Her face was very pale and her eyes were red.

'Oh dear,' said Virginia with a glance at the nanny who was standing with her arms folded. 'We don't look very happy today.' She held out her arms to her daughter, but the little girl made no move towards her.

'Is something wrong, Nanny?' asked Virginia.

'No, madam — at least, nothing so wrong that it can't be put right by proper discipline.'

'I see.'

Virginia did *not* see, but something in the nanny's expression dared her to enquire further into the reason for Victoria's obvious unhappiness.

'Aren't you going to kiss your mama?' Guy demanded, 'and your grandpapa? Don't I get a kiss today from my

25

little princess?' Victoria eyed them both forlornly, her grey eyes large with unshed tears.

'Toria's been crying,' said George conversationally. 'She's been crying for hours and hours and – '

Nanny Webster sucked in her breath sharply. 'That will do, Master George!' she cried. 'What have I told you about telling lies?'

George scowled as he gathered up his fallen animals and carried them over to his grandfather, who began to set them out in pairs on the table beside him.

Suddenly Victoria ran to the sofa and thrust her doll underneath it. 'You can stay there in the dark,' she cried with great vehemence. 'See how you like *that*, you bad, wicked doll!'

Virginia laughed. 'Oh, poor dolly,' she said. 'Whatever has she done to deserve such harsh treatment?'

George looked up. 'I suppose she's evil,' he said, 'like Toria and me.'

'Evil?' said Virginia, taken aback. 'But darling, of course you aren't evil.'

'We are,' he assured her. 'We are wicked and evil, aren't we, Toria?'

Victoria suddenly burst into loud sobs and hurled herself into Virginia's arms, clinging to her mother with desperation and mumbling incoherently. Over her head, Virginia again sought Nanny Webster's eyes.

'Whatever is all this about?' she asked as she smoothed her daughter's hair.

The nanny's expression was grim. 'I am afraid, madam, she has been very wilful lately and not at all amenable,' she declared. 'I will never tolerate rudeness and bad manners in my nursery. Children must learn how to behave and sometimes they don't enjoy the process.'

'Rudeness?' said Guy indignantly. 'Bad manners? That doesn't sound like our little Victoria.'

Nanny Webster stiffened visibly. 'I can assure you, sir, that your "little Victoria" is developing unpleasant characteristics and it is my duty to correct them – and the earlier the better.'

Virginia said, 'Perhaps you should sit down, Nanny.'

Nanny Webster attempted a smile. 'Thank you, but I prefer to stand and grow good, madam,' she said.

Virginia took out a handkerchief and dabbed at her daughter's tears.

'Now stop these silly tears, Victoria,' she said. 'If you have been rude or bad-mannered, then of course you must be punished and the best thing is to take your punishment and then forget all about it. Whatever it was, it's all over now, so let me see my little girl smile. Ah, that's better. Now go and fetch your dolly and we will –'

'I can't,' said Victoria sadly. 'She's got to stay in the dark because she's so evil.'

'*And* wicked,' said George. 'Don't forget wicked.'

'And wicked,' echoed Victoria dutifully.

Guy laughed. 'Upon my word, you are a queer pair,' he told them. 'Well, if the dolly must stay under the sofa, I suppose she must. Come over here, Princess, and look at your brother's animals.'

Victoria glanced at her mother, who nodded her approval. Then she looked at Nanny Webster. 'Do as you are told, Victoria,' the nanny snapped and the little girl hurried over to her grandfather.

Virginia said, 'Thank you, Nanny, you may go now. Please fetch them at four-thirty as usual.'

'Four-thirty,' repeated Nanny. 'Very well, madam. And George and Victoria . . .'

They turned guiltily and she wagged a reproving finger at them. 'No nonsense. Remember *exactly* what I told you before we left the nursery,' she said.

'Yes, Nanny,' they chorused.

When she had gone a little of the tension departed with her.

Virginia watched the children as their grandfather, with the wooden animals, did his best to make Victoria forget her tears.

'Look at that!' he exclaimed loudly. 'The lion's biting the elephant's ear. Ouch, says the elephant. Let go of my ear, you bounder. Oh! Now look what's happened. The elephant has trodden on the bear's foot. Ouch! says the bear. That's my toe you are standing on, elephant. You're a cad, sir!'

Geoerge giggled obligingly. 'Ouch,' he repeated. 'You're a cad, sir!'

He nudged Victoria, but she only smiled wanly and Virginia felt a prickle of unease as she thought of her daughter's description of the unfortunate doll. 'Evil' and 'wicked' were strong terms for a four-year-old to use. Presumably they were Nanny Webster's words. And 'stay in the dark' – whatever had prompted that?

'Georgie, come here to Mama,' she said suddenly and he trotted over to her. 'Why was Victoria crying for hours and hours?' she asked him. 'I want you to tell me, Georgie.'

A look of panic crossed his face at this suggestion and he shook his head vigorously. 'I mustn't tell,' he said, 'because I mustn't be a tell-tale.'

'But darling, you can tell me. Telling your mother isn't telling tales.'

'Yes, it is,' he insisted. 'We are not to tell anyone at all. If we tell, the dreadful scissor man will come in the night and cut off our tongues and we will never be able to say another word. Not *ever*. Not even if we go to Hell.'

Virginia frowned. 'Then just tell me what Victoria said that Nanny thought was rude.'

He hesitated and said, 'Nothing. She didn't say anything.'

'Then why did Nanny punish her?' his mother persisted. The child's confusion was evident and he wriggled uncomfortably under her scrutiny. 'I don't remember,' he said at last. 'I forget.'

'Now Georgie, I don't think you do forget,' said Virginia, trying to keep her patience. '*Was* she rude or bad-mannered?'

'She didn't do anything,' George insisted.

Virginia sighed. 'Then who had to stay in the dark?' she asked.

To her dismay, his expression changed at once to one of real alarm. 'No one,' he cried. 'No one had to stay in

28

the coal-hole. We didn't!' He looked panic-stricken and his lips trembled.

'Never mind then, darling,' said Virginia soothingly. 'We will say no more about it.' She smiled. 'Shall I read you a story or do you want to go back to your Noah's Ark?'

He was torn by indecision but as he hesitated, the door opened and Alex entered the room. One look at his face was enough to tell Guy and Virginia that Charlie Abrahams had died.

'Oh, Alex dear, was it dreadful?' asked Virginia, rising to her feet and crossing the room to put a hand on his arm in a gesture of sympathy.

Alex shrugged. 'He died peacefully – very peaceful way to go, I suppose.' He rubbed his eyes tiredly. 'I left a neighbour laying out the body. Poor old Annie! Do you know, she tied a breast of mutton to the old man's feet?'

'A breast of mutton?' echoed Virginia.

Alex nodded. 'To drive out evil spirits, or so she assured me. A Romany superstition, apparently.'

'Romany stuff and nonsense!' growled Guy. 'It didn't save him, did it?'

'It was to help his soul, not his body,' said Alexander. 'Anyway, I didn't want to argue with her at such a time. No doubt she felt she was helping.'

The two children had been edging further towards their father and now they clung to his legs, clamouring for his attention. He smiled and bent to put an arm round each one. 'And how are my little chickens today?'

They both began to talk at once, vying with one another to gain his ear. Virginia watched with a forced smile, for it secretly grieved her that her husband had such an easy rapport with them while she did not.

Guy winked at Virginia. 'We're "de trop" as usual,' he told her. 'Once their Papa comes in, we might as well give up.' But he spoke proudly, for he was fond of his son.

Virginia nodded absent-mindedly, for she was still thinking about Nanny Webster and the children. She decided she would have a word with Alex about it as soon as an opportune moment presented itself. Nanny Webster was very much a law unto herself, for she did not have a nursery-maid under her since none of them would stay with her for more than a few months. Her sharp tone and critical attitude repeatedly drove them to give notice and the previous year had seen three such hopefuls come and go. One of these had hinted that Nanny Webster was cruel and 'a mite too fond of the gin', but these allegations Virginia had disregarded as motivated by a desire for revenge.

What went on behind the baize door of the nursery was known only to the children and to Nanny Webster herself, and the children were obviously unwilling or too frightened to talk about it. The nanny would hardly admit to being cruel to her charges and Virginia did not really suspect her of such extreme behaviour, but she did wonder if the nanny's regime might be too strict for such young children.

She sighed. Yes, she would definitely discuss her apprehension with her husband as soon as she could, but at the moment another problem was dominating her thoughts. Lucien was coming home and she would have his company for only four days before he abandoned her in favour of Berkshire and the charms of Eleanor Sharp. Virginia was considering ways and means of prolonging his stay at Berwick House. She knew she could not detain him indefinitely, but thought she might try to persuade him to delay his visit to Berkshire by one more day. Let Eleanor wait for him. Let Eleanor wonder about the relationship between Lucien and his sister-in-law. Let her *suspect* . . . Virginia sighed again and wondered what Lucien had told Eleanor about her. Had he said that she was beautiful? Had he mentioned her age? She hoped not; there was too great a disparity in their ages for Virginia to feel any superiority on that score. How had he described her? She imagined Lucien's face, his eyes glowing. 'She's sophisticated and very witty. An excellent hostess, too. And her children adore her.' Well, perhaps that was going too far but she did, surely, have attributes which Eleanor lacked. She was a mature woman and

Eleanor was a mere girl. Girls were selfcentred, vain and devoid of intelligent conversation. *Surely* she, Virginia, must compare very favourably with the upstart Eleanor. What could she do now to hold his attention when he came home? She had never seriously tried to attract Alex's brother, but now suddenly it seemed a matter of considerable importance. She meant no disrespect towards Alex and certainly had no intention of putting her marriage at risk in any way, but it might be fun to pit her own charms against those which Eleanor possessed. If she succeeded, it would be a feather in her cap and no harm done. She pushed the children to the back of her mind and applied herself to the problem of Lucien.

Chapter Two

Grace muttered crossly under her breath as she eased Ivy Cummings' bath-chair down the path of Salter's Cottage and along the uneven pavement. Her employer had returned limping from her visit to Westminster Hall with what she insisted was a sprained ankle, alleging that on alighting from a train she had somehow tripped and fallen. The doctor had found nothing wrong, but had obligingly prescribed 'rest'. After his departure Ivy had called him 'a fool and a humbug' and had announced herself quite unable to manage the five-minute walk to the shops. Hence the bath-chair.

'Do look where you're going, Grace,' she grumbled. 'You'll tip me out if you are not careful. You don't just have to push the chair, you know, you have to *steer* it. You're jolting my insides. Oh, go carefully, I tell you!'

They passed the postman, who gave Grace a sympathetic wink, and then a large black dog ran out from a doorway and began to snap at the wheels of the bath-chair in a frenzy of excited yapping. Ivy kicked out feebly at it but missed and it was abruptly called back inside the house. At last they were outside the butcher's.

Ivy Cummings would give her weekly order and Grace knew exactly what it would be: a pound of best pork sausages; a pound of beef suet finely chopped; a brace of rabbits and a pound and a half of venison. The giving of this predictable order would, however, take some time to accomplish, for Ivy and the butcher would exchange titbits of local gossip and discuss the latest newspaper headlines at great length.

Ivy's trip to the butcher was one of the highlights of each mainly uneventful week. She had known John Strange for many years and trusted him implicitly. It was a matter of pride with her that she was always his first customer of the morning for, as she frequently told Grace, she liked to shop 'when the meat is at its freshest' and was therefore outside and waiting to enter the moment the shutters were rolled up. Today he came out to perform this task just as Grace was helping her employer out of the bath-chair and on seeing Ivy he commented sympathetically as she had hoped he would.

As Ivy limped into the shop Grace, left outside, gave herself up to the luxury of her thoughts.

It was now ten days since she had met Alex Latimer and he had been in her thoughts constantly. When she woke each morning the thought of him brought an instant smile to her lips, and at night she fell asleep with his image before her. She had written about him at great length in her diary and longed to go back to Berwick House in the hope that she might see him again, but so far she had had no excuse to go and certainly no time. Opportunities to visit her brother were rare and Grace knew that she might not set eyes on his employer again for four months or even longer. It was now May and Ivy's annual holiday was never taken until late September when she and Florrie visited their elder sister, Agatha, in Exeter, where she and her husband ran a small guest house. Grace always remained at home, for Ivy travelled with Florrie and Florrie's maid looked after both sisters. In September, then, Grace would have a little time to herself, although not as much as she might have hoped since Ivy always left a long list of household tasks which Grace must carry out in her absence. The devil would have no chance to tempt Grace if Ivy Cummings had her way.

As she waited outside the butcher's Grace snuggled down into her collar, for the wind was gusting and the sun's rays as yet had no real warmth in them. She allowed her thoughts to wander to a favourite fantasy in which Alex stood beside his wife's grave and glanced up to see Grace Martins on the opposite side. Quite how Grace came to be invited to the funeral was a problem she had not yet solved, but she thought she looked rather well in black and in the fantasy Alex was inexorably drawn to her. And she to him, of course. It was a great pity that he adored his wife . . . Grace wished that she *could* visit John again in order to check on that point. Did he actually *adore* Virginia, or did he simply love her? Or had John misunderstood the relationship? Perhaps Alex only found Virginia reasonable company. Perhaps, Grace thought hopefully, he had simply married her for her money or to please his parents. It was a comforting possibility.

Grace leaned her arms on the back of the bath-chair and surveyed the village street. The High Street branched almost opposite the butcher's and for a while she was entertained by a small traffic jam caused by the antics of a young lad trying to round a corner with a very large handcart, the wheels of which seemed determined to go in another direction. Red-faced, he was being harangued by the swarthy driver of a coal cart who was urging his two black Shires up the hill and a brewer's dray that was coming down the hill and trying to turn left towards Romsey. Other smaller vehicles were also involved and the chaos grew minute by minute. Suddenly Grace felt sorry for the boy and leaving the bath-chair, she ran forward to help him.

'Here, give me one of the handles,' she told the boy. 'I'll help you push it.'

Their combined efforts finally managed to propel the cart in the desired direction, then the rest of the traffic began to sort itself out. Grace returned to the bath-chair and relinquishing her dreams on the subject of Alex Latimer, began reluctantly to consider the problem of Alfred Harris. She had noticed that his visits to Salter's Cottage were growing more frequent. When she first went to work there, he had visited his aunt perhaps once every three weeks. Now it was once a week and on each occasion he managed to find time and the opportunity to have a few words with Grace alone. Cookie was very impressed with him and thought Grace should make more of an effort in his direction.

'He will look quite different in his best clothes,' she had insisted. 'He may not look anything special now, but if you saw him dressed up in his Sunday best you'd be quite impressed. He's quite handsome in a way and you could do a lot worse. I'd be after him if I was your age and wanting a husband.'

'But I'm not wanting a husband,' Grace had told her. 'I'm happy the way I am.'

'Maybe you are but things change. People die and the old girl won't last for ever. Every girl wants a husband and family — at least she should.'

At this point Ivy re-emerged from the shop and Grace's reminiscences were cut short as she tucked the blanket round her employer.

'And don't dawdle on the way home,' said Ivy. 'Alfred is probably coming this afternoon and I want you to put a duster round the parlour before he arrives.'

'But I gave it a good clean-up yesterday,' Grace protested, as she released the brake and turned the bath-chair round, 'after the sweep had gone.'

'I know,' said Ivy, 'but soot lingers in the air. You should know that. You will dust it today and you will probably have to dust again tomorrow, so you might as well put a good face on it. And as soon as you get back, tell Cook to make a dozen raspberry buns; they're Alfred's favourites. He really is such a dear boy; Florrie doesn't know how lucky she is to have such a son. Always so considerate and helpful — and his manners are impeccable. If the Lord had seen fit to give me a son, I should have chosen someone exactly like Alfred.'

Grace wondered whether Ivy would leave Alfred all her money. Salter's Cottage belonged to her and she hinted occasionally at the possession of stocks and shares about which Grace understood very little.

'I have told Florrie,' Ivy went on, 'that it's high time the boy found himself a wife, and she has spoken to the vicar on the matter.'

'The vicar?' Grace echoed, surprised.

'Of course. He knows most of the people in the village, and if there is anyone who will make Alfred a suitable match the vicar will know of it. He has promised to do what he can. Alfred has expectations and he should not be allowed to throw himself away on the first girl he takes a fancy to.'

Grace wondered uneasily if this was a reference to herself. 'What sort of expectations . . .' she began, but just then the black dog reappeared and repeated his earlier assault on the wheels of the bath-chair; the owner came out to apologize and they were passing the church before Grace was able to repeat her question.

'Why, his grandmother's money, of course,' said Ivy. 'She has left it in trust until he is twenty-four; Florrie says it is a considerable sum. Then there are his own prospects in his employment; the Post Office offers excellent opportunities for men of the right qualities. Alfred will not be a clerk for the rest of his life, I am quite certain of that.'

'Supposing Alfred does not like the wife that the vicar chooses for him?' Grace ventured.

'Not *like* her?' said Ivy. 'Of course he will like her if he's got any sense at all. Alfred will no doubt . . . oh, do be careful, you stupid girl! Why don't you look where you're going? You will have me out of here.'

'I'm sorry,' said Grace.

The bath-chair with its occupant was heavy and she found it difficult to push it up the hill.

'Being sorry won't help me if I'm tipped out into the roadway. When Alfred took me out yesterday, I felt not the slightest jolt – not *one* jolt – the whole time we were out. He steers me *round* the bumps and potholes, but . you push me straight through them.'

'I'm *sorry*,' Grace repeated ungraciously.

'And so you should be!'

The conversation languished after this small exchange and Grace was glad when they reached Salter's Cottage once more. After Ivy had vacated the chair, Grace pushed it round to the back of the house and put it away in the shed. She was surprised on entering the kitchen to find Alfred Harris already seated at the table enjoying a cup of tea.

'Surprise!' laughed Cookie.

'It is a surprise,' said Grace. 'I'm supposed to put a

duster round the parlour before you arrive. Does she know you're here?'

'Not yet. Perhaps I ought to go away and come back again?'

His dark hair, parted in the centre, was combed back on either side in a series of waves. His expression was earnest, his complexion a little sallow and he gave the impression of being larger than he was because his suit was a fraction too small, so that too much of his wrists and ankles was revealed.

'I have come a bit early, Grace, on purpose to see you,' he told her.

'Me?'

Alfred picked up his teacup and put it down again without drinking from it. His nervousness was obvious.

'I came to ask you something,' he began. 'It's to invite you to something. There's a Post Office social on the fourteenth of June. We can take a friend if we wish and I do. At least, I hope . . .' He picked up his cup again, gulped down the remainder of his tea and replaced the cup in the saucer. 'You'd come as my guest, of course,' he told the astonished Grace, 'so it wouldn't cost you anything for the ticket – and there's going to be a tea and entertainment. I thought you might like to come.'

'Well,' said Cookie, 'how exciting!' She looked expectantly towards Grace. 'A Post Office social! My word. What's the matter, Grace, has the cat got your tongue? Aren't you going to answer Mr Harris?'

'Of course I am,' said Grace, 'but I don't know what to say.'

'Say "Yes",' prompted Alfred.

'I would like to,' said Grace, 'but – '

'But what?' Cookie demanded. 'There's nothing to stop you going.'

'I don't know,' said Grace. 'I'd have to get permission. I'd have to ask Miss Cummings.'

Alfred smiled. 'Well, she won't say no if *I'm* asking you,' he said. 'Would you really like to come?'

'I'd love to,' said Grace, 'but I don't know . . .' She stopped again, thoughts of the conversation she had just

37

had with her employer making her doubtful. She did not want to disappoint him, but she could not match Alfred's optimism.

'It's very kind of you to ask me,' she said, 'and I'll come if I can.'

His normally mournful face was wreathed in smiles. 'I thought I'd ask her for you,' he offered.

'Ask me what?' demanded another voice and they turned to see Ivy in the doorway. 'What are you going to ask me?' she repeated.

'Why, if you will allow Grace to come to the social with me,' said Alfred. 'I was sure you'd say yes.'

'What social is this?'

'The Post Office Summer Social,' he explained, 'to be held in the chapel. There'll be a tea followed by an entertainment. I've asked Grace and she would like to come.'

'I'm sure she would,' said Ivy, 'and it's most generous of you to ask her, but I am not at all sure . . .' she hesitated, 'I am not at all sure it will be convenient – ' she said, then seeing her nephew's face fall, she added hastily, 'but of course I'll think it over.'

'You will? Oh, thank you, Auntie!'

'Don't thank me yet,' she said. 'I haven't given you my answer.' She looked at Grace. 'Perhaps instead of chattering here you could take a duster and do as I asked you; then I can take my nephew out of the kitchen and into the parlour.'

'Yes, ma'am, I will,' said Grace and snatching up a duster, she rushed out of the room.

Five minutes later Ivy and her nephew were alone in the parlour and Ivy was trying to persuade Alfred that the idea of Grace as a partner was not a good one.

'I really don't think, Alfred – although I couldn't say so in front of the girl – that Grace would be a suitable companion for you at the social,' she began.

'Oh, but Auntie – ' he protested.

Ivy held up her hand and obediently he left his sentence unfinished.

'I am only thinking of you,' she went on. 'If you are hoping for advancement within the Post Office, you really

38

must be more circumspect. A man's wife or companion is very important and his superiors would want to know that he could choose wisely.'

'I'm not asking her to marry me,' Alfred protested. 'I'm only inviting her to the social because I have no one else to take and I don't want to be the only one without a guest.'

'I see that, Alfred, but is the wrong guest better than no guest?'

'I think she'll do.'

Ivy sniffed. 'You are young, Alfred, and not altogether wise in these matters. Surely there is someone else you could invite. A friend of your mother's, perhaps?'

'No, Auntie,' he said. 'Oh, do please let her come. I am sure she won't let me down in any way. You've told mother yourself how sensible she is, and she doesn't get much fun out of life – at least,' he amended quickly, 'she doesn't get the opportunity to go to a social very often.'

'That's as may be,' said Ivy. 'I am still not happy about her as a companion for you. Whatever will your mother say? Grace is simply not in your class.'

To her dismay, she saw that her nephew's face was settling into stubborn lines.

'My mother isn't taking her to the social,' he said, 'and I've already invited her and she's very keen to come. If you won't allow it, then I shan't go at all.'

'Now there's no need to take that attitude,' she told him. 'I simply said I was not at all *happy* about it. I didn't say I would not allow the girl to go with you. Of course, if you are so determined and as long as you don't make a habit of inviting her out, then perhaps I will agree.'

'Oh, thank you,' he cried. 'You are a dear!'

Before she could protest, he had jumped up and planted a kiss on her withered cheek. 'You've made me so happy. I'll go and tell her,' cried Alfred and he rushed out of the room.

As she looked after her favourite nephew, Ivy could see that his delight was genuine and she was glad. She did, however, wonder what Florrie would have to say about it – but that, she told herself, was Florrie's problem. If she had found a suitable young woman for Alfred, then none of this would have happened.

*

Nanny Webster sat with George on her right and Victoria on her left as the dog-cart bowled along the outlying streets of Southampton.

'Nanny, can we go and see the ships?' asked George.

'We can *not*,' replied Nanny Webster.

'Can we go to Queen's Park, then?'

'We can *not* go to Queen's Park,' she told him.

'The Common, then,' George persisted. 'Can we go on the Common?'

'We can *not*,' she said again. 'We are going to Plummer Roddis to buy some material for your new shirts, Master George, and lace for your sister's collar, and that is all.'

'I want a toffee apple,' said Victoria.

'You know what happened to "I want".'

'But I *do*,' said Victoria. 'We always have a toffee apple when we come with Uncle Lucien.'

'*I* am not Uncle Lucien,' Nanny reminded them, 'and there will be no toffee apples. Toffee apples are bad for you and your uncle has no right to buy such rubbish.' She leaned forward and tapped the driver on the back.

'Take us to Above Bar Street,' she told him.

'Why can't we go and look at the ships?' asked George. 'Uncle Lucien takes us to see the ships. He *always* does!'

'I have already told you that I am not your uncle. He does not arrive until tomorrow.'

'I like Uncle Lucien,' said Victoria. 'He buys us toffee applies.'

'We could go on a tram,' George suggested. 'I love the trams because the horses go so fast. Uncle Lucien – '

'That's quite enough about your uncle,' Nanny told him. 'In fact, you are talking too much altogether, Master George. I have told you before that children should be seen and not heard. Now not another word out of you until we reach the shops.'

'If he does have another word, will he be wicked and evil?' asked Victoria.

'Yes.'

'I do like toffee apples,' said the little girl wistfully.

'That will do! Another word out of either of you and I will wash out your mouths with soap.'

Both children were silent as John manoeuvred the dog-cart alongside the kerb and jumped down to assist his passengers.

'And don't wander off, Martins,' Nanny told him. 'We shall probably be no more than a quarter of an hour. There will be no time for refreshment, so I will thank you not to leave this spot.'

'I'll be here,' he promised.

'See that you are.'

Nanny Webster bent to straighten the collar on George's sailor suit and adjusted Victoria's bonnet. As she stood up and took the children by the hand, an elderly gipsy woman made her way towards them through the people who crowded the pavement.

'Lucky heather, lady!' she wheedled. 'Buy a sprig of lucky heather?'

'Certainly not.'

The woman was small and dark, a bundle of shawls and petticoats. Her weatherbeaten face was wrinkled and her feet were bare. Over her arm she carried a basket and now she dipped her hand into this.

'Buy a flower then, lady?'

'No. Go away at once.'

'Pegs, then lady? All hand-made.'

'I have *told* you to go away.'

The woman was retreating before Nanny, edging backwards across the pavement, buffeted by the passers-by. For some reason she persisted. 'Lucky rabbit's foot, lady. Bring you luck, that will.' Her eyes did not leave those of Nanny Webster as she stepped back on to the foot of a stout gentleman who pushed her to one side with a muttered oath. Nanny Webster, embarrassed by her persistence, grew shrill.

41

'Go away from me,' she cried, 'or I will call a constable.'

The old woman muttered something under her breath and a gentleman who was passing gave Nanny Webster a meaningful glance.

'Most likely cursing you,' he told her. 'You want to be careful!'

'Cursing me?'

Briefly the idea of a curse frightened Nanny Webster and impulsively she grabbed the gipsy by the sleeve.

'What did you say just then?' she demanded. 'Tell me exactly, or I'll have you locked up for molesting innocent people.'

The gipsy pulled her arm away and offered the rabbit's foot once more. 'Bring you *good* luck, this will,' she said, wisely declining to repeat aloud what she had said.

Nanny Webster's fear gave way to ill-temper. 'Give me that,' she cried and, snatching the rabbit's foot, she threw it away over the heads of the small crowd that was already collecting. Then as the gipsy began to protest, she gave her a push which sent her and her basket flying backwards. Someone said, 'Hey, steady on!' but Nanny Webster was entirely unrepentant.

'Disgusting creature!' she declared as two women helped the old gipsy to her feet. 'Molesting decent people. It ought not to be allowed.'

The two children exchanged glances. Had the gipsy woman put a curse on Nanny Webster? Would anyone *dare* to do such a thing?

They followed her through the crowded store, past the haberdashery and ribbons until they reached the rear of the shop where they found themselves among bales of materials. Here Nanny Webster purchased two yards of shantung for George's shirts and the necessary cottons to go with it. For Victoria she bought lace for a new set of collars and cuffs and then the shopping was complete.

Nanny Webster's bad temper was caused by Lucien's imminent homecoming. In her experience, his visits did more harm than good to her two small charges, for in her opinion he spoilt them hopelessly and left them

42

unmanageable. She was thankful that this time the visit would be shorter than usual, as rumours had it that he would be moving on to Berkshire to stay with friends. His departure would not come soon enough for Nanny Webster.

As they made their way back to the dog-cart, George said, 'I wish I had a lucky rabbit's foot. I could make wishes.'

'Rubbish!' said Nanny. 'Superstition is not godly and I won't listen to such talk. You certainly won't go to heaven if you repeat superstitious claptrap.'

'Has Charlie Abrahams gone to heaven?' George asked.

'Mr Abrahams is dead and buried.'

'So, has he gone to heaven?'

'We can only hope so.'

'But has he?'

'If he was a good man and did not tell lies, then I expect he has. If not, he will be roasting in Hell, prodded by forks and wishing he had lived a better life.'

'And has Annie gone to the Union?'

'I don't wish to hear about either of them,' said Nanny firmly.

'Annie was a gipsy,' George went on recklessly, 'and Mama said she had to go to the Union, but Papa said he didn't like the idea at all. If Annie is a gipsy, could *she* put a curse on you like that other gipsy?'

Nanny turned on him swiftly, grabbed his shoulder and shook him hard. 'What did I tell you?' she said. 'I want to hear no more about gipsies. Now you will have no tea today and perhaps that will teach you to do what you are told the first time and not wait for a second telling.'

As soon as they reached the dog-cart, John jumped down from the driver's seat. 'Where to now?' he asked with studied innocence. 'Queen's Park?'

'Certainly not,' said Nanny. 'We are going straight home. Southampton has never been one of my favourite places. It's dirty, it's noisy and it smells. The sooner we go back to Beaulieu, the better I shall like it.'

*

Virginia was checking the household accounts when Fanny knocked and came into the morning room to say that Casey, the new gardener's boy, wanted to see her urgently. Virginia raised her eyebrows at the last word.

'Urgently?' she repeated. 'What impertinence! What can he possibly have to say that is urgent? It's very tiresome, Fanny. I'm going out shortly to meet Mr Lucien from the station.' She glanced at the clock and sighed irritably. 'Tell him I can spare him five minutes at the very most. "Urgent" indeed!'

Fanny gave a small bob. 'Yes, madam.'

She withdrew and returned a moment later to show Patrick Casey into the room. He was a large lad of seventeen, heavily built for his years, with a round face and anxious brown eyes. He carried his cap in his hands and twisted it nervously as he stood before the mistress of Berwick House. The splendour of the room astonished him and added to his apprehension.

'Well, Casey?' asked Virginia in her iciest tone. 'What is it that is so *urgent* that you have to interrupt me when I'm busy? Why can't you speak to my husband? I'm going into Southampton shortly, so whatever it is you must be quick about it.'

'Yes, madam,' he began, kneading his cap into a shapeless mess with his large hands. 'It's my brother Harry, madam. He's got me a job, like, on the *Mauretania*.' He spoke with the heavy accent of the Liverpool Irish. 'To be a trimmer, ma'am, like himself, and it's too good a chance to miss. There's chaps would give their right arm for the job, and it's only come my way because of him and my father. He was a trimmer but now he's a fireman – that's a stoker to you, ma'am.'

'I see.'

'See, you work your way up, ma'am,' he explained eagerly. 'First off it's trimmer, then coal-passer, then fireman. It's a good chance, ma'am and the *Mauretania*'s a lovely ship and I'd be on the same ship as my brother.'

Virginia frowned. 'But my husband told me you wanted very much to be a gardener. You've only been here a few months. Why the sudden change of heart?'

44

'Well, ma'am,' he explained, 'it wasn't me, like, that wanted to be a gardener; it was me Ma was so set on it. She didn't want me to go to sea like the others, because of the dreams she had, like, 'fore I was born. Dreamed that I was drowned at sea on a big ship, and she never forgot that dream. Doesn't want me to go to sea, so I came after this job just to please her. Just to keep the peace, like, because she did go on so. But we've always been at sea. My father says it's in the blood. Salt water in our veins, he reckons.'

He stopped to draw breath and Virginia said, 'But why don't you like gardening? It's a healthy, outdoor life — '

'It's not right for me, ma'am,' he insisted. 'I only took it to please my Ma. My heart's not in it and I'd like to work alongside my brother. Trimmer's hard work, but I'm fit enough.'

To prove this, he clenched his right fist to show off the muscles in his arm.

'But what about your mother?' Virginia asked. 'She won't be very happy, will she, if you go to sea against her wishes?'

The boy's face clouded momentarily. 'No, she won't, but my brother says she'll come round.'

'What does a trimmer do exactly?' asked Virigina, her curiosity momentarily aroused.

'They work in the coal bunkers, shovelling the coal to the chute, where it goes down into the passer's wheelbarrow. He takes it to the firemen and *he* throws it into the furnace that's under the boiler, ma'am. See, we're called trimmers because we keep the trim of the ship steady. If we took all the coal from one side, she'd develop a list. We work from both sides of the bunker.'

'But surely that's awfully boring work,' Virginia protested. 'A whole day shovelling coal?' His face, she observed, was beginning to assume a dogged expression.

'It's not a whole day, it's four-hour shifts, ma'am,' he told her. 'Four on, four off, and there's the other lads to talk to — not that you can hear that much above the racket, my father says — and it's dirty work, mind, but I

45

don't care. The black gang, that's what they call the men in the stoke-holds.'

Virginia glanced at the clock and saw that his time was nearly up. She was also rapidly losing interest and eager to be in Lucien's company again.

'Well,' she said, 'I don't think Mr Latimer will be very pleased to know that you've deserted us so soon, but I won't try to dissuade you. We'll soon find a replacement. You won't get paid for a whole week, naturally. Where are we? Ah yes, it's Wednesday. So that's three days' money.'

She reached into her bureau, took out a cash tin and counted out what was owing to him. 'There you are, Casey,' she said. 'You can leave at once.'

He took the coins, checked the amount and pocketed them gratefully. 'Thank you very much, ma'am.' He touched his forehead with a massive forefinger. 'I'm much obliged.'

He hesitated, but she closed the bureau lid and stood up.

'You can go,' she told him and watched him walk towards the door. 'Oh, and Casey, try not to get yourself drowned!'

He grinned widely. 'Oh, I won't drown, ma'am, don't you worry about me. I can swim. That was only a dream. Daft, my Dad says. He says women gets silly fancies when they're that way – Oh! Begging your pardon, ma'am. No offence meant!'

But Virginia had finally lost interest. She waved her hand peremptorily and said, 'Oh, for goodness sake, go if you're going,' and began to close her account books and tidy her pens.

After an awkward silence, the young man mumbled a 'Goodbye' and left the room and Virginia immediately forgot all about him.

*

Lucien sat back in his comfortable seat and tried not to stare at the woman who sat opposite. Instead, he stared around him at the already familiar first-class carriage

46

with its floral upholstery, gleaming leather arm-rests, decorative ceiling and highly polished woodwork. His army greatcoat, folded, was in the rack above him with his bag. He was well aware that his uniform added to his attractive appearance because the young woman opposite had given him several encouraging glances already, but her mother sat beside her and for this reason Lucien deemed it prudent to ignore the girl's obvious interest. He himself sat between a middle-aged matron on his left and a small businesslike gentleman on his right. The latter, engrossed in his copy of *The Times*, showed no interest in the other passengers and the middle-aged matron was busy with her knitting. As she controlled both needles and wool with deft fingers, she accompanied her actions soundlessly, moving her lips in repetition of the pattern. She was entranced with her work and from time to time as she finished each row, she would hold up the garment with small cries of satisfaction.

Lucien was dividing his thoughts between Eleanor Sharp and his sister-in-law, who had written to say that she would come herself to meet him at the station. This puzzled him slightly, as it was usually considered enough to send Martins to collect him, but Lucien was shrewd enough to wonder whether Eleanor Sharp was the reason for Virginia's solicitude. He had hoped she might be a little jealous of Eleanor, but now he wondered if it might be diplomatic to play down his feelings for Miss Sharp. 'Hell hath no fury,' he mused and made up his mind to be particularly nice to Virginia. He greatly admired his sister-in-law, but thought her a very unsuitable wife for his brother. Alex took his pleasures quietly, whereas Virginia craved fun and excitement. Lucien flattered himself that he provided this for her during his brief visits home, and this time must be no exception. Virginia was a good friend, but he did not doubt that she could easily become a very worthy enemy.

And Eleanor? He smiled to himself. Eleanor was a bewildering mixture of innocence and sophistication and Lucien found this intriguing. He half suspected that her innocence was contrived but if so, it was well done and

47

for the time being at least he gave her the benefit of the doubt. She was eighteen, but looked younger, and her wide china-blue eyes gave her a doll-like appearance. Her shape was 'comfortable' and a few more pounds would tip the balance towards plumpness, but Lucien did not object to this. He felt clumsy in the presence of small fragile women and Eleanor's well-rounded figure pleased him. For the same reason, he found Virginia's height reassuring.

At exactly ten minutes to three the train shuddered to a halt with a loud hiss of escaping steam and at once windows were lowered and doors opened along the length of the train.

'Southampton Central!' bellowed the porter.

Newspapers were quickly folded and knitting was stowed away as all the passengers stood up and those with luggage in the rack reached for it. Lucien pulled down his greatcoat, and bag and put on his cap. Then he followed the knitting lady out of the carriage and began at once to search the crowds for a glimpse of Virginia. Passengers with a lot of luggage whistled for porters who darted in and out of the crowd with their trolleys; dogs barked, doors slammed and cheerful voices were raised in greeting as travellers were met by waiting friends.

Lucien began to make his way towards the barrier, glancing from right to left in search of his sister-in-law. Suddenly he caught sight of her pushing her way through the crowd towards him and his face lit up at the sight of her. She looked quite perfect, he thought, in a coat and dress of soft green. Her hat was a delicate creation of matching feathers – new, of course, and designed to impress him. Smiling, Lucien confessed himself bowled over. She clutched at the hat with her left hand while her right was outstretched to grasp him.

'Lucien, there you are,' she cried breathlessly. 'It's so good to see you. You look marvellous!'

He kissed her cheek and her free arm went round him in a hug.

'It's good to see you,' he said. 'You look wonderful too. Have you missed me?'

'Not a bit.'

'Oh, you heart-breaker!'

Virginia laughed. 'Of course I have missed you. Dreadfully. Desperately. Catastrophically!'

He laughed. 'Is there such a word?'

'There should be,' she told him, slipping her arm through his. 'But dear Lucien, you are here now and that's all that matters. Is it good to be home?'

'Of course it is,' he assured her.

They reached the barrier, queued to get through, handed over their tickets and made their way outside to the forecourt where John was waiting with the brougham. He jumped down at once with a welcoming smile.

'Good afternoon, Mr Lucien, sir,' he smiled. 'Glad to have you back!'

He helped Virginia into the carriage.

'Nice to be here, Martins. Is the weather going to be kind to me, do you think?'

John, throwing the rug over their knees, glanced up at the overcast sky and said doubtfully, 'I reckon we'll have a bit of rain tonight or tomorrow, but it shouldn't be too much.'

'I hope you are right.'

While John resumed the driving seat, Lucien tucked the rug more securely around Virginia's waist, saying as he did so, 'It *is* good to be home!' Her smile was radiant.

'Straight home, sir?' John asked, for sometimes Lucien had a few calls to make in the town.

Today he said, 'Straight home, please, Martins,' and they were soon wending their way out of the station and into the street.

'So, what's been happening in the wilds of Southampton?' Lucien asked.

Virginia considered the question seriously, her head on one side. 'Not a great deal,' she told him. 'They are talking about knocking down some of the old houses in Silkshop Yard. They may even have started, I don't

49

know. Apart from that, I don't think the town's very different.'

'And Berwick House?' he asked. 'Still standing, I hope!'

She laughed. '*Exactly* the same as when you left it in the New Year,' she said, 'except that poor old Abrahams died and his wife has gone into the Union.'

Lucien frowned. 'Old Annie?' he cried. 'In the Union? Oh, surely not!'

Virginia shrugged elegantly. 'What else could we do with her?' she said. 'If we let her stay on after her husband died, they will all expect the same treatment. We cannot have all the cottages filled up with widows. The new man is due to start next week and where else should he live?'

As they turned a corner into Shirley Road, a small crowd of bare-footed boys began to run alongside the carriage, holding up their hands and crying, 'Give us a penny, mister!'

Good-naturedly, Lucien reached into his pocket and threw out a few coins.

'You're too soft-hearted,' Virginia told him. 'Oh, and young Casey, the gardener's boy – he had just started with us when you were home last. He's left. Half an hour ago, to be precise. Gone to be a sailor, like his brother.'

'The youngster from Chapel?'

Virginia nodded. 'The same,' she said. 'Apparently his sailor brother came home on leave and gave him such a glowing account that he couldn't resist it. He's going to be a trimmer on the *Mauretania*.'

Lucien pulled a face. 'It doesn't sound very exciting,' he said. 'I don't know why he didn't stick to gardening.'

'I put that point to him, but he said he wanted to work with his brother. A pity, really; he was a nice lad.'

'Was he any good as a gardener?'

'Not really,' Virginia admitted. 'He'll be no great loss, but the burning question is – will he be any better as a trimmer?'

They both laughed and for a few moments neither spoke again as the brougham weaved its way in and out of trams and carts. Underneath the travelling rug he reached for her hand and squeezed it. 'Let's talk about me,' he said. 'Have you missed me?'

'I always miss you.'

'You don't mind about Eleanor, do you?'

'Lucien!' Her laugh was convincing. 'Good heavens, no! I'm delighted for you. I hope you're going to tell me all about her; I'm sure she's very beautiful.'

This remark Virginia knew would be difficult for Lucien to answer. If he said 'Yes' that Eleanor *was* very beautiful – then she, Virginia, might take offence. If he said she was not, he would be disloyal. Lucien, however, was not to be caught out.

'Beautiful?' he said. 'Oh, I've not really thought about it. She has such tremendous charm and vivacity – and a good brain. Certainly she isn't ugly, and she's got beautiful eyes. She's only eighteen, but she has a sensible head on her shoulders. I'm sure you'll like her. What did Father have to say about it?'

Virginia considered her answer carefully, not wanting to hurry him into matrimony. 'He's very keen,' she said. 'He thinks you should marry as soon as possible.'

As she had expected, Lucien at once resisted the idea.

'Who's talking about marriage?' he demanded. 'She's just a nice girl and I'm very fond of her.'

'Is she equally fond of you?'

'I haven't actually asked her. There's plenty of time – so if you get the chance, do disillusion father on that score.'

'I will,' she said and thankfully changed the subject.

Chapter Three

The day nursery was a large gloomy room at the far end of the house. Next to it a smaller room served as the children's bedroom, beyond which a large room served Nanny Webster as both sitting and bedroom. The nursery itself was sparsely furnished, with a large square table in the centre of the room. Drawn up to this were two chairs for the children and a third for Nanny. There was a large chest containing the children's clothes and a large free-standing cupboard containing their toys. The two windows were tall and somewhat narrow, draped with brown velvet curtains. Heavy lace covered the glass panels and only when this was lifted were the children able to take a glimpse of the world outside the nursery. This forbidden luxury was only to be enjoyed when their nanny was busy in one of the other rooms, for she maintained that all the children's needs were catered for in the nursery and that prying into what did not concern them was an unpleasant trick to be firmly discouraged.

The floor was covered in a dark-patterned linoleum, but there was a rug in front of the fireplace on which the children were allowed to sit when the weather was extremely cold. When the fire was alight, it was mostly hidden from the children's view by their clean clothes which hung over the large fireguard to air.

Nanny, it seemed, had a great many responsibilities. It was apparently her responsibility that they did not over-eat, become self-indulgent, speak unless they were spoken to, question authority, become round-shouldered, become pigeon-toed, spoiled or pampered. George, at six, was considered old enough to understand the great burden that these responsibilities were to a nanny, and for most of the time he accepted that this was so.

On this occasion he sat at the table opposite his sister with his hands in his lap, his back straight and his head up. He looked neither to left nor right and his lips were firmly closed. Victoria copied him as well as she could. Nanny sat between them in the same rigid posture, but her eyes were on the clock.

'Three minutes to go,' she announced.

There was always a ten-minute silence before each meal, when the children were not allowed to speak or move. This time was to be spent in contemplation of God's goodness in providing food for them each day, but to the children ten minutes was an eternity. Another minute passed in complete silence.

'Two minutes to go,' Nanny announced.

Surreptitiously, George stretched out a finger and scratched his leg, but Nanny's head immediately jerked towards him as though tugged by an invisible string.

'Did I see aright?' she asked. 'Are you scratching, Master George?'

'My leg itches,' he protested.

'*My* leg itches, but I am not scratching it,' Nanny told him.

Victoria did not want to be left out. 'My leg itches,' she announced.

'Don't tell lies, Miss Victoria. Your leg does not itch.'

'It *does*.'

'I tell you it does not. One minute.'

The clock ticked on as they all waited for footsteps which would herald the arrival of their lunch. The nursery meals were chosen by Nanny, who ordered on Monday for the following week.

'One o'clock,' said Nanny and almost immediately there were footsteps followed by a knock on the door.

Nanny called out, 'Come in!' and the door opened to admit Fanny the parlourmaid – a slim girl with brown hair, rosy cheeks and a cheerful disposition. She carried a large tray and bustled across the room with a bright smile for the two children.

'Here we are then, Master George and Miss Victoria. Shepherd's pie today and carrots.'

She put the tray down on the far side of the table and Nanny leaned across to inspect the meal, picking up and examining each knife, fork and spoon. Unable to find any fault, she gave a slight nod and Fanny prepared to leave the room.

'Enjoy your dinner,' she told the children.

'Thank you, Fanny,' they chorused dutifully.

Shepherd's pie was not their favourite for the simple reason that occasionally it contained gristle which neither of the children liked. Since they were not allowed to leave any food on the plate, gristle – if there was any – had to be swallowed and that was not as easy as it sounded for George. He looked anxiously at the tray.

'And what are you staring at, Master George?'

'Nothing, Nanny.'

'Then turn your head back, please, and wait until the food is put in front of you. Time enough to look at it.'

'What's for pudding?' he asked.

'Wait and see.'

'It isn't tapioca, is it?'

'I said, "Wait and see".'

'I hate tapioca, so does Toria.'

'Nonsense,' said Nanny. 'We don't *hate* any of our food. Food is to make us grow big and strong, it is not to be liked or hated. It is simply to be eaten.' She served the food and put a plate in front of each child. They all bowed their heads.

'For what we are about to receive, may the Lord make us truly thankful.'

'Amen.'

Nanny picked up her own knife and fork, the children did the same and for a few moments they all ate in silence.

'Why is it called shepherd's pie?' asked George.

'Don't ask silly questions. Get on with your dinner.'

'What is a shepherd?'

'A shepherd is a man who looks after sheep.'

George giggled. 'Minced shepherd?' he said. 'It can't be.'

'Don't try to tell me what can and can't be, Master George,' said Nanny, 'or there will be no pudding for you at all.'

The two children exchanged a wordless glance and the meal continued for some time in silence. After a little more thought, George smiled at his sister and whispered, 'We can't eat people, can we?'

'Don't talk with your mouth full, Master George.' Nanny leaned across and slapped his hand so hard that the fork fell from his fingers and splattered brown gravy on to the clean white cloth.

'Now look what you've done, you naughty boy!' she cried. 'You'll stand in the corner for that when you've finished eating.'

George relapsed into a sulky silence as Nanny thrust the fork back into his hand.

Victoria asked, 'Is it jam tart? I like jam tart!'

'It is not jam tart.'

Victoria's eyes lit up hopefully. 'Is it jelly?'

Carefully Nanny removed Victoria's knife, then slapped her hand.

'That's for asking silly questions,' she said. 'You will find out all in good time.'

A moment later a piece of shepherd's pie fell on to Victoria's bib.

'Clean on this morning,' said Nanny furiously and the little girl received another slap.

Then the inevitable happened. George's next mouthful of minced beef contained a small piece of gristle and he pushed it into the side of his mouth while he swallowed the rest. Nanny Webster's sharp eyes, however, had missed nothing.

'What are you doing, Master George? Open your mouth at once and show me.'

Reluctantly he did so.

'Ah! A piece of gristle,' she said triumphantly. 'Close your mouth and swallow it at once.'

George knew she was pleased. He sensed, as he always did, that she was going to enjoy the ensuing battle. He closed his eyes, closed his mouth and tried to swallow the offending gristle. It would not go down.

'Open your mouth and show me,' demanded Nanny Webster. 'Ah! It's still there. I said swallow it.'

He tried again.

'I can't,' said George and his voice trembled slightly. Opposite him, Victoria's eyes grew wide with fright.

'You can and you will,' said Nanny.

Leaning across the table, she put one hand on the top of his head and the other beneath his jaw so that there was no way he could open his mouth. 'Now swallow,' she ordered.

He tried to free his head, but her grip tightened. He tried to say, 'I can't,' but was unable to open his jaw and get the words out. Nanny Webster's face was very close to his and he could see the dark hairs on her upper lip and the very small wart on the side of her chin. Her eyes were half-closed and she was breathing very fast. Panic flared suddenly within him and he endeavoured once more to swallow the offending gristle which then stuck in his throat. He tried to cough, but his head was still clamped between Nanny's hands.

'Swallow it!' she cried. 'Swallow it, I say.'

In spite of himself, George felt the tears prickling at his eyes as his desperation grew. Nanny would be pleased if he cried; she would feel that she had won, but tears would give her an excuse for further punishment.

Suddenly she shook his head roughly. 'Swallow it!' she shrieked. 'What sort of example do you think you are setting your sister?'

To spare himself further humiliation, he made one more attempt to swallow the gristle but this time he felt himself choke. He was going to be sick! He was sure of it. Frantically, he pulled and jerked his head and somehow managed to free himself from the vice-like grip of Nanny's hands, and at once spat the gristle out of his mouth on to the tablecloth. Nanny gave a furious gasp and for a moment there was no sound apart from the ticking of the clock.

'You nasty, disgusting little beast!' cried Nanny. 'How dare you spit? How dare you behave like that? You are no better than a pig.'

She jumped up from her seat and, seizing him by the

shoulders, jerked him bodily from the chair in one fierce movement, then shook him violently.

'You hear me,' she cried, her face contorted with anger. 'You are a filthy little pig!'

She slapped his legs three times, then rushed him into the corner of the room.

'You will stand there until you learn better manners,' she told him, 'and you will have no pudding. Turn your face to the wall and don't you dare turn round. I don't want to look at a pig. You will stand there until you see the error of your ways and then I shall expect a proper apology. You disgust me, do you hear? Well, do you?'

He nodded.

'Don't nod your head, answer me!'

'Yes,' he said through the beginning of tears.

She returned to the table and glared at Victoria whose lips were trembling. 'And don't you dare cry,' she told her sharply, 'or you will find yourself in the other corner. Here, give me that fork. You will be all day at that rate.' She scooped up meat and potatoes and thrust it roughly into Victoria's mouth. Almost before the child had a chance to swallow it, another forkful was waiting to go in.

'And take that look off your face,' cried Nanny. 'Anyone would think that I was going to eat you ... There now, the plate is clean.'

In the corner, George began to sob and Victoria looked at Nanny beseechingly. 'He didn't mean it,' she said.

'Be quiet. Sit there quietly while I finish my dinner and Master George, you'd better stop that snivelling or I shall fetch my slipper to you.'

Five minutes later there was a knock at the door and Fanny came in with another tray containing three plates of stewed apple and custard. She hesitated half-way across the room and glanced enquiringly at George, who stood in the corner.

'Oh dear,' she said. 'Poor Master Georgie.'

'Poor Master Georgie, my foot!' said Nanny. 'He's disgusting, his behaviour is quite abominable. We shall only want two of those puddings, thank you.'

'Oh, but Cook says . . .' Fanny hesitated. 'Cook won't be very pleased,' she amended.

'And why not, pray?' Nanny Webster's angular body stiffened with anger.

'She says she's tired of throwing away good food.'

'Does she indeed? I shall have something to say to Cook when I see her next. Tell her that from me.' She watched in a furious silence as Fanny cleared away the dinner plates and left the two plates of pudding.

As she carried the tray to the door Fanny, greatly daring, called out defiantly, 'Cheer up, Master Georgie!'

Trembling with rage, Nanny rose to her feet and pointed to the door. 'Get out of here at once and mind your own business.'

To everyone's surprise, Fanny, her face flushed, stood her ground.

'He's only a kid,' she said. 'He's only six. Cook says they should have a proper dinner no matter what they've done.'

Nanny drew herself up to her full height. 'It is quite obvious that Cook knows nothing about the management of children,' she said. 'That is why her job is to cook the food and mine is to run this nursery. I will run it my own way with no interference from anybody else. Do you understand?'

Fanny glared at her but did not answer.

'Do you understand?' Nanny repeated but Fanny, with a toss of her head, turned and stalked out of the room, banging the door behind her.

*

She marched back into the kitchen and banged the tray down on to the well-scrubbed table so that the crockery jumped.

'What's the matter with you?' asked Cook and then her glance fell on the tray and she added, 'Oh, not again!'

'Again,' said Fanny. 'Those poor kids – she makes their lives a misery.'

'Who is it this time?' asked Cook.

'Master Ceorgie. He's standing in the corner crying his

eyes out. Lord knows what terrible sin he's committed.'
There were murmurs of sympathy from the rest of the
staff.

Mrs Wade, the cook, was a large woman in her fifties,
shapeless but warm-hearted with grey hair that somehow
managed to stay curled in the steamy atmosphere of the
large kitchen. She had been at Berwick House for a good
many years and could remember Guy's wife, frequently
describing her as 'The nicest woman that ever walked on
two legs'. Her constantly recurring complaint was that
since the death of the old lady life had never been the
same. Mrs Wade was a good cook with a particularly
light hand for pastry; she knew her worth and was paid
accordingly.

Dot was the scullery-maid, a tall, angular girl with a
large mouth and teeth to match. She had broad hips and
strong legs and worked tirelessly without complaint. She
was reasonably content with her lot, but her ambition
was to get married to the first man who asked her. Now
she regarded Fanny indignantly.

'That miserable old woman,' she cried. 'I'd like to
strangle her with my own bare hands. I know what I'd
do if I was the mistress – I'd sack her and that's a fact.'

Fanny sighed helplessly. 'I just don't know why the
children don't tell their parents. They get plenty of
chances.'

'Too scared, I should think,' said Mrs Wade. 'Scared
of what the old battleaxe will do to them. I wouldn't like
to be in her nursery, I tell you straight.' She picked up the
plate of apple and custard and asked, 'Anyone hungry?'

Dot said reluctantly, 'It's Fanny's turn,' and Fanny
took up a spoon and began to eat.

Mrs Wade looked thoughtful. 'How many times this
week is it,' she said, 'that one of those kids has gone
without a proper meal? Either it's no egg at breakfast or
it's no pudding, or it's no cake at tea-time – '

Dot put in, 'Don't forget the bread and water when
they've been *really* naughty. For a whole day sometimes.
It's a wonder they're not starved to death.'

Mrs Wade shook her head again. 'I'd like to tell the

mistress what's going on, but I hardly dare and it's not my place to go telling tales.'

'That's the trouble,' said Fanny. 'It's nobody's job to tell what's going on, but she ought to know.'

Dot moved to the table, her eyes rolling expressively. 'What about an anonymous letter? Then they wouldn't know who had written it.'

Fanny looked doubtful. 'They might check up on the handwriting,' she said.

'We could disguise it, or use capitals – or cut bits out of the newspaper.'

'You read too many books,' said Mrs Wade, 'that's your trouble. We all know what happened to the nursery maid – she complained and the old cow got her sacked. It could happen to any of us.'

At that moment the back door opened and a small elderly man came in carrying a basket of vegetables. Mr Trott – Sid to his associates – was the gardener and his muddy knees and permanently dirty hands gave proof of this, if any were necessary.

'Morning, one and all,' he said predictably, as he dumped the basket on to the corner of the table.

'My clean table!' cried Mrs Wade. 'How many times do I have to tell you, Sid. Put it on the draining-board.'

Sid ignored her and began to poke about amongst the vegetables.

'There's a few carrots here,' he said, 'but that's about the last of them – and a cauliflower, the largest one I could find and . . .' He held up a small potato triumphantly between finger and thumb and waited for applause.

'New potatoes already,' said Mrs Wade.

'Just a few.'

'I love new potatoes,' said Dot. 'I could eat them on their own with butter. I could make a whole meal out of new potatoes.'

'Well, you won't get the chance,' he told her. 'There's just a few here for the family. The likes of you will have to make do with the old ones.'

60

Mrs Wade took the potato from him and examined it. 'Very nice,' she told him. 'Clean as a whistle.'

He nodded proudly.

'How did they escape the little varmints?' asked Fanny.

Sid waged a permanent war with the wildlife that surrounded the kitchen garden. Wood-pigeons from the nearby forest regularly attacked the young plants. The newly planted peas were eaten by mice; squirrels found their way under the netting and played havoc with the strawberry crop and rabbits nibbled the carrot-tops and helped themselves to the lettuces. Sid's war with 'the little varmints' had become a standing joke in the kitchen.

Before Sid could answer, Fanny put down her empty plate. 'We were just talking about Nanny Webster,' she told him. 'Poor Master Georgie was stood in the corner when I went up there and no pudding for him again.'

'What's he done now?' Sid asked.

'Probably nothing,' said Fanny. 'She said he was disgusting. I ask you, how can a kid of that age be disgusting? He doesn't know the meaning of the word.'

Sid sucked in his breath sharply and shook his head. 'That's a lady I wouldn't like to be on the wrong side of,' he said.

'*Lady*!' cried Fanny. 'I don't call her sort a lady. Monster, more like it.'

Sid sat himself down on one of the chairs which was the cue for Mrs Wade to ask, 'Cup of tea, Sid?'

'Thank you kindly,' he said.

Fanny said, 'So you've lost young Casey?'

Sid nodded. 'Gone to sea,' he said. 'Rather him than me! I tried to talk him out of it, but he would go. Now I'm on my own again and God only knows when they'll find me another lad!'

'Master Lucien's home,' Fanny put in. 'At least, he should be at any moment. The mistress has gone to meet him.'

'Has she now?' said Mrs Wade. 'Kind of her.' She made it sound as though there was more to this than met the eye. Dot caught her gist immediately and grinned.

'Never!' she said. 'Not her and him. She can't fall for him; he's young enough to be her son.'

'Not quite,' said Fanny, 'and he is rather handsome, but I can assure you it's not her and him.'

'Oh?'

Fanny had their attention now and she grinned self-consciously. 'I just happened to overhear something,' she said and there was an immediate and amused outcry.

'Oh, just *happened*,' grinned Mrs Wade. 'I suppose your ear just happened to be at the keyhole.'

'What if it did?' retorted Fanny. 'Nobody tells us anything. If we want to know what's going on, that's the only way to find out. Anyway, do you want to know or don't you?'

They crowded round as Mrs Wade poured Sid's tea.

'Well,' said Fanny, 'it seems that Master Lucien has found himself a young lady. Her name's Eleanor Sharp, and he's not spending all his leave here like he usually does, but spending some of it at her home meeting her family.'

Mrs Wade and Dot exchanged meaningful looks.

'Meeting his family?' said Dot. 'Then it's serious.'

'Could be,' agreed Fanny.

'Oh dear,' said Mrs Wade, 'I hope he doesn't do anything rash. He's only young.'

'So do I,' said Dot. 'If he gets married, he'll go and live somewhere else and then we shan't see him any more. It's always such fun when he's around.'

'Fun?' said Fanny. 'You didn't think it was such fun when he shut you in the broom cupboard last time.'

'I didn't at the time,' Dot admitted, 'but afterwards I did. He only meant it as a joke.'

'He always was the wild one,' Mrs Wade told them. 'Always in trouble as a boy, he was. I thought the Army would quiet him down a bit, but I don't know that it's done much good.'

'Well, I don't want him to be "quieted down",' said Fanny. 'I like him the way he is.' She giggled. 'I'll never forget Christmas Eve,' she said, 'on the stairs. Pressing me back against the banisters and buttering me up. I thought he was going to kiss me, I really did. My heart was going pit-a-pat. He had his arms right round me, but all the time he was tying my apron strings to the banisters! Made me look a right fool, but I had to laugh.'

'Do you think we'll get invited to the wedding?' asked Dot. 'If he marries this Eleanor?'

'Course we won't,' said Fanny. 'They'll get married where the bride lives and that's miles away from here.'

'Never mind,' said Mrs Wade. 'We'll get to see the photographs. they're sure to have a photograper, everybody does these days.'

'Lucky things,' said Dot. 'I wish it was me getting married. *You* don't feel like settling down, do you, Sid, with a nice young wife?'

Everybody turned to look at Sid, who sucked in his breath again and said, 'Oh dear me no!' with another gloomy shake of his head. 'No, no, no. Marriage is something I couldn't abide. Never did marry and I'm not going to start now.'

Dot winked at Fanny and said, 'Not even if I promised to darn your socks, Sid, and cook you a supper every night?'

'I darn me own socks and I cook me own bit of supper.'

'There's *other* things,' Fanny suggested with a grin.

He snorted. 'I'm too old for *that* sort of nonsense,' he told them. 'I've done without it all my life and I can do without it a bit longer.'

'But I can't,' said Dot. 'I'd like a husband and my own home. I'd like to do my own washing-up instead of somebody else's. I live in hopes.'

'When pigs fly . . .' said Mrs Wade.

Dot tossed her head. 'I can dream, can't I? No harm in that.'

Fanny wagged a finger at her. 'Make it a Monday,' she told her.

'A Monday?'

Mrs Wade smiled. 'You know what they say — Monday's dreams come true.'

'Do they really?'

'No harm in trying. Think hard about a young man proposing and then you might dream about it.'

Dot thought it over for a moment, then asked, 'Do you mean Sunday night so you wake up and it's Monday morning, or Monday night so you – '

'Don't tell her,' laughed Sid. 'She'll spend all her time dreaming and none working!'

They all laughed, but Dot shrugged her shoulders. 'Actually, I think the postman has taken a bit of a shine to me,' she said. 'Leastways, he always manages to touch my hand when he gives me the letters. D'you know what I mean? I can tell he's doing it on purpose.'

'There you are then,' said Fanny. 'We'll all come to your wedding if we can't go to Master Lucien's.'

Sid sighed dubiously. 'Very over-rated, marriage,' he said. 'You tell them, Mrs Wade.'

'I don't know,' she said. 'It's not so bad. Marriage? Well, it's ups and downs.' Glacing at the clock she cried, 'Good lord, is that the time? We're doing too much gossiping. Thanks for the vegetables, Sid; now you drink your tea and be on your way. And you, Dot, get on with that washing-up. When Mr Lucien does get back he'll put his head in to say "Hullo" and I don't want this kitchen looking like a rubbish-tip. So, all hands to the pump, please!'

Sid got up. 'All hands to the pump?' he repeated. 'Gone a bit nautical, haven't we? It should be you who's going to sea, not young Casey!'

*

Grace glanced up at the clock and saw that it was nearly half-past ten. With difficulty, she stifled a yawn. She sat beside what was left of the kitchen fire and her employer sat opposite her in a creaking rocking chair. Ivy was dozing off, but she was not prepared to go up to bed and until she did Grace would have to remain downstairs also. Ivy had been reading but now the book lay unheeded in her lap as her head fell slowly towards one shoulder. With a grunt, she jerked herself upright again and stared suspiciously at Grace.

'There's no need to stare at me,' she said.

'I wasn't, ma'am,' Grace protested. 'I was glancing at the clock, that was all.'

Since Ivy's return from London she had slept badly, complaining of the pain in her ankle and ringing her bell at all times of the night to bring Grace to her side.

'Talk to me,' Ivy demanded and Grace looked up from her sewing in surprise.

'Talk to you about what?' she asked.

'Anything,' said Ivy irritably. 'Just talk to me. Tell me how the new blouse is getting along.'

Grace held up the garment on which she was working, which she was hoping to finish by the time she went to the social with Alfred Harris.

'I've put one sleeve in,' she said. 'It's gone in quite well.' She put it aside and tried to think of something to talk about. 'When you were in London,' she said, 'I went to visit my brother at Berwick House. Do you know it?' Her tone was as casual as she could make it.

Ivy said, 'Berwick House? In Beaulieu, do you mean?'

'Yes, ma'am. My brother's head groom there.'

Ivy looked surprised. 'You didn't tell me that before,' she said accusingly.

'You never asked me about him. I didn't think it was of any interest.'

'Then why tell me now?'

'Because you asked me to talk to you. It was a topic of conversation, that's all.'

'I have heard of Berwick House,' Ivy told her. 'A daughter of a friend of Florrie's worked there for a short time as a nursery-maid.'

'I met Mr Latimer,' said Grace. 'He came down to the stable to talk to John about one of the horses. He seems very pleasant.'

'The name sounds familiar,' said Ivy, 'but I really know nothing about the family, simply that the young girl in question left after only three months. It seems the nanny made her life quite intolerable – a real dragon, from all accounts. I am afraid that power goes to the heads of some people. My own nanny was not at all like that; she loved us dearly and called us her "three little pets". Of course, we adored her.'

'John told me there are two children,' said Grace, 'but I didn't see them. I saw one of the tiny ponies though. Mr Latimer was very kind; he seemed to care.'

'Care?' repeated Ivy. 'Care about what?'

'Care about people. About me,' said Grace. 'He asked me if I was happy and had enough to eat.'

'Good gracious! What did you say?'

'I said "Yes" on both counts,' Grace told her hastily.

'I should think so too,' said Ivy.

Grace wanted to go on talking about Alex, but she dared not pursue the topic since it so obviously did not meet with Ivy's approval. She stole another look at the clock and saw that five more minutes had passed. Ivy caught the direction of her glance and said sharply, 'What's the matter with you? Why do you keep looking at the clock? You aren't tired, surely? A girl of your age.'

'Of course not,' said Grace. 'Would you like me to read to you, perhaps?'

Ivy shook her head pettishly.

'Shall we play cards?'

'I think not,' said Ivy. 'I can never concentrate late in the evening.'

Grace had a brainwave. 'Shall I read your palm?' she suggested. To her surprise, this idea was promptly accepted.

'I didn't know you could read palms,' said Ivy.

'My grandmother taught me many years ago,' Grace told her. 'Hold out your right hand and let me look at it. Yes,' she said after some consideration, 'this is what we call a pointed hand. You see the hand has a pointed shape, rounded at the bottom of the palm and narrowing towards the tips of the fingers. A pointed hand suggests that you tend to be rather highly-strung and emotional.'

Ivy nodded eagerly.

'The long, delicate fingers suggest sensitivity,' Grace went on. 'That means you rely a lot on your intuition.'

'That's very true,' said Ivy. She was leaning forward now and Grace realized that perhaps she had made a mistake in suggesting a little palmistry. Ivy now showed no desire at all to sleep; she was wide awake and quite animated. Perhaps, thought Grace hopefully, if she went to bed late she would sleep later in the morning. At least she might sleep more soundly and Grace might escape the sound of the bell which so regularly disturbed her nights.

'Your fingers are long in relation to your palm,' she said. 'Do you see? That suggests refinement, patience, a cautious nature. I am looking now at the setting of your fingers at the bottom.' She nodded. 'This finger, the smallest finger, we call Jupiter. On your hand it's set very low, which is another aspect of your cautiousness. This means you are very slow to build up friendships.'

Again Ivy nodded vigorously. 'Quite amazing,' she told Grace. 'So far you have been very accurate. I had my palm read once by a gipsy when I was still a young woman. She told me I would never marry. It was uncanny really . . . but go on.'

'This is the head line,' said Grace, tracing it with her finger. 'A long head line means intelligence. Above it is the heart line, here. Yours is well-shaped and quite strong. It starts here below the Saturn finger and that suggests a tendency towards selfishness – '

Ivy snatched her hand away and turned to stare into her palm. 'Selfishness?' she said. 'I hardly think . . . show me.'

Grace traced the line for her. 'It's only a *tendency*,' she said, 'and a tendency can be balanced by another line. It doesn't necessarily mean you are a selfish person.'

Ivy frowned impatiently. 'I should hope not. Can't you tell me something about the future? I don't want to be told I'm selfish when I'm not. Am I going to live to a ripe old age? Which is the life line? Have another look, child – and do try to get it right.'

Obediently, Grace looked at the hand again and frowned. The life line was not very long. 'It's this one here,' she explained. 'It's not particularly long but – '

'But what? What d'you mean, not particularly long?

Is it short?' Her tone was agitated and Grace tried to find something reassuring to say.

'The length of the life line doesn't necessarily indicate the length of your life,' she told her. 'A long line could mean a short life, a short line could mean a long life. In a way it's the *quality* of life which is shown by the life line.'

'Well, I've never heard that before,' said Ivy. 'That would mean the quality of my life was short and that doesn't make any sense. Mumbo-jumbo, all of it. Tell me some good news. Am I ever going to be rich? Am I ever going to be *happy*?'

Surprised by the sudden anguish in her employer's voice Grace looked up, but Ivy snatched her hand away, annoyed with herself for the give-away question. 'I think that's probably enough of that,' she said firmly. 'Look at the time. We should both be in bed. I shall feel like a rag doll tomorrow.' She stood up and tucked her book under her arm. 'I shall go to bed now,' she said. 'Please bring up a glass of hot milk and honey in exactly ten minutes.'

'I'll do that,' said Grace.

Ivy was half-way to the door when she turned again. 'Oh, by the way, Florrie tells me that Alfred is really very taken with you. *Very* taken indeed. Well, why do you look at me in that way, Grace? You should be very grateful that such a nice young man has taken an interest in you.'

'I am, of course, ma'am.'

'Well, you don't look it. I may say *I'm* not at all happy about the idea myself. I need you here and I don't want you getting any romantic ideas about Alfred or anyone else. Florrie, however, is only interested from her son's point of view. She has asked me about your character and I have been as honest as I can.'

'I've no plans to marry,' Grace told her quickly, 'but I didn't think it would do any harm to go to the social with him.'

'It will do no harm at all,' Ivy told her, 'unless you encourage him to think more deeply about you. That would be most improper for a girl in your position.'

'I shan't encourage him, you can be sure of that.'

'But, on the other hand,' said Ivy, 'you must be properly appreciative of the fact that he has *paid* for your ticket.' Grace nodded and Ivy sighed again. 'I have always been fond of Alfred,' she said, 'but he is inclined to be headstrong and he might let his feelings carry him away. It's up to you to keep the matter in perspective. A young woman can always inflame a young man.'

'I'll do my best not to inflame him,' Grace assured her, struggling to keep her face straight.

'Good. As long as we understand each other.' Ivy turned and began to go up the stairs, then looked back and said, 'One spoonful of honey. Ten minutes exactly.'

Chapter Four

The following day dawned fine and settled and Lucien proposed that he and Virginia should take the children to Buckler's Hard for a surprise picnic. Refusing to listen to any objections, he left Virginia to organize the food and headed at once for the nursery. He took the stairs two at a time, banged on the door, and burst in shouting, 'Who's for a picnic?'

To his surprise, the children were nowhere to be seen. Nanny sat darning by the window and she now rose indignantly to her feet.

'Is that a suitable way to enter a nursery?' she demanded. 'I think at least – '

'Where are they?' asked Lucien. 'I've come to collect them. We're going on a picnic.'

'I'm afraid not,' said Nanny firmly. 'The children are in disgrace and have been sent back to bed. There will be no picnic.'

Lucien refused to be cowed. 'To bed – at this time of the day? Then they'll just have to get up again.' He moved purposefully towards the bedroom door.

'Stop!' cried Nanny, her voice shrill. 'I forbid you to go in there. The children are in *my* charge and *I* decide what they do with their day. That's always been understood.'

He turned to face her and his smile was charming. 'Not by me, Nanny,' he said. 'I'm only the uncle.'

'They are *my* charges,' repeated Nanny.

'They are *my* nephew and niece,' retorted Lucien, 'and I have planned a picnic for them.'

'I am afraid I cannot allow – '

'What nonsense!' said Lucien. 'They cannot have done anything terrible enough to warrant missing a picnic.' Without another word, he opened the bedroom door and walked in. Startled, the two children sat up in bed.

'Uncle Lucien!' cried George.

'Get up, chickens,' he told them. 'We're going on a picnic to Buckler's Hard.'

Nanny appeared in the doorway behind him, her face grim, her arms folded. 'You aren't going anywhere,' she told them. 'Lie down again *at once!*'

Obediently they lay down, but Lucien – still managing a smile – took a few steps forward and pulled the bedcothes from each one of them. They were in their nightclothes. He turned to face the furious woman, keeping his tone light with an effort.

'This is quite ridiculous,' he said. 'What on earth have they done that is so terrible?'

'That's between them and me,' she told him. 'Now you will please leave the nursery. The children will not be accompanying you today. Another day, perhaps, if their behaviour improves and I am properly consulted beforehand.'

The children remained silent and despairing but he reached down and pulled each one of them into a sitting position. 'Out of bed with you!' he said. 'Now, where are your clothes?'

Nanny Webster was white and trembling with rage. 'I tell you I will not allow it,' she cried. 'They are to stay in bed.'

The children looked doubtfully from one adult to the other, but Lucien refused to show any anger.

'Find your clothes and quickly, children,' he said. 'Your mama is waiting downstairs and Martins is bringing round the pony-trap. There's no time to waste.'

George turned appealing eyes from his nanny to his uncle. 'Our clothes are in the other room,' he whispered.

To Lucien's surprise, Nanny suddenly spread out her arms to block the doorway and fixed the children with a look that dared them to push past her.

Lucien faced her. 'Please move to one side, Nanny,' he said, 'and allow us to go through.'

'I will not,' said Nanny. 'I will not have the discipline of my nursery – '

Lucien lowered his voice and, leaning forward, whispered, 'If you won't move aside, I shall have to lift you out of my way.'

Her mouth fell open with shock. 'You wouldn't dare,' she gasped.

'Wouldn't I?' he asked in a low, calm voice. 'It would make you look rather foolish,' he pointed out, 'but that's for you to decide. I am here to take the children on a picnic with Mrs Latimer and nothing you can say or do will make me change my mind. Now, will you please move to one side and let us pass.'

The children watched wide-eyed as Nanny stared back at Lucien, her eyes full of hate. It seemed for one long moment that she would not comply and George, whose sharp ears had caught what was said, hoped that his uncle *would* move her bodily from the doorway. At last, however, she gave in and stepped reluctantly to one side. The children ran into the other room with cries of excitement and rushed to the chair where their clean clothes were neatly piled.

'If you think,' hissed Nanny, 'that I am going to help them into their clothes, you are mistaken.'

'Don't worry,' said Lucien cheerfully, 'I'm sure we can manage. You are very busy with your sewing and we wouldn't want to distract you from that.'

Eagerly, the children struggled into their clothes, helped by Lucien's awkward fingers. Under Nanny Webster's hostile gaze, it seemed to take a very long time, but at last they were ready.

'Our hats, Uncle Lucien,' cried George.

Lucien turned to Nanny questioningly, but she looked him straight in the eye and said, 'I don't know where they are.'

He hesitated, not wanting to prolong the hostilities. Then he smiled at the children. 'Then we'll buy you each a new one,' he told them. 'Come along.'

'Will we be able to paddle, Uncle Lucien?' asked George.

'I don't know about that,' he said, 'but we might buy a kite on the way down. How would you like that?'

'A kite!' cried Victoria. 'I'd like to fly a kite.'

'Come along then. Say goodbye nicely to Nanny Webster.'

'Goodbye, Nanny,' chorused the children, feeling safer now that they each held one of Lucien's hands.

Nanny remained where she was and her expression was truly terrible.

'Goodbye, Nanny,' said Lucien quietly. 'We will take good care of them and will bring them back later on this evening.'

He led them out of the nursery and closed the door behind them with a sigh of relief. He had not heard the last of the matter – he was aware of that – but at least he had won the first round.

An hour later he and Virginia were installed on a rug beside the water at Buckler's Hard. Virginia sat beneath a large parasol and Lucien sprawled beside her. The children were trying to fly the kite, a large red creation with a red and green tail. Both were bare-footed; George's trousers had been rolled up to the knee and the skirts of Victoria's dress were pinned up round her waist, giving her a little more freedom. They both wore hats to protect them from the sun.

The river was busy with boats of all shapes and sizes, those at their moorings being rocked gently by the wash of craft that were on the move. The sky was scattered with small clouds, but the sun was warm for the time of year and there was very little breeze to cool the air. The grass stretched around them in all directions and for once the water was more blue than green. Everywhere children played while their parents sat back and enjoyed the sunshine. Two little girls threw a ball backwards and forwards with squeals of excitement, while two boys at the water's edge squabbled over a toy sailing-boat. A young mother made her way slowly along the beach with a very new baby in her arms and a small poodle prancing at her heels. A mother, father and little girl approached sedately from the other direction and as they passed, George and Victoria glanced curiously at the little girl, but none of them spoke. An elderly couple sat side by side on high-backed chairs and further to the left a young nurse in a grey uniform supervised a small group of children who were playing 'Tag'. Overhead, the sky was bright with a number of kites and the air was plaintive with seagulls.

'Poor little pets,' said Virginia, referring to George and Victoria. 'They do look so hot in those clothes – they really are most unsuitable for a picnic.'

'Yes, I'm sorry about that,' said Lucien, 'but I dared not stay there a moment longer. I thought Nanny might have devoured all three of us; she looked quite capable of it. She really is a bit of a dragon. Goodness knows what the poor little things are supposed to have done.' He glanced at the children. 'But don't worry about them now,' he said. 'They're obviously enjoying themselves.'

Virginia sighed. 'I must speak to Alex about Nanny,' she said. 'I keep meaning to do so, and then it slips my mind.' She turned to smile at him. 'But let's talk about you,' she went on. 'We have so little time together that we must not waste it. Now that Eleanor is going to take you away from me, every moment is precious.' She gave him a rueful smile.

'Eleanor won't make any difference to us,' he said.

'Won't she? Oh Lucien, I do hope not!' She gave him a look which suggested that their own relationship had been much closer than in fact it had.

'Of course it won't,' he insisted.

'But there will be no more trips to London, Lucien. No more visits to the theatre.'

'But why ever not?' he asked.

'There won't be time, Lucien,' she pouted prettily. 'You are bound to spend more and more of your life with Eleanor; that's only fair. But I shall miss you and I can't pretend otherwise. We shall all miss you. Who will play tricks on us and make us laugh?'

'You make it sound as though you will never see me again!'

'That's how it feels,' she said softly, 'as though I am losing you altogether.' She gave a little shrug and then laughed softly. 'Still, your father thinks it will do you good – nice steadying influence.'

'Hardly that,' laughed Lucien. 'Eleanor is not that kind of girl.'

'Isn't she?'

'Hardly steadying,' he told her. 'More a good sport really. I am looking forward to the autumn when they come to Berwick House. We shall have such fun, the five of us.'

'Five?' said Virginia.

'Isn't Alex to be included?'

'Oh, of course he is, if he has the time,' she said, 'but you know how he is – devoted to the estate.'

'It's a good job he was born first,' said Lucien. 'I would have been no good at all in his shoes.'

'Dear Alex, he does work hard,' she agreed.

She looked around her at the peaceful scene. A young woman was making her way along the water's edge with a basket of home-made fudge over her arm, and Lucien called her over and bought some for George and Victoria.

'You do spoil them, Lucien,' Virginia protested as the children ran off with their treat.

'That's what uncles are for, isn't it?' he asked.

In the water a few swimmers thrashed up and down, while further still a small boat passed, filled with sight-seers. A group of people sat down nearby, two elderly ladies on folding seats and a young man and woman on the grass.

Victoria called out, 'When's the Punch and Judy coming, Mama?'

'A little later,' Virginia told her. 'He isn't usually here until after three o'clock. Don't worry, we will see him when he comes down, you won't miss Punch and Judy.'

George came back to them. 'Mama, will you help us with our kite? It won't fly. It goes up in the air and then it falls down again.'

'Poor Mama is much too hot,' said Virginia. 'If I leave the shade of my parasol, I shall melt away.'

'Will you help us, Uncle Lucien?'

Lucien opened his mouth to say, 'Yes', but Virginia put a restraining hand on his arm and said, 'Uncle Lucien is tired, dear. You go ahead without us.'

'But we can't make it fly,' he protested.

'Well, you have plenty of time, dear. Now do as Mama tells you.'

To Virginia's surprise, as George turned away the young lady who had recently settled herself on the grass nearby turned suddenly and said, 'May I help you with your kite? I love kites. My name is Grace Martins.' She looked enquiringly towards Lucien and Virginia for permission.

'That's very kind of you,' said Virginia with a gracious smile.

Grace turned to one of the elderly women and asked, 'You don't mind, do you?'

'By all means,' said the woman, 'if that's what you wish,' and added, 'and if Alfred has no objection.'

The young man hesitated for a moment and then said, 'I dare say I could lend a hand,' and before anyone else could object, he and Grace had moved across to help the children. Before very long the kite was lifting upwards and the two children were watching it with rapt expressions.

Virginia whispered, 'How very odd.' She eyed the young man and woman speculatively. 'They're probably a young couple,' she said, 'glad to escape the eagle eye of the two mothers.' She moved a little closer to him. 'But tell me, Lucien, when are you planning to leave for Berkshire?'

'I shall have to go on Friday,' he said. 'First thing in the morning; they're expecting me in the late afternoon.'

Virginia nodded. 'I'm sure Eleanor is looking forward to seeing you again,' she said artlessly. 'I was hoping you might see the Hattons before you go. They're away at the moment, but due home any day. It's ages since we've all been together and I know they were looking forward to joining forces again when you next came home.'

So, she thought, Eleanor is expecting him on Friday. A plan was already materializing in her mind. She had made discreet enquiries from the Hattons' housekeeper and knew that they were due back in the evening. The Hattons, who lived on the far side of the village, had been friends of the Latimers for many years. All she had to do now was to drop them a note hinting that Lucien would be leaving on Saturday. Then with any luck they would suggest dinner on Friday night and Lucien might be prevailed upon to stay for one more day. If they did not rise to the bait, then she would have to let him go on the Friday because if she herself suggested anything for that evening, he would see through it at once.

Satisfied with her scheme, she allowed her attention to return to her children and, on impulse, called George to her and could not help noticing how happy he looked. It occurred to her that she rarely saw either of the children looking anything but subdued. Today George's face was flushed from the sun and breeze and his eyes shone with excitement and pleasure.

'Georgie, dear,' she began, 'I want you to tell me why you were sent to bed this morning?' To her dismay his carefree expression vanished, to be replaced by one of deep apprehension. 'I'm not cross with you,' she said gently, 'I just want you to tell me what happened.'

Reluctantly, after a long moment's hesitation, he said, 'It was Nanny. Nanny got hiccups and Victoria giggled. She giggled and giggled and Nanny told her to stop — and she couldn't, and then I started to giggle and Nanny's face went all red and she gave us both a smack for being such wicked children. I didn't cry,' he said proudly, 'although it did hurt, but Victoria cried and Nanny told her to stop crying at once but she couldn't, so Nanny gave her another smack and then another one and then I smacked Nanny.'

There was a long silence. 'You smacked Nanny?' said Virginia, astonished.

'Well, I tried to,' he said. 'I tried to smack her leg and then she said . . .' his eyes filled with tears at the memory, ' . . . she said we were little animals and we must go to bed.'

'Don't cry, dear,' said Virginia hastily. 'I am not at all cross with you. There's nothing to cry for. Have you told me all of it?' He nodded miserably. 'You are sure you didn't do anything else naughty?'

'No, Mama.'

'On your word of honour, Georgie?'

He nodded again.

'Then go back to your kite, dear, and forget all about it.'

He hesitated. 'But Nanny will be cross when we get home,' he said.

'No she won't, dear, because I shall speak to her myself. Go and fly your kite with Miss Martins and enjoy yourself.'

But to her surprise, he remained where he was and his expression didn't change. Suddenly he blurted out, 'I hate Nanny! I *hate* her!'

'Georgie, *dear!*' said Virginia, but at last the fear and dislike of Nanny Webster surfaced in the little boy. Totally overwhelmed by the emotions he had suppressed for so long, he found relief in a torrent of abuse as his voice became louder and more shrill and he passionately resisted all Virginia's efforts to silence him.

'I hate her! I do! *She's* the horrible pig, not us. She hits us both; she hurts us and she likes hurting us. She beats us with her slipper,' he cried, 'and ties us to the chairs and hurts us every way she can. *She's* the one that's wicked. *She's* the one that's evil!'

All heads were now turning in their direction. Victoria had turned in her digging and was now staring, white-faced, at her brother.

'Georgie, control yourself at once!' cried Virginia. 'Remember where you are. Hush, Georgie. Come to Mama.' She tried to take him in her arms, but he wriggled free and stood out of arm's reach, his face contorted, his arms flailing wildly.

'I hope *she* goes to Hell,' he cried. 'I hope she gets toasted in the devil's fire. I hate her! She's ugly and mean and she's – ' He pressed his hands over his eyes and, without warning, collapsed on to the grass, sobbing hysterically. People round them were beginning to mutter in astonishment or disapproval or both. Lucien reached out for his nephew but with a wild cry, George scrambled to his feet, a handful of loose soil clasped in each small fist.

'I hate her!' he screamed desperately and suddenly he unclenched his hands and flung the soil up into the air before turning to run in the direction of the water. By this time Lucien was on his feet and running after him, while Virginia also rose to her feet and made perfunctory apologies to those sitting closest to them. She then became aware that some of the soil had blown into Miss Martins' eye and hurried towards her.

'Oh my dear,' she said, 'I'm so terribly sorry. I'm quite at a loss – my son is not himself today. So very overwrought.'

'I understand. Please don't worry,' Grace said. She tried to smile, but her closed eye was obviously causing some discomfort.

'Perhaps I can help,' suggested Virginia.

Alfred intervened. 'I'll look after her,' he said. 'You see to your little boy, he's obviously very upset.'

'I just don't know what's got into him,' said Virginia. 'He's usually such a quiet child.'

Grace said, 'I'll be all right. Please don't scold him. It was an accident and it's nothing to worry about. I'll use the eye lotion when I get home.'

Just then a cry went up about fifty yards along the beach, which was taken up by all the children as the owner of the little theatre began to set it up on the grass.

'Punch and Judy! Punch and Judy!' they cried and within minutes, a small crowd of eager children had collected while their nannies and parents gathered behind them.

'Punch and Judy!' cried Victoria, hurrying over the grass. 'I like to see Punch and Judy.'

'You shall see it, dear,' said Virginia distractedly, taking her hand and leading her down to meet Lucien who was now returning with a very white-faced George in his arms.

'Is he all right?' cried Virginia.

'I think so,' said Lucien. 'He's a bit shaken up but you're all right, aren't you, old man?'

George nodded wanly.

Virginia kissed him. 'Don't worry, dear,' she said.

'We're not cross with you. No one is going to reprimand you. We shall say no more about it. Do you hear?' He nodded dumbly. 'But first you must come and say you are sorry to the young lady who was helping you with your kite, because some of the soil you threw went into her eye. Then we'll all go and see the Punch and Judy and forget about that horrid little scene.'

Lucien lowered George to the ground and he took his mother's proffered hand. Then Lucien picked up Victoria and swung her, shrieking with delight, on to his shoulders. 'Now you will be able to see the Punch and Judy all right,' he said. 'Come on!'

While Lucien took her to watch the Punch and Judy, Virginia returned to Grace with a contrite George beside her.

'How is the eye now?' Virginia asked her.

'A little sore,' said Grace, 'but I'm sure some boracic will soothe it. Please don't worry about me.'

'Nevertheless,' said Virginia, 'my son has something to say to you.' She looked at George meaningfully and his lip trembled under the scrutiny of so many adult eyes.

'I'm very sorry,' he mumbled. 'I didn't mean it.'

Grace knelt beside him and put her arms round him in a quick hug. 'Of course you didn't, George,' she said. 'We all know it was an accident and you are not to worry about it any more.'

'I think perhaps,' said Virginia to Alfred, 'that you should take your wife to a doctor to check there is no permanent damage to her eye.'

'He's not my husband,' put in Grace quickly, but just then Ivy decided to stand up and introduce herself.

'Grace is my paid companion,' she said. 'I shall see that the doctor examines her eye if I think it necessary.'

'Well, I insist on paying for any doctor's fee,' said Virginia, taking a small card from her reticule. 'This is my calling card; please send the bill directly to me. Now, if you will excuse us, we will join George's sister at the Punch and Judy show.'

*

80

During the evening Grace made several trips to the mantelpiece to glance at the small neat white calling card: 'Virginia Latimer, Berwick House, Beaulieu'. So that was the adored Virginia, she told herself and George and Victoria were Alex's children. Despite her inflamed eye, she was thankful that she had had the chance to meet the rest of his family. She wondered who Lucien was and wondered, too, what had provoked the little boy's hysterical outburst. She half-hoped that a visit to the doctor would be necessary so that Alexander would once more be made aware of her existence — *if* he even remembered her name. She had bathed her eye with a solution of boracic powder, but it felt no easier.

Ivy had grumbled repeatedly about the child's behaviour and the irresponsibility of parents, but Grace argued that childhood should be a happy time. Ivy was not convinced, insisting that the world was a vale of sorrow and God had meant it to be just that. Nothing would persuade her otherwise and finally Grace gave up trying.

The next morning Grace sat up in bed with the blankets tucked around her and brought her diary up to date:

28th May 1910. I almost met him yesterday but not quite. On the beach at Buckler's Hard we happened to meet his wife, Virginia, and the two children, George and Victoria. They were with another younger man. He seemed very fond of Virginia and she of him; perhaps he is her brother. Poor little George threw a tantrum about his nanny, who sounds quite fearsome, and then he accidentally threw soil into my eye. It is quite painful and I think I shall have to see the doctor. If only Alex had been there!! I know we can never mean anything to each other, but just to see him again would make the whole world bright for me. Maybe I'm being foolish, but I don't care. I love him and the fact that only a few miles separates his home and mine, gives me hope that one day I may catch another glimpse of him. Now I must make an early start because today is window-cleaning day. How I hate that job, but it has to be done and at least I can think of Alex while I work. I do so hope Virginia is kind to him. I couldn't bear it if I thought he was unhappy.

She closed the little notebook almost reverently, put it into her bedside cabinet with the pencil and slid out of bed. Later that morning, as she had expected, Ivy insisted on calling in the doctor who told Grace that the eye was slightly scratched but assured her there would be no permanent damage. He prescribed a lotion with which to bathe the eye and recommended that she keep a bandage over it for twenty-four hours to discourage the movement of her eyelid. Grace protested that this was unnecessary, but Ivy insisted that she carry out the doctor's orders. The doctor charged three shillings and sixpence for his visit and Ivy at once wrote a letter to the Latimers enclosing the bill. Grace did not know whether to be pleased or sorry. She was ashamed that Ivy was making so much fuss, but pleased that her own name would possibly be brought to Alexander's attention once more.

*

While Grace was cleaning windows at Salter's Cottage, Virginia was waiting nervously in the morning room for Nanny to appear. She had sent for her to discuss the events of the previous day, and to try to discover the reason for George's extraordinary outburst. When she mentioned the matter to Alexander, he had suggested that in fairness they should hear the nanny's side of the story.

'Please sit down,' she said as soon as Nanny Webster came into the room. 'I have something to discuss with you which is rather disturbing me, and I do beg you to be quite frank with me. We both have the children's welfare at heart . , .'

'Of course, madam.'

Her expression was distinctly unfriendly. When returning the children to the nursery the previous day, Virginia had refused to discuss the earlier scene in which Lucien had featured.

'As you know,' Virginia began, 'my brother-in-law and I took the children to Buckler's Hard yesterday for a picnic. While we were down there, poor George became extremely distressed for no apparent reason.'

Nanny's eyes narrowed. 'Distressed? In what way, madam, may I ask?'

'He began to shout and scream,' said Virginia, 'and became quite unmanageable. Almost hysterical really. I was very shocked and worried. He seemed so very, *very* unhappy.'

'Unhappy about what, madam? Did he say?'

'This is all rather awkward for me,' said Virginia, 'but I am sure you will understand that it has to be said.' Nanny waited as she searched her mind for a tactful way of explaining the problem.

'I am afraid he said some very unpleasant things about you, Nanny,' she said. 'At least, he said – now I am only quoting him, Nanny, so you must bear that in mind. He is only six and was obviously very upset at the time.'

Nanny nodded without comment and Virginia continued. 'He said that he hated you and that you hate him; that you were unkind to them and that you liked to punish them. His emotions were entirely out of control and we were all exceedingly alarmed to see him in such a state. At one point he was in a state of collapse. As you can imagine, he attracted a great deal of attention and I found the whole situation quite intolerable. I would be grateful if you could throw some light on this, Nanny.'

For a moment Nanny Webster's eyes glittered with what might have been malice, but she quickly lowered her eyes. When she looked up again there was no trace of guilt in her expression.

'I half-expected this, madam,' she said with a show of reluctance. 'As you obviously know, the children were forced to watch a most unseemly scene yesterday.'

'I don't think that is relevant – ' Virginia interrupted, but Nanny held up her hand peremptorily.

'Ah! But it *is* relevant, madam. You see, the children are used to proper nursery discipline. That is my responsibility. Your brother-in-law deliberately undermined my authority and that obviously had a most damaging effect on the children. I pleaded with him to restrain himself, but he ignored me completely. He insisted on rousing the children from their beds and *dragging* them from the nursery. We were all considerably distressed and obviously poor Master George has suffered more than any of us. He is a very sensitive child, madam, and for him your brother-in-law's interference obviously proved disastrous. George is highly-strung and I have worked very hard for years to help him control this wildness. If I may be completely honest, your brother-in-law's behaviour — if you will pardon the expression — set a very bad example to the children and I was both shocked and humiliated.'

Virginia hesitated. 'Lucien did tell me there had been some kind of problem,' she said.

'There certainly was, madam, but it was none of my doing,' said Nanny firmly. 'I was given no advance warning that a picnic had been proposed or I would have prepared the children. As it was, I was forced to allow them to leave the nursery in unsuitable clothing and in a state of acute confusion. If I am not to be allowed to run the nursery in the way I see fit, then perhaps I should consider tendering my resignation.'

'No, no, Nanny,' Virginia intervened quickly, 'no one is suggesting such a thing. I merely wish to establish if there is any truth in what George alleged. I would like to know your feelings for the children, Nanny. Do you love them?'

It was Nanny's turn to hesitate. 'I am as fond of your two children as I have ever been of any other children in my care. I cannot allow myself to *love* them. They are not mine; they are with me for a limited period.'

'And what do they feel for you, Nanny? Do they love you?'

'I trust not,' said Nanny. 'Their love should be reserved for their parents. It would be quite wrong of me to try to steal their affection — that is most certainly not a nanny's role. I have nothing but contempt for any nanny who tries to woo the children away from their parents. That is quite despicable.'

Virginia hesitated. 'Of course, but – '

'Pardon me, madam, but there are no "buts". My job is to care for the children twenty-four hours a day during most of their young lives – to encourage decent habits: cleanliness, politeness, a respect for authority – '

'That's as may be,' said Virginia. 'My own nanny achieved all those aims, yet I was always aware that she loved me.'

Nanny Webster's mouth tightened. 'Then that was very wrong of her. Children have a certain amount of love to give, and whatever is stolen by the nanny is lost to the parents.' Virginia was disconcerted by this argument. She had expected contrition on the nanny's part and possibly an admission that she had been at times a little too harsh with George and Victoria. Instead she had managed to blame Lucien for the débâcle and Virginia was somewhat at a loss.

'Well, I really don't know what to say,' she said after an awkward silence. 'I will discuss the matter further with my husband. I do wonder if perhaps the children are too much for you on your own, Nanny. It might be a good idea to advertise for another nursery-maid who could help you. You pointed out that your hours are long and your duties certainly are unremitting.'

Now at last it was Nanny Webster's turn to look apprehensive.

'There really is no need, madam,' she said. 'I am perfectly capable of looking after the children single-handed *if* I am left to my own devices and if my work is not undermined. I do not expect an apology from your brother-in-law, although some people might consider it suitable, and I am prepared to forget the whole unfortunate matter. I do not relish the idea of trying to train another nursery-maid. Three in the past two years, and none proved at all suitable.'

Virginia let this pass and tried a new approach. 'You must remember, Nanny, that the children are very young. I think perhaps too much discipline can be harmful. They do seem to spend a lot of time in the nursery.'

'That is where they belong,' said Nanny Webster.

'But we have large gardens, Nanny. Fresh air cannot harm them – a walk now and then in the sunshine. Today perhaps.'

'As you wish, madam, but it is very easy to unsettle children. They get over-excited, as they did yesterday.'

Again Virginia thought it wiser to ignore the insinuation and thankfully drew herself up. 'Well, I hope we understand each other a little better,' she said, rising. 'You may go now.'

Nanny Webster also rose and said, 'I would appreciate a guarantee that nothing like yesterday's events will happen again.'

Virginia wavered. To give such a guarantee would surely be to admit that Lucien had been in the wrong. Perhaps he was; she felt very uncertain. The nanny's manner was so matter-of-fact that she was almost convinced.

'I will consider what you have said and will talk to my husband this evening,' she said.

'Thank *you*, madam,' said Nanny without a smile or a nod, and she turned and walked out of the room.

Virginia sank down on to the chair and put a hand to her head. While she was still trying to collect her thoughts, Lucien came in with a letter on a tray. Pretending to be Fanny, he took small mincing steps and then curtseyed with mock humility.

'A letter for you, ma'am,' he said, but Virginia refused to be amused. 'Oh, really,' she exclaimed. 'What now? This really is proving to be a most unpleasant day.'

'What did the old dragon have to say for herself?' he asked as she opened the envelope.

'She managed to lay the blame at *your* door,' Virginia told him with a slight frown. 'She really is impossible. I am beginning to think I detest the woman. She always manages to give the impression that she's doing us a favour by working here. Anyone would think that George and Victoria were monsters.'

'Take no notice of her,' said Lucien.

But Virginia was reading the contents of the letter and her frown deepened until finally she threw the envelope and its contents on to the table with a gesture of exasperation.

'A doctor's bill,' she said, 'with a note from that odious woman we met on the beach. It seems the young girl's eye has required medical treatment. Well, I shall let Alex deal with it. My nerves are quite frayed by all this unpleasantness.'

'You shouldn't let it bother you,' he told her. 'Come for a walk with me in the garden.'

It was on the tip of her tongue to refuse his invitation. What she really wanted to do was retire to her bedroom and lie down with a whiff of her smelling-salts, but as she looked into Lucien's handsome face she thought of Eleanor and forced herself to smile instead and say, 'What a sensible idea. You are such a dear, Lucien. A walk in the garden might calm me.'

'Oh dear,' he said with pretended dismay, 'is that the effect I have upon you? I had hoped that my company was more exciting.'

This time her smile came a little more easily. 'I refuse to comment on that suggestion,' she said. 'I shall entrust myself to your care.'

'You won't regret it,' he promised with a little bow. 'Perhaps a stroll under the trees away from prying eyes?'

'Lucien!' she exclaimed. 'How very naughty of you! It's a good job I know you or I might think you had ulterior motives.'

'Perhaps I have,' he parried, lowering his voice. 'Perhaps I intend to ravish you in the shrubberies where no one will hear if you scream for help.'

Virginia's smile widened delightedly. 'You are quite impossible,' she told him, 'and I shall call your bluff. I shall accept your invitation to walk under the trees and I shall no doubt return unscathed to the house in due course. Are you going to offer me your arm?'

'Once,' he said, 'I offered you my heart and you turned me down.'

Virginia laughed. 'But you were only sixteen!'

'I offered it again a year later. I asked you to come away with me to foreign parts!'

'You've always been very persuasive,' she said. 'Perhaps if I had been single — who knows what might have happened?'

'But you will walk in the shrubberies with me.'

'Yes, indeed.'

'I might guide you to the summer-house.'

She raised her eyebrows in mock dismay. '*Not* the summer-house!' she protested. 'Would I be safe there with you?'

'I rather think not,' he said. 'I might just kiss you.'

'Why would you do that?' she asked. 'You have someone else to kiss.'

'Maybe for all the "might have beens",' he said softly. 'Shall we go?'

He offered his arm with exaggerated gallantry and she slipped her left arm through his and laid her right hand on his sleeve.

'You are such a dear, Lucien,' she said. 'I don't know what I shall do without you.'

*

The summer-house was a fragile structure, built many years earlier at the instigation of Guy's wife who used it as somewhere to hide from her overbearing husband. It was made of wood in an insubstantial hexagonal design of her choosing and Guy had likened it to a bandstand. The upper wall panels were of trellis and the roof rose to a central shallow point. Years of neglect and weather had faded the colour of the wood to a pale grey and it was now a forlorn shadow of its former self. Inside, a wooden seat ran round the walls and the wooden floor was rotten in places.

Virginia and Lucien stood on the grass outside and looked at it critically.

'We used to love this place when we were boys,' Lucien told her. 'Pity it's been allowed to deteriorate. Sometimes it was a fort — it made a good fort, because you could stand on the seat and fire arrows through the trellis. The gardener had three boys and they used to be allowed to play with us.' He smiled at the memory. 'None of us wanted to be the enemy, that was the trouble, because the enemy was always outside trying to get in. We used to toss for it and I had a two-headed coin so we always won. That meant we were the defenders and could go inside the fort. The others had to be attackers and they had no real base.'

'It all sounds great fun,' said Virginia, 'but I'm surprised at you cheating with that coin. I thought you were honest!'

'Honesty doesn't always pay,' he told her with a grin. 'You can have too much of it. Harry, Bill and . . . what was the other one called? Ah yes, Eddie – he was the youngest and a bit slow. He always had to be killed so that we could bury him. We were good at funerals, we used to do them with full military honours – that's if he was on our side. If he was a Zulu or a Red Indian, he didn't get such a good send-off.'

'Who were you then?' asked Virginia.

'Who were *we*?' He pretended indignation. 'Why, Her Majesty's loyal soldiers, of course!'

'With bows and arrows?' Virginia raised her eyebrows. 'We surely didn't fight the Zulus with bows and arrows?'

He laughed. 'Don't be so pernickety,' he said. 'Those things didn't matter; we just fought. Sometimes it was bows and arrows, sometimes sticks and stones – until their father put a stop to it . . . the stones, I mean. Ruining his grass-cutter, he said; spoiling the blades, so then Father put his foot down. No more stones.'

Virginia was losing interest in his reminiscences and looked up at him with a sudden provocative sweep of her lashes. 'Well, are you going to carry me over the threshold?' she asked.

His expression changed at once at the prospect of a different kind of skirmish and he lowered his voice. 'It would be an honour,' he replied.

As he lifted her off the ground, she put her arms round his neck and let her hair brush against his cheek. They stepped inside and he lowered her to the ground.

'Thank you, kind sir,' she said with a smile and added, 'You've never really kissed me, have you, except in fun?'

'Kiss you?' He raised his eyebrows in mock horror. 'And risk a duel with Alex? Pistols at dawn and all that stuff!'

'I'm serious, Lucien,' she told him, lowering her eyes and smoothing the folds of her skirt so as to avoid looking at him directly. 'You never have kissed me, although I know you've always wanted to; I've seen it in your eyes.'

'Was it so obvious?' His tone was no longer bantering.

'To me it was.' She swallowed, annoyed with herself for her unaccountable nervousness. If only Lucien would take command of the situation, she thought. That was *his* role – she should not have to give a lead, it was hardly ladylike – but he was holding back and time was very short.

Glancing up, she asked, 'Have you never wondered about me? About whether or not I *wanted* to be kissed?'

'I thought Alex – '

She fought down her irritation and said, 'I don't want to talk about Alex.'

'Then, no . . . I didn't ever think you wanted me to kiss you. I always imagined you were just flirting – amusing yourself at my expense, maybe. I'm sure teasing your brother-in-law is – '

She put a finger to his lips. 'I don't tease,' she said. 'I don't play games. I've always wanted you to kiss me.'

At last he took hold of her hands and as he pressed them against his chest his face was very close. She leaned towards him breathlessly as slowly his lips came down towards hers. At last he kissed her . . . a tentative, hurried kiss, but a kiss none the less, and she felt a thrill of triumph. Almost at once, however, he drew back and she knew intuitively that he was thinking of Eleanor.

She freed her hands and, taking hold of his, placed them around her waist. Then she put her own arms around him and pulled him close. 'This is how it's done,' she whispered.

The next kiss was stronger and lasted longer.

'Lucky Eleanor,' she said, half mocking. 'I'm beginning to envy her.' She allowed her body to press against his.

'Good God, Virginia!' he gasped.

Suddenly he stepped back and she could tell she had managed to arouse him.

'Does Alex . . .' he began, then fell silent, the question unfinished.

'Does Eleanor?' she answered lightly. 'Don't ask questions, my dearest Lucien; they're always unanswerable.' She lowered her voice. 'Isn't it enough that we're here together, just this once, and that you've kissed me?'

By way of answer he pulled her close again and kissed her fiercely. 'I've always wanted you,' he told her. 'Always envied Alex, waking each morning to find you beside him.'

'Lucien!' She struggled a little but without conviction, then relaxed suddenly into his arms and began to return his kisses with equal passion. If Eleanor could see them now, she thought with satisfaction. The wretched girl might be younger than her, but she would give Lucien something to remember! His arms began to explore her body and then he was fumbling with the buttons of her bodice.

'Please!' he whispered. 'Just let me look at them. Those lovely breasts – I've imagined them so many times.'

'Oh no, Lucien!'

'Just once. It's our last chance, *my* last chance! Just to see them, to touch them . . .'

Virginia was beginning to feel flustered. She had not intended to go further than a few kisses, but now she wondered how far Lucien had gone with Eleanor and longed to go even futher.

'I don't know . . .' she began, but her doubts came too late. Lucien pushed her back until she sat heavily on the seat. His fingers were so urgent and his eyes so intense that she could not bring herself to deny him. Her breasts, yes, she decided . . . but no more. She leaned back with her eyes closed as he knelt in front of her.

'Oh, Virginia! You sweet, beautiful, desirable woman!' Then her breasts were free and he was kissing them and she abandoned herself to the exhilaration of the moment, stroking his head with her hands until a sudden sound

91

jolted her to her senses. Frantically, she covered her breasts.

'What was that?' she whispered. 'I heard something, I'm sure I did. Oh, Lucien, *stop* it!' She pushed his hands away. 'I tell you I heard someone outside. I *did!*'

'There's no one,' he told her. 'Please, Virginia – '

'Stop, I tell you!' In a panic, she began to fasten the buttons of her bodice. 'Didn't *you* hear someone?'

'No, I didn't. You're imagining things. Oh Virginia, don't hide them again just yet. Let me – '

'*No*, I tell you. For God's sake!'

'But there's no one. I heard nothing.' His voice was sulky. 'I'll take a look outside.'

'No, don't!' She sprang to her feet as he stood up. 'Keep quite still and *listen!*'

Together they froze, listening, but hearing nothing.

'I'm certain . . .' she began. 'Oh, Lucien, I was so *sure*.'

'Then let me take a look.'

'No. If there *is* anyone, they'll see you.' They waited, hardly daring to breathe, but heard nothing untoward and Virginia's panic began to subside.

'Maybe I was wrong,' she said at last.

'You *were* wrong. There's no one it could have been.'

Virginia drew a deep sigh of relief. If she had been seen like that, with Alex's brother! Her fingers trembled as she fastened the last button and straightened her collar.

'I'm sorry,' she said lamely. 'I expect you think me a fool.'

'No, I don't.' He brushed the dust from the knees of his trousers, avoiding her eyes. They were both aware that the moment of romance was irretrievably shattered.

Lucien turned away to hide his disappointment and Virginia, her panic subsiding, cursed herself for the fiasco – but she had been so *sure*.

'Perhaps it was just as well,' Lucien said abruptly. 'I might have forgotten that you are my brother's wife.'

'I'm sorry, Lucien, I really am. It was so foolish . . .' Her voice trailed off into silence as she regarded Lucien's back, stiff and uncompromising – probably thinking of Eleanor now, and regretting what had happened. Virginia bit her lip. She had wanted it to be a beautiful experience for him; a comparison with the hateful Eleanor. Now the memory of it would be an embarrassment to both of them.

'Lucien.' She touched his arm and he turned round to face her. 'Say you're not angry with me. I'm truly sorry.'

'It doesn't matter, Virginia.'

They looked at each other wordlessly – Virginia longing for a few kind words, a little flattery to lessen her humiliation – but he looked as though he was longing to walk away and forget the whole incident.

After a moment, he walked to the doorway and looked around.

'There's just the two of us,' he told her.

'Thank heavens for that,' she breathed.

'Perhaps we should go back to the house?' Lucien suggested.

'Perhaps we should.' She patted a few stray hairs into place and sighed. 'Am I tidy?'

'Fine. Perfect,' he said, with only the merest glance. 'Shall I go on ahead? Would it look better?'

Virginia felt irritated by his lack of sensitivity.

'If anyone's going on ahead, it should be me,' she said curtly and managing only a brief smile, she pushed past him and walked quickly away from the summer-house towards the house.

*

Later that evening Virginia handed Ivy's note to her husband.

'From that Cummings woman. We must pay it, of course,' she said. 'It really was most unfortunate.'

He frowned as he read it. 'Grace Martins,' he said. 'That name sounds familiar.' Light dawned. 'Of course, Martins' sister; the young lady I met in the stables. How extraordinary. At least, I presume it is her. What did she look like?'

'Does it matter, dear?' Virginia asked. 'Just pay the bill and forget about it.'

'But if she's John's sister . . .' he began. 'She was a

pleasant girl. I should not care to think that the eye had suffered any lasting ill-effects.'

'A speck of soil? It's hardly a major catastrophe.'

'Hardly,' he agreed, 'but perhaps in a week or so we should write and enquire if the eye is quite cured.'

'Quite unnecessary,' said Virginia. 'It would only encourage this ridiculous Ivy to produce another bill.'

'Sight is very precious,' he told her.

'You are playing into their hands, Alex. Please let us forget the whole matter. The question which worries me is Nanny Webster. We must get a nursery-maid; I feel sure she's over-worked, but too proud to admit it. In spite of her protests, I think we must give her some assistance. I thought I would make some enquiries in the village and if we do not find anyone suitable there, I will contact one of the agencies in London. George's outburst was really quite frightening and I don't want it to happen again.'

'Has it happened before, I wonder?' said Alex.

'Nanny Webster says not. She blames Lucien, of course, but I can't accept that. Maybe the boy *is* highly-strung. The point is that he'll be going away to school before long and I don't want anything of this kind to happen there. We mustn't risk a recurrence.'

'Of course not. Poor lad! Do whatever you think best, dear. A nursery-maid would take some of the pressure off Nanny — if only we can keep her!'

'It's worth trying.'

Just then the gong sounded for dinner and he reached out his hands to Virginia to pull her up from her chair.

'Cheer up,' he said. 'Put a brave face on it, dearest, for Lucien's sake. He will be off to Berkshire tomorrow and we shall both miss him. We must make his last evening a cheerful one.'

Virginia agreed, although in fact she had other ideas for the following day. She was still hoping to delay Lucien's visit to Berkshire, and to that end had sent a cleverly worded note to the Hattons which she was hoping they would act upon. If they did, there would almost certainly be an invitation to dinner for tomorrow night which Lucien would find difficult to refuse. Anthony Hatton had bought land and a house on the opposite side of Beaulieu and the two families had been close friends for more than thirty years. Margaret, Anthony's wife, was also a local girl and had once been very fond of Guy. Unfortunately, he had not returned her affections and she had then married Anthony. Their only child, a son, was a year older than Lucien and the two boys had been inseparable. They had both attended Winchester School, but when Lucien went into the Army Reggie took up medicine and was still studying in London. Virginia knew that if Reggie was home, Lucien would definitely accept an invitation to dinner. Reggie was engaged to a young nurse at St Thomas's and Virginia was sure that Lucien would want to boast to him about Eleanor. They had always been great rivals in a friendly way. Whenever they swam together as boys, they raced; whenever they went fishing, each boy tried to catch more fish than the other. They competed against each other at point-to-points. No, thought Virginia, Lucien would never pass over an opportunity to see his closest friend and as she preceded her husband out of the room she crossed her fingers.

By noon the next day, however, her hopes of success were dashed. The invitation had been forthcoming, as she had hoped, but Reggie was in London and so Lucien turned it down. There was nothing for Virginia to do but hide her chagrin behind a smile and look forward to Lucien's next leave.

Chapter Five

The Social had been organized to raise funds for an event to be held later in the year. This was 'The Outing', a picnic by the sea – usually Bournemouth – for the poor children of the town. Alfred Harris had recently been voted on to the Social Committee; he was extremely proud of this fact and deeply aware of the responsibilities of office, attending every meeting and contributing to all discussion with great earnestness. The Committee consisted of a retired accountant, a school-teacher, a butcher and an undertaker – all worthy men in Alfred's opinion, although the undertaker had been known to miss an occasional meeting. Although there were no ladies on the Committee, they were always in evidence before any social events, making things to sell, baking cakes or collecting saleable items of jumble. They also organized 'Lucky Dips', made hundreds of lavender bags and verbena sachets and were equally invaluable when it came to preparing the refreshments.

These ladies were the wives of Committee members and Alfred had felt his single state to be a distinct disadvantage, experiencing a fierce pang of envy when the butcher said, 'My missus will bake a couple of sponges.' He looked forward to the time when he could make a similar offer. Could Grace Martins bake a sponge, he wondered, or better still, a 'batch of orange rock-cakes'? The school-teacher's wife was making the latter and the school-teacher had hinted, on being pressed, that 'a batch' was probably three or four dozen. The accountant's wife had promised a huge date and walnut slab cake while the undertaker (who had buried his wife several years ago) had ordered a hundred currant buns from the baker and would pay for them out of his own pocket. He was a wealthy man and could easily afford such an extravagant gesture, but Alfred could not. Finally

Florrie had agreed to make two dozen jam-tarts and Alfred felt that honour had been satisfied. A mother lacked the cachet of a wife, but the jam-tarts would taste as good as rock-cakes.

Alfred expected the Social to be a great success and he hoped Grace would be impressed by the special part he had played in its organization. To him had fallen the task of arranging the entertainment and the results – displayed on a poster of his own designing – made uplifting reading.

When the great day arrived, he proudly led Grace into the hall foyer and lingered by the notice board until her eye fell on the programme of forthcoming delights.

' "The Midnight Air" – duet for piano by Samuel and Olivia Bridges,' Grace read aloud. ' "A Forsaken Bride" – monologue by Amanda Lane; "Gypsy Dance", by the Misses Staines. It's a very varied programme, Alfred.'

Alfred smiled, delighted by her praise. 'I do hope so,' he agreed. 'It was quite a problem. Quite a headache, really. You know how it is – everyone wants to sing and nobody wants to recite. Funny, that. Then old Mrs Carter, who always plays the violin, had to drop out because her sister's been taken ill and she's had to go over to Castleleigh. That meant two people would have been singing one after the other, and I had to rearrange it all again.'

'Poor you,' sympathized Grace.

'Do you sing at all?' he asked hopefully.

'A little. I'm not very proficient. I sing for Ivy some-times, but she usually wants hymns. She plays and I sing. I'd like to be able to play the piano, but we could never afford the lessons. We had a piano once, but after my father died Ma had to sell it. But I don't see your name on the list. Don't you sing?'

'I'm there.' He pointed to the seventh line. ' "Choir – a selection of well-loved favourites." I sing tenor,' he told her, 'but let's go on in and I'll introduce you to the rest of the Committee. They're sure to be around somewhere.'

He was very pleased with the way she looked, with her hair swept up under the dark straw hat and a small

97

cameo brooch at the neck of her white lace blouse. He liked the soft line of her shoulders, her neat waist and well-kept hands. No one would mistake her for anything less than a lady's companion, he thought, and wished his mother was not so determined to marry him off to one of the vicar's protégées. Grace Martins was very much to his taste, but his mother insisted he could do better.

The hall was decorated with crêpe paper artistically draped over windows and doors and a long low trestle table in front of the steps held a variety of potted plants and cut flowers. The food, on further trestles, had been arranged along one side of the hall and consisted of numerous plates of sandwiches and cakes, a huge tea-urn and jugs of lemonade. Circular tables had been set out all over the body of the hall with four chairs to each table, so that before and after the meal the audience could watch the concert. In all, about a hundred people would be accommodated.

'It all looks very grand, Alfred,' Grace told him. 'I do think it's well done.'

He positively glowed with pride at this compliment and took the unprecedented step of slipping his arm through hers, something he had never dared to do before with Aunt Ivy's eagle eyes constantly upon him. As Grace gave no sign of disapproval he tightened his arm a little, his spirits soaring. She had always seemed rather aloof on previous occasions but perhaps now, away from Aunt Ivy, she would reveal her true feelings for him. A brawny man approached them with hands outstretched in greeting, followed by an equally brawny woman.

Alfred made the introductions. 'Mr Gordon Woodley, the butcher, and his wife, Norah – Miss Grace Martins.'

They all shook hands and he was aware that Gordon was eyeing Grace with ill-concealed admiration, a fact which had not escaped Norah who was looking none too pleased.

Hastily, Alfred said, 'Your sponge looks very good, Mrs Woodley. Very good indeed. I shall make sure I sample a slice.'

Her taut features relaxed a little. 'How kind of you to

say so, Alfred. Try the orange one. I think it's the best, although of course raspberry jam and cream is a favourite with most people.'

Taking her cue, Grace said, 'Orange sponge! It sounds delicious.'

'Do you cook?' asked Norah. 'I mean, is it part of your duties? You're a companion, Alfred tells us.'

'That's right,' said Grace. 'No, it's not part of my duties since we have a cook, but I can cook, naturally — although sponges aren't my speciality.'

Norah smiled. 'What *is* your speciality, Miss Martins?'

Grace felt Alfred's fingers close around her arm and did not want to let him down.

'I find I have a bit of a way with pastry,' she invented. 'Pies and tarts, that sort of thing.'

'Hot-water crust?'

'Er . . . no.'

'Ah!' Norah's tone made this omission sound rather significant but before Alfred could rush to Grace's support, John Smart, the undertaker, was bearing down on them and more introductions had to be made. A few minutes later the school-teacher and his wife arrived, followed almost immediately by the accountant and his wife, and Alfred was pleased to see that Grace — being younger if not prettier than the other women, was much admired by the men.

When at last the time came for the Social to begin, the first half of the programme was presented to an appreciative audience. Tea was then served and the various refreshments were devoured and appraised. The second half of the entertainment followed, including Alfred's own contribution in the choir. Grace, he could see, was enjoying herself tremendously and the excitement had brought a soft rosy flush to her face which enhanced her appearance.

While Alfred was on the stage he was annoyed to see the undertaker leaning a little too close to Grace and became rather uneasy. The man was well-endowed financially and was a widower — and although he had never spoken of remarrying, one could never be sure with people like that and Grace *was* a very attractive girl. Alfred was beginning to see Grace in a rather different light – no longer as the poor companion who would be fortunate to land a husband like Alfred Harris, but as a desirable woman who could attract someone like John Smart. The idea was so outrageous that for a moment Alfred's firm tenor voice faltered and he received a pained look from the choir-master. John Smart and Grace Martins? No, it was not possible . . . but the undertaker *was* a wealthy man and not every woman felt a distaste for his profession. Suddenly Alfred made up his mind to propose to Grace as soon as was seemly instead of waiting a few more months as he had intended. He was so disturbed by the novel idea that she might marry someone else that he had to resist the urge to rush from the platform and propose to her then and there!

The concert ended at nine o'clock and after interminable 'Goodbyes' he walked Grace back to Salter's Cottage; when they reached the gate she asked him if he would care to come in for a cup of cocoa.

'No, thank you,' said Alfred, afraid that his aunt might have stayed up past her bedtime to chaperon them. 'Look, Grace, I've something to say to you . . .' he began, determined to ask for her hand but wishing he had had time to prepare a suitable speech with which to preface the proposal. 'I've had it in mind for some while now that it's time I thought about settling down – that is, moved away from my mother and made a home of my own. Do you follow me, Grace?'

'Of course,' she answered, 'but won't your mother be rather upset? She does rather . . . well, let's say she relies on your company, being a widow. And where would you go? Find a room, do you mean?'

He took a deep breath. 'Not a room, a flat,' he corrected her. 'I mean *marry*, Grace. I want to settle down with a wife in a home of my own and, well . . .' he shrugged, 'have a family.' To his surprise, Grace did not appear to 'follow' him. At least, she said nothing and seemed unaware of the honour he was doing her. 'Grace, I mean *you*,' he said. 'You and me.' He fancied he saw alarm in her eyes, but hurried on. 'I mean, why don't you and me get married? You and *I*, I mean. What I'm trying to say is – look, Grace, I'm trying to tell you – oh, for Pete's sake! I'm *proposing* to you, Grace.'

Too late he realized that his proposal was not particularly appealing and certainly not romantic. If only he had had more time, he thought. She looked positively wretched.

'Oh, Alfred,' said Grace. 'I do wish you wouldn't. We hardly know each other really.'

'Hardly. . . .' He shook his head in exaggerated astonishment. 'Grace, I've known you ever since you came as Aunt Ivy's companion and that's nearly a year now.'

'Yes, but we've hardly had time to get to know each other properly,' she protested. 'I didn't know you felt this way – at least, not enough to propose. I don't want to hurt your feelings, but . . .' She sighed.

Alfred could hardly believe it. She was going to say 'No!' She was going to turn him down. It must be that beastly Smart fellow; the undertaker had turned her head. He tried hard to remain calm.

'Look, Grace,' he said. 'You must know I've always admired you. In fact I *love* you.'

'Oh, *please*, Alfred,' she said. 'Don't.'

'But why not? I love you, Grace, and I want to marry you. I'm asking you to marry me. Not straight away, of course, but after a suitable engagement. A year or two maybe. But we could make plans and I could start furnishing a home. What do you say? I'll make you a good husband. I swear it!' He waited.

'Alfred, I'm very flattered,' she said at last, 'and I do like you – and I respect you as well – but I can't accept because I don't love you, Alfred. I do want to *love* the man I marry. Love, honour and obey, it says, doesn't it? I'd have to be sure I loved you, wouldn't I, or else how could I make you a good wife?'

Alfred opened and shut his mouth. She *was* turning him down!

'It's that swine Smart!' he cried, his disappointment

101

overcoming his discretion. 'I saw him while I was singing. He was ogling you.'

Her denial had a genuine ring to it. 'Mr Smart? The undertaker! Oh, Alfred, how could you possibly think that about me and Mr Smart? He's so *old*. Old enough to be my father!'

'But he was ogling you,' he persisted.

'He was telling me an awful joke,' said Grace, 'about a mix-up in the coffins. One day they found that they were burying the wrong man. One man had only one leg and the – '

'Grace!' cried Alfred. 'I don't want to hear jokes! I want you to give me your answer now. Yes or no?'

'Then I'm afraid it will have to be "No".'

'Grace Martins!' he warned. 'Be careful what you say. I won't ask you twice; I don't think you quite know what you're saying.'

He was struggling now to keep his irritation in check as his indignation gave way to frustration. 'Most girls in your position would welcome the chance of their own home – a chance that doesn't come every day. I'll have you know that I'm sticking my neck out, asking you like this.'

'Are you?' She looked startled.

'Yes, I am. My mother thinks you quite unsuitable and she'll be very upset indeed if I tell her I've made you a proposal. It's nothing personal, but she thinks I could do better than a paid companion; she made that quite clear when I told her I was inviting you to the Social.'

Grace's expression changed. 'Then she'll be delighted that I've said "No",' she observed. 'At least I've made somebody happy.'

Alfred's flash of irritation subsided as quickly as it had risen.

'You could make *me* happy,' he told her, 'if only you would think it over. Oh Lord, I'm making an awful hash of this. Of course I'll ask you again, Grace. I'll give you time to think it over carefully; that's only fair. I was just so afraid that wretched undertaker was putting ideas into your head . . . and I'm sorry about what I said about mother.'

'You're not going to tell me now that she *does* approve of me?'

'No.' Too late he regretted his indiscretion. 'Not exactly – but of course she doesn't really know you.'

'Ivy isn't keen on the idea of me marrying you either,' said Grace. 'She's made that quite clear. Nothing against you in particular – '

'I should jolly well hope not! I'm her nephew!'

There was an uncomfortable silence which was eventually broken by Alfred. 'So, you'll think it over then?' he asked, subdued.

'I don't think I'll change my mind,' said Grace, 'but I'll think about it if you like.'

'You do that,' he told her. 'Never mind about my mother or Aunt Ivy. It's you and me that matters, Grace. We'd have a good life together, you know. I've been asked to go on the committee of the Rambling Club and I *have* been thinking about buying a new bicycle.' In fact he had never even considered such a possibility, but now it seemed a good idea. 'A *tandem*,' he added.

She smiled briefly and greatly encouraged, he rushed on. 'Yes, I think I could promise you a pretty good social life and my prospects at work are quite considerable. Slow but steady advancement – that's what Mr Brown promised me when I joined.'

'I'm sure you'll do very well, Alfred,' she said, 'and I'll think it over, only . . . please don't count on it. I'll most likely still say "No".'

It was his turn to smile and he laid his hand on her arm. 'I'm very hopeful you'll say "Yes",' he said. 'You've got a sensible head on your shoulders, I know, and you'll see reason. I'll ask you again by and by.' She nodded.

'And you did have a good time at the Social?' he asked.

'Yes, I did, and thank you awfully for taking me.'

'Good girl,' he said heartily. 'Shall I kiss you good-night?'

'If you like.'

He kissed her and she was every bit as wonderful as

he had imagined. His senses leaped with excitement as he felt her warm body within his arms and his kiss became two kisses and then three. As she began to struggle, his arms tightened round her and his kisses became more intense until, when she finally struggled free, she was breathless and flustered.

'Alfred Harris!' she gasped. 'I could hardly breathe!'

Panting, Alfred reached for her again, but she dodged backwards and closed the gate between them.

'Ivy will be waiting up for me,' she hissed. 'I must go, Alfred. She's probably watching from the window.'

'No, don't go yet!' he cried, fumbling with the latch of the gate, but she was already at the front door and he heard her key go in the lock.

'Grace! Dammit!'

For a moment she was silhouetted against the hall light, her hat awry, her hair dishevelled. Suddenly he wanted to make her more dishevelled! Blast and dammit! He had never felt so excited by a woman.

'Grace, come back here!' he hissed urgently.

But the door closed and she had gone.

*

Grace had been in bed and asleep for several hours when something roused her. She opened her eyes and listened sleepily, dimly aware that something was wrong. Usually she slept deeply and only the ringing of Ivy's bell inter-rupted her dreams. But this time the bell was not ringing and her senses told her that it had not been rung. She waited. A delicate rattle sounded against the open window-panes and was followed by a soft pattering on the linoleum. Something had been thrown in through the half-open window!

Her heart began to thump uncomfortably as she reached for her dressing-gown which lay across the bottom of her bed. Someone was outside in the back garden! Suddenly she guessed who it was.

'Oh, no!' she whispered as she tied the cord round her waist.

104

'Grace! Grace Martins!' came Alfred's voice from the darkness below the window.

As she crossed to the window she stepped on to the tiny pebbles and, cursing under her breath, went back to the bed for her slippers.

'I'm coming,' she muttered.

What in heaven's name was he up to, she wondered and – more to the point – whatever would Ivy say if she knew? The whole business about the proposal would come out, and Grace was in no mood to cope with the endless arguments which she anticipated when it became known that she had effectively turned down Alfred's offer. She opened the window further and looked down into the moonlit garden where he was clearly visible. He was looking up at the house and although it was not light enough for her to read the expression on his face, intuition told her that he was the worse for drink. She groaned.

'Alfred! What do you want?' she asked, keeping her voice as low as possible for fear of waking Ivy who slept in the next room.

'Oh, Grace! Grace!' His slurred voice was louder now that he had seen her. 'I've got to talk to you. You must come down. I wasn't . . .' He swayed slightly.

'We'll talk about it tomorrow,' she hissed. 'You must go home, Alfred, do you hear me? Go home to bed.'

'No!' he cried thickly. 'Not until – not until your –' He swayed again.

Grace wondered desperately what she should do. He hardly seemed in a fit state to be allowed on the streets alone. Would he be able to find his way home, she wondered, even if she could persuade him to try. At this time of night there would be few vehicles on the road for him to fall under, but he might conceivably get lost. Presumably Florrie knew that he was missing from his bed and Grace could imagine what a panic she would be in. Reluctantly, she came to the conclusion that she would have to take him home.

'Grace!' he shouted. 'I want to marry you. Yes! That's it! I want . . . ooh!'

To Grace's surprise, he began to fumble with the buttons of his trousers but just as it dawned on her what was about to happen, the window next to hers opened and Ivy put her head out.

'Who's down there?' she called in a quavering voice. 'Who is it? I shall call a constable if – '

The sight of Alfred urinating over her favourite standard rose silenced her abruptly and gave Grace time to withdraw without being seen. Clapping a hand to her mouth to stifle an attack of giggles, she waited to see what would happen next. Eventually, she heard Ivy's incredulous voice.

'Alfred? Is that you? It *is* you. Oh, how could you do such a thing? And do you know the time? It's past one o'clock.'

'I must . . .' Alfred began again. 'I must speak to Grace. I mean to marry her. Where's she gone? Grace!'

Grace toyed with the idea of pretending to be asleep but it seemed unlikely she would get away with it. She looked out of the window and saw Alfred trying ineffectively to re-button his trousers. From the next window Ivy, her face surrounded by a halo of curling-rags, glared at her.

'It's Alfred,' Grace ventured unnecessarily. 'He's been drinking, I'm afraid.'

'Drinking?' Ivy was scandalized. 'I'll have you know my nephew never drinks – at least, not in the way you mean. The *occasional* glass of elderberry wine, maybe, but *drinking*, no. He must be ill.'

Alfred shouted again. 'Grace! Say you'll marry me. That's all I want to hear. Just say . . .' He swayed and clutched at the clothes-prop for support, but the prop was resting against the clothesline and now it slid along and fell to the ground, taking Alfred with it. There was a muffled moan and then silence.

Ivy screamed. 'He's hurt!' she cried. 'Oh, poor Alfred! What will Florrie say? He's not moving, he's unconscious!'

Grace said, 'He fell on to the grass so he can't be badly

106

hurt. Should we bring him inside, do you think, if we can lift him?'

'Bring him in? Yes. Yes, of course! That's the best thing.' Ivy hesitated. 'Bring a blanket from your bed. We'll put him on the sofa. Oh dear! Perhaps we should call Doctor Edwards. What a thing to happen, I can't understand it at all!'

'Don't upset yourself,' said Grace. 'I'm sure he'll be fine. It's just the drink and he'll sleep it off by the morning.'

Ivy snorted in disbelief and withdrew her head. Grace paused to strip back the coverlet and tug the top blanket free. Folding it awkwardly, she then decided that a little light might be useful and lit the candle that stood beside her bed. Hurrying to the door, she let herself out into the passage in time to see Ivy heading for the stairs. She, too, was carrying a blanket but had not bothered to fold it and it was trailing on the floor. Even as Grace opened her mouth to call out a warning, Ivy stepped on the trailing end of the blanket and plunged headlong down the stairs. There were several thuds and then silence.

'God Almighty!' cried Grace and, dropping her own blanket, she rushed forward and looked down the stairs. Ivy lay at the bottom with her arms thrown out, one leg twisted under her.

'Please, God!' whispered Grace. 'Oh, please don't let it be serious.'

She rushed down the stairs calling Ivy's name as she went, but there was a stillness about the crumpled form and Grace felt a terrible certainty that she was dead. Kneeling beside her, she peered into her eyes but they were wide open and apparently sightless. She could find no pulse in the thin wrist.

'Ivy!' whispered Grace helplessly.

For a full minute she knelt beside her employer, shocked and fearful, while her mind refused to function, but slowly her wits returned and she was able to consider the situation. Alfred lay in the garden (unless he had regained his feet by now) and Ivy was unconscious beside her. Doctor Edwards must be summoned immediately.

Infinitely grateful for the invention of the telephone, Grace ran to it, called up the operator and gave their number.

'Doctor Edwards – and please tell him it's urgent,' she said. The operator, recognizing the number, said, 'Oh dear, it's not Miss Cummings, is it?'

'Yes, she's had a bad fall. Please hurry.'

She hung up the receiver before the inquisitive operator could waste further time by asking questions and went back to Ivy. She did not dare move her, but covered her instead with one of the blankets. Was she still alive? Grace offered up a short prayer.

'I've called Doctor Edwards,' she told her. Looking down at the apparently lifeless body, she thought how mortified the prim old woman would be at the prospect of being seen by the doctor with her hair in curlers. 'I'll see to Alfred first,' Grace said, 'then I'll come back and take them out for you.'

Hurrying out into the garden, she fought back tears. Surely this was not the end for Ivy. It was so unexpected, so utterly improbable, so *undeserved*. Death had no right to steal up on people this way.

In the garden she found Alfred on his knees staring up at the house. 'I gotta talk to Grace – ' he began.

'You're talking to her,' she told him severely. 'This is *me*, Grace. Now I'm going to take your arm and you are going to get up. Do you understand? You're going to come into the house . . .' She tried to pull him to his feet.

'Say you'll marry me,' he begged. 'Say you'll . . . Ar!' Just in time, Grace jumped aside as he doubled up and the contents of his stomach erupted on to Ivy's neat lawn. She closed her eyes despairingly and prayed for patience.

'Do you feel better now?' she asked him when it was over. 'Good. Then please get to your feet, Alfred, or else I shall have to leave you here. Doctor Edwards will be here shortly – at least, I hope he will.'

Somehow, with a mixture of coaxing and bullying, she got him to his feet and half-carried him into the kitchen where she propped him in Ivy's rocking-chair and gave him a mug of cold water to sip.

'I'll be back,' she said and returned to her employer. Ivy had not moved and showed no sign of life but, as she had promised, Grace sat beside her and gently unwound the curling rags. She had just finished this task when there was a ring at the front-door bell and Grace hurried thankfully to let in the doctor. She explained what had happened and, together, they turned Ivy over and the doctor examined her. Finally he shock his head.

'I'm afraid there's no hope, Miss Martins,' he told her. 'None at all. I imagine the fall killed her instantly and at least she would have felt no pain; it was all too sudden, you see.'

Grace had known in her heart what the diagnosis would be and yet the confirmation stunned her.

'I can hardly believe it,' she whispered. Then a fresh thought struck her and she said, 'Oh dear. Poor Florrie! However will I tell her?'

The doctor closed his bag and at that moment Alfred appeared in the doorway, staring blearily at them.

'I wanna marry Grace,' he announced.

Grace said hurriedly, 'I was going to tell you, doctor. Alfred's been drinking a little too much and he's a bit under the weather. It's a complicated story.'

The doctor stood up. 'I think perhaps I should hear it,' he said.

*

17th June. Poor Ivy died two days ago after a fall down the stairs. It was the worst night of my whole life. First Alfred proposed after the Social and I tried to say 'No' kindly, but he turned up drunk as a lord in the middle of the night. Ivy fell down the stairs going to let him in, so in a way it was Alfred's fault but in a way it was mine, too. Strange to think that if I'd said 'Yes' she would still be alive. Florrie has taken Ivy's body over to her house and I am here alone with Cookie tidying the place up and waiting for the funeral and wondering what to do next. Look for another job, I suppose. Poor Alfred is in such a state, what with me not saying yes and his aunt dying and his mother knocked all of a heap. The funny thing is that I miss her – Ivy, I mean. She used to nag and grumble, but now she's gone I think she was a lot better than some and I was really quite comfortable here.

Alfred asked me again to marry him and this time I managed a definite 'No'. Florrie doesn't know whether to be pleased I've refused him (because she doesn't approve of me) or cross because I didn't fall over myself with gratitude for her son's offer. I know he means well, but I can't marry him or anyone else. I just keep seeing Alex Latimer's face. Thinking about him is the only thing that has made the past two days bearable. I wish! I wish! But what's the use of wishing. He belongs to Virginia and he ADORES her. Lucky Virginia! And it's so long since I last saw him. He called in to ask about my eye one day, but I was in the back garden and Ivy told him I was fine, so I didn't get a chance to speak to him or even to see him. Still, he must have cared about me a bit to bother to call. At least I like to think so. Well, that's enough about my dearest Alex. The big question is, what am I to do now Ivy has gone?

On the nineteenth of June Ivy was buried in the church-yard of St Michael and All Angels which appropriately was set half-way between Salter's Cottage and her favourite butcher. A thoroughly chastened Alfred stood beside the grave, one arm supporting his mother whose face was hidden by a heavy black veil. Grace had stationed herself on the other side of Florrie and the rest of the small group of mourners were neighbours and friends, but Cookie was absent, having stayed away to help Florrie's cook prepare the funeral repast.

'Ashes to ashes, dust to dust . . .'

The rector spoke the well-known words in a voice that held genuine sorrow. Grace was trying hard to pay proper attention to the service, but found it difficult to concentrate for she had other matters to consider. The position of nursery-maid at Berwick House had recently been advertised and her brother had promised to approach his 'guv'nor' on her behalf. She had wonderful fantasies in which she saw herself sharing the same roof as Alex Latimer. If she could get the job she would see him again, and that glittering prospect had helped her through the gloom of the past few days. Another problem was Alfred's refusal to accept 'No' as an answer to his proposal. He insisted that she was too confused and upset to think rationally. Her rejection seemed to have made her doubly desirable in his eyes and he assured her he would wait for a 'long, long time' before he gave up hope. To make matters worse, he had given his mother such a glowing account of Grace's actions on the night of Ivy's death that Florrie's earlier objections had been modified to some extent, and now she was prepared to say that Grace just *might* make a suitable daughter-in-law. The job as nursery-maid at Berwick House offered Grace an escape and she saw the advertisement in the *Southampton Times* as Fate at its kindest.

Forcing her thoughts back to the present, she glanced down at the gleaming wood of Ivy's coffin and wondered if Ivy's spirit was somehow among them or if it had already departed to a better place. And how did Ivy feel about her abrupt change from life to death? Could she still experience emotions? Was she annoyed with herself, Grace wondered, for that one careless step that had precipitated her down the stairs and into another existence? Perhaps she was enjoying herself – congratulating herself on the loss of all her earthly cares – or had met with the spirits of her parents and any other friends or relations who had preceded her. Death was no stranger to Grace, for she had seen her own parents laid to rest as well as two aunts and an uncle. Familiarity had not bred contempt, though – rather, a healthy respect – but it had removed some of the dread. For Grace, curiosity outweighed grief.

Yet in Ivy's case it all seemed a little *unreal*, for five days ago she had been alive and well and full of grumbles and now she was stiff and cold, silenced for ever by a moment's carelessness. She was dead, Grace knew, but still it did not seem entirely impossible that she might suddenly materialize beside them with, perhaps, a word of criticism for the rector about the speed with which the organist had galloped through the final hymn!

Grace tried to concentrate on the rector's words, but after joining in on 'Amen', her attention wandered – again this time to the two Latimer children for whom she might soon be partly responsible. George and Victoria. Victoria had seemed a nice enough child, but poor George! She wondered about the nanny as George's pale impassioned face came clearly into her mind. 'I hate her! I hope she dies!' What a strange comment for such a young boy. Suddenly Ivy's words came back to her – 'the nanny made her life intolerable. A real dragon – ' Grace began to feel rather uneasy. Could anyone be that terrible? Perhaps so, if seen through the eyes of a child.

The first spadeful of earth was scattered over the coffin as the rector finally closed his prayer book.

'Poor, *poor* dear Ivy,' sobbed Florrie and Grace patted her arm sympathetically while Alfred offered her another clean handkerchief. Grace was impressed in spite of herself, for this was the third handkerchief and to set in a store of them seemed to her an incredible piece of foresight on his part.

When it was all over, she and Alfred guided Florrie away from the grave and back to the waiting carriage. The three of them were whisked back down the hill and out along the Romsey Road to Florrie's house.

'It was a beautiful service,' said Grace as they alighted. 'I'm sure Ivy would have approved. And all those flowers!'

Florrie made no answer until they were safely inside the house. Then she removed hat and veil and gave her nose a final blow.

'It *was* very pleasing,' she said, 'except for that last hymn which was much too fast. Quite unseemly, I thought. I shall have a word with the rector about that when I see him again. But now, let us go into the dining room. I have no heart to eat, but I confess I am feeling rather faint and I must look after my health.'

Chapter Six

The Union was housed in a long single-storey building
and its grey stone walls and small windows were not
unattractive. The front garden, however, boasted no grass
or flowers and there was something about the place
which chilled Alex's heart as he approached the main
door . . . something intangible, but grim. Matron was a
sour-faced woman in late middle age.

'I've come to see Mrs Abrahams,' Alex told her after
he had introduced himself.

'When was she admitted?'

'Early in May,' said Alex. 'Annie Abrahams.'

'The gipsy?'

He nodded. 'How is she settling in?' His expression
was anxious.

Matron shrugged. 'A difficult woman. She rarely
speaks to anyone; just shakes her head when people
speak to her. Some of the others have given up on her.'

His anxiety deepened. 'Is it normal – this reluctance
to talk? Is she likely to come round? Do people often
go through a phase of not talking when they are first
admitted?'

'Sometimes – for a few days . . . maybe a week. I've
never known it persist.' She shrugged. 'Still, she's not
harming anyone but herself. Without conversation it's a
long day, but it's her own choice.'

'Could it be the shock?' Alex persisted. 'Has a doctor
seen her?'

'A doctor?' Matron seemed to take offence at this
suggestion. 'She's not ill, she's just stubborn. We can
only afford doctors for the sick and Abrahams is plain
awkward.'

He gave up. 'I'd like to see her,' he said.

'Well, you'll get no change out of her, but it's up to
you.'

Alex followed her down a long corridor where their footsteps rang on the paved floor and through a low-ceilinged room where a small group of young women were nursing babies; their eyes followed him, but they made no answer to his cheerful greeting. Then Matron led the way across a small grassed area where children were playing – two young girls squabbled over a hairless rocking-horse, another played listlessly with a few picture blocks and a boy threw a ball up into the air and caught it. They, too, paused to stare at the visitor, but none of them returned his smile.

They found Annie in a large, sparsely furnished room which accommodated them day and night. Apart from nearly a dozen beds, there were one or two wooden chairs and a large chest of drawers. The floor was stone-flagged and there were no carpets, but a text on the wall reminded them of the love of Christ and a long list of rules was pinned above the mantelpiece.

Annie sat in a window-seat, gazing out at a walled courtyard where elderly men were walking in twos and threes.

'Abrahams, you've a visitor,' said the matron sharply, 'so try to find something to say for yourself.'

She left them together with a loudly disparaging sniff as Annie turned from the window and looked at him in astonishment.

'Mr Latimer, sir! Oh, you *shouldn't!*' she protested. 'This is no place for your sort. Oh, you shouldn't have come.'

Alex took one of the old woman's hands and smiled. 'How are you?' he asked. 'I wanted to see for myself how you were settling down.'

By way of answer, she waved a hand to indicate her room-mates. Two of the women were very old and bed-ridden, a third sat in a chair staring vacantly ahead and a fourth leaned heavily on two sticks and watched them with avid interest.

'If there was any drink here, which there isn't, they'd drive me to it,' Annie told him wryly.

114

Alex pulled up a vacant chair and sat beside her, relieved that with him she was behaving quite normally.

'I'm told you don't talk much,' he said gently. 'It's not good to – '

'I've nothing to say to them!' she interrupted him firmly. 'They're not my sort at all and they smell. It's not their fault, but we've nothing in common. Nothing at all. I've no need to talk to the likes of them.'

'But what on earth do you do all day,' he asked, 'if you don't talk?'

Annie drew her shawl more tightly around her shoulders and gave him a straight look.

'I *think*, sir,' she said. 'I remember things about me and Charlie. Memories, sir. That's all I've got left now, but they're good ones. My memories are worth remembering.'

Alex was silent, filled with admiration for her stoicism in such bleak surroundings; sure that in her place he would die of misery.

At last he said, 'Annie, have you no relatives at all who might take you in? I know about the tribe and you having to leave it, but I can't bear to see you like this. I should never have let you come here. Something must be done, but I don't know what.' He spread his hands in a gesture of despair.

She shook her head. 'No one as I know of,' she told him, 'and I won't go back whining with my tail between my legs. I broke the rules, Mr Latimer, and I knew exactly what I was doing. They won't take me back. No sir, but don't you fret over me. You've more important things on your mind I'm sure. I had a lot of good years with Charlie and if this is the price – ' She broke off to wave her hand as the old woman with the two sticks drew nearer. 'You get away!' she told her sharply. 'This is a private conversation between me and Mr Latimer.'

The old woman mumbled incoherently, but obligingly turned and prepared to leave them.

Alex tried again. 'Would you like me to go to Norley Wood and make a few enquiries? Would it do any harm to try? I won't if you feel strongly about it, but it could be a way out.'

'You can try,' she said with a shrug of her thin shoulders, 'but I don't give much for your chances, sir, and that's the truth. I did have a sister Rosa, but I 'spect she's dead and gone. She was ten years older than me. Poor Rosa, she did cry when I left. Married to a man half her size, a useless good-for-nothing with mean little eyes. He's no good, I told her, but she wouldn't listen. I don't know why my Dado allowed it.'

Seeing his puzzled look she said, 'That's "Father" to you, sir,' then sighed. 'No, I'll make out here, sir, as long as they leave me to myself. I've got my memories, Mr Latimer, and no one can take them away.'

Alex stayed with her for nearly an hour and was pleased to see that his visit had cheered her. He had felt unutterably depressed, however, and he left determined to do what he could to improve the quality of her meagre existence.

*

On his way back to the house he called in at the stables to ask about Caradox, who was now causing some concern. The stables consisted of a long, low building some distance from the house and at right-angles to it; one end led out through double doors into the paddock, and at the other end there was a large tack room. Between these, a row of six stalls housed the various horses and ponies and a hay-loft above ran across the stalls. A walkway linked the stalls and two stable-doors opened from it on to the larger cobbled yard.

The horse was off its food and the vet had been called in, but with little success to date, and Alex had told John to send for the gipsy horse-doctor who was well-known and respected in the area. After cursory greetings had been exchanged, Alex asked John, 'Did he come?'

'He did, sir,' John told him. 'He asked if we had any saffron trees, but I said I didn't reckon so, leastways not as I'd heard of.'

Alex drew his brows together. 'Saffron trees?'

116

'Yes, sir. He was on about the male and the female tree, but I told him straight I'd never heard of any round these parts. Couldn't make head or tail of it, to tell you the honest truth. So then he said to try elecampane mixed into his bait.' He grinned. 'He swears by it. Says he's even taken it himself and it'll cure a cold quicker than anything else!'

Alex laughed. 'Rather him than me,' he said. 'So, did he leave us any?'

'Yes, sir, and he offered to fetch us a bit more in a day or so, but I thought I might send the lad to Norley Wood first thing tomorrow.'

Alex nodded his approval and went into the stall with John to have a look at his favourite horse. After more discussion, the two men walked back along the cobbled courtyard, John describing the events of his day and Alex nodding abstractedly.

'By the way, sir,' said John, 'I told Lee you'd see him right. I had no money about me, so I couldn't pay him.'

'That's fine. I've got to go down there about poor old Annie.'

In a few sentences he explained her plight and his intention to try to trace a sympathetic relative who might give her a home. He looked at John. 'They called her Abrahams in the Union. No "Mrs", not even "Annie". I couldn't bear it. I think that troubled me more than anything. It puts her on a level with common criminals. Abrahams!' He shook his head.

He was just closing the gate on his way back to the house when John hurried after him, a look of some embarrassment on his face.

'Sir!' he called. 'I was just wondering . . . if you'll pardon the liberty, Mr Latimer, but I did hear whisper of a position going up at the house for a nursery-maid?' As Alex nodded, he went on. 'I was just wondering, sir, if my sister Grace might stand any sort of chance. She's lost her place as companion through no fault of her own.'

He described Ivy's accident and its tragic consequences. 'Grace is a bit down, naturally, sir. She was fond of the old girl and – '

117

'Haven't I met your sister?' Alex put in. 'Wasn't she here one day?'

'That's right, sir. And you were kind enough to pay the doctor's bill for her eye.'

'Was I?'

'Yes, sir. Grace, her name is. She had dirt in her eye from Buckler's Hard and the doctor said it was scratched and –'

'Oh yes, I remember.' He looked at John dubiously. 'Has she any experience with children?'

'Well, not really, sir,' he confessed, 'but she's fond of them and she's very keen to learn.'

Alex smiled. 'Do you think she'd survive our Nanny Webster?' he asked. 'Not many of them do.'

John hesitated. 'Well, she's got plenty of spirit, sir. I reckon she'd make out as well as any other girl, maybe better. She's a cheerful girl by nature.'

'Hm.' Alex considered the idea. 'Well, I don't see why she shouldn't at least have an interview. My wife's seen two girls already and neither were suitable.' He nodded. 'Yes, why not! Tell her to come up tomorrow between twelve and one and I'll warn my wife to expect her. Mind you, I can't promise anything, but let her come by all means. Just don't raise her hopes too high.'

*

The following day, in a state of great excitement, Grace arrived ten minutes early for her interview. She was shown into the library by Fanny who, knowing of the relationship between Grace and John, felt it necessary to give her a few words of advice.

'Don't let Mrs Latimer see you're scared,' she said, 'even if you are – but on the other hand, don't sound too smart. See, they like to think they're the smart ones; we're just servants. And call her ma'am – well, I expect you know all that, having been a companion. I've often thought about being a companion. Not that I'd give up this job, but if ever I had to find another place. Is it a good job, d'you reckon?'

'It's not bad,' Grace conceded. 'It all depends on who

you're with. Ivy wasn't a bad old thing really, all things considered. I think after someone's dead, you see them in a different light.'

Fanny nodded. 'John's nice,' she said, 'your brother, I mean.'

Grace fancied her tone was wistful and she grinned. 'We get along,' she said. 'Mind you, we didn't as kids. He was older than me and I adored him but, of course, I suppose I was a bit of a pest as far as he was concerned. I don't see him very often now.'

'Mr Latimer thinks very highly of him. I heard him say so.' She winked. 'If you keep your ears open, you hear lots of things.'

'Are there any other girls coming for interview?' asked Grace.

Fanny shook her head. 'Only you today. There's another one tomorrow – but only if you don't get the job. I do hope you do.'

The two girls exchanged a look, shyly promising friendship, for each had already formed a favourable opinion of the other.

'I'll try my best,' Grace assured her. 'Fingers crossed!'

'Ditto,' said Fanny. 'I must go. Anyway – good luck.'

'Thanks.'

Left alone, Grace decided to take a closer look at the rows of books which completely covered every wall. A few were very old and battered, but many were handsomely bound in leather. Pulling one carefully from the shelves, she opened it gingerly and was glancing through it when the door opened behind her. She turned, expecting to see Fanny or Mrs Latimer, but to her delight it was Alex Latimer who stood there. Her heart contracted with joy at the sight of him, but she also felt her cheeks flame as she held out the book.

'I hope you don't mind,' she said. 'They're so beautiful. I was admiring the bindings.'

To her relief, he came forward smiling, took the book from her and glanced at the title.

'Ah, Thackeray,' he said. 'I confess I haven't read it. It belongs to my father.'

'I love reading,' she told him, 'although, of course, there's never much time.' With a flash of inspiration, she added rather grandly, 'I look on a good book as a luxury.'

'Do you now?'

He seemed about to smile but changed his mind and returned the book to her, watching without further comment as she carefully returned it to its place on the shelf.

'I really came to find you and satisfy myself that your eye was quite recovered,' he said.

'Yes, thank you. It really wasn't that bad. Just sore for a day or two.'

'I was sorry to hear of Miss Cummings' death. It must have been a tremendous shock to you.'

'It was, sir. I just wish I could undo those few seconds when she tripped, then she'd still be here.'

But even as she uttered the words, Grace recognized the lie. She did not wish Ivy any harm, but if she *were* still alive Grace would not be at Berwick House talking to Alexander Latimer.

He glanced at the clock and said, 'My wife will be ready to see you now. I'll show you the way.'

Grace followed him along a broad passage and into the last room on the left.

'I've brought Miss Martins,' he said. 'Do be nice to her, Virginia. She looks rather nervous.'

With a smile, he left the room and Grace turned to face his wife who sat beside a large highly polished table. Virginia nodded towards the seat opposite her and Grace sat down at the table. If only Alex were interviewing her, she felt sure he would give her the job. He was so kind.

Virginia wasted no time on pleasantries.

'I have spoken to your brother about you, Miss Martins, and to my husband. You are older than most nursery-maids, but that may be an advantage. Some of them are *so* irresponsible. I don't see why you shouldn't be suitable. Nanny Webster, as you have probably gathered, has a very sharp tongue and is a keen disciplinarian, but you would be working under her and her word is law. You may not relish that idea; I imagine a paid companion has a little more freedom.'

Grace, remembering Fanny's advice, searched for a way to answer which would sound neither scared nor smart.

'I'd do my very best,' was the rather unsatisfactory result.

'I certainly hope so. Nanny Webster has been with us ever since George was born and she came with the highest recommendations.' Virginia hesitated. 'So far we have not found a nursery-maid who could work with her, but they were all so young. I think that a more mature person might be able to cope.'

'To *survive*,' amended Grace silently as aloud she said, 'Would there be any chance of promotion, ma'am?'

'Nanny Webster would, of course, train you. Eventually you might then be able to secure a position as nanny in another household. That training will be reflected in your salary, so it would not be much – eleven pounds a year to be exact, all found.'

As companion to Ivy Cummings Grace had received twelve pounds all found, but she was willing to relinquish the difference if it meant she could be near to Alex Latimer.

'Eleven pounds is quite satisfactory to me,' she said. 'Do you think I may be suitable, then?'

Virginia regarded her critically. 'You might do,' she said at last. 'We'll see.'

Grace, nodding, crossed her fingers.

'Your uniforms would be provided and you would serve a probationary period of six months which I believe is usual. You would start work at six-thirty and *if* you went out in the evening after the children are in bed, you would have to be back at a reasonable time. Nanny Webster would decide that; she wouldn't want a nursery-maid who is exhausted, so no doubt she will want you in bed quite early.'

'Yes, ma'am. I understand.'

'Would you like the job?'

'Yes, I would. Very much.'

'Then we'll consider it settled.'

Grace wanted to shout for joy, but somehow she hid her elation and merely said, 'Thank you, ma'am.'

'I want you to take the heavy work from Nanny Webster's shoulders,' Virginia went on. 'She likes to have sole charge of the children, but there are many other tasks to be attended to which you can do. Carrying trays up and down ... Fanny does it at present, but it's not her job; cleaning the grates; emptying slops and so on. I hope you're not afraid of hard work?'

'I'm not, ma'am,' said Grace.

'Your brother says you are an adequate scholar.'

'I like to read –' Grace began.

'I imagine there will be very little time for reading. There will be plenty for you to do – washing, ironing and mending the children's clothes, for example. Nanny Webster's word will be law.'

'In other words,' thought Grace, 'I shall be at the old dragon's mercy and can't count on anyone else for help if she makes my life a misery. If it weren't for Alex, I should take great pleasure in turning the job down.'

'If you settle down well, we might review your wages in six months. It will depend on Nanny Webster's opinion of you. The fact that your brother works for us will not earn you any favours.'

'I understand,' said Grace. 'I don't expect any.'

'The children will call you Grace. Victoria is no problem but as you will recall from our earlier meeting on Buckler's Hard, George is highly-strung and needs careful handling. Do you have any questions?'

'Yes, ma'am. Do I get *any* free time. An afternoon off, for instance?'

'Oh yes, of course. One afternoon once a fortnight and one whole day once a month.'

'Does Nanny Webster take time off?' Grace prayed she did.

'She has not done so for a long time, but now I shall insist. She drives herself too hard. Well, I think that's everything.'

In spite of her misgivings, Grace felt absurdly grateful.

122

'I'll take you along to the nursery wing,' said Virginia, 'and introduce you. Then you can start tomorrow morning. Your brother can fetch you and your things from wherever you live at present.'

'It's Lyndhurst, ma'am.'

'Oh yes. So it is.'

With a sinking heart, Grace followed Virginia back along the passage and up a short flight of stairs to a green baize door. On the other side of this was another passage, but this one was narrower, darker and the floor boasted nothing better than linoleum. When they went into the nursery Grace received her first shock, for George was sitting in a chair to which his arms were bound by a length of white sheeting. His face was pale and his expression was sullen. Victoria sat in the window-seat holding a doll on her lap, her eyes full of tears.

'Oh dear,' Virginia faltered. 'We seem to have chosen an unfortunate time to look in.'

Nanny Webster rose from her chair and laid down her sewing.

'Not at all,' she said. 'Discipline is part of growing up. Master George is learning that certain disgusting habits are not tolerated in polite society.'

'Disgusting habits?' Virginia repeated, her dismay obvious. 'Oh, Georgie!'

'Picking at a scab on his knee,' stated Nanny Webster, 'but he'll learn. And Victoria is learning to mind her own business and not meddle in her brother's affairs.' She turned her attention to Grace with obvious disapproval. 'So this is a nursery-maid, is it?'

'Grace Martins,' said Virginia, 'is sister to our head groom.'

'That's a strange recommendation,' said Nanny Webster. 'Let's hope you're not afraid of hard work. I shall keep you busy, have no doubt on that score, and I expect a high standard of cleanliness – no dirty finger-nails, no greasy hair, no bad language and speak when you're spoken to. Otherwise you get on with your work. Is that understood?'

'Yes, Nanny.' Grace met her eyes as calmly as she could.

'She's going to start tomorrow,' said Virginia, her eyes going unhappily to George who was gazing at her imploringly. She gathered up her courage. 'We did agree, Nanny, when we had our little talk about the children, that – '

'I remember, madam. Every word.'

'Then don't you think . . .'

Nanny's gaze met hers unflinchingly and Virginia's sentence was never finished. Instead, she turned to George and said, 'Do please try to be a good boy, Georgie darling. For *my* sake.'

The little boy made no answer and Virginia wrenched her gaze away to confront the nanny once more.

'I thought . . .' she began. 'That is, my husband and I hope that now you have an extra pair of hands in the nursery you will find more time to – to give the children a little more freedom. I have spoken of this before.'

Nanny Webster's mouth tightened ominously. 'Freedom? Freedom is a dangerous thing,' she said. 'It is most unsettling unless it is based on a firm discipline and discipline has to be *instilled* into the young alongside knowledge. The children's lessons come first. *If* they do them properly, there is time for a little play, but I regret to say they do not do them correctly. That is why we can spend so little time in the garden enjoying what you choose to call freedom.'

'That may be,' Virginia persisted, 'but Martins says that George never rides his pony now which is a great pity. They do spend rather a lot of time in the nursery and the garden is always available . . .' Her voice trailed off into silence as Nanny Webster folded her arms.

'The garden may be always available,' she said, with a strange glint in her eyes. 'It is not, however, always the most suitable place for young and innocent minds. We did take a walk in the garden on one occasion, but I was forced to cut the venture short for reasons which I do not wish to discuss.'

Grace was puzzled by the tone of her voice and the

124

expression in her eyes. She found them somehow disturbing, but Virginia appeared to find nothing amiss.

'Well, Nanny,' she said firmly. 'I'm sure you will bear my wishes in mind and now that you have Miss Martins to help you, I shall hope for some changes.'

The older woman looked at Grace disparagingly, but said nothing.

Virginia hesitated, then turned and led Grace from the room. Closing the door behind her, she drew a deep sigh of relief.

'She means well,' she said. 'I know that her motives are of the best, but she is *so* highly principled and sometimes I think she forgets quite how young they are. Poor George!' Another sigh escaped her. 'I do wish they smiled more . . . had more fun.'

Grace met her eyes squarely and said softly, 'I'll do what I can, ma'am, I promise. Certainly on Nanny's day off.'

'Oh yes!' Virginia's expression relaxed a little. 'Nanny's day off. I quite forgot to mention it to her, but I will insist.'

Impulsively she held out her hand and Grace took it. 'Well, Miss Martins, you start tomorrow.'

Chapter Seven

Stanley Marcus put down *The Autocar* and drummed his oil-stained fingers on the table-top. He was a good-looking young man with a generous mouth, well-shaped nose and light brown eyes flecked with gold, and his thick hair was the colour of straw. Slowly and painfully he was coming to a decision. He thought hard, then picked up *The Autocar* again and read the advertisement for perhaps the tenth time, checking the date at the top of the page. The second of July – so it wasn't out of date and he still had time to apply.

'Dammit, I will!' he said aloud.

He threw down the magazine, pushed back his chair and crossed to the window to gaze out across a maze of Bradford's roof-tops and chimneys. Stanley felt that he hated it all. He wanted to be anywhere in the world but Bradford, because here he would never be able to forget the girl who had rejected him for another man. Even now he could not hate her, but he *could* try to forget her and he damned well would! Cissie Marchbanks' betrayal still hurt after eleven days and nights of cursing her and feeling sorry for himself, but now he could see a way out. He would go south and be a chauffeur and make a new life. No more clocking on and off at the factory. He would exchange his place at the work-bench for the driver's seat of a Daimler Landaulette. A job with prestige! He would say a fond farewell to the day-long clamour of machinery, and would earn the weekly sum of one pound nine shillings and sixpence plus board and lodgings. He would be respected for his skills as an individual instead of being a nameless worker liable to be bawled out by the foreman whenever the latter was in a bad mood. He, Stanley Marcus, would at last *be* somebody.

The more he thought about it, the more he liked the

idea. He had seen plenty of chauffeurs and secretly envied them their smart uniforms — cheesecutter hat, double-breasted tunic, cord breeches, highly-polished leggings and boots. They 'cut a dash'. Stanley rather fancied himself in maroon with grey trim, but he had noticed that a chauffeur's uniform was frequently chosen to match the car he drove, so the choice of colour was rather flexible.

He tried to imagine the reaction of his friends and relations when he told them he was going south to Southampton to be a chauffeur to a Mr Alexander Latimer. Well, he couldn't get much further south than that! To Stanley, the very name and address promised excitement and a glamorous new way of life.

As he left the window and sat down again, his mouth was set in a determined line. Cissie Marchbanks would soon see how little he cared! If she thought he would moon around Bradford, hoping for a change of heart on her part, she could think again, he told himself. She would realize her mistake, but it would be too late. She would *miss* him and serve her right.

He sat back, folded his arms and began to consider the letter he would send to Mr Latimer. He believed his engineering qualification to be reasonable and he *had* driven a car. (No need to say that it was for a distance of five hundred yards.) He was also reasonably well-educated and of a cheerful disposition. (Except of late and his present mood was entirely attributable to the unforgivable behaviour of a certain female and not to any flaw in his character.) Was he honest? Clean about his person? *Unattached* and ambitious? Yes, he was. After a few years with Mr Latimer, he would move on to greater heights. Chauffeur to an earl, perhaps.

'Cry your heart out, Cissie Marchbanks!' he muttered. It would soon be abundantly clear to her and everyone else that her rejection was the best thing that had ever happened to Stanley Marcus.

With a burst of enthusiasm, he rushed for paper and pen and began to draft a letter.

Dear Mr Latimer,

I am writing in reply to your advertisement in this week's *Autocar*. I am twenty years old and a fully-trained engineer (qualifications enclosed). At present I am engaged as a factory hand, but am desirous . . . [He looked doubtfully at the last word, crossed it out and wrote 'keen', then crossed that out and wrote 'eager'.] . . . eager to advance my prospects. I have some experience of motor cars and would like to be considered for the position of chauffeur which you are offering.

Yours truly, Stanley P. Marcus.

He read it through with growing confidence and then re-wrote it, paying greater attention to his handwriting, spelling and punctuation.

Later that evening, after he had posted the letter, he tried to recall everything he had ever heard about motor cars and how to drive them, but this amounted to very little – no more than isolated snippets of information culled from friends or overheard in the bar at the Six Bells – and he was forced to admit that it was not a very impressive collection. Motor cars were started by means of a starting handle which could break your wrist if it was not used properly; there was another method which involved 'bringing in the clutch' (whatever that might be) while running the car downhill; there was a carburettor to be adjusted, and a magneto; headlights were fuelled by acetylene gas, and tyres were prone to punctures and had to be changed.

He shrugged philosophically and decided that as long as Mr Latimer knew less than he did (if, as he hoped, the Daimler was the fellow's first motor-car), then the scales were weighted in Stanley's favour and he might get away with it. There was certainly no harm in trying.

His mother looked up from her darning.

'What's up with you, lad?' she asked. 'You've not said a word this past hour. You weren't writing to that no-good Cissie, were you?'

Stanley raised his head and a broad grin spread over his face.

'No, Ma,' he said. 'She's lost me for good, more fool her. I'm going south to be a chauffeur!'

*

Within three weeks Stanley's boast became reality and he arrived at Berwick House with all his worldly possessions in a tin trunk. He was soon installed in a room above the stables which had been hastily adapted for human habitation, and was then taken by his new employer to the kitchen where the staff dinner was about to be served.

'This is Mr Marcus, our new chauffeur,' Alex told the assembled staff. 'This is Mrs Wade, our cook; Fanny, the parlour-maid; Dottie Baines, the scullery-maid and Grace Martins, the nursery-maid. I'm sure they'll look after you.'

With a brief smile, he was gone, and Stanley found himself the subject of close scrutiny from four pairs of eyes.

'So you're the new chauffeur,' commented Cook. 'Right old rumpus you've caused, I can tell you! Well, sit yourself down, lad. You're just in time for a bit of boiled ham. Set another place, Dot, and then mash those spuds.'

Dot did as she was told, pausing only to flash a radiant smile at Stanley.

'Rumpus?' he repeated. 'How's that, then?'

Fanny smiled at him. 'Oh, it wasn't much,' she said, trying to soften Cook's words. 'Just a bit of . . . well, you know.'

'No?'

Fanny looked awkwardly at Grace, who said, 'I'd better get back upstairs, but it's nice to have met you.'

When she had gone, Fanny explained. 'It's her brother, John. He's head groom, you see, and doesn't take kindly to the master buying a car.'

Light dawned. 'I see,' said Stanley. 'Doesn't like the competition.'

Cook began to slice the ham. 'Course he doesn't,' she said. 'Stands to reason. He's probably been dreading it.

And then to make matters worse, he's lost one of the tack rooms for a — '

'Tack room?' he echoed.

'Where they keep the horse's tackle. Saddles and suchlike. The master's taken it for a garage for the car when it comes; it's been on order for weeks now.'

Dot rested her arm for a moment and said, 'Carried on alarming, John did, when he heard. "Bloody motor cars!" That's what he called 'em.'

'That will do!' snapped Cook. 'You know I won't have that sort of language in my kitchen.'

'But I'm only saying what *John* said,' Dot protested.

'That makes no difference,' Cook turned to Stanley. 'But don't let it worry you. It's natural enough, if you think about it. Folks are afraid of change. He'll come round in time, he's a good old stick, is John.'

Fanny raised her eyebrows. 'Old? John's not old.'

Dot scooped the mashed potatoes into a tureen. '*And* you're living in the room over the stables,' she said. 'John was hoping that room would do for an assistant groom. Now, because of the car, he's not getting one.'

Stanley gave what he hoped was a carefree laugh. 'Well, I won't lose any sleep over it,' he said. 'If this John's got any complaints, it's Mr Latimer he should tackle, not me.'

They all sat down at the table and Cook began to pass along the plates. 'Oh, John won't say anything,' she said. 'It's not his place to, is it?'

They helped themselves to carrots, peas and potatoes and Stanley's eye gleamed as he noted the generous portions with which they filled their plates. He had also seen a large pie cooling on the draining-board and a jug of custard. There was obviously no shortage of food in this establishment and since he had a prodigious appetite, Stanley felt distinctly cheerful. Looking at Fanny and Dot and remembering Grace, he thought that with these three young women around, life could be a lot of fun. He seemed to be the only eligible bachelor – except this John fellow, perhaps.

'So the nursery-maid is the groom's sister,' he said. 'I hope she's not against me, too.'

Cook gave him a sharp look. 'No one's *against* you,' she corrected him. 'So don't go getting your hackles up. Just you put yourself in John Martins' shoes and see how you'd feel. He's always driven the master everywhere, and the mistress – the whole family, in fact. Now I suppose there'll be times when the master uses the car instead.'

'Lots of times, I should think,' said Stanley through a mouthful of boiled bacon. 'Let's face it, the motor-car is the transport of the future. It's here to stay and all the John Martins in the world can't turn back the clock. The motor-car is *progress*.'

Three pairs of eyes regarded him uneasily.

'Well,' said Fanny, 'I shouldn't go on about it *quite* like that if I was you, and specially not in front of John or Grace. It's a very touchy subject.'

Dot leaned across the table to reach for the salt. 'She's new here, Grace is. Only been here a few weeks. Not that we see much of her. She's stuck upstairs in the nursery, poor thing, with Nanny Webster. Leading her a terrible dance, she is – Nanny Webster, I mean. Making her life miserable every way she knows how. I wouldn't be in her shoes for all the tea in China.'

Fanny nodded. 'Your problems with John are nothing to what poor old Grace has to put up with, so don't you go upsetting her with talk about progress and motor-cars because she's got enough to worry about.'

It was Cook's turn to nod. 'We all have our problems,' she said, 'but we all have to rub along together. If you remember that, Stanley, you won't go far wrong.'

Stanley raised his hand to his forehead in a mock salute. 'I'll remember, captain!' he promised with a broad grin. 'Any more of that boiled bacon?'

*

Grace opened her eyes and a smile spread over her face. Today was Thursday and Nanny's day off, so she would have George and Victoria to herself again and could try

131

to make up to them for the wretchedness of the rest of their week. Virginia, true to her word, had insisted that Nanny Webster should take a whole day off once every ten days. She had tried to make it a weekly event, but Nanny had wanted it to be fortnightly so a compromise had finally been agreed. The trouble was that Nanny Webster had nowhere to go and therefore remained firmly ensconced in the nursery, but this gave Grace the excuse she wanted to take the children outside. Previously, their only 'outings' had been an occasional trip to the shops in Southampton, but Grace had decided to take things fairly slowly so that Nanny Webster would be less likely to notice any changes in the nursery routine.

Today Grace washed and dressed herself and then went downstairs for Nanny Webster's breakfast tray which she then took to her in her room. This meant that breakfast in the nursery could be a more relaxed affair than usual, for Grace did not enforce Nanny Webster's 'no talking' rule but allowed quiet conversation.

Victoria and George eyed her hopefully. 'What will we do today?' asked George in an exaggerated whisper as he spread marmalade thickly on his toast. 'Could we go for a walk in the garden?'

'I should think so,' said Grace. 'I should think we might even play some games.'

'Games?' cried Victoria, her eyes like saucers. 'What sort of games? Oh, Georgie, we're going to play *games!*' She spooned boiled egg into her mouth absent-mindedly, her thoughts on the excitement ahead.

George's eyes clouded. 'We don't know any,' he said, 'except kites. We could play kites.'

'*You* don't know any,' Grace smiled, 'but I do! I know lots of games. Indoor games and outdoor games. Quick games. Slow games. Dull games. Exciting games. Take your pick!'

Victoria stuffed two small fists into her mouth to help contain her excitement.

'Which *outdoor* games?' whispered George with an uneasy glance at the door.

Grace held up her left hand and began to count off on

132

her fingers. 'Let me see now, there's "Hide and Seek" and "Tom Tiddler's Ground" . . .'

The two children looked at each other in delight.

'Tom Tiddler!' cried Victoria, relishing the sound of it.

' "Fox and Hen",' Grace went on, 'and maybe "Mary's Gone A Milking".'

'What's that?' asked George. 'How do you play "Mary's Gone A Milking"?'

'Well,' said Grace, 'one has to be "mother" and all the others are the children and they join hands and sing questions and answers. It would take rather a long time to explain it all. Let me think a moment — what else is there? Oh yes, we might play with bubble-pipes. But no, we could play with them indoors, so we'll save that for a rainy day.'

' "Fox and Hen"?' repeated George. 'How do you — ?' He broke off in dismay as the door opened and Nanny came into the room. Both children immediately busied themselves with their food, their eyes fixed on their plates. Even now, one word from Nanny could put an end to all their hopes for the day.

' "Fox and Hen",' Grace began, ignoring Nanny's sudden appearance, 'is a chasing game.'

Nanny walked slowly to the table and even Grace fell silent.

'Straighten your back, Master George!' she snapped. 'I've told you before. If you don't sit up straight, you'll grow into a hunchback and everyone will jeer at you.'

George straightened up, his eyes on Grace's face, imploring her support.

'That's splendid, George,' said Grace.

'And Victoria!' Nanny went on. 'Your mouth is too full. You cannot chew your food properly if your mouth is too full. If I've told you that once, I've told you a hundred times. Really, Miss Martins, you must make more effort to maintain good standards or I shall be forced to make a complaint about you to Mrs Latimer.'

'I'm sorry, Nanny,' said Grace. 'I'll remember in future.'

Much as she longed to quarrel with Nanny's regime,

Grace knew that she dared not push her too far. Already it was obvious that Nanny Webster was only waiting for an excuse to get rid of her and she was determined not to give her one. She was also aware that her own presence in the nursery was very important to the two children, and that already they looked upon her as an ally. During the few weeks she had been at Berwick House she had grown fond of them, and she did not want to be separated from them. As nobody else spoke, Nanny hesitated, reluctant to leave them in peace but unable to find further cause for criticism.

' "Fox and Hen",' Grace began again, as though Nanny's continued presence was of no significance, 'is great fun. Someone has to be the fox and the others are the hens. The fox sits in his den and the hens creep nearer and nearer. They keep asking him the time and he tells them all sorts of different times. Half-past one, quarter to three and *then* – '

'Yes?' The two small voices sounded as one as the children stared at her wide-eyed.

Grace lowered her voice dramatically. 'The fox says it's *midnight* and – '

'What rubbish!' snorted Nanny. 'Filling their heads with silly nonsense. You ought to know better. You'll get them over-excited and we all know where that leads. Tears!'

'It's just a game,' said Grace, keeping her voice light with a great effort, determined not to give Nanny the chance to spoil their day. So far they had not experienced a true clash of wills, but Grace knew only too well that Nanny Webster's position was far stronger than her own.

'We'll talk about it later, children,' she said with a smile. 'Now finish up your breakfast and then I'll take the tray downstairs.'

Still Nanny Webster lingered, unwilling to leave. Suddenly she leaned over and picked up the china 'house' which held the marmalade pot.

'Toast crumbs!' she cried triumphantly. 'Someone's been putting their *knife* into the marmalade instead of using the proper spoon. Who was it? I want to know and I shan't move from this spot until I do know!'

George went very pale but sat with his lips tightly closed, aware that an admission of guilt would give Nanny the longed-for excuse she needed.

'Oh dear!' said Grace. 'I'm the guilty one, I'm afraid. How very naughty of me!' She pulled a wry face and slapped her own hand with mock severity. 'I'm sorry, children. I won't ever do it again. Now, have you both finished eating? Good. Then we'll say grace.'

Together, under Nanny's furious eyes, they said, 'For what we have received, may the Lord make us truly thankful.'

Grace tried to appear oblivious of Nanny's continued presence and smiled at the children. 'Now, we'll wash our hands and then we'll be off.'

'The trays,' said Nanny. 'I hope you don't expect *me* to take them downstairs?'

Grace smiled at her disarmingly. 'Oh no, Nanny. This is your day off and well deserved it is, too. We shall take the trays down on our way out. Cook likes to see the children now and again.'

'*I* don't encourage it,' Nanny said at once. 'All that fussing and petting upsets the children.'

'Oh, really?' Grace looked at her in pretended amazement. 'I don't find that at all.'

'And don't let Cook give them anything to eat. No biscuits or cakes. It ruins their appetites. I'm afraid Cook has no idea how to deal with children. None at all.'

'Cook? Oh, but you're wrong; she's a grandmother,' Grace smiled. 'Didn't you know? She has a grown-up daughter and two grandchildren.'

While Nanny digested this remark, Grace bustled about, helping George and Victoria to wash their hands and put on their coats and hats. Then she piled the breakfast things on to the tray, brushed the tablecloth clear of crumbs and put on her own hat and coat.

'The table must be laid for lunch,' cried Nanny as they finally headed for the door.

'I shall do it when we get back,' Grace told her firmly.

135

'We don't want to miss the sunshine. Open the door, Georgie, that's the way, and say "Goodbye" nicely to Nanny Webster.'

As they went downstairs, they all breathed more easily. They were free! If only it was 'Goodbye' to Nanny for ever, thought Grace. That *would* be something to celebrate!

Downstairs they found the kitchen buzzing with excitement. The new car had arrived and the driver was being regaled with tea and cake.

'The motor's absolutely marvellous!' Fanny told them. 'You'll have to go and see for yourselves. We've all had a quick look and Stanley is wearing himself to a frazzle polishing it.'

Grace's heart leaped. 'Is Mr Latimer there?'

'No, it's all right,' said Cook, misunderstanding the reason for her question. 'He's on the estate somewhere and Sid's been sent off to look for him. They didn't expect the car until later this afternoon, but the driver here started off early and made an overnight stop in Winchester. It's dark green and gleaming with brass. Just imagine riding in a machine like that with no horses!'

'I'd be scared,' said Dot.

'I wouldn't,' cried Fanny. 'Stanley is as proud as a peacock. You'd think it was his car. He's going to have a uniform to match it – the same shade of green. Bottle, I suppose you'd call it. Bottle-green with white braid.' She glanced down at the children and grinned. 'You go with Grace to see the new motor. You might be lucky enough to ride in it one day. Wouldn't that be a treat?'

George and Victoria began to tug at Grace's hands.

'We'll be off to the stables then,' she said. 'We'll see the car and maybe the horses, too. I'll ask John. Then we'll play some games.'

Cook rushed to the biscuit tin but Grace said, 'I'm afraid they're not to have biscuits or cakes. Nanny Webster's strict orders.' Lowering her voice, she added, 'She might ask and I don't want them to have to tell lies.'

Cook tutted, disappointed, but then brightened. 'What about an apple? Did she mention apples? No? Right then,

136

my little pets, Cook will find you an apple. An apple a day keeps the doctor away. That's what they say, anyway.'

Five minutes later Grace and the children let themselves in to the large cobbled area that formed the stable-yard. At one end John and the stable lad were grooming Caradox, their faces turned resolutely away from the new motor. At once Grace was aware of friction and her heart sank. John's face wore an expression of stern disapproval, while Ben looked merely sulky.

'Morning, John,' she said. 'Hullo, Ben.'

They merely grunted in reply.

George and Victoria, prompted by Grace, made their greetings too and suddenly John saw his chance.

'Hullo, Master George and Miss Victoria,' he said loudly. 'Come to see the *horses*, have you? Well, so you shall. You shall see them all!' He smiled down at George. 'Not much good buying Dixie, was it?' he teased. 'You hardly ever ride him.'

George said, 'Nanny won't allow it because I'm so evil and I don't know how to behave properly. Perhaps when I do know, I'll be able to ride him.'

John and Grace exchanged exasperated looks at this further proof of Nanny Webster's power.

'You'd better hurry up and behave then, Master George,' said John, 'or poor little Dixie won't recognize you. It's so long since you've been down to see him. Let's find him now shall we, and you shall give him a sugar-lump.'

Unfortunately, as John strode off, George hung back and looked appealingly at Grace. He had seen his pony before, but he had never seen a motor-car.

'Go on,' urged Grace. 'Follow John. We'll see the motor later I promise. There's plenty of time.'

Still George hesitated. Because of Nanny Webster's discouraging attitude, he had only had two riding lessons and still found the pony a rather formidable animal. He felt sure it would either bite or kick him, whereas the new motor would presumably do neither.

'George!' hissed Grace. 'Come *on!*'

Meanwhile John had opened the door to Dixie's stall

and was leading the tiny Shetland out into the yard. George still had not moved, so Grace took his hand and gave him a gentle tug, but at that moment Stanley gave a couple of 'toots' on the car's horn and the pony, startled, rolled his eyes and began to tug at the halter.

In what his mother would have called a 'high-falutin'' voice, Stanley cried, 'Who's for a ride in the motor, then?'

The two children squealed with excitement but Grace, sensing trouble, grabbed at the children and held on to them as John turned in the chauffeur's direction, his face thunderous.

'You young idiot! You keep that damned machine of yours quiet!' he roared. 'You ought to have more sense.'

Stanley, his hands in his pockets and a cleaning rag draped over his shoulder, strolled towards John with studied nonchalance.

'The horses will have to get used to a few noises,' he said. 'Motors do make a bit of noise, I grant you, but they don't drop stinking dung all over the place like horses.'

Still trying to steady the fractious pony, John cried, 'But they fill the air with stinking poisonous fumes from their exhausts and you can't put that on your roses!'

Ignoring him, Stanley turned to the children. 'Coming to see the new motor-car, then?' he asked. 'I might let you toot the horn.'

'Oh no, Stanley,' cried Grace. 'Please don't let them. It frightens poor little Dixie.'

'Frighten him my foot!' said Stanley. 'Horses'll play up at anything – a rabbit, a bird, even a shadow. That's the trouble with animals. John's a bit of an old woman where horses are concerned; all grooms are. It's the nature of the beast. They'll just have to get used to motors because they're here to stay.'

Grace gave him a very straight look. 'Please, Stanley,' she said. 'If you two have to be like this, could you just call a pax while we're here? We won't stay long and John *is* my brother.'

A little of his swagger deserted him and his laugh, when it came, was apologetic. 'Just for you, then, fair lady,' he said. 'I never could resist grey eyes.' He took a step nearer to her and lowered his voice. 'And yours are the greyest I've ever seen. For grey eyes, I'd do anything. I'm a *slave* to them.'

She had to laugh at his nonsense, but then she saw that John was watching them.

'We'll look at the horses first,' she told Stanley. 'It won't take long. Then we'll come back to the motor.'

However, she had reckoned without John who deliberately made the inspection last as long as possible, showing the children all the horses, describing all the harnesses and finally giving both George and Victoria a ride on Dixie's back. Under Grace's warning eye, neither of the children dared complain, but eventually they had seen everything there was to be seen and were able to thank John and move over to the motor.

Stanley stood back with them, hands on hips, as they all admired the gleaming machine. The glass windows sparkled, as did the deep green glossy coachwork. The head-lamps were of brass and the walls of the newly-washed tyres were white.

'What a beauty,' said Stanley. 'Look at that line!' He waved his hand vaguely and Grace and the children nodded with suitable solemnity. 'I'm trying to put it back in tip-top condition before Mr Latimer sees it,' he confided. 'He should be here soon. You should have seen it when it arrived – all dusty on top and the wheels all splashed with mud.'

'So you gave it a wash and brush up,' said Grace. 'Well, children, what do you think of your Papa's new motor-car?'

'I like it,' said Victoria with an earnest nod of her head.

'So do I,' said George. 'Can we sit in it?'

Grace made doubtful noises. 'That depends on Stanley,' she said and two pairs of wide eyes turned on him beseechingly. He looked at Grace and grinned. 'What's it worth?' he asked in a low voice. 'I might let them, just for you – but you'd have to make it worth my while.'

'I've no money,' said Grace, pretending not to understand the drift of his conversation.

He lowered his voice even more. 'One kiss,' he told her. 'A very quick one!'

'Certainly not!' cried Grace, though she was secretly amused and flattered by his impudence.

'Just one very quick kiss,' he insisted, his eyes never leaving hers. 'One quick kiss and then I'll let them sit in the back.'

'Stanley!' she protested. 'That's not fair.'

'I'll let them sit in the driver's seat and hold the wheel.' He had raised his voice a little so that George and Victoria could hear exactly what he was offering.

George's eyes widened and he turned to his sister. 'He's going to let us sit in the front!' he cried. '*And* hold the wheel! Oh, I do hope Grace kisses him.'

Grace tried to look cross, but the attempt was a failure. Stanley Marcus was an attractive young man, there was no denying that, and she had no real objection to a quick kiss. If she said 'No' now, the children would be heartbroken, so she laughed. 'You cunning devil! You know I can't refuse. Make it a *quick* one, then,' she told him, and then to Victoria, 'Now then, ladies first.'

While Stanley helped Victoria into the place of honour, Grace glanced round to make sure that John would not be a witness to what he would undoubtedly consider a betrayal on her part. As she turned back, Stanley's arms went round her and his mouth was on hers. It was certainly not the quick kiss he had spoken of, but it was enjoyable and she made no protest. When it ended, Stanley's brown eyes were warm but he made no comment and Victoria sat in the driving-seat for several minutes while Stanley showed off the various features of the machine and George hopped up and down in a fever of excitement, hardly able to bear the suspense.

Then Stanley leaned towards Grace. 'Is George going to get a turn in the driver's seat?' he asked innocently.

Grace took several seconds to take his meaning and then she simply had to laugh at his effrontery.

'Stanley Marcus!' she cried. 'You cheat! You really are

the limit. What if it had been Nanny Webster who brought them down? You wouldn't have blackmailed her. So why me?'

'You've got grey eyes,' he grinned. 'She hasn't. I fancy you, but I don't think I could touch Nanny Webster with a barge pole! So, what do you say? The last one wasn't so bad, was it? Didn't turn your stomach or anything?'

'N-no,' she admitted, 'but you said *one* kiss.'

'You might get to like them. Or perhaps you already do. You must have been kissed lots of times; I've heard all about this Alfred fellow.'

Grace tossed her head. 'There's nothing to hear,' she said. 'He asked me to marry him and I said "No". It's not my fault if he won't take no for an answer.'

'Fanny said he wrote you a letter.'

'He did.'

'Did you answer it?'

'Yes. I told him "No" again.'

His smile broadened. 'Am I better-looking than him?' he asked.

Grace tried to look severe. 'It's not just looks a girl goes for, Stanley Marcus, it's . . . it's a kind heart and honesty and lots of other things. So before you . . .'

But Stanley was lifting Victoria down. 'Ooh Georgie, it's lovely!' she cried, her face flushed with triumph. 'It's ever so exciting.'

George looked at Stanley for permission to climb aboard and Stanley looked at Grace.

'Please, Grace,' begged George.

'Oh, all right!' she laughed. 'You win!' And while George climbed up into the car, Stanley kissed her again. It was a long kiss which ended abruptly.

'Ahem!'

They jumped apart and turned guiltily to see Alex Latimer regarding them with a look that Grace found hard to read. Stanley began to stammer apologies, but George saved them.

'Look at me, Papa! I'm driving the car. I'm really driving it. Only it's not going along.'

'So did I!' cried Victoria. 'I did, Papa! You didn't see me, but I did. Really and truly.'

Grace was grateful for their timely interruption which distracted their father's attention, but she was terribly mortified that the kiss had been seen by Alex – and to make matters worse, Sid was in the background, grinning proudly at their discomfiture.

Alex, however, made no further comment but turned to Stanley.

'Marcus, I understand the fellow who delivered the motor is still around. Is that so?'

'Yes,' replied Stanley. 'He's in the kitchen.'

'*Sir,*' said Alex.

Stanley looked puzzled.

'In the kitchen, *sir,*' said Alex. 'I've told you before.'

'Oh! I see.' Stanley nodded to show that he understood and added, 'Sorry.'

'Sorry, *sir,*' persisted Alex.

'Sorry, *sir.*'

Alex sighed. 'Well, I'll have a word with him presently. Let's see how she goes, Marcus. Put her through her paces.' All eyes turned eagerly towards Stanley.

'Right now?' he asked.

'Why not?'

Stanley shrugged and said, 'Right, then,' but he looked rather unhappy. Slowly he helped George down from the front wheel and wiped his hands on the cleaning rag. Everyone watched with bated breath as he slowly took his place behind the wheel.

'Motors do vary a lot, of course,' he said, '*Sir.*'

'Of course,' said Alex. 'It will take you time to get used to her, I realize that. Just a brief demonstration – run her to the end of the yard and then reverse back.'

'Reverse? Er . . . let me think a minute – '

Grace thought she detected a note of panic in his voice and also knew with a sudden flash of intuition that Alex minded about the kiss and was about to punish Stanley for it by making him look foolish in her eyes. As though by magic, John and Ben emerged from the tack room and stood with folded arms, hoping to watch Stanley fail.

Grace found herself crossing her fingers for him. Frowning with a great show of concentration, Stanley twiddled various knobs and half-heartedly moved the gear levers. Then he found the starting-handle and carried it round to the front of the machine, where he inserted it and swung it valiantly several times. Each time the children squealed with excitement, but each time the engine remained silent.

'She's stubborn, this one,' Stanley remarked as though from a wealth of previous experience.

'Is she?' said Alex.

George looked at the motor in surprise. 'Is it going?' he asked. 'I can't hear anything.'

'Not yet,' said Grace. 'It's very difficult and Mr Marcus isn't quite used to it.'

She longed for Stanley to succeed, but suddenly he looked up. 'Perhaps,' he suggested, 'we should let the *driver* demonstrate it first since he's the expert and he's come all this way. I wouldn't want to steal his thunder.'

To Grace's surprise, Alex turned to her. 'What do *you* think, Miss Martins? Should we call in the expert, or shall we let Marcus handle it?'

At last Grace understood. Alex did not know if Stanley's kiss had been welcome or not, and was giving her the chance of revenge if she wanted it. She smiled at him gratefully. 'I think we should call in the expert,' she said.

As his eyes still held hers, she saw again that indefinable something in his expression which she could not recognize but at last he turned back to Stanley.

'Go and fetch the fellow then, Marcus.'

The demonstration was all that they could have desired – a revelation. The car jolted to and fro over the cobbles, stopping and starting, turning left and right and reversing. Everyone in the yard had a ride in it (with the exception of John, who declined the offer) and by the time it was all over the Daimler Landaulette was declared a huge success. Finally, it was time for Stanley to be initiated into its mysteries and Grace took the children back into the garden. There was only time for one game, so they played 'Hide and Seek' and returned to the

nursery in high spirits in time to wash their hands for
lunch. The morning had been a great success and the
children were full of their adventure. When Grace took
them downstairs at four o'clock to see their parents, Alex
and Virginia were astonished and delighted to see them
so cheerful and after Grace had collected them once more
Alex looked at Virginia. 'That young woman is a real
find,' he said. 'The children seem quite devoted to her.
Do you think she'll stay the course?'

   She looked at him for a long time before answering.
'Yes,' she said at last. 'I rather think she will.'

Chapter Eight

Later that same day Fanny arrived in the stable-yard and at once sought out John. She was carrying a tray with three mugs and a plate of cake on it. Ben set down his pail and took his mug of tea, his eyes widening at the sight of the three thick slices.

'Crikey! Caraway-seed cake. My favourite. What's got into Cookie?' he asked, taking a large bite.

'It's her birthday,' Fanny explained. 'She's feeling generous, I suppose, but we're to keep it quiet. She made it specially for us.'

'Mum's the word,' he assured her. 'How old is she, then?'

'Nobody liked to ask and she's not letting on.' Fanny looked round. 'Where is everybody?'

'Mr Martins is in the end stall with Caradox and Stanley's taken the motor down to the village to buy some more petrol. He won't be long, more's the pity.'

Fanny shook her head. 'I don't know why you all have to be so awkward,' she said. 'If the motor's here to stay, you can't blame Stanley. He just *drives* it.'

'And don't we know it!' said Ben, spluttering indignantly through his cake. 'He must lord it over everybody, that's what annoys me. To hear him talk, you'd think the horse and carriage were already on the scrap-heap. He says he hates horses, too, but I reckon he's scared of 'em and won't admit it. Yesterday he called himself "one of the new men"! Mr Martins gave him a proper telling-off. "If you're one of the new men," he told him, "then thank God there's plenty of the old ones still around." A "jumped-up puppy" – that's what Mr Martins calls him. And he's so blooming conceited. Insufferable. That's Mr Martins' word for him – as well as a few others I wouldn't like to repeat. Might singe your delicate ears!'

'Such as?' she asked curiously, but he assured her his

145

lips were sealed. 'If you must know, you'll have to ask Mr Martins,' he added.

Fanny decided that she had talked to Ben for long enough. She was longing to see John, so she now made her way through the stable to the end stall where Caradox, tied to a ring in the wall, was being groomed.

John stood beside the horse with his left hand across its back. In his right hand he held a small brush which he drew across and down the animal's coat in firm, smooth strokes. He glanced up as Fanny appeared, but made no effort to stop what he was doing. As he worked, he whistled softly and tunelessly through his teeth, much to Fanny's amusement.

'Do horses like music?' she asked curiously.

'Yes, they do,' replied John. 'At least, they like the sound. You see, while I'm whistling Caradox knows I'm still around and it's me that's touching him and not something else. Horses are like us; they get nervous and need reassurance.'

Fanny said nothing. She was secretly admiring his brawny arms revealed by the rolled-up sleeves and the back of his neck where the hair began to curl.

'I've bought you some tea,' she told him, 'and it's Cookie's birthday so there's cake as well.'

'Fine.'

He had reached the hind-quarters and now he reached up and took hold of the horse's tail in his left hand.

'Why d'you do that?' Fanny asked.

'Stops him from kicking while I brush his hind legs.'

'Is he fierce, then?'

'Fierce? No, of course not. A bit ticklish, that's all.'

Nervously, Fanny stood well back as John completed the horse's near side and moved round to repeat the performance on the off side. He began by brushing the head and then lifting up the mane to brush the neck beneath it. Fanny, still holding the tray, was content to watch until John glanced up suddenly.

'You can leave the tea. I'll have it when I've finished here.'

'There's no hurry,' she assured him. 'I like to watch if you don't mind.'

'Makes no odds,' he remarked laconically. 'Like horses, do you?'

Fanny hesitated. With her limited experience, she found them large and mostly unpredictable. Once when she was five years old the baker's horse had nibbled at her hair, and later she had seen a man knocked down and killed in the street by two runaway horses pulling an Army wagon.

'I don't know much about them,' she compromised, adding hopefully, 'but I could learn.'

This answer seemed to please him, for he gave her a quick smile which thrilled her.

'Right then,' he grinned. 'Lesson one. This is his near side, that's his off side. These are the withers, shoulder, postern, hock, fetlock. Got all that? This is a dandy brush, and that there's a curry comb for cleaning the brushes. Ever sat on a horse? Like to try?'

'No fear!' cried Fanny, then an idea occurred to her and she said quickly, 'I mean, yes, I will.' Surely, she thought, John would have to pick her up or else how could she reach that broad, gleaming back. 'Will he mind?' she asked.

'He trusts me,' he assured her and without warning he seized her round the waist and lifted her up into the air.

'Throw your leg over,' he told her, 'tuck your skirt up a bit – and hold on to his mane.'

Fanny was terrified. The animal seemed so much larger than he had done when viewed from the ground and John seemed to be so far below her.

'I'm going to fall!' she cried. 'I am! I'm slipping off!'

'Of course you won't fall,' John told her, but to steady her he clamped a firm hand round her ankle. 'Talk to him. Pat his neck,' he suggested.

She did so, but the horse at once swung his head round and the eye that she could see rolled expressively.

'He doesn't like me,' she squealed. 'I can see it in his eyes. I'd better get down, John. *Please*, John! Get me down.'

147

But he stepped back, leaving her stranded on the horse's back. Clinging on to the silky mane as best she could, Fanny closed her eyes, reasoning that if she stayed on John would admire her pluck and if she fell off he'd blame himself and would have to pick her up. If she pretended to be unconscious, he might even *carry* her. But John only laughed and closed the gap between them.

'Come on, I'll help you down,' he said. 'That tea will be getting cold.'

Fanny allowed herself to be lifted down again.

'Did you like it?' he asked with a grin. 'Of course, you didn't have a saddle. Then you could have sat side-saddle. Not very ladylike, I'm afraid – bare-back.'

'He's so big,' said Fanny. 'And from up there he looks even bigger – but thanks, anyway.'

'Don't want a job as a stable-maid, then?' he laughed and she shook her head vehemently. 'Pity. I could do with an extra pair of hands to muck out and polish the tackle.'

He gave the horse an affectionate slap and led the way out of the stall, along to the door and out into the yard, but just as he was drinking his tea a loud spluttering and clanking heralded the return of the Daimler and with a muttered curse, he abruptly ducked back inside the stable, leaving Fanny on her own.

Slowly, hiding her disappointment as best she could, Fanny made her way towards the motor with the remaining mug of tea. Stanley parked the car and climbed out, his manner deliberately jaunty and his voice loud.

'There and back in less than half an hour,' he announced. 'Not bad going, that. There's real horse-power in that little engine.' He took off his cap and mopped his face, then took a cloth from the car and wiped his hands.

'Tea,' said Fanny, 'and cake. It's Cookie's birthday.'

'Tell her many happy returns,' said Stanley and took the cake eagerly.

Ben emerged from the door at the end of the stable and glared at Stanley, who immediately retaliated with a rude gesture. Unfortunately he was holding his cake at

148

the time and somehow it crumbled and fell to the cobbles, where several watchful sparrows swooped on it. Ben's mocking laugh rang out and Stanley's face clouded over.

'I'll get those two one of these days,' he muttered. 'I'll settle the score before I leave.'

'Before you leave?' cried Fanny, surprised. 'Are you leaving, then?'

'Of course I am, you ninny!' he snapped. 'I've got ambitions, I have. Not like those two, content to potter about here all their lives, raking out manure and polishing bits of harness. And when I go, I shall take a certain someone with me.'

Fanny's eyes widened. 'A certain someone? Meaning who?'

'A wife,' he said with a broad wink.

She gasped with excitement. 'You don't mean Grace?'

He put a finger to his lips. 'Don't tell her,' he warned. 'I'm going to break it to her gently. She doesn't know yet.'

'You mean you haven't asked her?'

'I'm getting round to it.'

Fanny relapsed into giggles. 'You've got the cheek of the devil, Stanley Marcus. I bet she doesn't.'

'We'll see then, won't we? If it's between me and Alfred Harris – '

'Where are you going, then?'

He shrugged. 'Up the ladder. I aim to be chauffeur to a lord before I'm done. Cottage in the grounds or flat over the garage – a proper garage, that is, not a converted stable. I'll have my own superior accommodation and a wife and kids to put in it.'

'Suppose she says "No"?'

'Then I might ask you.' She shook her head firmly, but he laughed. 'You might do a lot worse,' he said. 'I'm what's known as a catch.'

'You're what's known as a big-headed, conceited, bumptious – '

'You're just flattering me,' he said, grinning. 'Now, you'd better get yourself back to the kitchen. *Some* of us have work to do!'

She collected the mugs and went back slowly, forgetting Stanley and replaying the moments she had spent with John. Was *he* the marrying kind, she wondered, deciding to ask Grace when she came down to the kitchen later with the children's tea-tray.

When approached, Grace looked doubtful. 'The marrying kind? John?' she repeated. 'I honestly don't know. He's thirty and still unwed, so maybe he's not going to. Do you – that is, are you really that fond of him?'

'I'm head over heels about him,' Fanny confessed. 'Always have been. Only you must promise not to tell him. If you ever breathe a word to a soul – '

'Of course I won't.'

'I think sometimes that he's so wrapped up in the horses he'll never think about marriage until it's too late,' Fanny said earnestly. 'He'll end up a lonely old bachelor and that would be a shame. Don't you think he needs a woman to look after him? He should have a home and a wife and family. He's not getting any younger.'

'No, he's not,' Grace agreed. 'The trouble is that he's not the romantic kind. John's always been quiet and sort of steady.'

'Well, there you are then!' declared Fanny. 'I don't go for the flashy sort of man. John's my kind of man, only he never really looks at me and I was just wondering . . . well, hoping really . . . that you might sound him out about me. Or even about women in general – or his plans for the future?'

'I'll try,' said Grace, 'but I can't promise anything, mind. He might tell me to mind my own business.'

'I don't mean I want to get wed right away,' Fanny explained, 'but it would be nice to have some sort of hope for the future. If he said he liked me a lot, or something like that. I keep worrying about the barmaid at the local; he goes down there with Ben sometimes.'

Grace smiled. 'I don't see barmaids as John's sort,' she said. 'I promise I'll see what I can do, Fanny, but don't expect miracles.'

And with that Fanny had to be content.

*

The following evening after the children were in bed, Nanny Webster granted Grace's request for a quarter of an hour's free time. She went out into the garden and sat on the swing, pushing herself gently to and fro and thinking about Alex and his wife. Was it true that he adored her? If so, did she adore him in return? Whenever Grace saw them together, they seemed perfectly amicable and even Fanny had never heard them quarrel although they argued. But was *not* quarrelling proof that they adored each other? Grace had no idea how married people behaved, since her own father had died when she was only four and her mother had remained a widow until her death.

Virginia had a ready smile, but to Grace it seemed to lack spontaneity, as though she smiled only with her mouth and kept her true feelings well hidden. Her brown eyes were so dark that at times they looked almost black, and Grace could easily believe Cook's theory that she was of Spanish origin. Inscrutable, thought Grace. Could a woman with inscrutable eyes be warm and adoring? Cook said that Mrs Latimer's first husband had shot himself because he was bankrupt, and that when Virginia married Alex she hadn't got two halfpennies to rub together. Grace longed to know more about the woman who shared Alex's bed. She tried to imagine them in bed together, but could not do so. Her picture of their shared existence was a very sketchy one, and the rest of the staff had started to tease her about her frequent enquiries.

Overhead, the sycamore bough creaked rhythmically and Grace found the sound soothing. Her eyes closed wearily — she had been working non-stop since the moment she got out of bed that morning, and she had the strong suspicion that since Nanny Webster could not drive her out by unkindness, she was trying to wear her out physically.

The creaking of the bough masked approaching footsteps, so that Grace was startled when a large figure materialized suddenly beside her.

'Sorry,' said the young man. 'I didn't mean to creep

151

up on you. I'm Pat Casey and I used to work here as the gardener's boy.'

Grace smiled. 'I'm the nursery-maid. You must have left before I came. Are you looking for someone?'

He took off his cap nervously, then put it back on his head.

'I was only wondering, like,' he confided. 'Is my old job gone?'

Grace thought about it. 'We've got a gardener's boy, if that's what you mean. He's been here for some time.'

'Ah!' His disappointment was obvious. 'Well then, that's it. I just thought . . .' He fell silent, scuffing the toe of his boot into the grass.

'You out of work then?' Grace asked him.

He began a rambling account – which Grace only half understood – about a dream his mother had had before he was born and his brother who was on a ship called the *Mauretania*. She finally understood that he had sailed to New York, but had been attacked by an unidentified fever on the journey home. The fever had persisted, so he had been unable to sign on again after the ship turned round in Southampton. Then his job had been snapped up by someone else and now he had nothing.

'Oh dear,' said Grace, genuinely concerned. 'Do you want to go up to the house and enquire? They're probably just starting dinner, but you could wait.'

'Don't *you* know?' he asked. 'Wouldn't you get to hear of it, like, if they were looking for someone?'

'I don't think they are,' Grace told him, 'but I could ask my brother John; I expect you know him, he's head groom in the stables. I don't think they're short of a stable lad, but there's no harm in asking; he can't bite your head off.'

Actually, he *could*, she reflected – the mood he was in lately – but Pat Casey need not know that.

'Let's try,' she suggested.

Stanley was in London taking a course of driving lessons, but Ben appeared from the tack room and greeted Pat Casey cheerfully, for they had been good friends during the short time Pat had worked in the

152

garden. Ben shook his head gloomily when he learned the reason for Pat's visit.

'Not very likely we need someone,' he said, 'now that they've got *that* thing.' He pointed to the half-open door of what was now a garage, through which the motor-car was just visible.

'A motor!' cried Pat and together they inspected the usurper.

'They're more likely to get rid of someone,' said Ben, 'and that someone could be me! It's a good thing the mistress doesn't go a lot on motors. Monsters, she calls 'em! While she still wants the brougham, we'll be safe, but if she's ever won over to the likes of that it'll be curtains for us. Curtains! Mr Martins says it's only a matter of time.'

John's voice broke into their conversation. 'What's only a matter of time?' he asked and then, recognizing Pat, added, 'Hullo, what brings you here?'

Pat launched into a second account of why he was looking for a job, but John could offer him no hope.

'The damned motor has a lot to answer for,' he told him. 'I was hoping to get a new lad – there's too much work for the two of us – but the "guv'nor" got himself a chauffeur instead and a real cocky little brat he is, too. Telling the guv'nor he could drive, and he doesn't know one end from t'other! Gone to London now to learn how to do it. More expense. Motors! Huh! You might as well pour your money down the drain. No, lad, I'm afraid I can't help you. You'd best find yourself another ship; there's nothing for you here.'

Grace walked as far as the road with the dejected Pat. 'I know how you feel,' she sympathized. 'I was a companion and then the old lady died. I was lucky to get this job, although if Nanny Webster has her way she'd get rid of me tomorrow. Here . . .' She pulled a florin from her pocket and handed it to him. 'It's not much. No, take it, please. It'll maybe help a bit. See you through a couple of days. You might get another ship now you're better.'

He didn't want to take it from her but when she

insisted, he mumbled his thanks and stood with his eyes fixed on the ground, ashamed of the need that made him accept her money and unsure how to take his leave.

'Did you like it on the ship?' she asked. 'Better than gardening, I mean?'

His head came up. 'I loved it! It was grand.' A brief smile lit up his face. 'And all the lads – we used to lark about, like, when we were off duty.' He shrugged wistfully and Grace patted his arm briefly. 'Keep trying then, for another ship,' she told him. 'You might be lucky. I'll keep my fingers crossed for you.'

She watched him set off back home and hoped that someone would give him a ride for at least part of the way. It was quite a journey from Beaulieu to Southampton, and if he had to walk he would not be home until the small hours of the morning.

*

A few weeks later, Grace and the two children were sitting round the nursery table when there was a knock at the door and Alex came into the room.

'Am I interrupting anything?' he asked with a smile. 'You all look very busy.'

Before Grace could answer, George piped up, 'We're playing a game with lots of letters. Grace made it for us out of paper and I'm winning. You have to make words and I can make them. Look, Papa, I've made "dog" and "jam" and yesterday I made "fog" and then—'

'I can make words, too,' cried Victoria. 'I'm *nearly* winning!'

'You're only nearly winning because Grace helps you with all the words,' George said. 'Nobody helps me; I can make the words myself.'

Alex stood beside George while Grace explained the rules of the game.

'It's really just a way to help them learn to spell,' she told him. 'I thought it would be fun. It's not actually Nanny Webster's day off, but she's gone into Southampton to choose material for our new uniforms.'

He nodded. 'You do seem to be enjoying yourselves,'

he said. 'I wonder if I dare suggest you finish the game later? I thought it would be nice to take the children to see old Annie. She was always so fond of them, but it's a long time since she's seen them. She's still in the Union I'm afraid, and I'm rather worried about her. It's such a gloomy place and she doesn't get on very well with the other inmates. And that awful word – *inmates*. I'm trying hard to make other arrangements for her although my wife thinks I'm wasting my time.'

Grace nodded. 'It must be a great worry,' she said, unable to think of anything more constructive.

'I can but try,' said Alex. 'Anyway, that's not your problem. I think seeing the children will cheer her up more than my solitary visits.'

'It's a lovely idea,' said Grace. 'I'm sure they'd love to go.'

However, George wrinkled his nose. 'I don't want to,' he grumbled. 'I want to finish the game.'

Victoria, taking her cue from George, said, 'I don't want to, either. I don't like her. Who is old Annie?'

Grace and Alex exchanged amused looks.

'You probably don't remember her,' said Alex. 'She's an old lady who is rather lonely since her husband died. She isn't happy, so I thought we should cheer her up – and a ride in the motor would be fun.'

At the mention of the motor-car, George wriggled off his chair without further bidding. 'Is Mama coming with us?' he asked.

'No, she's rather busy this morning,' said Alex. 'I did ask her, but she didn't think she could spare the time. So there'll be just the three of us.'

Grace helped Victoria to get down from her chair. 'I'll fetch their outdoor clothes,' she said.

Victoria looked up at her father. 'I want Grace to come with us,' she declared. 'Why can't she come?'

Busy at the wardrobe, Grace felt her heart leap, but she allowed no change in her expression as she carried back the hats and coats.

Alex hesitated. 'There's no reason why she shouldn't,'

he said. 'Would you like to come with us, Miss Martins?
I'm sure Annie would be pleased to see you.'

'I'd *love* to,' cried Grace. 'And a ride in the motor!
How exciting.'

September was not living up to expectations and the
day was overcast with a cool wind, but in no time at all
the children and Grace were warmly clad and waiting
downstairs in the hall while Alex departed to fetch his
greatcoat. They were still waiting for him when Virginia
came out of the morning room and asked them what
they were doing there.

Grace told her of the proposed visit to Annie, and
Virginia was obviously displeased.

'Is there really any need for *you* to go, Miss Martins?'
she asked. 'I'm sure you have plenty of work to do in
the nursery and Nanny Webster will expect you to be
here when she returns.'

Grace began to stammer an explanation but just then
Alex returned and, realizing the drift of the conversation,
he turned to his wife.

'I asked Miss Martins to join us,' he said, 'but it was
Victoria's idea – and a jolly good one, too!' He tweaked
her nose gently and the little girl squealed with delight.
'We're all going to have a ride in that monster of mine.
I think Miss Martins is quite looking forward to the
adventure.'

'I am, sir,' said Grace anxiously, 'but if Mrs Latimer
thinks I shouldn't – '

'Of course she doesn't.' Alex spoke firmly before
Virginia could answer. 'It will do you good to get out of
the nursery. Blow the cobwebs away. The same four
walls, day in, day out – can't be good for you.'

Virginia had stiffened visibly. 'Miss Martins is *paid* to
spend her time within what you choose to call "these
four walls",' she began. 'I'm sure she has some mending
to do. You will waste her morning, Alex, and then she
will have to sit up half the night to catch up with her
work. I am only thinking of her . . . but please yourself.
If I had not been so busy, I should have come with you
myself.'

Victoria tugged at her father's coat, crying, 'When are we going, Papa?' and George said, 'Can I sit next to Grace in the motor?'

'No, *I* want to!' cried Victoria.

Neither of the two children had expressed any regret that their mother was not going to accompany them and Virginia bit her lip.

'I really must insist that Miss Martins stays here,' she said, her voice rising angrily. 'She is not paid to go gallivanting around and you, Alex, should not encourage her to do so.'

There was a sudden silence and Grace felt her face burn, while Victoria clutched at her hand and George looked up at his father with a worried expression. Alex's eyes narrowed, but he made an effort to keep his temper under control as he said quietly, 'I have asked Miss Martins to accompany us and I have no intention of changing my mind.'

Grace dared not look at Virginia's face, but she saw that her fists were clenched with impotent fury.

Alex turned to Grace and smiled. 'Now,' he said, 'perhaps we can make a start.'

'May I sit next to you?' Victoria asked.

'You shall sit one on either side of her,' announced Alex, 'and I shall go in front with Marcus.'

George considered this. 'Can I sit with Marcus on the way home?' he enquired.

The question was an innocent one, but it was immediately obvious to the three adults that such an arrangement would put Alex in the back of the motor with Grace.

'Certainly not!' cried Virginia while Grace, to hide her face, knelt hurriedly beside Victoria and pretended to fasten one of her coat-buttons.

'We'll worry about that when the time comes,' said Alex lightly. 'Now children, say "Goodbye" to Mama.'

The 'Goodbyes' were very brief, for the children were eager to take their places in the motor which at that moment came chugging up to the front door. Within minutes Stanley had installed Grace and the children in

157

the back. As he covered their laps with the rug he gave Grace a huge wink and called her 'my lady' which made the children giggle, but Grace put a warning finger to her lips for Virginia had followed them out and now stood furiously at the top of the steps. She gave no answering wave as the equipage moved off and Grace was uncomfortably aware that by coming on the trip she had probably earned her mistress' enmity. She could have offered to withdraw from the outing, but that would have undermined Alex's obvious intention to take her with them. It had become a tug-of-war and indirectly Grace had supported Alex, but despite her misgivings she was glad that she had done so. He had risked his wife's displeasure for her sake and she was ridiculously grateful and secretly very flattered that he had thought her worth the argument. If Alex valued her company, Grace did not care about Virginia's disapproval.

'I don't care a fig!' she told herself rebelliously. 'She had her chance to go on the outing and she turned it down.' And putting the problem resolutely out of her mind, she gave herself up to the wonders of the newest form of travel.

The motor-car was certainly not the most comfortable way to travel. The wheels seemed to seek out every pothole in the road and the passengers were frequently shaken from side to side, but this the children found hilarious and their laughter was infectious. They shrieked every time the motor turned a corner and George did his best to fall off the seat until a quiet word in his ear from Grace sobered him up. They waved to passers-by and laughed aloud every time Stanley sounded the horn. George declared stoutly that he *never* wanted to ride in the brougham or the dog-cart again and Victoria quickly agreed with him. Grace would willingly have endured a much more severe shaking for the sake of seeing Alex's head and shoulders through the window that separated them, and knowing that for an hour or so the three people she held most dear were hers alone.

Annie Abrahams was so thrilled to see them that tears

of joy ran down her cheeks. Alex had brought her some honey and eggs, which she accepted gratefully.

'You really are too good to me, sir,' she repeated. 'I shall have one of them there eggs for my tea. And brown ones, too! They taste the best, you know, brown eggs. Don't ask me why, but they do.'

At first George and Victoria were rather shy of the old woman, but they soon relaxed and began to chatter away to her, telling her about George's pony and the games they played with Grace. After a while Annie produced a box of buttons for Victoria to sort through, while for George she found some ancient toy soldiers.

'Your father used to play with those,' Annie told him. 'Him and your Uncle Lucien. They loved those soldiers. Course there were more of them then — twelve I believe — but over the years they went astray. Oh yes, they loved those soldiers. They used to set them all up and then knock them down. And my poor Charlie used to help them. He loved children, did Charlie.' She turned to Alex. 'Do you remember those days?'

'I do,' he told her. 'We loved to visit your cottage.'

Annie turned to Grace. 'Lucien always wanted the best soldiers — the ones in red, you know — and how he'd carry on! Talk about airs and graces! Proper little devil, he was. He'd stamp his foot in a real paddy. "That foot of yours will go right through the floor one of these days," I told him, "and you'll have to stay here for ever and ever!" Course, Mr Latimer here would always give in to him because he was the big brother and Lucien was a good bit younger.'

Alex, searching his mind for snippets of news, told the old lady about Lucien and Eleanor and this brought a sparkle to her eyes as she clasped her hands joyfully.

'So it might be wedding-bells again!' she cried. 'That would be a bit of excitement, that would.' She broke off, stiffening visibly as an elderly man shuffled within earshot of the conversation. 'You get away!' she called. 'This is not for your ears. You go back to whatever you were about.' The old man retreated and Annie shook her head and lowered her voice. 'Poor old devil. He never has a visitor, but that's no reason for him to share mine. Got no one left, you see.' Then, more loudly, she continued, 'So Master Lucien might be getting married? Well, I never. It seems only yesterday that he was playing with these very soldiers.' She turned to Grace suddenly. 'And what about you?' she asked. 'Have you got a young man?'

'No,' Grace told her. 'I've got my hands full at the moment with these two scamps and I'm not thinking about finding a husband.'

'Well, never mind, dear.' Annie patted her knee consolingly. 'One of these days the right man will come along. You'll see. "There's a man for every woman", my mother used to say – and there'll be one for you.'

'Miss Martins isn't short of admirers,' said Alex but Grace, recalling Marcus' kiss, gave him an appealing look and he promptly changed the subject.

The next hour passed very quickly, but at last Alex decided they must leave before the old lady became overtired by her lively young visitors. They left, promising to visit her again, and then it was time to get back in the motor. George rushed ahead and clambered up beside the driver's seat and Grace held her breath while Alex deliberated.

'Will he be safe there?' he asked. 'I'm not too happy about it.'

'Oh *please*, Papa!' cried George.

'Safe as houses,' Stanley assured him. 'And I'll take it very steady, round about ten or twelve miles an hour. That is, if you're not in a hurry, sir.'

'There's no hurry,' said Alex. 'Very well then, George, but you sit well back and keep quite still. Do whatever Marcus tells you, you understand? Any nonsense and we'll have to change places.'

George nodded and Alex turned to the rear of the motor where Grace had seated herself at the window with Victoria beside her. He got in and sat down and began to tuck in the rug.

'I can't see!' wailed Victoria. 'I don't want to be in the middle. I want to sit by the window.'

'Well, why not?' said Alex. 'You sit here. Climb over me – that's it.' He smiled at Grace. 'I hope you don't mind.'

'Not at all,' she said breathlessly.

He took his place next to her and then leaned across and tucked the rug round her. His proximity and kindly concern brought a sudden tightness to her throat and she had to look out of the window as tears of joy pricked at her eyelids. His arm and thigh were pressed against hers and she could feel the warmth of his body. She had never in her wildest dreams imagined such wonders and as they set off back to Beaulieu she was ecstatically happy and wished the journey could last forever.

*

31st July. Yesterday I went to the Union with Alex and the children to see an old gipsy woman called Annie. She was so pleased to see George and Victoria she cried tears of joy. Alex was so kind to her and she kept saying 'Bless you, sir.' Alex is trying to find her niece who also married outside the tribe and who might take her in. Mrs Latimer didn't want me to go with them and she must have had a word with Nanny W. while we were out, because when I got back there was a huge pile of mending waiting for me. I guessed Nanny W. was wanting me to complain so I didn't say a word. It took me until nearly midnight to finish it and I was too tired to write in here, but it was worth it just to sit in the back of the car with my lovely man. Maybe he doesn't really adore Virginia as much as they say, but I don't want her to make him unhappy because of me. If only I could be the one that makes him happy, but I know that's what Ma used to call 'crying for the moon'.

Another letter from Alfred. I do wish he would stop. Everyone is teasing me and Stanley is getting cross and behaving as though he owns me, all because of those two silly kisses. Alex sent Stanley to Peckham in London for some driving lessons with a Mr Roberts, and he seems to drive very well now but Mrs Latimer doesn't appear to like the car much. She says it's too bumpy and keeps breaking down, which it does. Usually a tyre bursts.

Nanny Webster is getting worse. I sometimes wonder if she is quite right in the head. Yesterday I'm sure I could smell gin on her breath. She makes me sick, always on about evil and hell-fire, yet she doesn't seem to think *she's* evil, tormenting the children the way she does. Yesterday she thrashed George with a slipper and then told him that if he told his father he would get another thrashing. I was all set to tell Mrs Latimer, but Cook and Fanny talked me out of it because they say I'll get the sack like the others and then Nanny will have the children all to herself again, which will be worse for them. I wish I knew what to do. The children are such dears, but I mustn't let myself love them too much. That's what nannies do, Cook says, and it always ends in tears. . . .

*

In the dining room, Virginia pushed her plate aside and smiled at her husband across the table. Alex nodded to Fanny, who stepped forward to take away the dinner plates and condiments, replacing them with trifle, an apricot pie and a jug of custard. As she left the room, Virginia's smile wavered and finally vanished.

'What are you thinking, Virginia?' Alex asked.

'It's nothing.'

'You don't seem very happy since Lucien went to Berkshire. I fancy you've – '

'It's nothing to do with Lucien!'

'But you usually enjoy the summer so much,' he reminded her. 'This year you seem somehow preoccupied and quiet. It's August already, and before you know it the summer will be over. You've hardly ridden this year and you haven't even taken much pleasure in the garden.'

'I just don't feel like it. Don't bully me, Alex,' she said irritably.

'Bully you?'

'You know what I mean. Anyway, you are hardly the most charming companion this summer. You seem to prefer Miss Martins' company to mine.'

'Oh, don't be so ridiculous!' he protested. 'That stupid little episode was of your own making and well you know it. You made a mountain out of a molehill. No, something is bothering you and I wish I knew what it was. It's useless to protest because I *know* you, Virginia, and I know you're not yourself.'

She was silent and then suddenly indicated both desserts with a peremptory wave of her hand, waiting for him to choose.

'The pie please, but not too much,' he said.

Virginia served him and then helped herself to a small helping of the trifle, toying with it absent-mindedly until Alex spoke again.

'Are you upset about Marcus going to London?' he asked. 'I know it was an added expense, but it was well worth it. He's come back full of confidence and a perfect mine of information. The Hattons are planning to buy a car and they are going to send one of their grooms there. The idea of a proper course of instruction for motorists is catching on. Their second groom's very keen to drive, so when they get their car – '

'It's nothing to do with Marcus,' she burst out. 'It's this wretched house party. If you must know, I'm dreading the 24th and I wish we'd never agreed to it. All those people – and I'm not really feeling up to it.'

He reached out and took her hand in his. 'So that's it. Aren't you well? If not, you should see the doctor. He'll give you a tonic.'

She snatched her hand away. 'I'm perfectly well, Alex, so please don't start fussing about doctors.' She pushed her plate away peevishly. 'I do wish Cook wouldn't put so much sherry in the trifle; it's much too rich. I tell her again and again, but she never listens to a word I say. Servants! They are more trouble than they're worth.'

'Do you want to cancel the weekend then?' he asked. 'It's rather short notice, but I will if you wish me to.'

Virginia hesitated. She was only dreading the weekend

163

because she would have to watch Lucien with his young lady friend and was afraid her jealousy would make her spiteful – and that the reason for her spitefulness would be obvious to everyone. She would have a lot of extra work – Eleanor was bringing her brother and an American friend with her – and all for nothing. Eleanor would no doubt flaunt her power over Lucien and she, Virginia, would feel old and useless and good for nothing more than arranging for everyone's creature comforts. If only she had had the courage to complain earlier, they could have cancelled the whole thing, but now it was Monday and the visitors were due on Friday evening. The menus had been drawn up, extra food had been ordered and the bedrooms were ready. It was too late to withdraw.

'Of course I'd like to cancel it but I can't,' she said irritably. 'It's much too close. We'll just have to go through with it but I'm not looking forward to it, that's all.'

'Poor Virginia,' he said. 'Suppose we take on another pair of hands just for the weekend? Would that ease your burden a little?'

She smiled gratefully and felt a sudden small burst of affection for him. He really was a very good husband, she thought, and she knew that many women envied her. It was simply that temperamentally they were poles apart – a perfect example of the attraction of opposites. Her own fiery temperament had been drawn to his quiet, gentle manner but now, if she was honest, that same gentleness bored her. Alex had not altered – he was still the man she had married – but *her* needs had changed and as the years went on, she yearned for the excitement she had never known as a young woman. Married to her first husband at seventeen, she was pregnant with her first child by the time she was eighteen. The child, a boy, had died just before his first birthday and then two years after that her husband had died in what the local newspaper had been kind enough to describe as 'a shooting accident'.

She had turned gratefully to Alex who offered her love, comfort and security, but she had never loved him. She

164

had hoped that gratitude might grow into love, but it had not done so. Now she wanted a little more out of life than playing mistress to a house that could easily be run by the servants without her help. Even the children, she thought, seemed to exist in a world of their own where a mother was quite superfluous. Tears of self-pity welled into her eyes but she pressed her fingers against her eyelids, willing herself not to cry. Alex was quite blameless and she did not want to cause him any pain. Her present problems were her own and she had no one in whom she could confide. She could hardly tell Alex that she had allowed his brother to go too far that last evening in the summer-house, and that now she did not know how to face Lucien let alone watch him with another woman. *And* (and this was a real fear!) suppose he had told Eleanor! She went hot and cold at the thought – but no, surely he would not be so indiscreet? Possibly he had already forgotten the episode, or maybe to him it was just a silly prank. Oh, it was all quite unbearable. In Lucien's eyes, he had probably made a fool of her and she had only herself to blame.

'Virginia?' Alex broke into her train of thought. 'You're miles away. I asked if you would like some extra help in the house? We could get someone for a whole week starting tomorrow, and that would give you plenty of rest before the weekend.'

'Thank you, Alex,' she said with a wan smile. 'That would be a tremendous help.'

Damn him! she thought illogically. His kindliness merely compounded her guilt. Why, oh why, had she married him, she thought wretchedly. She was not good enough for him, she had never made him truly happy and she had made herself unhappy.

'Oh, darling!' she cried, suddenly full of contrition. 'Forgive me. I've been such poor company for you, but I will try to pull myself together.'

Jumping up from her chair, she went round the table to put her arms round him. 'You're so good to me, Alex. I'm very lucky, I know, and I promise to cheer up and make you happy.'

Alex pushed back his chair and pulled her down on to his lap. 'Then why don't we go away together for a holiday after the weekend – back to Marienbad, perhaps. Just the two of us if you like, or we could take the children?'

'Oh yes, Alex! We will,' she cried, but then her face fell. 'But not Nanny Webster. I couldn't bear it if we had to take Nanny Webster.'

'Could you manage the children on your own?' he asked. 'You usually find them so tiring.'

'Maybe not. Oh dear! Why is everything so difficult?'

'We could take Miss Martins instead. How would that suit you?'

Virginia stiffened and then straightened up. 'No,' she said, '*not* Miss Martins. The children are getting much too fond of her and it's not a good thing. I think she's getting fond of them, too.' She looked at him anxiously. 'I don't want to take her, Alex.'

'Please yourself, Virginia.'

Slowly she got up, walked back to her place and sat down. 'Perhaps we should leave the children here after all. It will be just like old times without them – second honeymoon.' She retrieved her plate of trifle and finished it without speaking.

At that moment there was the sudden sound of racing footsteps, a hurried knock on the door. Before either of them could answer, it burst open and Grace tumbled into the room, flushed and breathless.

'What on earth – ?' cried Alex.

'I don't care what you do to me!' cried Grace, her eyes blazing. 'You can dismiss me, I don't care, but that woman is a *monster!* She's shut them in the coal-hole – the *coal-hole!* And she's going to leave them there *all night.* Do you hear me? She's a wicked, scheming old bitch and it's time you knew it!'

Shocked, Alex rose to his feet. 'Miss Martins, please calm down. No one is going to dismiss you.'

'Oh, but you will,' Grace told him. 'You will when you hear it all – when she tells you I shook her. Yes, it's true. Shook her and pulled her hair! I did and I'd do it again. She's hidden the key and she won't say where it is. I lost my temper, but the children are – '

'You shook Nanny Webster?' Virginia's expression was a mixture of shock and triumph. 'Really, Alex, Miss Martins has gone too far!'

Alex held up a hand. 'I'm more interested in the fate of the children,' he rebuked her. 'The rest can wait.'

'And I say it can't,' snapped Virginia. 'If this girl has had the effrontery to *shake* Nanny Webster, then she'll – '

'I'm not going to say I'm sorry,' Grace cried. 'She deserved it.'

Alex said calmly, 'Please, Miss Martins, tell me about the children. Tell me briefly what has happened.'

Grace took a deep breath. 'She's so crafty!' she began. 'She sent me to the post-box just to get me out of the way and then when I came back, they were gone. She's hidden the key and she won't let them out. They're screaming the place down. I think Nanny Webster is mad!'

Virginia rose to her feet, white-faced. 'How dare you say such a thing?' she began. 'You're hysterical!'

But Grace was not to be silenced. 'I tell you she's a monstrous, crazy old woman and she's not fit to look after a dog, let alone two young children. Please, Mr Latimer,' she begged, 'don't leave them down there. It's pitch-dark and dirty, not to mention rats and spiders. It's inhuman. Oh, for pity's sake! Don't just stare at me – *do* something, can't you!'

She burst into angry tears and Alex took her arm and guided her to a chair. Then he turned to his wife. 'I'll deal with this,' he said and hurried out of the room before she could protest.

*

When Alex reached the nursery, he found Nanny Webster visibly shaken but determined.

'That girl has got to go,' she declared. 'I won't tolerate her interference a moment longer. I knew she was unsuitable right from the start, and I should never have agreed to give her a try. She has done nothing but try to under-

167

mine my authority ever since she came, and now she has actually laid hands on me! Quite out of control, I'm afraid. That hysterical little nobody will never set foot in this nursery again, I hope that's absolutely clear.'

'Where are the children?' asked Alex, ignoring her speech.

'They are where they belong.'

'And where is that?' His voice was ominously low.

'In the coal-hole.'

'Please give me the key at once, Nanny.' He thought he could smell alcohol on her breath.

'Certainly not. They have to be punished,' she said. 'In the morning, if they are truly sorry, then maybe – '

'The *key*, Nanny.' His grey eyes were cold as steel and Nanny Webster hesitated.

'It's for their own good,' she protested. 'They have to be disciplined. A night in the coal-hole does them no harm.'

Alex held out his hand. 'The key, please. They will not spend another moment in that awful place; they are only *children.*'

She looked at him with the dawning of disaster in her eyes. 'That nasty Miss Martins is to blame,' she blustered. 'Coming here with her smarmy ways. She's spoilt them . . . ruined them. That's why they're so difficult to handle. She's undone years of my work with all her foolishness, years of work. She's undermined me at every turn and she's nothing but a wicked little trouble-maker.'

Quietly Alex said, 'If you don't give me the key *at once*, I shall be forced to break the coal-hole door with an axe and then I should be forced to charge you for its repair.'

Nanny Webster opened her mouth to protest, changed her mind and closed it again. Abruptly, she crossed to the mantelpiece, took the key from behind the clock and held it out.

'Thank you,' said Alex and he took it from her and walked out.

Downstairs he found Fanny and Dot outside the door

of the coal-hole trying ineffectively to quieten the screaming children. They stood back as he approached and Fanny said, 'It's not the first time, sir. They've been in there before.'

Without answering, Alex unlocked the door and as it swung open the two children fell out. They were covered in coal-dust and their faces were streaked with tears. Victoria's eyes rolled hysterically and George was trembling all over as Alex knelt down and took them both into his arms. His expression was grim, but his voice was tender as he soothed them.

'I heard a rat,' sobbed Victoria. 'I did, Papa. It was scratching. A nasty big rat!'

George nodded, white-faced. 'It lives there with all its brothers and sisters. Nanny Webster told us; she said they would nibble our toes. Oh, Papa! I don't like rats.' The little boy buried his head against his father's shoulder.

'Hush now,' comforted Alex. 'Don't cry, Victoria. You are quite safe now and you wll never, *ever* go in there again. You have my word on it. Never! Do you hear, Victoria? Then don't cry any more, little one.'

George said, 'I tried not to cry, but I couldn't help it.'

Victoria lifted her head. 'Cry-babies go to Hell. Nanny Webster – '

'Of course they don't,' said Alex. 'If I were shut in there, I think *I* would cry.'

George's lips quivered. 'Would you, Papa?'

'I certainly would.' He kissed them and when at last they had recovered from their fright, he gave them into Fanny's care with a final hug and instructions that they should be cleaned up.

'Then give them each a mug of warm milk,' he ordered, 'and a few biscuits. I'll send Miss Martins down to collect them later.'

He made his way back upstairs and went into the nursery where he found Nanny Webster in her bedroom, boiling a kettle to make herself a pot of tea. She turned as he came in, the brown china tea-pot clasped in her hands.

His voice was low and even.

'Nanny Webster, I'm afraid we can no longer employ you here,' he told her, 'and I am very sorry I did not make the decision sooner. I am sorry, too, that I cannot give you a reference, for I genuinely believe you to be a quite unsuitable person to be in charge of young children. Instead, I shall give you three months' wages in lieu of notice and you will leave tonight. Martins will take you to Southampton in the dog-cart to catch the six-thirty train back to London. If you need help with your luggage, ask Martins to carry it downstairs for you. I have nothing more to say to you.' He walked out of the room and she stared after him.

'Sacked, am I?' she whispered. 'Sacked! After all I've done for those children.' She stared round her at the familiar room which she was soon to vacate. 'Sacked,' she repeated.

Suddenly she flung the tea-pot into the fireplace where it smashed to pieces, splattering the carpet and her own skirt with hot tea. Hands clenched, she looked slowly along the mantelpiece until her gaze fell upon a vase which also belonged to the house. With a choked cry, she snatched it up and smashed that also. 'They can't do this to me,' she said and began to drum her fists wildly against the mantelpiece. The edge of the shelf hurt her hands, but she revelled in the pain until at last she had exhausted herself. Painfully, she stretched her cramped fingers and inspected her flesh for bruises. Finally, she dropped her hands to her sides and stared straight ahead with dull, unseeing eyes. An idea was forming in the darkest recesses of her mind, an idea which gave her a crumb of comfort. For a long while she did not move but at last her lips trembled and she clenched her right fist and shook it in the direction Alex had taken.

'Don't you think you've finished with me, Mr Latimer,' she whispered with a gleam of malice in her eyes. 'Don't think you've paid me off because you haven't. I'll make you sorry, you see if I don't.' She smiled thinly and her eyes glittered with malice. 'Oh no, Mr Latimer,' she repeated. 'I've not finished with this family, not by a long chalk. Three months' wages and no reference? We'll see about that. Your trollop of a wife will rue this day for the rest of her life!'

Chapter Nine

Friday was cloudy at first, but by midday the sky had cleared and preparations were in hand for the arrival of the visitors. The house had been polished from top to bottom and the guest rooms were bright with fresh flowers and fragrant with the smell of beeswax. In spite of the extra pair of hands, Cook was overworked and snapped at everyone as she rolled, cut and crimped pastry and iced interminable cakes. Outside, the yard was full of duck feathers and Fanny was complaining bitterly that it was not her job to help prepare food. Dot was peeling mountains of vegetables, her fingers raw from the cold water, but her thoughts were on Stanley Marcus to whom she had taken a great fancy – her fantasies about him making life a little more bearable. Ida, the extra pair of hands (a dull, somewhat dumpy girl) was polishing the silver cutlery.

Virginia was having her hair dressed by the hairdresser who had been brought in from Southampton at great expense. She had finally reconciled herself to the weekend by a decision to flirt with either Eleanor's brother or the American friend. Or both . . . She would show Lucien that his attentions were no longer necessary to her self-esteem and that she could easily attract other men if she wished to do so. There was no way she would let him see her true feelings. She would be utterly charming and her sophistication would make Eleanor look coltish and gauche by comparison. As she watched the hairdresser's deft fingers, she admired her reflection and felt happy and excited.

In the stable-yard, Stanley was polishing the car and making a few minor adjustments to the engine while he whistled loudly and tunelessly. John was attending to the two horses which would pull the brougham. It had been decided that both car and carriage would go to

Southampton to meet the visitors from the London train, but John had mixed feelings about this arrangement and had protested that the motor would frighten the horses. However, Alex had insisted that they must get used to it. John now worked with his back to the motor and its chauffeur, his face set in angry lines as he tried to ignore Stanley's whistling which he rightly guessed was intended to annoy him.

Grace and the children arrived as the brougham was wheeled out for a last-minute check and they all admired it dutifully, which cheered John a little.

'I really came to remind you about Victoria's pony,' Grace told him. 'Mr Latimer did say she was to have one, but he's leaving the choice of the animal to you.'

'I know,' said John, 'but I just haven't got around to it. I meant to nip down to Norley Wood and see what the gypsies have got; they can break in a pony better than anyone, but it's finding the time. I haven't forgotten.' He smiled down at Victoria. 'So you're going to have your own pony, eh? Lucky girl.'

'When will I have it?' she asked.

'Soon as maybe,' he told her. 'Soon as this weekend's over, I'll have a bit of spare time hopefully. Then I'll find you a nice little pony and we'll teach you to ride.'

'Will you teach Georgie, too?' she asked.

'Well, now, Master George *can* ride. He used to ride when he was only three, although he didn't get much chance when old Nanny Webster came. I don't think she approved of horses. Come to that, I don't think she approved of anything – but never mind. She's gone now and you've got a new nanny. How d'you like her, eh?'

'She's ever so lovely,' said Victoria and to prove it she flung her arms round Grace's legs and hugged them.

Grace smiled. 'I'm only on probation as Nanny,' she reminded her brother. 'Mrs Latimer made that quite clear. But I'm doing my best and hoping a lot. I'm getting an extra three pounds a year and if I do get the job it will mean another five!' She lowered her voice. 'I think *Mr* Latimer would make it permanent, but she's not so keen.'

'You'll make out,' he told her. 'Don't worry yourself about it.'

Just then Stanley called out to the children to 'come and look at the motor' and they scampered away with shrieks of delight. Ignoring their desertion, John said, 'It might be best to give Victoria George's pony and get him a new one. He's outgrown it really.'

'Do whatever you think's best,' said Grace.

She too wanted to have a word with Stanley, but she was reluctant to offend John so she waited until Ben needed his advice in one of the stalls and then took the opportunity to follow the children to the far end of the yard.

'Well, here I am,' she said to Stanley. 'What's the news?'

He gave her an odd look. 'Didn't Fanny tell you?' he asked.

'No, she just said you had some news for me.'

'So I have.' He lowered his voice. 'Your admirer was here this morning, asking for you.'

Her expression changed abruptly. 'Oh no! Not Alfred?'

'The same. I'll say this for him – he's a stickler for punishment.'

'Oh dear, poor Alfred! I do *wish* he'd be sensible. What happened?'

'Your brother sent him packing.'

'Oh dear!' she said again.

'Oh dear!' he mocked. 'Perhaps you haven't been firm enough. You have to be cruel to be kind, you know, Grace. Write him a letter and tell him straight out you don't like him.'

'But I do *like* him,' said Grace. 'I don't *love* him and I couldn't marry him, but he's not a bad sort. I don't want to be unkind – '

'You'll have to, Grace, or else he'll never give up and then he'll never find anyone else. If he shows up here again, I'll box his ears for him! That might make it clear to him if nothing else does.'

'Box his ears?' She glared at him indignantly. 'Stanley

Marcus, you'll do no such thing. Don't you lay a finger on him.'

'But he's got to be told,' Stanley insisted. 'He's got to know you're my girl now, not his.'

Grace's eyes widened. 'I am *not* your girl,' she said.

He grinned. 'Be nice if you were, though. You do like me, don't you?'

She nodded. 'But only *like*,' she said. 'I like Alfred, too.'

'And if you had to choose between him and me you'd choose me.'

'But I don't have to.'

'If you did?' He picked an imaginary speck of dust from the bodice of her dress. 'You'd choose me, now, wouldn't you? Admit it.'

She hesitated. 'Yes, but – '

'There you are then. *Quod erat demonstrandum.*'

'*Quod* what? Whatever are you on about, Stanley?'

'Just a bit of Latin I picked up in London,' he told her airily. 'It means "which was to be proved". I bet Alfred Harris doesn't know any Latin.' He leaned closer. 'I dare you to give me a quick kiss!'

'Don't be saucy.' She laughed. 'If Alfred gets the prize for persistence, you get it for cheek!' She turned to the children. 'Now George and Victoria, have you seen enough? If so, we might have time to play "Fox and Hen". What do you say?'

' "Fox and Hen!" ' cried George and Victoria clapped her hands and they at once relinquished the charms of the motor-car and ran off towards the front lawn.

Stanley watched them for a moment, then said, 'They're different children since the old battleaxe left. You've got a way with kids, Grace. You ought to have some of your own.' He was no longer teasing her. 'I wish you'd take me seriously. We ought to get to know each other. I shan't always work here, you know. I've got ambitions and I'm going places. You could come with me, Grace. We could have a lot of fun, you and me.'

'Leave Berwick House?' cried Grace. 'But how could I? The children need me. And I've got ambitions, too, you know. If I get the job permanently, I'd be a fool to throw it away. So don't include me in your plans, Stanley Marcus.'

He did not seem in the least perturbed by her discouraging declaration of intent. 'You'll change your mind,' he said with a grin. 'My charm will sweep away all your objections. Just give me a few months.'

'We'll see,' she said, returning his smile.

He shook his head, bemused. 'Don't you ever want to settle down with a home and a man of your own?'

'Yes, I do,' she confessed. 'But . . .'

She sighed. She could hardly explain that she was in love with her employer. Stanley would tell her that there was no future in it and she had already worked that much out for herself.

*

Promptly at five minutes past five the house-guests arrived at Southampton station, descending from the train in high spirits. After hasty but cheerful introductions, there was a rush to the guard's van to collect their various pieces of luggage before the train moved off again. Eleanor was much prettier and more vivacious than Virginia had expected, but the latter hid her dismay and greeted her as warmly as the others. Her brother, Archie, was very like her, with the same large eyes and eager expression, but his hair had more red in it than Eleanor's and he was shorter and almost plump. He looked like a good-natured overgrown schoolboy, and Virginia could not imagine herself accomplishing anything of a romantic nature with him. The American friend, however, more than compensated for this disappointment. Lawrence Scott was perfect! He was dark and handsome and wore his clothes in a casual way that instantly appealed to her. His handshake was almost too firm as he said, 'Virginia! You're every bit as beautiful as Lucien promised.'

Lucien put an arm briefly round her shoulders and said, 'She certainly is!'

Lawrence still held her hand and now he covered it

with his left hand also. 'My friends call me Larry. I hope you will, too.'

Archie warned, 'Don't let him dazzle you, Virginia. He's a terrible heart-breaker. I didn't want to bring him because he spoils all my chances.'

Eleanor slapped his arm playfully. 'You toad, Archie! That's not true. The two of you are practically inseparable But – ' She turned to Virginia. 'Where's your husband? I've been so looking forward to meeting him.'

Fleetingly it passed through Virginia's mind that Eleanor might well turn Alex's head, but she found that idea less depressing than the fact that the wretched girl had stolen Lucien from her. Alex was not that kind of man, she reminded herself; she had never known him to flirt with another woman.

'Alex will meet you all later,' she replied. 'He sends his apologies that he couldn't be here, but he had some business to attend to.'

'Let me guess,' said Lucien. 'He's doing a good deed somewhere. I know Alex.'

'Actually, you're right, Lucien,' she said. 'He's collecting Annie Abrahams from the Union and taking her to a niece's house. He's made some financial arrangement for her, but I don't know the details. He couldn't bear the thought of her spending her last days in that dreary place.'

'He sounds terribly decent,' said Eleanor, impressed.

'Oh, terribly,' mocked Lucien. 'Galahad's my brother's middle name.'

Virginia bridled. She might have allowed him a few liberties when they were very close, but now that he had removed himself from her she decided not to let the jibe pass unchallenged.

'You make that sound less than a compliment,' she said. 'Whatever happened to brotherly love, Lucien?'

'What indeed?' he asked with a smile. 'I've spent the best years of my life trying to ponder that very question – ever since he let my mouse out of its cage!'

Eleanor found this very amusing and Virginia noticed that even her laugh was attractive. She was forced to admit that she could not fault Lucien's taste in women but if this young woman were to become her sister-in-law – could they ever be friends, she wondered.

Stanley arranged most of the luggage on top of the car but Eleanor's two hat-boxes and one valise went into the brougham. Naturally, the visitors all exclaimed over the new Daimler, much to John's secret annoyance, but after some discussion it was finally decided that Virginia, Archie and Larry Scott should ride in the brougham, while Eleanor and Lucien would motor home.

'And no racing, you two!' Lucien warned the respective drivers. 'We all want to get there in one piece.' They set off home with much hilarity and Virginia, with her two escorts, felt her mood expanding and thought that perhaps she might after all enjoy herself. If she did not, it certainly would not be for want of trying.

*

They reached Berwick House a little after six and found Grace and the children waiting in the drawing room as instructed. More introductions were made and Nanny Webster's absence was explained briefly to Lucien, who declared that in his view they were well rid of her. George and Victoria were admired and fussed over for ten minutes or so and then Grace was told to take them back to the nursery.

'Now,' said Virginia, 'I'll call Fanny in a moment to show you to your rooms and jugs of hot water will follow. Our neighbours, the Hattons, are coming to dinner, but we don't dine until eight so there'll be plenty of time for a stroll in the grounds – drinks, croquet or whatever you fancy.'

'Wonderful!' cried Eleanor. 'I'm dying to explore the garden and the old summer-house. Lucien has told me so much about it.'

Virginia felt suddenly cold and then hot. Surely, *surely* he had not told her?

But turning to Larry, Eleanor went on, 'He and Alex used to play there for hours. Sometimes they pretended it was a castle, at other times a fort. You know how boys are.'

'Tomorrow I thought we might play tennis,' Virginia said quickly, 'in the morning before it gets too hot, and then we could go for a picnic maybe or hire a boat and go down the river. Then on Sunday – '

Lucien held up his hand to interrupt her. 'Let me guess. Church parade!'

They all laughed and Virginia said, 'You don't have to – I just thought . . .'

To her surprise, Eleanor flashed her a supportive smile and said, 'Well, I shall certainly go because I simply adore country churches. They're so friendly and not awe-inspiring at all. I do so hate to be awed when I'm in church. I like to feel comfortable and at ease while I'm asking for my sins to be forgiven!'

It was not a wildly amusing remark, but obligingly everyone laughed and Virginia thought what an attractive man Larry Scott was and admired his laugh which was deep and rich. She liked his perfect white teeth and well-shaped mouth too and thought him infinitely eligible. A godsend, in fact. She hoped he would continue to pay her a lot of attention so that Alex and Lucien would feel jealous.

After they had dispersed to their various rooms, Virginia put a hand to her head and thought rapidly. She would try to arrange things so that she and Larry sat next to each other at meals and maybe next to each other in church . . . and on the boat if they hired one. He was making no secret of the fact that he found her attractive and the next two days would offer plenty of opportunities for them to become more closely acquainted. By the time Alex arrived home, he found his wife bright-eyed with excitement and was pleased to see that she was obviously enjoying the weekend she had so recently wanted to cancel.

*

During dinner that evening Virginia had plenty of time to study Eleanor and soon realized how completely she

179

had won Lucien's devotion – and why she had done so. She was every bit as attractive and vivacious as Lucien had claimed, but she also appeared to offer everything that Lucien could possibly want from a woman. By gazing at him with shining eyes and hanging on to his every word, she made it plain to everyone that she admired him tremendously. She also laughed at all his jokes, passed the salt and pepper before he had a chance to ask for them and warned him most solicitously to 'be careful of the bones' when the fish course was brought in. In addition she looked quite radiant in a gown of pale green taffeta, simply but perfectly cut. Virginia was forced to acknowledge silently that although her own gown, in cream oyster satin, flattered her well enough, Eleanor had youth on her side and no one could fail to appreciate her flawless complexion and sweet young face.

Eleanor was also clever and showed an intense and apparently genuine interest in Lucien's regiment, a subject about which Virginia had never felt the slightest curiosity. She had to admit that Eleanor was playing a good hand.

'Tell them about Minden, Lucien,' Eleanor urged, with suitable enthusiasm. 'Do tell.' He protested that no one wanted to hear about the Army, but she insisted. 'You're much too modest, Lucien – isn't he, Virginia? Of course they want to hear; it's too fascinating for words.'

Lucien still declined to elaborate on the subject so Eleanor, undeterred, launched into the account herself.

'Minden was a very famous action and the Hampshire regiment won a battle honour for it. They were only foot soldiers, you see, but they fought and won against the French *cavalry*. In the Seven Years War, it was, in the eighteenth century. When was it exactly, Lucien? I forget?'

Cleverly, she had drawn him into the account.

'1759,' he said. 'As Eleanor said, foot soldiers had never advanced on cavalry before and in fact they shouldn't have done so then, only someone who shall be nameless gave the wrong order. Of course, the men obeyed and the result was a victory that surprised everyone.'

'That's why the red rose is in their badge,' Eleanor went on, 'because on the way to the battle they picked red roses and — ' She broke off, seeing Lucien shake his head. 'Oh dear, have I got it wrong? You tell them, then, darling.'

For a split second Eleanor's eyes met Virginia's and the message came across clearly: 'He's mine and I know how to keep him.' Then her eyes were again on Lucien as she listened to his version of the story and Virginia did not know whether to be amused or annoyed by the girl's impudence.

'The rose in the badge is Lancastrian,' he explained, 'and it was granted to the pikemen and bowmen by Henry V after Agincourt. The rose that they wear only on Minden Day is tucked behind their cap-badges.'

Eleanor smiled round at everyone. 'Isn't that romantic?' she demanded. 'I think it's quite beautiful.'

There were murmurs of agreement and Mrs Hatton asked, 'So you have no regrets, Lucien, about making the Army your career? We did wonder when you went in. I said to Reggie, "Is he cut out for the Army?" It's a very rigorous life.'

'Not at all,' he answered promptly. 'It's an interesting life, full of incident. Never a dull moment. Plenty of good company — you're never short of friends — and there's a certain unity of spirit which I doubt you would find anywhere else.'

'It sounds wonderful, doesn't it?' cried Eleanor with a little pout. 'Men really are the most lucky beasts. What can a woman do that is half as exciting?'

'She can *marry* a soldier,' said Alex and they all joined in the laughter.

Virginia, a little piqued by the way Eleanor was dominating the conversation, decided suddenly that she would have to take a belated interest in the Hampshire regiment and turned to Lucien with a smile.

'What would you say was the most exciting day in your Army life so far?' she asked.

He hesitated and Guy said, 'I know what mine was. It

was the battle of Kabul, in 'seventy nine. A damned good show, that was.'

At once Eleanor turned the full power of her wide-eyed charm on the old man.

'Oh, were you in the Army, too? Lucien didn't tell me. How naughty of him.'

'Same regiment,' Guy told her proudly, 'but I had to come out in '81. My elder brother, Rupert, died and I had to take over the running of this place. I wasn't at all pleased, I can tell you, but there was nothing else for it. Poor old Rupert.'

'How awful for you,' said Eleanor, 'especially if you'd set your heart on the Army. Fate can play some really cruel tricks. Still, it must have made you feel a little better when your son went into your old regiment.' She turned back to Lucien. 'You haven't told us *your* most exciting moment, darling.'

He smiled at her in a way that made Virginia's heart contract painfully. 'It was the day Princess Henry presented our new colours at Portsmouth,' he told them.

Larry looked puzzled. 'You'll have to explain,' he said. 'Forgive an ignorant American, but I didn't know you had a Princess Henry.'

'Princess Henry of Battenburg,' Lucien elaborated. 'She's a niece of Queen Victoria and Governor of the Isle of Wight, so she was asked to present the colours. Maybe "exciting" isn't the right word. Perhaps "moving" is better. It was three years ago, while I was still a very impressionable ensign. It really is a most solemn occasion; the old colours are trooped and then the new colours are consecrated by the Chaplain-General.'

Eleanor sighed. 'I think that's just too sweet,' she said. 'I wish I'd known you three years ago.'

The look they exchanged pierced Virginia's heart, but as she hastily averted her eyes her gaze fell on Larry Scott and she realized suddenly that he was not listening to Eleanor or Lucien but giving *her* his full attention. For a moment she thought that he had read her expression, but then he smiled lazily and lowered his right eye in a wink! Surprised, but pleased, she smiled back at him and wished that she had seated him nearer to her. Archie's words came back to her: 'He's a terrible heart-breaker.' Did she want her heart broken? He certainly was an attractive man. She tore her gaze away and tried to concentrate on what Lucien was saying.

'The weather had been absolutely foul,' he told them, 'but on the actual day the sun broke through and it was such a relief.' He laughed. 'Of course, it was a wonderful excuse to eat a damned good lunch and drink a sight too much wine. June the 9th – I can still remember the date because it was the first time I'd been on parade on such an important occasion.'

'De Winter, wasn't it?' put in Guy. 'Colonel de Winter, if my memory serves me well.'

Lucien nodded. 'That's right. He presented all the officers to the Princess, including "yours truly", and then Mrs de Winter presented the wives. The Princess was terribly pleased, too, because the band played one of her own compositions – a march she had written for the 5th Volunteers. It was all very regal and truly memorable.'

Guy said, 'Well, you'll be the last of the Latimers, Lucien, to join the "Tigers". Young George will have to step into Alex's shoes when his time comes; there'll be no Army career for him.'

'A pity,' said Lucien. 'He's a lively little chap – would probably enjoy Army life.'

While they chatted, Ida moved quietly among them removing empty plates and substituting clean ones, while Fanny brought in the tureens of vegetables followed by the roast beef.

Mrs Hatton then asked how the children were faring with their new nanny, and Virginia was pleased to find herself the centre of attention once more.

'They seem to like her,' she said. 'Mind you, Miss Martins is rather young and inexperienced for the position, but Alex thought that now that Nanny Webster has left, we should give her a trial period. I thought she should have some help as it's such a long day for her, but we haven't taken on anyone else yet.'

Alex said, 'Fanny gives her a break most days, even if

it's only for half an hour. It gives her a chance to stroll in the garden or to relax with the rest of the staff.'

Virginia raised her eyebrows. 'Really?' she exclaimed. 'This is news to me, Alex. May one ask when Fanny gets a break?' Her disapproval was obvious.

'Fanny has her afternoon off once a week, as she has always done,' he told her, 'whereas Miss Martins is with the children twenty-four hours a day.'

'Except for the time the children spend with *us*.'

'Sometimes that isn't very long,' Alex pointed out. 'The girl needs a little time she can call her own; she's a great reader – '

'She *reads?*' asked Virginia with exaggerated surprise.

'Yes, indeed. She's very keen to improve her mind and I've told her she can borrow books from the library.'

'Improve her mind?' laughed Mrs Hatton. 'Do you remember our Nanny Brown? *Her* mind was beyond improvement and it turned out that all she thought about was "the gee-gees".'

'Damned right!' her husband agreed. 'A real terror, she was! Used to send the gardener down to the village to put her bets on for her – all in our time, of course. It was nearly a year before we found her out, but fortunately by that time our son was almost ready for prep. school and we could let her go without worrying about replacing her.' He shook his head gloomily. 'Staff aren't what they used to be, not by a long chalk. I can remember my own nanny when I was a boy. I adored her – small, plump and cuddly, she was. I was eighteen when she died, but I cried my heart out, I don't mind admitting it. Oh yes, I shed a few tears for my dear old nanny, God rest her soul!'

'I don't think children should get too fond of their nanny, do you?' said Eleanor, turning wide eyes on Guy. 'We used to call our nanny "Sharky" behind her back because her name was Marjorie Sharks. It was Archie who started it, but then I used to giggle and get into trouble. He was awful.'

Archie protested good-naturedly, but she rounded on him. 'Oh yes, you were, Archie – you really were a beastly bore! Putting my pigtails in the inkwell, not to mention spiders in my bed! Still, you did get a spanking for that and quite right, too!'

Archie laughed heartily at this and a piece of beef went down the wrong way, so Mrs Hatton had to pat him on the back.

'Well, I think Miss Martins is a great find,' said Alex. 'I hope she stays. The children are so much happier with her.'

'I shall choose a strict nanny for my children,' said Eleanor, 'so that they will love me best.' She turned to Margaret Hatton. 'Did you love your mother more than your nanny?'

'I didn't have to make a choice,' she answered. 'My mother died when I was seven and my grandmother came to live with us. Nannies seemed to come and go without making much of an impression on me. One married the postman, I remember, and another stole something and was packed off in rather a hurry, but now I can't even remember their names.'

'Let's hope Miss Martins doesn't have any followers,' said Lucien. 'She's pretty enough.' He wiped his mouth with his napkin and leaned back. 'That was very good; Mrs Wade's excelled herself today.' He turned to Mrs Hatton. 'Have you thought any more about a motor? Alex says you're on the point of buying one.'

Virginia made a gesture of disapproval and turned to Mrs Hatton. 'Don't allow it!' she exclaimed. 'I refuse to set foot in ours; it really is such a monster. Alex, you must admit the brougham is more reliable. At least we know we shall get there on time without a burst tyre or something equally dreadful. And that chauffeur!'

Alex grinned. 'Young Marcus? What's wrong with him? Since he came back from London there's nothing he won't tackle.'

'Attractive, too,' said Eleanor, 'if you like boyish good looks – and some women do.'

'He's a splendid mechanic,' said Alex. 'He can change a wheel in less time than it takes to talk about it.'

'He's had so much practice!' Virginia laughed. 'That's why.'

She, too, placed knife and fork together on the plate and dabbed discreetly at her mouth. 'I don't suggest he doesn't know his job,' she went on, 'but it's his lack of respect I object to. He simply has no idea how to speak to his superiors. None at all. It's never "Yes, sir," – it's "Right-oh!" '

Alex joined in the general laughter. 'Virginia's right,' he said, 'but what we all have to remember is that he's never been in service before and doesn't have any idea how things are done. He's only worked in a factory – an engineering works, to be more exact – and it's a very different kettle of fish there. They clock on and off and when they've done their hours they can go home and they're not responsible to anyone. Their time's their own. They don't live in tied accommodation, either. Marcus sees himself as an employee and not as a servant; he just isn't used to the system.'

'Then he should *get* used to it,' Virginia insisted.

Ida reappeared and, seeing that everyone had finished eating, began to clear away while Fanny brought in a large rhubarb fool, an open plum flan, a big bowl of cream and a tray of fresh fruit. She also arranged coffee cups on the sideboard before withdrawing once more.

Alex was still trying to convince everyone of the worth of his chauffeur. 'Marcus doesn't mean any discourtesy,' he said. 'He and I understand each other. I like the lad and I don't know what I'd do without him. That engine can be very temperamental, but let Marcus loose with a spanner and in no time at all she's purring like a kitten.'

Lucien leaned forward. 'You may like him, but poor John Martins certainly doesn't. I thought they'd come to blows last time I was in the stables. They're like a couple of terriers, always spoiling for a fight. In fact, I've heard that – '

Virginia held up her hands appealingly. 'Please!' she cried. 'We mustn't bore our guests with domestic problems. Let's talk about something a little more elevated – art or music, perhaps?'

Archie groaned. 'Art on a full stomach? No, it can't be done.'

Eleanor's laugh rang out. 'Do stop it, Archie! You're trying to embarrass me. Stop him, Lucien. Kick him under the table if you can reach him!'

As the wine loosened their tongues, the talk flowed on and Virginia thought with satisfaction that the evening was being a great success. Mrs Wade *had* done well and she would give her a special 'thank you' in the morning. If only Eleanor had not been quite so perfect! Still, she was a pleasant guest. If there was one thing Virginia dreaded it was shy guests; they were such hard work and if she had any say in the matter were rarely invited a second time. If Eleanor married Lucien everyone would adore her and there was nothing Virginia could do to prevent it. She must accept defeat with as much charm as she could. Even Guy was already very 'taken' with his son's young lady.

As she straightened her shoulders she saw that Larry Scott was regarding her keenly again with a slight frown on his face. She returned his gaze boldly and suddenly something intangible passed between them, something that was insubstantial yet positive. Virginia sensed in his interest a desire to know more about her and felt a flutter of anticipation, while her heart leaped with gratitude. Perhaps Larry Scott was not besotted with Eleanor's youth; possibly he appreciated a more mature woman. A tawny port instead of the *nouveau beaujolais* as Alex had once said.

Suddenly Larry plucked a small flower from the table-centre and beckoned Fanny to him. 'Give this to your mistress,' he said clearly. 'To a most gracious English hostess from an American admirer.'

The rest of the conversation died and Virginia was aware that all eyes had turned in her direction as she took the bloom from Fanny and laughed delightedly.

'I shall wear it next to my heart!' she announced with mock gallantry, but her eyes held his and in the silence their eloquence was deafening.

*

The following day just before one o'clock, Dot staggered in from the garden with a loaded tray and set it down with a crash of relief on the draining-board.

'I wish I was rich,' she declared. 'Tennis and then lunch under the trees. Blooming marvellous, isn't it? I could really enjoy being rich. The tennis must have given them an appetite because they've cleared all the salmon mousse. I was hoping to get a taste of that.'

'What I reckon's so unfair,' said Fanny, 'is why are rich people so good-looking? They say you can't have your cake and eat it, but *they* do. Dot's right. I know who I'd rather be if I had to choose between them and me.'

'They're good-looking,' said Cook, 'because a beautiful woman can always find a rich man to marry her. Then they have good-looking children and *they're* rich, so they choose good-looking partners when they grow up. Even an ugly man can find a beautiful woman willing to marry him if he's got money, so then he doesn't have ugly children.'

'Well, it's not fair,' Fanny repeated.

'Stop moaning,' said Cook, 'and take out the salad – and you, Ida, take out the plates. No, not those; they're dishes. Can't you tell a plate from a dish, girl?'

Ida scowled. She was not proving a great success, being rather sullen and not very willing.

'Dot, you take the ham and the pickles. Not in the jar! Whatever is the matter with everyone today? You ought to know better than that. Put it into one of the white bowls. You really are . . . I don't know. I could do it myself in half the time and have time left over for the Lord's Prayer.'

Just then the back door opened and Stanley put his head in. 'I'm starving!' he announced. 'When are we going to eat?'

'When they've finished,' Cook told him. 'And don't ask me when that will be, because they've only just sat down. That wretched tennis! It went on and on.'

'Where's Grace?'

'In the nursery – and before you ask me, no, you can't

188

slip up for a quick word. I've had strict orders from Grace; she was very cross about you going up yesterday and blamed me. So from now on, the nursery is out of bounds. Anyway, they're eating their dinner. Ah, there you are, Fanny. What kept you so long? There's bread rolls here and butter. I meant to do butter curls, but there just wasn't time. I don't know if I'm on my head or my heels.'

Fanny rolled her eyes expressively at Stanley. 'Hullo — goodbye!' she muttered as she rushed out again.

Cook lifted a large apple charlotte from the oven. The top — a crisp golden brown — was sprinkled with brown sugar and chopped nuts and Stanley whistled his approval.

'There'll be precious little left,' Cook told him, 'so don't get too excited.' She set it on the draining-board and straightened up, a hand to her aching back. 'Where are they off to tomorrow?' she asked him. 'Any idea?'

'They're going down to the river,' he said, 'for a picnic. We're driving them to Buckler's Hard and then they're taking a boat.'

Cook paused for a moment to mop her perspiring face. 'What do you think of Mr Scott?' she asked. 'Handsome devil, isn't he? I must say I've rather taken a shine to him. And his clothes! Perfect cut and such beautiful cloth; you can tell he's a gentleman just by looking at him. And the way he speaks in that drawl they have over there. I'm not usually one for the men, but I could listen to *him* all day.'

Stanley considered, his head on one side. 'I suppose he *is* handsome,' he conceded. 'I wonder what he does. I mean, where does all his money come from? He hasn't robbed a bank, has he?'

'A man like that doesn't need to,' said Cook. 'People like Mr Scott are born to money. You can always tell; they take money for granted because they've always had it.'

Fanny had returned and, overhearing, she said, 'He might not. He might have made it by stocks and shares and things like that — that's how some people make money.'

Stanley laughed. 'Hark who's talking!' he said. 'What do *you* know about stocks and shares? I bet you wouldn't recognize one if it bit you on the ankle!'

She gave him a withering look. 'Well, I would then, because I keep my ears open and *learn* things. They're things you buy and then the price goes up and down and you look in the *Financial Times*, so there! Then when they go up, you sell them again and make a profit!' She stuck out her tongue. 'So I *do* know. Anyway, just now he was telling them about Harland and Wolff.'

They all regarded her blankly.

'Harland and Wolff?' echoed Dot. 'What's that when it's at home?'

'It's a firm that builds ships,' Fanny told them. 'He must be something to do with the firm because he seemed to know a lot about it. In Belfast, it is.'

'But he's an American,' Stanley objected. 'Belfast's in Ireland.'

Fanny adopted an expression of exaggerated amazement. 'No! It never is! Did you hear that, Cook? Belfast's in Ireland.'

Cook grinned. 'Well, I'm blowed! I thought it was in Australia!'

'Anyway,' Fanny continued loftily, 'they're building ships for the White Star Line and Mr Scott came over on the *Adriatic* because that's their biggest and best ship to date. *And* all their boats end with "ick" — that is IC — like *Adriatic*, *Baltic*, names like that. He was telling Mrs Latimer and she was looking up at him with her eyes all shining. I think she's a bit smitten.' She struck a pose and said in a false voice, 'Oh, Larry, how terribly fascinating. *Do* go on!' For added effect, she fluttered her eyelashes and Stanley laughed.

'You'll get into trouble, my lady, one of these days,' said Cook, 'snooping the way you do. You see if you don't.'

'I wasn't snooping, I was overhearing,' Fanny protested. 'I was clearing things a bit slow like and just happened to overhear. No crime in that. Anyway, when he said he's coming over again next year Mrs Latimer said, "Oh, how perfectly splendid, Larry," and looked as if she'd burst out of her stays with excitement.'

At that moment Grace came into the kitchen to bring back the dinner plates and collect the nursery desserts, and Fanny quickly brought her up to date with these latest snippets of information.

Then she went on, 'And he's coming over in the spring of next year, so he can travel back to America in the new ship, if he can – on her maiden voyage. That's another "ick" – the *Olympic*. He's probably got shares in the White Star Line – or else in the shipyard.'

'Or both,' said Stanley gloomily. 'More likely both.'

'But the White Star Line *is* the shipyard, isn't it?' said Cook.

Fanny shook her head. 'I didn't say that. I said the shipyard – that's Harland and Wolff – builds the ship for the shipping line – that's White Star.'

Grace was looking troubled. 'You don't really think she's fallen for Mr Scott, do you? She's got a very nice husband of her own. I know Mr Scott's very handsome but Al—' – she corrected herself hastily – 'Mr Latimer's much nicer. Just because he's not the flashy type, that's not to say . . .' She hesitated as she caught sight of Stanley's expression and went on defiantly, 'What I mean is, I don't think Mr Scott can hold a candle to Mr Latimer.'

Surprised by this, Cook, Fanny and Dot stared at Grace, who coloured faintly under their scrutiny.

'Grace!' cried Fanny. 'I do believe you're *blushing*. I reckon it's *you* that's smitten with Mr Latimer.'

'Of course I'm not!' cried Grace. 'I just think he's a lot nicer than Mr Scott.'

'Course he is,' said Cook, coming to her aid. 'Take no notice of Fanny; we've no time for idle gossip. The children will be wanting their puddings, bless their hearts. I made them an orange jelly because the rest are having apple charlotte and the children aren't so keen on it. If you like to wait for yours, there'll be some charlotte later.'

191

Grace declared herself quite happy with the jelly and disappeared upstairs with the tray. Before anyone could make further comment, Ida rushed into the kitchen clutching her hand and complaining that she had been stung by a bee. In the excitement of carefully removing the sting and applying a blue-bag, Grace was temporarily forgotten.

*

As the departing visitors gathered on the steps with their luggage prior to their return to the station, the weekend house party was voted by all to have been an outstanding success. Even the weather had been kind to them, for the sun had shone relentlessly on all their activities.

Eleanor had been pleasantly surprised by Virginia's kindness towards her, and was also pleased to know that she had made a favourable impression on the rest of the family.

Archie had enjoyed himself in his own way. He liked good food, and the meals at Berwick House had been entirely to his satisfaction in both size and quality. As usual, he had eaten much more than he needed with a complete disregard for his expanding waistline, so now he felt wonderfully full and well pleased with life generally.

Larry Scott had probably enjoyed the weekend more than anyone, for he had fallen in love with Virginia Latimer. He had therefore valued every moment spent in her company, whether they had been sharing a picnic, inspecting the horses, playing tennis or singing a duet at the piano after dinner. His joy was only marred by the knowledge that he must leave her, but he was a resourceful man and had worked out a possible solution to this problem. Though this was not perfect, it was the best he could contrive in the relatively short time at his disposal. As the Daimler appeared, followed by the brougham, he suddenly pretended to have lost his wallet, slapping his pockets with a look of exasperation on his face.

'What is it?' asked Virginia.

'My wallet,' he told her. 'I seem to have mislaid it. Oh,

this is too annoying. I'll just nip back to my room and have a quick look around. It can't be far – on the bedside table, I guess.'

He hurried back into the house taking the steps two at a time, and after a moment Virginia followed him. When she went to the door of his room, however, he was nowhere to be seen.

'Larry?' she said softly.

Two more steps took her into the room and suddenly the door swung to behind her and she turned to see Larry with his back to it and a finger raised to his lips.

'You startled me!' she began. 'Whatever – ?'

He held up a hand and she fell silent immediately. 'We don't have much time,' he told her, 'but I simply had to speak to you. The wallet is safe in my breast-pocket but Virginia, you *have* to know how I feel about you.'

Virginia, startled but not at all surprised by his words, put a hand to her heart which was beating furiously. Before she could speak, he went on, 'I can't just walk away like this – I've got to see you again. I'm half out of my mind, Virginia. How do I tell you? How do I convince you that this is something real, something that's going to *last*? I know you're married and I know I've no claim on you – you have every right to reject me – but please don't do that.'

Virginia was thrilled by his outburst, for she had hoped for just such a declaration, but now it had come she felt the need to step warily.

'But Larry, I daren't – ' she began.

'No, please don't interrupt,' he begged. 'We have so little time. All I ask, all I *beg*, is that you let me write to you. Somehow it must be possible for us to keep in touch. I'm so afraid of losing you altogether. I want to tell you how I feel and here . . .' – he waved his hands helplessly – ' . . . under your husband's roof it's impossible. Just tell me you feel something for me in return? I thought I saw it in your eyes, but I hardly dared to hope.'

For a moment Virginia struggled with her conscience. He was rich and exciting, handsome and infinitely eligible, but Alex, the children and Berwick House were all precious to her and not to be risked lightly. Yet if all he asked was a correspondence. Was it possible? Was it reasonable to take such terrible risks for a few love-letters? What would happen if Alex ever found out? As if reading her thoughts, he said, 'No one need ever know, I swear it. Just let me write to you. *Please*, Virginia!'

She was so flattered and excited that her doubts began to lose their validity as she imagined the thrill of reading and answering his letters. It would be a most exhilarating and dangerous secret and Virginia longed to agree. It would add colour and sparkle to her life and keep the spectre of boredom at bay. It was too good to refuse.

'You may write,' she said at last, 'as long as . . .'

The pleasure in his eyes was reward enough for the step she had taken. Seconds passed and neither spoke; and then he lifted both her hands, put them to his lips and kissed them, his eyes looking intently into hers.

'Oh, Larry!' she whispered. 'This is such folly, but – '

'But you won't regret it? You won't change your mind?' From below they heard someone calling and Virginia clutched his arm with a desperate haste.

'The letters?' she cried. 'How on earth can we do it? Alex will see them.'

'No, I've thought it all out,' he told her urgently. 'I'll write to you under your maiden name and send the letters to the Post Office – then you can send one of the servants to collect them. And you will answer them? You promise? I know I have no right to ask, but just to keep in touch. If you were free, Virginia, you'd be my wife before the week was out! Just say you return my feelings. Say you love me – '

At once she was alarmed. 'No, no! I can't say that!'

'No, I see . . . I'm sorry. But *I* can say it and I do!'

There were footsteps on the stairs. The opportunity was slipping away.

'Someone's coming!' she cried. 'Oh Larry, I think I do love you. Yes, it's true. Oh, my dear!'

From the end of the passage they heard Lucien calling, 'Did you find it? We're all going to miss the train if you don't hurry.'

With a supreme effort, Virginia arranged her features into a smile and stepped out of the room.

'It had fallen down beside the bed,' she told him breathlessly as Larry followed her out on to the landing.

Passing Fanny on the stairs she told her to ring the station and tell them to hold the train for a few minutes, then hurried with Larry to rejoin the others on the steps. They quickly took their places, Virginia had to sit in the brougham with Archie and Alex while Lucien, Larry and Eleanor went in the motor. At the station the 'Goodbyes' were necessarily brief, but Virginia managed to whisper her maiden name to Larry under cover of the hissing of the train engine and the shouts of the station staff. The train started and as it gathered speed, Larry put his head out of the window and Virginia watched him as long as she dared. From now on, she thought, that could never be long enough.

Chapter Ten

A week went by and then two — and still Virginia could not pluck up courage to send someone to the Post Office to ask for a letter in the name of Forster. This was partly because she was afraid of the suspicion this might arouse, but also because deep in her heart she doubted that there would be a letter. On reflection, it seemed so unlikely that a man as rich and handsome — and as *desirable* — as Larry Scott should have fallen in love with her. It was altogether too fantastic... the stuff of which dreams were made. She was also fearful of where embarking on an illicit correspondence might lead and reluctant to take the first step along a path of deceit and intrigue. A hundred times a day she asked herself if she really wanted an affair of the heart, but in spite of the disadvantage the truthful answer was invariably 'Yes'. She felt strongly attracted to Larry Scott, but then all women who met him must have been equally drawn to his relaxed, confident manner, his ready expansive smile and his eyes which could be eloquent or inscrutable. Yes, she could never deny his personal magnetism, but she had not entirely fallen under his spell — at least, not as passionately as he appeared to have fallen for her — and she felt sure that if they did not meet again she would eventually be able to forget him. If they corresponded, however, he would occupy more and more of her thoughts until her own deeper feelings and desires would be aroused also. She had only flirted with him to make Lucien jealous, but it seemed that her efforts had misfired. Lucien had been engrossed with Eleanor, but the effect on Larry Scott had been much more effective than she had intended.

Allowing him to write to her had further encouraged him... and she had said that she loved him. So now she must take responsibility for her actions. Someone must be sent to the Post Office soon. Should it be Fanny or

Dot – or maybe Grace Martins? Should she insist on their discretion and reward them in some way, or would that arouse further suspicions? Surely there must be a way to hide her own involvement. Virginia thought long and hard about it and finally sent word for Grace to come to her in the morning room.

'I want you to take the children for a walk,' she said, busying herself with a few letters on her bureau desk, 'as far as the Post Office. I have offered to collect any letters that may be left there for a friend of mine; the name is Forster. Mrs Forster.' She hoped that Larry would have the sense to use only her initial. Provided he used only a 'V', she could in future refer to her friend as Vera Forster.

'Yes, ma'am,' said Grace. 'Shall we go after lunch or now?'

Suddenly it became a matter of urgency to Virginia to know whether he had written or whether perhaps he had thought better of his rash declaration. The suspense was becoming unbearable.

'Oh . . . now, I think,' she decided.

'Yes, ma'am,' said Grace, then hesitated. 'May the children have a penny each to spend? It's such a thrill for them and it doesn't happen very often.'

'Of course!' Too eagerly, Virginia took the coins from her cash-box and handed them to Grace. 'But see they don't eat the sweets until *after* lunch or they will spoil their appetites. And here's a sixpence for you – you may see something you fancy.'

Grace's surprise was obvious and Virginia felt at once that the generous gesture had been a mistake, but it was too late for regrets.

'About this friend of mine, Mrs Forster,' she went on. 'She has some difficulties which do not concern you, and I have promised to be as discreet as possible over the letters. I would like you to be equally discreet.' Grace was looking at her rather blankly, so she hurried on, 'In other words, I don't want you to talk about the letters to anyone else. Do you understand?'

'Of course, ma'am. I won't say a word.'

'I'm sure she will be most appreciative.' Virginia

197

glanced at the clock. 'Good gracious, it's nearly eleven o'clock. You must hurry. And bring the letter straight to me – that is, if there is one. There may not be. Now do get along!'

When Grace had gone, Virginia crossed her fingers. If there was no letter, after all her scheming, she thought she would die of disappointment. However, she need not have worried, for when it arrived the letter – addressed to Mrs V. 'Foster' instead of 'Forster'; Larry had obviously misheard her – was everything she could have hoped for.

My dearest Virginia, [he had written in a strong, sloping hand] It was so generous of you to allow me to write to you and I trust you have not had second thoughts. I need so desperately to tell you how I feel about you and those few poor words when we parted were woefully inadequate. Quite simply, my darling girl (if I may presume to call you that) you have quite bowled me over and I hardly know how to deal with my emotions. Of course there have been other women in my life, and many of them professed to have loved me 'to distraction' as they say, but I was never able to match their feelings. To tell the truth, I believe I rather scorned them for their inability to control their emotions and pitied them for their single-minded devotion. That is not meant to sound boastful, but to explain to you what a profound shock it was to find myself in a similar situation, for here I am hopelessly, helplessly in love with another man's wife.

Dearest Virginia, what am I to do? I am torn between joy and despair – the former because I have found a woman who has transformed my life; the latter because you belong to someone else. When I left you at the station it was a terrible effort to appear normal, but at least you had been kind to me and said we could correspond. Now my great fear is that you will change your mind. Please, I beg you with all my heart, never make such a decision. All that makes life worth living is the thought of your letters in answer to mine.

Guiltily, Virginia glanced at the date on the envelope and saw that he had posted the letter the day after he left Berwick House. So he had already been waiting nearly two weeks. And when was he going back to the States? She read on anxiously:

I know that probably you can never be mine, but if I know that you return my feelings I shall not feel quite so alone. It is all so unexpected and I hardly know if I am on my head or my heels. Me, in love! My darling girl, you have turned my whole world upside down and I adore you. I am returning to America at the end of the week so will put my home address at the end of the letter. However, I shall find an excuse to come back to England, probably in the early spring. Dare I hope that when I do you will agree to meet me somewhere? Paris, perhaps, or London – or am I asking for the moon? The thought that somehow, sometime we could spend a few stolen hours together will have to sustain me through the long, lonely months ahead.

Do write to me. I shall live for your letters. Forgive the ramblings of a madman – I am indeed out of my mind with love! Say you care for me just a little!

Your devoted Larry

The address followed and then he had added a row of kisses. Virginia read the letter again dazedly, savouring every word. It was true, then: Larry Scott was in love with her. Truly, sincerely, *helplessly* in love. Slowly, she lifted the letter and put it to her lips. She would have to answer it; she would write to him kindly, confessing that she certainly did care for him but reminding him that she *was* married and could never allow herself to match his passion. In the spring perhaps they would meet, although she was not sure how this could be arranged. At all costs, she thought, she must not allow herself to become infatuated with him, for that way lay disaster. The affair would remain a secret joy for the two of them to share. Alex must *never* find out.

'Oh, Larry!' she whispered. 'I want to love you so

much in return, but I daren't.' And she kissed the letter again and began carefully to re-read it.

*

Summer faded unwillingly into autumn and high winds wrought havoc in the grounds of Berwick House, stripping the leaves from the trees, while the first night frosts blackened the late roses. Inside the house life went on much as usual and on the surface, at least, the household functioned from day to day as it always did. November passed into December without incident and then the inhabitants suddenly discovered that the Christmas season was upon them and preparations were put in hand. The Christmas puddings had been made long since, but there was mincemeat to be made for the pies and a dozen other things to think about and the kitchen staff were torn between the natural excitement engendered by the season of goodwill and the knowledge of all the extra work which it entailed.

In the garden Sid was nursing the Christmas vegetables – sprouts, parsnips, thyme and parsley – for the potatoes had long since been stored underground and covered with a layer of straw to keep out the light. There were hedges to be given a last trim and leaves to be swept up daily, and this gave Sid the excuse for numerous bonfires which kept the raw air from his bones. He managed to plant a few new roses before the first light fall of snow set him to clearing paths, a job he detested.

Upstairs the children's enthusiasm for Christmas was infectious and Grace helped them to devise and make small gifts for their parents as well as decorations for the nursery. Earnest deliberations on the part of the children resulted in small but urgent messages to Santa Claus and these were whisked up to the night sky by way of the nursery fire. Strenuous, almost superhuman, efforts were made by George and Victoria to 'be especially good', and each night after they had gone to bed Grace worked on her presents for them. It was a happy time and when at last the snow came their joy was complete; they donned

200

warm clothing and went outside to make the inevitable snowman.

However, for the first time in her life, Virginia could feel no enthusiasm for the Christmas spirit since all her thoughts and energies were directed to the letters she sent to Larry Scott and those she received from him in return. She lived for the days when Grace's trip to the Post Office Store would result in an envelope bearing its familiar American stamps, and it did not occur to her to wonder what the nanny thought about these mysterious letters. Grace Martins was a servant and as such was not expected to hold opinions on anything at all. She was there to run errands and hold her tongue. Virginia's letters to Larry were pages long and adding to them each day was an eagerly anticipated labour of love. Since their parting she had received thirteen letters and had sent five to him. Christmas without him could mean nothing to her and although she attended to the extra duties associated with the season, she did so with a degree of indifference that did not go entirely unnoticed. Even John Martins, her loyal admirer, found her moody and unpredictable.

After her initial reluctance, Virginia had later allowed herself to be carried away by the romance of the illicit correspondence, and as the weeks passed her imagination wildly exaggerated the intensity of their relationship so that – although in fact they had never even kissed – she convinced herself that their affair was of a most intimate nature. Her letters to him were full of physical longings and his to her, couched in similar terms, fanned the flames of her passion. She hid the love-letters in the bottom of a trunk where she was certain no one would find them. Although she was conscious that Alex must be aware of her changed manner she was too much in love to care, assuring herself that he was busier than ever with the estate and would never have time to investigate the matter further. On the morning of Christmas Eve, however, she was shocked to receive a letter on another matter which immediately shattered her complacency. It was written in an uneven hand on a scrap of paper which had apparently been torn from a notebook. One section of the writing was slightly blurred, as though a liquid had been spilt across it.

Dear Mrs Latimer,
You will no doubt be surprised to learn that I was a witness to you and Mr Lucien in the summerhouse on the sixteenth of May. I was shocked that you should allow such liberties, but I kept my mouth shut. Now I am in need of ten pounds, as without a reference I cannot find another place and the money your husband gave me is all gone. Bring it here. If you don't, I shall go to your husband. You won't like that. People like you are the scum of the earth. You have ruined my name but I could ruin yours. This is no idle threat. I mean every word, so do it or you will be sorry.

The letter was unsigned, but there was an address: 11, Challis Court, Southampton. A great blackness swept over Virginia as she finished reading and she thought she was going to be sick. Her fingers closed instinctively over the page, crumpling it before hurling it violently across the morning room.

'Nanny Webster!' she whispered. 'Oh, dear God!'

She leaned forward, resting her arms on the desk as fear churned inside her. The shock had numbed her brain and for a moment all she could say was, 'No, no, *no!*'

As the minutes passed her senses gradually returned and she was struck by the irony of it all. She had been so clever about her affair with Larry Scott, and now here was that foolishness with Lucien, come back to haunt her like a ghost from her past . . . Lucien, who now meant so little to her compared with Larry.

'Please, God, don't let this be happening to me,' she begged. 'Take pity on me. Forgive me. Don't let her tell Alex.' At last she rose unsteadily to her feet and made her way across the room to retrieve the letter, picking it up gingerly between thumb and forefinger as though it might burn her.

With trembling lips she re-read the scrawled words:

'... witness to you and Mr Lucien in the summer-house ... I was shocked ...'

'The malicious, evil old witch!'

But how on earth had she seen them? She so rarely came into the garden. Presumably she had brought the children out for a walk – oh God! Had the children seen them too? She went hot and cold at the thought of it. No, surely not. But Nanny Webster *had!* That was abundantly clear. She had even made a note of the date.

Virginia shook her head helplessly. If only they hadn't sacked the wretched woman ... but they had had to do it, and Alex had been generous to a fault over the money. Nanny Webster had known about the summer-house but had said nothing. She had waited all this time to have her revenge. Not for a moment did Virginia doubt that she would carry out her threat. Whatever happened, she must give her some money, but presumably it would not end there. The blackmail would continue. Regrets flooded in. Why oh why, had she let Lucien take advantage of her on that one foolish occasion, when he had already turned his attentions towards Eleanor and their own relationship was at an end? It was all so unnecessary – except for her own pride. If she was honest, she must admit that at the time the incident had helped to lessen her disappointment. She had *wanted* it to happen and had been a willing partner in all that took place. Her cheeks burned as she remembered his hands exploring her body ... and Nanny Webster had been *watching!* Nanny Webster had been defiling it all with her hateful beady eyes. It was too horrible to think about and now the vindictive old bitch was going to make use of that knowledge.

The letter itself puzzled her. Nanny Webster was an educated woman and her handwriting was particularly neat and well formed. Had she been drunk, perhaps, when she wrote it? Virginia could not imagine it, but a terrible despair welled up in her heart as she imagined similar letters stretching ahead into the future. She put a shaking hand to her mouth, her eyes were dull with shock and revulsion. It was all so dreadfully *ugly*.

203

Then a fresh thought struck her, increasing her panic. How on earth could she find the money without Alex knowing? She had a little money of her own which remained from a legacy from her grandmother, but Alex had access to all the accounts and would be sure to notice if she withdrew anything. He always teased her for extravagence, but she always had something to show for it – a pair of kid gloves or a jewelled pin. Now she would have nothing. She wondered if she could pawn something . . . but no! That, too, was out of the question, for she would never be able to redeem it. If she *sold* a bracelet or a brooch Alex might ask where it was and she would be unable to explain its disappearance.

There was a knock at the door.

'What is it?'

Cook came into the room and Virginia looked up distractedly. 'Excuse me for troubling you, ma'am, but I'm a bit bothered about the menu for Boxing Day,' Cook began. 'So far I haven't been able to – '

'Not now, Cook,' interrupted Virginia curtly.

Cook's eyes widened in surprise. 'But ma'am, I can't make – '

'*Not now*. Are you deaf?'

'No, ma'am, but – '

'That will do, Cook! We'll talk about it at some other time.'

'Some other . . .' Cook's protest faded as she saw the look on her mistress' face and she withdrew hurriedly without another word.

Virginia read the letter again, her face taut with anger.

'Nanny Webster!' she muttered malevolently. 'I could cheerfully kill you!'

*

Christmas morning was a scene of bustle and excitement throughout the house as each member of the household reacted to the occasion in his or her own way. The kitchen staff got up an hour earlier than usual, but in reasonably high spirits. Guy woke up with a toothache and had to resort to oil of cloves but he bore it cheerfully enough, reluctant to let his own troubles spoil anyone else's pleasure. The children were awake very early and Grace allowed them to investigate the contents of their stockings in front of the fire which she had coaxed back into flames. Virginia awoke with a severe nervous headache and a sick feeling in her stomach, so had a perfect excuse not to attend church without resorting to subterfuge.

'Are you sure the fresh air won't help you?' asked Alex, a look of concern on his face. 'The rector will be so disappointed if you don't attend. You know how he is about Berwick House.'

'No, it won't help me,' Virginia snapped. 'If I thought it would help, I should not have suggested staying in bed. You will have to go without me and the rector will have to put up with it. He is the least of my worries.'

Alex picked up the slip at once. 'What are you worrying about, Virginia? I thought everything was – '

'I didn't mean . . .' she stammered, then recovered herself. 'Of *course* I have worries. This house doesn't run itself, Alex, especially at Christmas, and Cook is being particularly stupid. It's not surprising I have a sick headache. The only wonder is that I don't get them more often.'

Alex took her hand in his. 'I thought yesterday that you were not quite yourself,' he said. 'I've been worrying about you for some time. I trust you would tell me if you weren't happy about anything. I'm never too busy to – '

'Oh, for heaven's sake, Alex!' she cried. 'I am perfectly happy. Deliriously so! I just don't want to go to church – I mean, I don't feel well enough to go. Wish everyone a happy Christmas from me and say I will come down as soon as I feel able. And close the curtains again, please. The light hurts my eyes!'

He made no answer, but instead gave her a searching look which increased her uneasiness.

'And don't stare at me like that, Alex!' she exploded. 'I'm not a peepshow!'

She regretted her lack of control but could not hold the words back. The anger she felt towards Nanny

Webster and the dread with which she faced the forth-coming meeting with the woman made it almost imposs-ible to behave normally. Now she saw the concern in her husband's eyes change to suspicion as he sat down on the edge of the bed and took hold of her hands.

'Please, Virginia,' he said. 'There *is* something wrong, I can tell. You really must confide in me or else I can't help you.'

She withdrew her hands sharply and put them under the bedclothes.

'For the last time,' she said grimly, 'there is *nothing* wrong with me except a sick headache, but you seem determined to make it worse by all this wretched fussing. I shall ring down for some camomile tea.' Seeing that he looked entirely unconvinced, she made a supreme effort and managed a faint smile. 'Really, Alex, I shall be fine if I can only rest a little longer. Do please go down to breakfast.'

She reached for the bell-pull and was relieved to see her husband getting to his feet again. He gave her a long look, nodded briefly and went out of the room.

At once the lines of her face sagged again into an expression of misery, but when Fanny brought the tea she told her she was not to be disturbed and forced herself to drink the pale gold liquid.

She had secretly arranged with Martins that as soon as the household had been safely delivered to church, he would slip back and wait in the lane at the rear of the house on some pretext or other so that he could take her down into town. Unable to obtain any money, Virginia had decided to offer Nanny a small locket which she rarely wore and which hopefully Alex would not miss. If the very worst happened and he did notice its absence, she would pretend she had mislaid it. For the moment anger was keeping Virginia's fear at bay and had given her courage of sorts, and she was prepared to go to any lengths to protect herself from attack from any quarter. Thank heavens for Martins, she reflected gratefully. At least she had an ally of a kind. If she had made the mistake of embracing the new motor-car, instead of remaining loyal to horse and carriage, she would never have dared to enlist his help. God moves in a mysterious way, she decided.

When she heard the brougham draw up at the front door she went to the window and watched from behind the curtains as Fanny, Dot, Sid Trott and the gardener's boy – all arrayed in their Sunday best – climbed in and were whisked away to church. The motor-car then drew up and Alex, the two children and the nanny climbed inside. Virginia was pleased to note that on this occasion Alex sat in front. On several occasions in the past months she had been aware that her son was being allowed to ride with the chauffeur and the idea of her husband and the nanny sitting in close proximity in the back did not please her. On one occasion she had commented adversely but Alex, misunderstanding her objection, had merely laughed, explaining that it was a treat for George and there was no danger at all.

When she was sure that they had all gone, she got up out of bed and began to wash and dress as quickly as she could. Cook would never leave the kitchen on Christmas morning and Guy would not get up until the rest of the family were due back from church, so she would not be missed for several hours.

*

The streets in which they eventually found themselves were narrow and mean, and they had to make several enquiries before discovering that Challis Court was one of the roads which led from Orchard Lane. It was obvious when they did find it that the dark alleyway would not allow the brougham to pass through it. The narrow walkway was a gloomy place, cluttered on either side with dustbins and with lines of washing strung between the houses. Virginia's lips tightened grimly as the groom helped her down into the muddy remains of the recent snow. To make matters worse, a fine rain had started to fall and Virginia turned up the collar of her coat, for she had left home without an umbrella.

'I'd best come with you, ma'am,' John suggested, but

Virginia shook her head. She had no intention of satisfying his curiosity.

'You stay here with the brougham,' she said. 'We can't just leave it here.'

She looked round at the other people in the street, who either stared back at her with an insolent grin or returned her stare with sullen indifference. A boy ran up to them and held out his hand; he had legs like sticks and his cap was several sizes too big for him.

'Spare a copper, lady?' he cried.

Virginia looked with loathing at his bare feet and ragged clothes and shook her head.

'Go on, lady. Just a copper! Well, a halfpenny, then.'

'Nothing,' said Virginia, keeping her voice steady with an effort. 'Go away.' Turning back to John, she said in a low voice, 'Whatever happens, you are not to leave this spot. I don't want to find myself alone here when I get back.'

As he looked at her and saw the fear in her eyes, his respect for her deepened. Whatever her business in this insalubrious area it was no concern of his, but he could imagine what courage it had required to visit these mean streets.

'I won't budge, ma'am,' he assured her. 'I'll be right here waiting for you. Don't you fret.'

'Thank you.'

As she picked her way along the alley, Virginia felt the cold slush seep through her boots and shuddered. Faded paint flaked from all the doors and windows and there was an unpleasant smell of foul drains. Above each doorway a narrow shelf-like 'porch' offered little or no shelter from the weather, while the wooden shutters flanking the ill-fitting windows hung unevenly on rusting hinges and obviously would never close properly. Virginia's soul shrivelled in the miserable surroundings and in spite of her overriding anger, she felt a flicker of pity for Nanny Webster in her downfall. As she walked she was aware of faces at some of the windows and of eyes that followed her boldly. Challis Court after dark must be a daunting place, she thought, and prayed that if she ever had to visit it again it might be in daylight.

When she reached No. 11, she found neither knocker nor bell, so rapped sharply with her knuckles. There was no answer so she tried again, under the suspicious gaze of a small girl who appeared at the door of the house next door. Virginia had rehearsed the scene many times, but in none of them had Nanny Webster failed to open the front door.

The child next door was now joined by a thin woman with haggard eyes. 'She'll never hear you,' she announced. 'She'll be too far gone.' She raised an imaginary bottle to her lips. 'You'd best just go in.'

She withdrew, taking the girl with her, and the door slammed behind them. A mangy tabby cat with a battered ear sprang out from behind a dustbin and tried to rub itself against Virginia's skirts, but she sent it away with a surreptitious kick. Should she go in uninvited if, as the neighbour suggested, Nanny Webster was drunk?

Virginia knocked once more and tentatively tried the handle of the door, which suddenly swung open. Stepping inside, she found herself in a small, dingy room which smelled of boiled cabbage. The grate was full of ashes and there were no curtains at the grimy window. Virginia's instinct was to turn and run from the place, but even as she hesitated she heard the creak of bedsprings in the room overhead.

She called out, 'Is that you, Nanny Webster?'

The anger which so far had buoyed her up suddenly evaporated, leaving her nothing but fear and a deep resentment that she should have been forced into a situation for which nothing in her life had prepared her.

Stairs led upwards from an open doorway on the other side of the room and, receiving no answer, Virginia crossed to them and called again.

'It's me, Virginia Latimer. Please come down.'

Another silence greeted her words and disconcerted, she wondered whether she should go up, but as this was the last thing she wanted to do she continued to try to persuade Nanny Webster to come down. When eventually this proved unsuccessful, she realized that she had no choice and climbed the narrow stairs, her footsteps sounding on the bare wood. Mean stairs, she thought, in a mean house in an even meaner street. How did people survive in such ghastly conditions, she wondered. Presumably, to have any roof overhead was better than the gutter . . . but not much better.

At the top of the stairs she found two doors; one was shut but the other open and through this doorway she saw a sight that made her gasp with disbelief. Nanny Webster, once so prim and straitlaced, lay sprawled in a ramshackle, unmade bed. Incongruously, she was still wearing her uniform, but it was dirty and crumpled. In her right hand she held a bottle of gin that was already half-empty.

'Nanny!' gasped Virginia, entirely at a loss for words and almost forgetting the purpose of her visit for a moment in an unexpected rush of pity.

Nanny Webster sat up and waved the bottle. 'To celebrate – ' she began. 'To . . .' She fell back against the bedhead and took a quick drink from the bottle. 'It's so much . . .' she started again, 'so much better if you . . .'

Trying to focus her eyes a little, she sighed deeply and scratched her tousled hair. Her words were slurred and she reeked of alcohol. 'I forget – ' she said. 'That's the trouble. I keep forgetting . . .'

The bodice of her once neat uniform was spotted with food and her cap was askew. If she had not presented such a tragic figure, Virginia would have laughed. Her eyes travelled over the room, assessing the crude furniture; the colourless threadbare carpet; a sagging grey armchair that spewed horsehair from a split in one arm; tattered curtains and a cheap, spindly washstand which supported a swing-mirror with cracked glass. The picture of poverty and neglect was overwhelming. As though reading her thoughts, Nanny Webster made an effort to raise herself from the pillow again, propping herself precariously on one elbow.

'Nice little place,' she mumbled. 'Like it, do you? Well, it's your doing . . . yours and . . . your doing.' She belched and, since she had no free hand, put the neck of the bottle to her lips as she said, 'Pardon me.'

For a moment Virginia stared at her, horribly fascinated, then she swallowed hard. Her head throbbed painfully, but she struggled to retain what remained of her composure.

'I received your letter,' she said. 'I have no money. I brought this instead.' She drew the gold locket from her pocket and approached the bed. 'It's gold – eighteen-carat. It will fetch at least ten pounds, maybe more.'

As Nanny Webster allowed herself to fall back against the pillow, her left hand came up and Virginia dropped the locket into the upturned palm.

'Gold, you say?' The voice rose enquiringly.

'Certainly,' said Virginia, adding in what she hoped was a firm voice, 'And let that be an end to it.'

'An end?' Nanny Webster looked at her blearily. 'An end to . . . to what?'

'To this nonsense. The letter. Everything. I want no more letters,' Virginia repeated. 'You're a nasty-minded old woman and I want nothing more to do with you.'

Nanny Webster peered at the locket, spilling a little of the gin as she did so.

'Gold?' she asked again.

'Yes.'

'It's not very big. I wanted ten pounds – I wanted – '

'I've just told you that it's worth more than ten pounds,' cried Virginia. 'Sell it and keep away from me. Do you hear me?'

'Do I hear you?' Nanny smiled crookedly. 'I don't know. It's all so much better with a drink – yes, a drink – that's it!'

She held up the bottle to check the level of gin that remained and shook her head. 'It's going down. That's what it does, it goes down . . .'

Virginia drew herself up tall.

'I am going now,' she said. 'But remember – no more letters, or I shall fetch a constable. Do you hear me, Nanny?'

Nanny Webster wagged a finger at her and smiled

horribly. 'No, you won't. You won't fetch . . . you won't fetch anybody, because I saw you and him – '

Virginia paled. 'Stop it, you filthy old hag!' she cried. 'I won't hear another word. I'm going and I shall not come again, so don't bother to write any more letters.'

She spoke with as much conviction as she could muster. It seemed worth trying although she was almost sure the blackmail would continue. All she could hope for was a reasonable interval before the next letter so that she might have time to think of a way to deal with the problem. She retreated to the bedroom door and, turning, groped her way down the narrow stairway.

When at last she stepped outside into the rain, she was absurdly grateful that Nanny Webster had been too drunk to follow.

With her head well down, she retraced her steps on legs that trembled. If Miss Martins had not interfered, they might never have sacked Nanny Webster and none of this would have happened, she reflected bitterly. But that was less than fair. The children's welfare had been at stake and Nanny Webster had had to go. If only Alex had given her a decent reference . . . but that, too, was out of the question. Nanny Webster had to leave and without a reference. The true cause of Virginia's predicament was the incident in the summer-house and she cursed herself for her stupidity. If only she could turn back the clock, she thought miserably, but that was not possible. She had been guilty of a serious indiscretion, a fatal error of judgement, and there seemed no way she could ever rise above it. The cost of her folly would be very high indeed.

At the corner the grimy urchin still waited with hand outstretched. 'Give us a copper, lady? You can spare it.'

Virginia met the bold, dark eyes and read the mixture of hope and hostility in them and without understanding why, she gave him a penny. Perhaps it was conscience money. Perhaps she felt that her stay in the insalubrious street was a mercifully brief one, while he would live out his childhood in the shadow of the grey walls and peeling paint.

'Ta very much,' he said.

His eyes flickered briefly as he flipped the coin into the air, caught it and laid it on the back of his hand.

'Heads I win,' he said. 'Tails you lose,' and again the impudent eyes held hers.

Perhaps he was older than he looked, she thought. In a few years' time he would be a threat instead of a nuisance. A trouble-maker. Sharply she said, 'Now you leave me alone.'

By way of an answer, he put a thumb to his nose and said, 'La-di-dah, aren't we?'

But he made no effort to molest her further and seconds later she came in sight of the brougham and hurried thankfully towards it. John Martins jumped down as soon as he saw her and helped her into the carriage, asking solicitously, 'Are you all right, ma'am?'

Virginia was so pleased to see him; he looked clean and wholesome. She tried to smile, but her lips trembled and she realized she was close to tears.

'I am quite all right,' she whispered. 'Just take me home, please ... and Martins – this is for you.' She fumbled in her pocket and gave him a florin and he touched his hat.

'Not a word, ma'am,' he told her, and as he climbed back into his seat she wondered if the florin would prove the first of many.

*

When Alex came back from church he was pleased to see her apparently recovered and supervising the preparations for dinner.

'No, no, Dot,' she was saying. 'How many times do I have to tell you we use the *best* silver cruets at Christmas.'

'I'm sorry, ma'am.'

'I tell you every year. You have a head like a sieve!'

She turned to smile brightly at Alex. 'How was the service, dear? I did hate to miss it but I knew a rest would put me to rights.'

'I'm glad to see you looking better,' he said. 'A little

flushed, perhaps, but if you're sure you have no temperature – '

'None at all, Alex. I am quite well again. Was it a long sermon? You seem later than usual.'

He frowned. 'It wasn't the sermon that delayed us,' he said. 'It was that damned fool Martins. The fellow went off in the brougham and got back late with some garbled story about having to have a wheel fixed. He'd been for a drink, if you ask me. All the staff had to stand around in the rain waiting for him, and we could hardly leave for home in the motor until I knew for certain that they were going to be collected.' He looked at her closely. 'Virginia, you look very pale.' She had turned away from him, but he took hold of her hand and made her face him.

'You're *trembling*,' he said. 'Dearest, whatever is the matter?'

'It's nothing at all,' she stammered, not meeting his eyes. 'Maybe I am still a little feverish, but I do feel well enough to see the day through.'

Alex was on the point of remonstrating with her, but at that moment the door burst open and the two children bounded cheerfully into the room followed by Grace Martins.

'Oh, Mama, do *look!*' cried Victoria. 'We saw Mrs Gray from the Post Office Stores and she gave us each – '

'A sugar mouse!' cried George, not to be done out of his share in the story. 'She was in church and she had a new hat with a black bird on it, a pretend one, I mean, and it – '

'It wobbled!' giggled Victoria. 'It wobbled every time she nodded her head, and then when she knelt down to pray – '

'It fell off!' George's face glowed at the memory. 'And everyone was watching and started to laugh . . .'

He stopped, aware suddenly that their wonderful story was not receiving his mother's full attention. She stood with one hand to her heart and seemed not to be listening while her chest rose and fell.

'Are you quite well, ma'am?' Grace asked.

Virginia struggled to calm herself, but Alex's words had frightened her. She had thought herself so clever, yet in fact had come very close to disaster by misjudging the time it took Martins to make the journey to Southampton and back.

Alex was looking at her strangely. 'Virginia?' he said. 'Nanny is speaking to you.'

With an effort, she forced her thoughts back to the present.

'I said, are you quite well, ma'am?' Grace repeated.

Virginia looked at the younger woman.

'I am well enough, thank you,' she said. 'I do wish people would stop fussing.' Aware suddenly that she held one hand to her racing heart, she quickly lowered it.

Victoria tried again. 'The dead black bird fell off, Mama. It was *so* funny!'

'It wasn't *dead*, silly,' George corrected loftily. 'It was stuffed.'

'It *was* dead!'

'It wasn't!'

'It couldn't fly.'

'No, but – ' George hesitated, frowning.

Hastily Grace said, 'Tell your Mama about it later. Time to come upstairs now and take off your hats and coats, and then it will be time to open the rest of your presents.'

Immediately the two children forgot about Mrs Gray's unfortunate hat and, chattering excitedly, allowed themselves to be ushered out of the room.

Alex put an arm round his wife's waist and murmured, 'I haven't wished you a happy Christmas yet, dear.'

Virginia swallowed hard. 'Nor I you, Alex,' she said.

She longed to throw her arms around his neck and say, 'Help me!' but she must find her own solution. So she forced a smile and returned his kiss with as much enthusiasm as she could muster. He was a good husband and she did love him, of course – but beside her growing obsession with Larry Scott and the growing difficulties with Nanny Webster, the fact of his goodness paled into insignificance. The two matters which dominated her

215

waking hours could never be shared with him. For the first time for years she felt alone, and it frightened her. For her it was *not* a happy Christmas, but she must put a brave face on it. Soon it would be 1911 and she hoped the New Year might bring her the happiness she craved.

Chapter Eleven

The New Year began with snow which turned, in a day or so, to slush. For Alex Latimer January always brought the chance of a brief respite from his onerous duties, for there was less to do in the winter. Maintenance work on the cottages was shelved until the spring, it was too early for lambing and forestry matters were mostly in abeyance. Normally he looked forward to the free time at his disposal, but this year he found himself unable to relax. He felt apprehensive, aware that a gulf had developed between himself and his wife – a gulf that he could not understand.

On the thirteenth of January he sat alone in the library, an open book unread in his lap as he tried once again to analyse the situation. It seemed to him that Virginia had been peculiarly restless for the best part of a year, but during the last few weeks her behaviour had been quite unpredictable. Her mood changed from one day to the next – sometimes even from one hour to the next. She was at times depressed and withdrawn, irritable with the children, forgetful and quick to take offence. At other times she was determinedly cheerful, over-affectionate and apparently carefree. Some days nothing pleased her, but on others nothing seemed to ruffle her complacency. She seemed almost to be acting the role of wife and mother. When he tried to persuade her to talk to him, she protested with unnecessary and unconvincing vehemence that she had no worries and that he was making her nervous by his 'ridiculous suspicions'.

At first he had thought she was pregnant and hiding the fact from him. The birth of both children had been difficult, but the doctor had not suggested that a further child might be a risk to her health. She had decided that she wanted no more children and Alex had reluctantly agreed.

However, a word with the doctor had now reassured him that she was not pregnant. He had also wondered if she had taken a lover, but that seemed unlikely. She was extravagantly affectionate at times, almost clinging, and had once surprised him by asking, 'Do you still love me, Alex?' and more recently, 'Will you always love me, whatever happens?' It had occurred to him that she might be suffering from a mental breakdown of some kind, but he could see no reason for such a thing to happen when she was under no particular stress. The house was well run; they had no financial difficulties; the children were happier than they had ever been and the health of the family was sound.

With an unconscious shake of his head, he raised the book and made a determined effort to read it, but within minutes his thoughts had reverted once more to his wife. He recalled their courtship – himself young and eager; Virginia reluctant at first, but then allowing herself to be persuaded. She had told him frankly that she did not love him, that her heart belonged for ever to her dead husband, but he had accepted her on those terms – believing that in time she would learn to love him. Their lovemaking until recently had been satisfying, although Virginia would never reveal her true feelings. Did he even *know* her, he asked himself despairingly. They had shared the same bed for many years and had produced two lovely children, and to the rest of the world they were man and wife. But did they *know* each other? He was afraid he had failed her in some way.

'Virginia,' he whispered. 'What do you want from life?' And what did *he* want? He wanted a happy, loving family. Wasn't that enough?

Laying the book aside, he stood up and crossed the room where he rested his clenched fists one above the other on the mantelpiece and then leaned his head against them despairingly.

'For God's sake, what's wrong?' he demanded aloud.

His own wife was becoming a stranger to him and he felt powerless to prevent it. He stood there for a long time, until his unhappy thoughts were interrupted by a knock on the door.

'Come in.'

He had expected Fanny or Dot with a new scuttle of coal for the fire, but it was Grace Martins who entered the room.

'I'm only returning a book, sir,' she said. 'I can come back some other time, if it's not convenient.'

He straightened up and attempted a smile, wondering fleetingly if she had read the misery in his eyes.

'No, Miss Martins, now will do as well as any other time. What have you been reading?'

She laughed a little as she came towards him. 'It's Ballantyne's *The Coral Island*. I nearly gave it up half-way through – it's terribly gory – but I persevered.'

'Would you say you enjoyed it?'

She nodded, but added, 'Even though I had to skip some of the worst bits.'

Looking into her eyes, Alex was surprised to find a little warmth stealing into his chilled soul. There was something serene about the young nanny's face and for a long moment he let his eyes travel over it, admiring the full mouth, the soft hair tucked up under her cap, even the freckles that sprinkled her cheekbones. It was an open face with no pretence and suddenly he wondered about her. How did she view the Latimer family and – more interesting still – what did she think of him?

'Are you really happy with us?' he asked abruptly.

'Oh, yes, sir.'

He wondered what happiness meant to someone in her position. A secure job, a roof over her head and food to satisfy her hunger – was that enough for her or did she secretly long for a different life, with a husband and children of her own?

He frowned without realizing that he did so, but she said anxiously, 'I truly am, sir,' as though she thought he had doubted her word.

He did not reassure her, for his mind was suddenly troubled by the thought that one day she would leave them to marry. She had denied any interest in Ivy

Cummings' nephew, but there was still Stanley Marcus who was obviously interested in her – Alex remembered the kiss in the stable-yard. His brows contracted further as he looked at her, but then he became aware of her nervousness and smiled.

'Not thinking of leaving us, then, for pastures new?' He tried to make the question a casual one.

'No, sir.'

'No followers?' He smiled again to show that he intended the question humorously.

She shook her head and then said, 'That kiss, sir, was just Stanley's joke. It didn't mean anything – leastways, not to me. He's like that with everyone, it's just his way.'

'I see. So you think you'll stay with us, Miss Martins?'

'I hope so, sir – that is, if you're satisfied with me.'

He nodded gravely. 'We are – but you did say that when you had "found your feet", as you put it, you might be glad of a nursery-maid to help you. You do have a long day.'

'No longer than Nanny Webster's day,' she replied, 'and I'm younger. I look at it this way, sir. If I was married and had two children, I'd have to look after them without any help *and* I'd have a home to clean and shopping to do and a man to look after, so . . .'

Her reference to 'shopping' reminded him that he had seen her once or twice in the village.

'I saw you coming out of the village store one day last week – ' he began.

To his astonishment her expression changed at once and she hastily lowered her eyes. 'I was . . .' she stammered. 'That is – I had to post a letter for Mrs Wade.'

He laughed to cover his surprise. 'There's no need to look so guilty. You're at liberty to come and go in your own free time.'

This seemed to make matters worse.

'Oh, I do – unless it's not my free time, and then I always take the children. They love an outing and we . . .' Her voice trailed into silence.

In spite of himself, he said, 'Oh, so you post a lot of letters for Mrs Wade?'

It sounded as though he had caught her out in a lie and he had not really intended that, but to his consternation Grace now looked more troubled and confused than ever. Could she be hiding something, he wondered, feeling a rush of disappointment at the idea that she might not be as genuine as he had thought her.

'Yes,' she stammered. 'I mean, no, not a lot. Sometimes they're my own letters.'

Ah! he thought. Her own letters! So perhaps she *did* have a sweetheart and was keeping it to herself for fear of earning her employer's disapproval.

'Please, Miss Martins,' he said gently, 'there's no need to explain. You are entitled to a life of your own and you don't have to account to us for every move you make. You may send letters to whoever you please. I hope you don't think that we expect you to account to us for everything you do.'

She lifted her head and there was a look in her eyes that disturbed him. 'No, sir,' she said, 'I've never thought that.' She hesitated, her gaze never leaving his face. 'I swear I would never do anything to disappoint *you*, sir. Not if I could help it.'

'I'm sure you wouldn't. Please don't look so worried.' He wanted the unfathomable look to leave her face. She had come into the room looking carefree and innocent and now she looked ill at ease. He could not bear to send her away feeling less than happy.

'Well,' he said cheerfully, 'what would you like to read next? Dickens? Shakespeare? Have you read Barrie's *Peter Pan*? Or Carroll's *Alice in Wonderland*? What sort of books do you like?'

'I don't really know, sir.'

'Love stories? Adventure? Fantasy?'

'I don't think I want to bother with fantasies,' she told him and he was pleased to see that already her uneasiness had lessened. 'Something with a strong story and plenty of characters.'

'Plenty of characters ... hmm.' He considered. 'My wife enjoyed *Barchester Towers*; it has a clerical background.'

She hesitated. 'Did *you* like it, sir?'

Flattered, he said, 'I have to confess I haven't read it, but perhaps you could try it and give me your opinion on it. You never know, you might persuade me to read it.'

'Do you have time to read?' she asked. 'You always seem so terribly busy. You look so tired, sometimes, that I – '

This last comment startled him and looking at her face, he saw that she instantly regretted it. Neither of them spoke for a moment as he enjoyed the realization that she had cared enough to notice his tiredness. He *did* work hard, much too hard, but no one else seemed aware of it. Virginia's only reaction was one of impatience that he must spend so much time away from her. His father considered he 'mollycoddled' his employees and spent too much on their creature comforts. Yet here was the nanny actually concerned on his behalf. He felt ridiculously grateful.

Grace, however, obviously considered she had gone too far and was stammering an apology. 'That was impertinent of me, sir. I do beg your pardon.'

'There's no need to apologize,' he told her. 'I appreciate your concern. I think . . .' He smiled. 'I *know* you have a kind heart. Yes, I do occasionally find time to read. Here . . .' He took down the book and exchanged it for the one she was returning. '*Barchester Towers*. I hope you enjoy it.'

'I will, sir. Thank you.'

Again an awkward silence fell between them. She held the book against her chest and then smiled. 'It's a big book; it will keep me out of mischief.'

'I can't imagine you – ' he began and then stopped. No, that remark would be an impertinence on his part.

'I'd better go, sir,' she said with obvious reluctance and he nodded.

Still she hesitated, apparently about to add something, but she changed her mind and with a quick bob of her head, turned and left the room.

After a moment he whispered the words she had

uttered so impetuously: 'Sometimes you look so tired that I – '

The unfinished sentence intrigued him.

He took a deep breath, walked to the window and looked down into the garden. 'She really cares,' he marvelled and was strangely comforted.

*

13th January 1911. Today I had Alex all to myself for a few minutes. He was in the library and when I first saw him he looked so sad I longed to throw my arms round him and somehow hug him back to happiness. If only I had dared! He tried to be cheerful and was so kind, telling me to read *Barchester Towers*, which I will do, and asking me if I am happy and will I stay here. And do I have followers. How could I answer that except to say, 'No, but *you* do. I am your follower!' Then he spoilt it all by asking me about being at the village store and I got frightened and almost gave away about the letters. I'm sure he guessed something. How I hate those wretched letters. I suspect more and more that they are Mrs L.'s from Mr Scott because the stamps are American. And if they are for this Mrs Foster, why does Mrs L. look so disappointed when I come back empty-handed and so thrilled when there is a letter? I have been so tempted to tell her I won't collect them, but I'm afraid of antagonizing her. She doesn't like me. And now she's made me lie to Alex and I expect he thinks I'm lying on my own behalf. How I despise her. She is married to the dearest man in the world and if she prefers Mr Scott, then I don't think much of her judgement. Fanny heard them arguing again the other day. If only she realized how lucky she is, Mrs Latimer I mean. If only she would make him happy. I could forgive her anything. Oh Alex, do you really adore her? If so, I hope you never discover that she certainly doesn't adore you.

*

Larry Scott had promised a return trip to England and this was finally arranged for the Easter period. Virginia was in a fever of excitement at the prospect of seeing him again, but reluctant to invite him to Berwick House because she knew she would never be able to hide from anyone the way she felt about him. Her love would shine out in her eyes and ring in her voice whenever she spoke to him. He might be more practised at hiding his emotions, but Virginia could not guarantee her own behaviour. If Alex *should* guess, there would be the devil to pay! She dare not risk it and told Larry firmly that he must not expect an invitation to her home. However, this only created a new difficulty. Lucien was on leave again and would be visiting Eleanor. If Larry stayed with the Sharps, as he had done on his previous visit, Lucien might invite them all to Berwick House. Virginia begged Larry to stay in London instead and he agreed reluctantly to humour her.

He arrived at Southampton on March 20th, but the following day Virginia received a letter by hand which threw her into an immediate panic.

My dearest Virginia,

As you see, I am in Lyndhurst only a few miles away. I intended to go straight to London, but I could not do it. To be so near to you and to move on without seeing you would have been an agony and so, my darling girl, you must not be angry.

I am here under the name of Stuart Bell. Meet me here, I beg you, and let me hold you in my arms. Then I swear I will go on to London and wait for you there, although the waiting will be unbearable. Please, Virginia, do come for however brief a moment. I must see you and, from your letters, I believe that your longing for me is equally strong. Could we meet here? If not, will you suggest somewhere else? Forgive me, my dearest love, but I love you. It is as simple as that. Your devoted Larry.

*

Virginia sank into the nearest chair and, breathing deeply, tried to think calmly. She felt weak with shock and was at once thrilled by the knowledge of his nearness and terrified that he might be seen and recognized by some mutual acquaintance. She pressed the letter to her lips and closed her eyes.

'Oh, Larry! My dearest Larry. If only I could see you,' she whispered, but she dare not even consider the idea. Larry must be mad even to suggest that they appear in public together just a few miles from Beaulieu. Mad . . . or desperate. The thought brought a glowing smile to her face. Of course she must see him before he left for London. She had promised to meet him there, and had already prepared an excuse for that occasion, but this was a new challenge to her resourcefulness and she would not fail him. She must not let him think that her feelings for him were less strong than his for her. She began to pace the bedroom, the letter clasped tightly in her hands. Her beloved Larry was only a matter of miles away, and when she remembered his passionate letters her face burned.

But where to go? Where to meet unobserved? A safe rendezvous where they need not be continuously glancing over their shoulders? It came to her at last that the forest itself would offer the best place of concealment. She would meet him in the New Forest – at Norley Wood. Martins would take her in the brougham and then she would dismiss him for half-an-hour – no longer – and join Larry in his carriage. There was no need for Martins even to see Larry. That would be an unnecessary risk, she thought bitterly, remembering that Nanny Webster had made two further demands for money and doubtless would make more. It would never do to put Martins in a position where he also knew too much. Her experiences with Nanny Webster had taught her caution.

After long consideration, she penned the following words:

Darling,
   Of course we must meet. I will be at Norley Wood

tomorrow around three. I beg you to use the utmost discretion for my sake. I will not put my name to this for fear it falls into the wrong hands, but I live for tomorrow. If you are not there I will wait thirty minutes – no longer. I adore you –

Then she sent for Grace, and told her, 'I would like you to deliver a letter for me to the Crown Hotel in Lyndhurst. Take the children with you – it will be an outing for them. There will be no need to wait for an answer; just hand it in at the reception desk and leave.'

She held out the letter and added unnecessarily, 'It's for a Mr Bell.'

Grace took the letter without speaking and stood looking down at it with an expression which Virginia found difficult to interpret.

'Well, don't just stand there!' she said. 'Anyone would think you had never seen a letter before. What's the matter with you?'

Grace bit her lip but still made no reply, and Virginia felt suddenly cold with apprehension. The girl looked rebellious – surely she was not going to refuse!

Finally Grace raised her head. 'I'm sorry, ma'am, but I can't take it.' She held out the letter, but perversely Virginia did not take it from her.

'What do you mean?' she demanded, her voice shrill. 'Why can't you take it? It won't bite you!'

When Grace looked up her face was white. 'I *won't* take it,' she said. 'I . . . I don't like delivering messages.'

There was a moment's silence while they stared at each other; Grace white-faced, Virginia with a bright spot of anger burning in each cheek.

'*Won't* take it?' Virginia repeated, frantically playing for time. How dare this stupid little nobody defy her! Of course she must take the letter. Her thoughts whirled and now it came to her that of late the girl had been increasingly unwilling to collect the letters for 'Mrs Foster', and recently had refused the sixpence which she had earlier been willing to accept.

'I'm sorry,' said Grace, 'but I just don't want to be a

messenger any longer.' Her mouth had settled into a stubborn line and her expression was uncompromising.

Virginia hesitated in the face of such determination, for the last thing she wanted was a scene which might draw attention to the vital letter.

'You are being particularly stupid,' she said. 'May I ask why you will not take it?'

'I'm employed here as a nanny,' said Grace, 'and that's all I really want to do.'

'Really Miss Martins . . .' Virginia shrugged. 'I don't understand you. It's not much to ask and there is a shilling in it for you – are you sure you won't change your mind?'

'No,' said Grace. 'I'm sorry.'

'You certainly will be,' said Virginia as she snatched the letter from Grace's hand. 'You are a stupid, unhelpful, ungrateful young woman and I'm sure my husband will agree when he hears about your ridiculous behaviour!'

Grace gave her a long, hard look. 'I don't think you'll tell him,' she said flatly. 'May I go now?'

Virginia gasped. The audacity! The barefaced insolence! She longed to take the girl by the shoulders and shake her. They exchanged a long look which was full of hostility, but then Virginia bit back her fury as common sense surfaced. The girl must know something – or had guessed. It would be suicide to provoke her further.

She drew in her breath sharply and squared her shoulders.

'Yes, you may go – and send Fanny to me. Perhaps she will have the decency to perform a simple errand which you seem to think beneath you.'

Through tight lips Grace said, 'Thank you, ma'am,' turned on her heel and walked out of the room.

Virginia choked back angry words as the door closed behind the nanny and she stared desperately at the letter in her hands. The ugly scene had jarred more than she would admit, but there was no time for recriminations. As she waited for Fanny, an awful thought struck her.

Suppose she also refused? Suppose there was no way she could get word to Larry . . .

However, Fanny duly appeared looking quite uncomplicated and agreed cheerfully to deliver the letter. She seemed delighted at the prospect of a ride to Lyndhurst in the pony-cart. Overcome with relief, Virginia doubled her offer to a florin and watched Fanny's face light up. A thoroughly nice girl with a proper understanding of her place, she thought, and felt her anger begin to recede. She decided that in future Fanny would be her messenger. And Grace Martins? Her eyes narrowed. Grace Martins would learn what it was like to be out of favour.

*

Half an hour later a breathless Fanny was sitting next to John on the driving seat, dazedly wondering how Fate could have dealt her such a marvellous card. A ride into Lyndhurst alone with John! She was not to know that Grace had already turned down the chance, and would not have cared if she had known. It was enough that Mrs Latimer had given her this golden opportunity, and she did not mean to waste it. John had helped her up as though she were a lady and he was smiling – which meant that he did not object to the outing either . . . which might mean that he was looking forward to it. Well, perhaps 'looking forward to it' was going too far, she amended. Probably he 'did not mind', but Fanny meant to make it a positive pleasure and began by remarking on how well he handled the horses. That pleased him, she could tell, and she congratulated herself on a promising start.

As they sped along towards Stubbs Wood she chattered vivaciously, admiring the scenery, pointing out the yellow-brown bracken and exclaiming over the wild ponies that wandered the heath in small unconcerned groups.

'They won't mind us,' Fanny said artfully, 'because our horses trotting must be a sound they like – but motor-cars! I should reckon they hate motor-cars – nasty smelly, noisy things.'

'You can say that again,' said John.

'Filling the air with their beastly fumes,' she went on. He nodded.

'Frightening the birds . . . oh, look there! I saw a squirrel. There it goes, up that tree. Did you see it?'

'No, I didn't, but I saw a fox one time, a large dog fox. Late evening, it was. Nearly ran it down. Came out from behind a gorse-bush bold as you like. Handsome creatures, really, if you discount what they do.'

'What they do?' She turned large eyes towards him. Men liked to impart information; she had read that only a few weeks ago in a magazine.

John shrugged. 'They kill chickens and so on.'

'But they have to eat, don't they?'

'They kill for fun – bite the heads off and leave the rest. Kill half a dozen and only eat one.'

'Oh, that's horrible!'

'I heard of a woman once who had ten ducks and the fox came along in the night and bit off all their feet. There they were in the morning, still alive and couldn't walk or swim. Had to be put out of their misery.'

'Ugh! John!'

'I heard of another chap – '

'Don't tell me,' she begged. 'It's too awful!'

The conversation was not going in the direction she had intended and she searched her mind for a way to bring the talk back to a more cheerful subject.

'I saw an eagle once,' she told him. 'It was hovering in the air. Not moving, just hovering.'

'Must have been a kestrel. There aren't any eagles in these parts. Was it high up – between twenty and thirty feet?'

She nodded doubtfully.

'That was a kestrel then. A sparrowhawk keeps low. What was it after?'

'I don't know.'

'Kestrels go for small mammals on the ground – they hover and then swoop down. A sparrowhawk eats small birds.'

'I didn't know you knew so much about birds and things,' she said, genuinely impressed.

He turned and smiled. 'There's a lot you don't know about me,' he said.

Fanny tossed her head. 'There's lots you don't know about *me*,' she retorted. 'You probably never give me a second thought. I bet you don't even notice me half the time? I reckon I might as well be invisible.'

She waited hopefully for him to deny these assertions, but he merely grinned and shrugged his broad shoulders as he tapped the horses into a canter. A dog-cart approached from the other direction and John raised his whip in salute as the two vehicles passed each other, wheels rattling on the rough track, hooves clattering and harness jingling.

Fanny looked at him. 'It's not really the end of the horses, is it?' she asked. 'I mean, the motor-cars aren't really going to take over, are they? I can't imagine how it would be without horses; it would be a different world.'

John's smile faded. 'I wouldn't like to say but I certainly hope not. Be a sad day for England if those infernal machines – and their infernal drivers – ever get the whip-hand over us. A very sad day indeed.'

Fanny hesitated. She had no wish to spoil the outing, but she did want to make it quite clear that his way of life was hers; that he and not Stanley Marcus was her ideal man.

'The chauffeurs are as cheeky as the machines,' she said at last. 'Stanley's not all bad, no one is, but he's so full of his own importance. Conceited, I suppose!'

John snorted. 'When he gets behind the wheel of that motor, he thinks he's God. They all do. It's honk-honk! Get out of my way! That's their attitude.'

Fanny laughed. 'Well, he may think he's God and so might Mr Latimer, but I certainly don't. Mrs Latimer's got her head screwed on the right way.' She quoted primly: 'A well-turned-out carriage and pair shows a woman off to best advantage.'

He raised his eyebrows. 'And where did you read that?' he asked.

Fanny laughed. 'In a magazine.'

She did not tell him that the magazine in question also had an article on how to enlarge your bust, or that she was eagerly awaiting the arrival of Margaretta Merlain's secret process, which could be used in the privacy of her home and which guaranteed an increase of six inches within thirty days. She hoped that her new figure would rival that of the local barmaid and enhance her desirability in John's eyes.

Glancing down at the letter which lay in her lap, she picked it up curiously.

'Mr Stuart Bell,' she read aloud. 'I wonder who he is?'

'Best not to know,' he advised.

Fanny's surprise was genuine. 'Why ever not?' she asked.

He tapped the side of his nose. 'Ask no questions, hear no lies.'

'But what do you mean? Who *is* Mr Bell?'

He gave her a sideways glance. 'Did she give you a tip?'

'A florin.'

'Me too.'

'So? What does that mean?'

'Never you mind. Perhaps it's my suspicious nature.'

Fanny at once began to press him for more information, but he side-stepped adroitly, saying, 'So you don't fancy Stanley Marcus?'

'No, I don't.'

'Who do you fancy?'

For a second or two she almost cried, 'You!' but thought better of it.

'No one,' she said. 'Who do *you* fancy?'

'Ditto.'

'What's that?'

'Same as you — no one.'

This, Fanny decided, was getting her precisely nowhere.

'Actually, I do have my eye on someone,' she confided, 'but I'll never say who it is — not to a living soul. Unless he speaks first, of course. He should, shouldn't he? It's up to him.'

'I suppose so.'

They waited at the crossing for the train to pass and then went on towards Matley Wood. Overhead the sun shone but there was a cool breeze and Fanny huddled into the collar of her jacket, trying to hide her disappointment. She was not managing to arouse his interest – or if she was, he was hiding it pretty well. Maybe he was not interested in women. Perhaps he was what the magazine called 'self-sufficient'. Or maybe he had once been crossed in love and had vowed never to fall in love again. Perhaps he was not even aware that he did feel anything for her. Maybe she should try to make him jealous. She had hinted that there *was* a man in her life, and so he might well think on that. She resolved to give him a few days, then if he had made no move towards her by then, she might try to make him jealous. The trouble was that the only available and suitable male was Stanley, and she was treading on dangerous ground there. It would have to be quite clear that Stanley was after her and not the other way round. It would never do for John to think she had crossed over to the enemy.

She was silent for so long that John eventually said, 'A penny for them!'

Fanny shook her head. 'A penny? Is that all? You'll have to make me a better offer,' she laughed and, thinking hopefully that one day he might make an offer for her affections instead of her thoughts, she gave him an enigmatic smile as the outskirts of Lyndhurst came in sight.

Chapter Twelve

The following afternoon soon after lunch, Grace knocked on the door of Virginia's bedroom. When it was opened, Virginia said brusquely, 'Oh, it's you. What is it? I'm in a fearful hurry.'

She was wearing a new cream gown and matching coat and her hat, of soft green straw, was decorated with cream silk roses. Grace noted her sparkling eyes and flushed cheeks and thought unwillingly that she had never seen her look so beautiful.

'It's George,' she began. 'I'm not very happy about him, ma'am. He hasn't eaten his lunch, which is most unusual, and – '

Virginia interrupted her, irritation written large on her face. 'Please, Miss Martins, I hardly think you need run to me with every little problem. You are paid to be responsible for the children and it is entirely your own fault that you do not have a nursery-maid to help you. If the children are proving too much for you, we shall have to find someone else – someone who is *mature* enough to cope single-handed.'

'You don't understand,' said Grace when her employer drew breath. 'I *can* cope with them, but today George is – '

'He is a very highly-strung child and he needs careful handling.' Virginia gave her a spiteful look. 'I spoke to my husband only this morning, suggesting that perhaps you are too inexperienced for the post. Children need a firm hand and you may not be – '

It was Grace's turn to interrupt. 'Mrs Latimer! George is *unwell*. I think you should see him.'

She saw Virginia's eyes flicker towards the clock on the mantelpiece.

'Unwell?' she repeated. 'In what way unwell? I have an urgent appointment and Cook has made me late already, fussing about the butcher's bill. Tell me quickly, what's wrong with George?'

'He's very hot, feverish I'd say, and he complains of pains – either side of his neck. I think it might be his glands – '

Virginia's mouth tightened. 'What do you know of glands?' she snapped. 'Do you have any medical training?'

'No, but – '

'Then I scarcely think you are qualified to make a diagnosis.' The soft sparkle had completely gone from her eyes and a hard glitter had taken its place. 'If George is hot, then I expect you have allowed him to become over-excited.'

'I haven't. His head aches – '

'So does mine!' Virginia turned to examine the angle of her hat in the nearby mirror. 'And no wonder. First Cook and now you. Fuss, fuss, fuss – it's quite intolerable!'

'I'm sorry to fuss, but I'm really worried about him,' Grace insisted. 'I think we should ask Doctor Collett to take a look at him; he could be sickening for something serious.'

Virginia was picking up her gloves, pulling them on carefully, smoothing the fingers. She gave Grace a withering glance. '*I* shall decide when the doctor is to be called,' she said. 'I shall come up to the nursery and take a look at my son the moment I return.'

'But I don't think we should wait until then,' Grace began worriedly. 'Won't you *please* just take a look at him before you go. It wouldn't take long.'

Virginia leaned towards the mirror and ran a finger lightly over her eyebrows. Then, satisfied with her appearance, she turned to Grace.

'Ask Mrs Wade for a soothing drink for him. Rose-hip syrup, perhaps. Keep him quiet until I come home.'

'But how long will you be gone?'

'That's none of your business, Miss Martins. Please do try to remember your place. I really am beginning to regret taking you on. Had it not been for my husband's insistence that we give you a chance ... still, we can always rectify matters.' Her expression was triumphant as she looked at Grace. 'You really do not have the necessary experience and this fuss you are making over George proves it. Now, I must fly.'

As Grace still hesitated, she said, 'That will be all, Miss Martins,' and there was nothing for Grace to do but retreat on to the landing and watch as Virginia went downstairs in a swish of rustling silks and the merest hint of eau de cologne.

She returned to the nursery, where George lolled in a chair at the table, half-heartedly fingering the pieces of a jig-saw. His eyes looked heavy and his chin rested in his hand.

'Where were you?' he asked fretfully the moment Grace entered the nursery. 'I wanted you. My head hurts.'

'I'm sorry, dear,' said Grace. 'I went to speak to your Mama. I told you I would only be gone for a moment or two, and I ran all the way back.'

She put a hand to his forehead and her anxiety increased.

'Where's Mama? You said she was coming to see me.'

'I'm afraid she can't because she has to go out.'

George's face puckered miserably. 'I wish she would come.'

'She has promised to come the moment she gets back,' Grace told him. 'Now, shall I ask Mrs Wade for a nice drink for you?'

'And for me?' cried Victoria. 'I'm very poorly too!'

She looked the picture of health, but Grace said, 'Oh dear. Then you must have a drink. Some of Mrs Wade's best rose-hip syrup.'

Victoria pulled a face. 'But I don't like rose-hip syrup,' she protested.

'But if you're poorly – '

'I feel better now,' Victoria said quickly.

Grace smiled. 'What a quick recovery!'

The little girl turned to her brother. 'If *you* make a quick recovery, you needn't have any rose-hip syrup.'

Ignoring her, George scowled at the half-completed jig-

235

saw. 'The pieces won't go together,' he complained. 'The house has got no windows, because I can't find the pieces.'

Grace took his hot little hands in hers. 'Georgie, dear, I think you should let me put you back to bed. Then, while you drink your syrup I'll read to you. How about that?'

'I haven't been naughty,' he cried. 'I haven't! I don't have to go to bed.'

'No, no, George, I know you haven't,' she soothed him. 'Now think. Have I ever sent either of you back to bed for being naughty?'

George looked at his sister, who said, 'No. Never.'

'But Nanny Webster did,' said George.

'Well, I'm not Nanny Webster,' smiled Grace. '*I* put you to bed at night when you're sleepy – and in the day-time if you are poorly so that you can rest. You'll feel all comfy and then maybe your head won't ache so much. I suggest we try it.'

'Do try it, Georgie,' urged Victoria with a gleam in her eye. 'You could be the patient and I could be the nurse and wear my white apron.'

George wavered, reassured by Grace's words.

'When you are in bed, I could tell you a story,' Grace suggested. 'Or I could read to you from one of your favourite books.'

The little boy was feeling so ill that he surrendered gratefully to this tempting proposition and Victoria ran to the cupboard to look for the nurse's apron Grace had made for her a few weeks earlier.

Grace rang the bell and began to undress George while she waited for Fanny to arrive. She then told her that George was feeling unwell and asked for a glass of rose-hip syrup. Fanny had just turned to go when, without any warning, George gave a strangled cry and his legs buckled beneath him. Before Grace could catch him, he slipped to the floor, his face deathly pale, as his eyes rolled upwards and a little blood oozed from between his clenched teeth.

Fanny screamed, but clapped a hand over her mouth

to silence herself. Grace knelt over the small body, her lips moving in a soundless prayer. 'Please God, don't let him die!' She suspected it might be a fit, but had never experienced such a thing before and the blood frightened her. She fought down a feeling of panic, telling herself to keep calm. If anything happened to him . . .

'Oh, Georgie!' she whispered. She realized for the first time just how dear he was to her and knew she had committed the cardinal sin – she had allowed herself to love the children. His limbs began to twitch feebly as intuitively Grace seized one hand and began to rub it.

'George!' she cried. 'George dear, can you hear me? Don't be frightened, my pet, I'm here.'

Victoria tiptoed forward, her nurse's apron in her hand, but Grace – seeing her small shocked face – gestured to Fanny to look after her.

'Miss Victoria, you come here to me,' said Fanny, promptly taking the little girl by the hand. 'Master George will be better shortly. We mustn't crowd round him, must we? We must give him plenty of air.'

Grace turned George's head gently to one side and unfastened his collar and waited helplessly to see if the alarming symptoms would increase. She desperately wanted to go for help, but was afraid to leave him.

'Why does George look like that?' Victoria asked tremulously. 'Is he asleep?'

'No, dear,' said Grace. 'He's very poorly, but he'll be better soon.'

Fanny whispered, 'That blood round his mouth. Oh, Grace . . .'

Grace glanced up, keeping her voice steady with an effort. 'I think maybe he's bitten his tongue,' she said. 'Any chance of catching Mrs Latimer before she goes?'

'She's gone,' said Fanny, 'and I'll bet you a sixpence she's gone to meet –'

'Hush, Fanny!' cried Grace, with a warning nod of her head in Victoria's direction. 'Don't say anything.' She looked down at George and saw with a rush of hope that his eyes were still and the twitching had lessened. 'I think the worst is over,' she said. 'George, can you hear me?'

The boy murmured something inaudible, but at least it was a response.

'He's coming round,' said Grace thankfully.

Victoria asked, 'Who has Mama gone to meet?'

Fanny said, 'Oh Lord! Trust her!' and Grace shook her head, too concerned with George to worry over Fanny's indiscretion.

'*Who?*' Victoria insisted.

'Nobody,' Fanny told her. 'Now why don't I tie your apron for you?'

'No,' said Victoria, throwing it down. 'I don't want to be a nurse. I don't like Georgie; he looks funny.'

'He'll soon be well again,' said Grace, weak with relief, as George opened his eyes and stared dazedly into hers. The twitching had stopped, but as his jaw relaxed he tasted the blood in his mouth and his eyes filled with alarm, followed by tears. She gathered him up into her arms and held him close as he began to cry.

'There, there,' she soothed. 'It's all over now, but you cry if you want to. A few tears will make you feel better.'

'Boys don't cry!' protested Victoria, shocked by this unseemly behaviour.

'Yes, they do,' said Grace. 'I've told you before. Even grown-up people cry sometimes. I cry. Fanny cries, don't you, Fanny?'

'Oh yes, I do,' Fanny agreed.

'But not *men*,' insisted Victoria. 'Nanny Webster said — '

Grace and Fanny exchanged exasperated looks. 'Nanny Webster was wrong,' said Grace. 'Tears are for crying when you are unhappy.' She kissed the top of George's head. 'Are you feeling better yet?'

He nodded, but his face remained buried against her chest.

She looked at Fanny. 'We must have the doctor at once,' she told her. 'Please telephone him and explain what has happened.'

Fanny looked shocked. 'Call out the doctor? But shouldn't we wait for Mrs Latimer?'

'No,' said Grace, recalling her employer's recent words.

'I won't wait. She told me I was responsible, so I'll take the decision myself.'

'What about Mr Latimer?' Fanny suggested. 'I could send someone to find him.'

'Send for Mr Latimer, by all means, but in the meantime I want the doctor. He must look at George as soon as possible. If you won't telephone him, then stay here with the children while I do.'

Still Fanny hesitated. 'But Mrs Latimer will blame me if – ' Grace stood up. 'All right, I'll do it and Mrs Latimer can say what she likes about it. Please stay here, Fanny. No, Georgie, don't cry. I'm only going to the telephone to ask Doctor Collett to come and make you better. You like him, don't you? He always makes you laugh.'

Victoria nodded vigorously. 'Yes, he does, Georgie. He makes us laugh. He told us about the funny monkey that went up a pole and couldn't get down again.' She giggled at the memory and George obligingly managed a watery smile.

Grace hurried out of the room before her courage failed her. She was horribly aware that telephoning for the doctor without permission from one of her employers might not meet with their approval. In fact, Virginia would probably use it in her campaign to have her sacked. As she ran downstairs her heart quailed at the prospect ahead, but she reminded herself that George was ill and Doctor Collett must be summoned.

Fortunately the doctor was at home and, on hearing the symptoms, immediately agreed to call and was with them within ten minutes. By the time he arrived Grace had put George to bed with just a sheet over him and the rose-hip syrup had been brought up.

'He's so hot,' she explained as the doctor examined him. 'I don't like to make him any hotter. Mrs Latimer suggested the syrup before she went out.'

The doctor frowned. 'I'd like to speak to her, of course. When are you expecting her back?'

'I'm afraid I don't know.'

'But she saw him earlier?'

'No, she didn't have time. I think she had an appointment.'

'Hmm.' He gave her a shrewd look from beneath bushy white eyebrows. He was a tubby, elderly man who had been the family physician ever since he moved into the village and he was greatly respected. 'Have you ever come across a convulsion before?'

'No.' Grace decided that honesty was the best policy. 'I hope I haven't done anything wrong.'

'Not at all,' he told her. 'Quite the contrary. It seems that you remained calm, comforted the patient and called me in. There was not much else you could do, Miss Martins, and I think you are to be congratulated on your common sense. As for this young man . . .' He ruffled George's hair with a gentle hand. 'I suspect influenza. There are one or two cases in the village.' He lowered his voice. 'The convulsion is not usually a symptom, but I have come across it before and he is a nervous child. It doesn't mean he's developing fits, so don't worry. I doubt if he'll have another. He's . . . let me see . . . seven now. He'll grow out of them shortly. It was just bad luck.'

Grace said. 'I hope I haven't over-excited him. Mrs Latimer thought that perhaps – '

The doctor put away his stethoscope. 'Stuff and nonsense! Don't blame yourself. I haven't seen these two children looking so well and happy – yes, happy – for years. That is the key word: happy heart, healthy body. That's what my grandmother used to say and she was a wise old bird. Best day's work the Latimers did was in getting rid of Nanny Webster. Oh yes, I've had several encounters with her over the years. A very difficult woman to deal with . . . but I don't have to tell you that, do I?'

Grace smiled. 'So what is the treatment, doctor? What do I have to do for George?'

The doctor shrugged. 'Not a great deal, really. There's no cure yet for influenza and maybe there never will be. No magic pills. Just rest and fluids and a nourishing but light diet. You'll find his temperature will fluctuate – up one minute, down the next. When he's cold, keep him

240

warm and give a warm drink. When he's hot, give him a sponge down with a cold flannel; rub the skin briskly so as to bring the blood to the surface – it cools quicker that way. Doctors aren't miracle workers, Miss Martins, it's all common sense. A bit of know-how and a lot of luck. I'll call in again this evening. Must keep a close watch on him, poor little chap. It can prove dangerous if neglected – complications can set in. But that's not going to happen here.' He patted her arm. 'Don't look so worried, Miss Martins. We'll pull him through. A light diet, remember, little and often. Broth, milk puddings, that sort of thing. Mrs Wade knows what I mean so talk to her. Plenty of rest. Rest, rest and more rest!'

'I see.'

'Don't be afraid to call me if you have any further worries, day or night. I'd rather be called too early than too late.' He turned back to George, who was watching them both. 'You do what your nanny tells you and rest, then you'll soon be back on your feet. No mountain-climbing. No hundred-mile run. No trying to swim the Channel!'

George smiled faintly. 'I can't swim,' he said.

'Can't swim? Whatever next! Well, don't try to paddle across.'

He caught sight of Victoria, who was now struggling to fasten her nurse's apron. 'Oh, Nurse Victoria!' he cried, tying the bow for her, 'I didn't see you there. Now I want you to take good care of Master Latimer and I'll be along later to see how he is.'

Victoria giggled delightedly. 'Yes, doctor.'

The old man straightened up and shook Grace by the hand. 'I'll let myself out. Goodbye. Au revoir, etc.'

When he had gone, Grace drew a long shuddering breath of relief. So she had not called him out in vain! George had influenza – and his mother had not even been able to spare the time to look at him. Was Fanny right, she wondered? Had Virginia been to a secret rendezvous with the mysterious Mr Bell? John would no doubt know, but would he tell? And were Mr Bell and Larry Scott one and the same person? She would prob-

241

ably never know and suddenly she did not care. What did they matter, anyway? George and Victoria were what mattered and the doctor had promised that George was going to be fine.

*

When Virginia hurried back into the house just after four o'clock she was greeted by Fanny with a request that she go at once to the library where Mr Latimer was waiting to speak to her. Her guilty conscience misinterpreted the reason for her husband's peremptory summons and she stood in the hall, frozen in the act of removing her gloves, staring at the maid in consternation.

Fanny, savouring her mistress' obvious discomfiture, was enjoying herself immensely. Keeping her face expressionless, she added, 'He did say "immediately", madam.'

Virginia's hand fluttered to her throat, her suspicions deepening. Alex had somehow found out where she had been, but how? Only Martins knew and Martins was entirely trustworthy, she would stake her life on it. If Martins had not told Alex, then either someone had seen them or Alex had seen Larry's letter . . . but that was impossible for she had it with her. Her thoughts raced wildly.

'Did he say – ?' she began, but then shook her head, annoyed with herself for revealing the extent of her anxiety. It would never do to ask a servant for information. Glancing sharply at the parlourmaid, she was aware of a certain smugness in the girl's manner which increased her trepidation. Damn her! She knew something. What was it Virginia's mother had once said? 'Servants always know everything – one must simply ignore the fact.'

'Thank you, Fanny,' she said coldly.

When Fanny had gone Virginia remained in the hall, pulling off her gloves with fingers that trembled while she tried to decide how to counter her husband's accusation. She could confess her love for Larry, but then Alex would divorce her . . . unless perhaps she gave her word never to see him again. Could she bear that? The stolen hour in the forest had thrilled her and she knew that she would never again appreciate Alex as a lover . . . could never appreciate any other man. Only Larry Scott could unlock her emotions and only with him could she ever feel fulfilled. But divorce was synonymous with disgrace and she did not think she could survive it.

No, if Alex had no proof, then she must lie. She had prepared a story and that would have to suffice. If he did have proof. . . . She swallowed hard. She was wasting time; better to know the worst.

As she entered the library, Alex threw down his book and jumped to his feet, his face pale with suppressed anger.

'It might interest you to know, Virginia, that your son has influenza and that Miss Martins was forced to send for the doctor *in your absence*.'

For a moment she was too surprised to speak, for she had completely forgotten her conversation with Grace before leaving the house.

'Your *son*,' repeated Alex seeing her blank expression. 'George Latimer. You do remember him, I suppose?'

Virginia flinched at his words as her eyes widened with alarm. Alex never resorted to sarcasm.

'Of course I remember – ' she began. 'Influenza? Oh dear.' In spite of the shock, her heart leaped with relief. Alex had not discovered her liaison with Larry Scott! She took a deep breath and uttered a prayer of thankfulness.

'Oh dear!' he mocked. 'Is that your only comment? I understand from Doctor Collett that the child had a convulsion!'

'A convulsion?' she stammered, 'But he's never had such a thing before.'

'Well, he has now. And fortunately Miss Martins had the presence of mind to telephone for the doctor.'

That wretched young woman again! Virginia wanted to scream. Too late she realized her mistake, for Alex took a step nearer to her and his expression was furious.

'On her *own* authority,' he told her, 'because the child's mother, who *knew* that he was unwell, had not even bothered to visit him. If she had done, no doubt *she* would have made the telephone call. What was so important, Virginia, that you could not spare five minutes of your time for your son when he needed you?'

Virginia produced the excuse she had planned.

'I had a sick headache and I thought a little fresh air would cure it.'

'You have been gone since just after lunch, I believe. Shall we say since two o'clock, to be generous?'

'I really don't see why you should begrudge me a little fresh air, Alex.'

'I don't. You could have had all the fresh air you wanted – *after* attending to your son, who was ill.'

Virginia saw a passing straw and clutched at it desperately. 'I had no idea he was unwell,' she said defensively.

'That's not true!' He seized her arm in a painful grip. 'Miss Martins told you she was very worried, she described the symptoms and she asked you to call the doctor.'

Virginia pulled her arm free and rubbed it reproachfully. 'That's what she told you, is it?' she countered. 'And naturally you choose to believe the word of a servant instead of your wife.'

'I think she was telling the truth, yes. Why should she lie?'

Virginia tossed her head. 'Because she is a trouble-maker, that's why. She obviously had you fooled. Really, you are a bigger fool than I took you for, Alex.'

Her husband was looking at her with the eyes of a stranger and Virginia felt a small tremor of fear. She was doing her best to make light of the situation, but her uneasiness was increasing. His repressed anger frightened her and dimly she recognized that the so-called neglect of her son was a serious crime in her husband's eyes. Alex had never spoken to her in this way before and she did not know how to react.

Assuming an air of injured innocence, she asked, 'Don't you want to hear *my* version of what happened? Don't you owe me that much?'

He threw himself into an easy chair and said, 'Go

244

ahead and tell me your version, Virginia. I would really like to believe you.' But the hardness in his voice was still there and she knew she would have an uphill struggle to convince him.

'I was feeling ill,' she said, 'and decided I must take some fresh air. Just as I was about to leave, Miss Martins came to me and said that George wouldn't eat his lunch. I replied that this was hardly my concern since she is paid to see that he does . . . or words to that effect. She's such a silly little thing, she annoys me. I told her that we were considering finding a replacement as she is obviously incapable of assuming responsibility for the children's welfare – '

'*We* have not considered any such step,' he put in, 'but go on.'

'Well, *I* have. The woman is arrogant and . . .' she remembered Grace's refusal to deliver the letter – 'and unco-operative.'

He seized on the word at once. 'In what way is she unco-operative?'

Virginia cursed her runaway tongue. 'Oh, in lots of ways, I try not to bother you with them.'

'I would like you to bother me now. It's important.'

She waved her hand vaguely. 'I can't think of anything offhand. Oh, this is getting us nowhere. How is George? I must go to him.'

'Suddenly you are concerned,' he observed. 'How nice.'

'Naturally I am concerned. He's my son.'

'He was your son two hours ago, but you weren't concerned then. You thought a ride in the fresh air more important.'

'I tell you, I didn't think he was unwell. Miss Martins said nothing to me about him being ill.'

'She wanted you to call the doctor.'

'I didn't think it was necessary. I – ' As soon as the words were out she knew she had given herself away, but it was too late.

He stood up swiftly and this time he took hold of her shoulders. 'So, she *did* tell you he was unwell?'

Virginia stared at him. 'She may have mentioned something,' she stammered. 'I felt too ill – I don't remember.'

But now the anger had gone from his face and he looked suddenly weary as he turned away and crossed to the window.

'Miss Martins was being kind about you, then,' he said. 'I think you misjudge her, Virginia. To excuse the fact that you could not spare the time to see George, she pretended that you had an urgent appointment. I think that shows great tact on her part, don't you?'

'It shows nothing of the kind!' snapped Virginia. 'I *did* have – ' Her stomach lurched with sudden fright as she saw she had made another slip. 'I mean, I didn't have an appointment. I . . . oh, damn!'

Still he did not look at her. '*Did* you have an appointment?' he asked.

'No, of course not. That nasty little troublemaker – '

'Then you were in no hurry?'

Virginia was trapped and she knew it. She had to admit to either an urgent prior appointment or a lack of concern for her son. And in her mind Grace Martins' meddling ways had been responsible for her downfall. As she imagined Grace poisoning Alex against her and then sharing the details with the rest of the servants, a helpless rage welled up inside her. Somewhere, someday she would get rid of the girl if it was the last thing she did! All this unpleasantness had entirely wiped from her mind the wonderful moments she had spent with Larry and that made her want to weep. Frantically, she blinked back tears of frustration and misery.

'I won't answer any more of your questions,' she burst out. 'Damn you and damn Miss Martins! She's going – do you hear me? She will leave this house and we shall all be well rid of her!'

At last Alex faced her and Virginia saw the beginnings of disenchantment in his eyes. 'I'm disappointed in you,' he said quietly.

She wanted to shout, 'And I am disappointed in you. Larry Scott is worth ten of you!' But at least that secret was safe, she thought gratefully. At least she had someone in her life who appreciated and loved her. Larry Scott wanted to *marry* her! How she longed to shout it aloud and see the look on her husband's face. Larry Scott was younger, more handsome, he had more money, he was offering her *the world!* Yes, Alex might humiliate her with his hateful questions, but she had it in her power to shatter his complacency . . . and maybe one day she would.

'And Miss Martins stays,' he said. 'She is young, but she is learning fast and today she showed both common sense and initiative. The children adore her and she is good with them. You have said yourself – '

'*I* am the one who employed her,' she snapped.

'*I* am the one who pays her salary,' responded Alex evenly. 'Let me make something clear, Virginia. I shall not pay the salary of anyone else unless Miss Martins chooses to leave of her own free will – and not because you have made her life intolerable. So if you get rid of her, there will be no one to take her place and you will have to look after the children yourself.'

Virginia bit her lip. 'You don't seem to have a very good opinion of me,' she said. 'Suddenly I am regarded as some kind of ogre.'

'You are not the woman I married,' he told her. 'You have changed over the past year – I don't know why, but you have.'

There was a long painful silence. Virginia felt as though he had slapped her face and her mind was in a turmoil. Her husband no longer adored her! The knowledge came as a shock and although she told herself she did not care, she was not convinced. Never since their first meeting had there been a time when Alex had not loved her . . .

She remembered their first meeting now. Still deeply depressed after her husband's death, she had agreed with considerable reluctance to share a holiday in France with family friends. They had motored down to St Jean de Luz in June, where Alex and his family were also staying. Alex had been amongst a small crowd watching an artist at work on the quayside and she had joined them. As he turned to go, their eyes met and for him it had been love at first sight. For her part she had been flattered – amused, even – by the quiet, reserved young man many years her junior. Her friends had been surprised by their sudden friendship and somewhat alarmed by Alex's determination to marry her. He had told her later that he could not bear the expression in her eyes and longed to make her smile again.

Now, for the first time since that day in St Jean de Luz, he was looking at her with no love in his eyes and Virginia felt as thought her world was falling apart. Instinctively, she knew that her usual wiles would be to no avail. Alex had stepped away from her, had distanced himself, and she felt horribly alone and defenceless. If only Larry was beside her! She took a little courage from the knowledge that he wanted her – as wife or mistress, he did not care. But she did. She had experienced the full horror of notoriety when she discovered her husband lying dead across his desk, a pistol on the floor beside him. The gossip had been intolerable and the attention from the press had sickened her. Then she had been innocent of any misdemeanour, but if she ran away with Larry Scott she would be hideously guilty and she knew she could not live with the averted heads and hypocritical smiles. So Alex thought she had changed, and not for the better? Well, perhaps she had, but she felt that life owed her a great deal after all she had suffered in the past. If only she had met Larry that day by the quayside instead of Alex!

With a jolt, she realized that Alex was speaking to her. 'I said, "Perhaps you should take a look at George",' he repeated. 'The doctor will be calling again shortly and it will look rather odd if you still haven't visited him.'

She avoided his eyes. 'I will go now,' she said and walked out of the room, her flushed face at odds with the terrible coldness in her heart.

*

George's illness was mercifully short and without the feared complications, and he soon began to enjoy the advantages of being ill. His mother and father came to

248

the nursery to see him each day – although rarely together – and Fanny brought up delicacies from the kitchen – sweetbreads served with lemon sauce, minced steak with *no gristle*, egg custard, cream soup and Mrs Wade's special milk jelly. Victoria brought him a posy of flowers from the garden while his grandfather brought him a wooden horse and a copy of *The Boys' and Girls' Own Joke Book*. Grace nursed him tirelessly, but a week later Victoria succumbed to the disease and before both children had recovered Grace herself was taken ill and forced to take to her bed also. Mrs Drury, a professional nurse, was then engaged to care for all three of them. She was elderly but very competent.

Throughout this period, Virginia did her utmost to persuade her husband that Grace obviously lacked the stamina necessary for the job, but Alex refused to consider such a suggestion and the presence of Grace Martins in the house remained a sensitive subject between them which did nothing to heal the rift which had developed earlier. Although Virginia did her best to hide her resentment and Alex tried to put the matter from his mind, neither was wholly successful and the relationship remained an uneasy one.

By the last week in April both children were up and about and the nurse – used to dealing only with the sick – found them rather wearing and complained to Virginia that she could not manage without the assistance of a nursery-maid. Since it was impractical to take on someone for such a short period, it was decided that a young girl from the village should be employed to take them out each afternoon for two hours so as to give Mrs Drury a rest from their boisterous demands.

*

One morning Alex arrived in the nursery just as the children were finishing their breakfast and announced that he would take them out at nine-thirty.

'Where to?' they chorused gleefully.

'To see Annie Abrahams and take her some eggs and things.'

249

The children cheered through mouthfuls of toast and eggs, but Alex forbore to chide them for their poor table manners.

Nurse Drury said, 'How lovely! A trip out with Papa,' and added hopefully, 'And how long will you be gone, sir?'

Alex smiled. 'An hour or so. Annie loves to see them.'

'They won't be going near any infections, I hope?'

'Certainly not. Annie's as fit as a fiddle.' He tweaked one of Victoria's curls and asked, 'And how's Miss Martins? I'd like to have a word with her if that's possible.'

The nurse looked dubious. 'Well, she's still confined to her bed, sir. Another day or two perhaps . . .'

'I would like to see her today. The doctor tells me that she'll be well enough to resume her duties next week, but I would prefer to satisfy myself that she feels up to it.'

'Rather her than me. Oh, don't take me wrong, Mr Latimer, but the children are a real handful.'

'I know. I realize that she will hardly be bursting with energy. Would you ask her if I could talk to her for a few moments?'

'I will, sir, but she does sit up in a chair in the afternoon. Would that be more . . . proper?'

He laughed. 'I won't be available after lunch,' he told her, 'so it will have to be now. I promise to leave the door ajar so that you will hear her if she screams!'

Nurse Drury's smile was a little stiff, but she went into the bedroom and returned within minutes.

'She says to go in,' she reported, her disapproval tempered by the knowledge that she would soon be leaving Berwick House and need not concern herself with such breaches of etiquette.

Alex tapped on the door of Grace's bedroom and she called for him to go in.

He deliberately left the door open and approached only as far as the end of the bed. As he looked round the small room for the first time, he saw how sparsely it was furnished: a single bed with a wooden headboard, with a rickety bamboo table beside it; a chest of drawers topped by a swing-mirror; a narrow wardrobe of varnished wood and a marble-topped washstand. On the bare boards a strip of faded carpet ran alongside the bed. He felt a flash of anger that such drab surroundings should be considered suitable for her and a pang of guilt that he had never bothered to learn for himself how the room was furnished.

'I'm sure we can do better than this,' he said, indicating the room with a wave of the hand.

Grace said awkwardly, 'It's not too bad. I think Nanny Webster had some of her own furniture and she took it when she left. I didn't have any of my own.'

'But the attic's full of stuff. Go and pick out anything you fancy.'

'Oh, but – ' Grace hesitated.

'But what?'

'Mrs Latimer chose the furniture and she might not like it if I change it.'

'Nonsense. Whyever should she object? The furniture in the attic is not serving any useful purpose, merely collecting dust.'

Still Grace regarded him doubtfully. 'Perhaps you would mention it to your wife,' she suggested.

'I can do better than that. I'll come up with you and help to choose it. How would that do?'

'It's very kind of you, sir.' Her heart leaped at the prospect of a shared excursion, however mundane, but she could imagine the trouble it would cause if Virginia found out. And as for knowing that Alex had been into her bedroom! Grace's heart quailed at the thought as she tried to concentrate on what he was saying.

'The doctor tells me you have been very sick indeed, and he puts it down to the fact that you were overtired and your resistance was low.' He smiled. 'He says we have been working you too hard, and Nurse Drury tells me at every opportunity what a handful the children are.'

'Oh no, sir!' she began.

'Oh yes!' he said. 'Of course they are very lively, and I'm sure that when you resume your duties you will still be feeling rather under the weather. So I've decided to

251

keep on the girl from the village – whatever is her name? I can't remember.'

'It's Kitty, sir.'

'Ah, yes, Kitty. Well, I think if she's willing we will keep her on so as to give you a break each afternoon. What do you say to the idea? I warn you – it's either that or we shall employ a full-time nursery-maid. I'm not prepared to let you wear yourself out; it's not reasonable. You do a splendid job with the children and I understand that you don't feel able to manage a full-time assistant, so Kitty is a good compromise, I think.'

Grace was silent. She did not want to refuse her employer's generous offer, but she could imagine Virginia's reaction to the idea. It would add fuel to her argument that Grace was not competent. It was obvious to her that she had become a bone of contention between her employers, with Virginia trying to get rid of her and Alex equally determined to keep her. The fact that Alex was championing her cause gave her great pleasure, but she would never underestimate Virginia. A determined woman could always find a way and Grace feared her.

'You don't sound too enthusiastic,' he teased.

'I am, sir,' she told him. 'I'm most grateful.' She could not tell him what worried her, but he seemed able to read her thoughts.

'Don't worry about Mrs Latimer,' he said easily. 'I will explain everything to her.'

'Thank you, sir.'

Grace wished that she had had time to put on her best nightdress – the one with the blue ribbon threaded through the neck. She had combed her hair, thank goodness, but she was aware that the two plaits made her look very childish and not at all like a competent nanny. Aware of his gaze, she stared at the blanket, her fingers plucking nervously at a small hole. She could imagine how delightful Virginia looked in her bed, because Fanny had taken her up to the bedroom once when everyone was out. Virginia's own bedroom was decorated in shades of apricot and there were filmy drapes over the bed and a deep pile rug on the floor. There were gilt-

252

framed mirrors too and the air was full of the scents of powder and perfume. There were flowers and delicate white ornaments and Virginia's nightgown was of silk.

Grace glanced up at last to see Alex looking at her with that inscrutable expression which over the last weeks had become so familiar. 'So that's settled,' he said.

She nodded wordlessly, rendered speechless by a sudden longing for him to come closer – to reach down and kiss her. Hastily, she averted her eyes. He had a knack of reading her mind and he must never know that she loved him.

'Miss Martins?'

She looked up and to her astonishment he took a couple of paces towards her. Neither of them spoke, then suddenly he took hold of her hand and looked at it.

'Poor little hand,' he said gruffly. 'You've lost weight. We must feed you up. I'll tell Mrs Wade.'

Grace dared not speak – hardly dared even to breathe – while he held her hand in his . . . a single word might break the spell.

At last he released her and seemed at a loss for words, glancing away at the bare room.

'I'll get Mr Trott to send up some flowers,' he said and walked quickly from the room without a backward glance.

Chapter Thirteen

Virginia sat in the darkened box, gazing at the scene on the stage below her. The finer points of *La Traviata* were eluding her although Madame Tetrazinni, according to Larry, made a wonderful Violetta and John McCormack a superb Alfredo. She could not judge their performances for herself because she was not musically inclined, and she could not understand the plot because it was being sung in Italian. No hint of disillusionment would pass her lips, however, for she was with Larry Scott and that fact alone made the evening an outstanding success. He had dared to be seen in public with her at no less a place than the Royal Opera House, Covent Garden! On their arrival, she had swept up the broad red staircase on his arm, seeing the two of them side by side in the huge gilded mirror at the turn of the stairs – a handsome couple, she congratulated herself; no one could dispute that, she thought proudly. She looked positively breathtaking in a dress of rose-coloured lace, while Larry – immaculate in his evening suit – attracted the eye of every woman they passed. In the box she had been aware of admiring faces upturned towards them and in the interval they had mingled in the Crush Bar to great effect.

At any moment one or both of them might have been recognized, but for Larry that brought added spice to the evening. For her own part, she had half-hoped for such an event. If their attendance at the opera reached Alex's ears, then matters would come to a head. She was growing tired now of the constant need for lies and pretence and longed for the courage to do something positive – but doubted if she would ever have it. If only Fate would intervene . . . her darkest fear was that Larry would grow tired of the situation and would give her an ultimatum. Already she thought she sensed an impatience within him and she could not blame him. Their occasional meetings had so far been very brief affairs — a few stolen hours snatched while Alex was away on business — but tonight, sitting beside him, she had come to a decision. She had told Alex that she was visiting an elderly family friend and *might* have to stay overnight, but so far Larry was unaware of this. She had not felt able to tell him, but now her resolve hardened a little. If she was to hold Larry's attention, she must offer him something she had so far withheld. They had never been lovers in the fullest sense of the word and Virginia felt that by allowing this final step in their relationship, she would rekindle his interest.

After the performance they were going to have supper at the Louis XIV Restaurant at the Piccadilly. During the meal she would suggest that they book a room for the night at the Savoy Hotel — a double room — under an assumed name. She knew that kind of thing happened and prayed there would be no embarrassing questions they could not answer. They would share a bed for the first time and she would promise him other such occasions. Surely the gift of her body would convince him of the depths of her love for him and then their affair would soar to new heights.

Now that she had made the decision she longed for the performance to end, for she was eager to be done with the meal also. She was impatient to discover the delights of Larry's body and to reveal her own to him. Having three children had affected her very little physically and she was proud of her smooth pale skin, rounded breasts and long shapely legs. Alex found her beautiful and desirable and Larry would also.

As the music of the famous duet filled the theatre, she took a sideways look at her companion who sat leaning forward with his arms resting on the edge of the box, a rapt expression on his face.

'I will give you a greater thrill than all Verdi's operas put together,' she thought with satisfaction. 'I will give you a night to remember, Larry Scott.'

He was so good to her, so extravagantly generous. He had taken her to Kosminski's — the furrier in Berners

Street — to buy her a collar and muff, but at the last minute her courage had deserted her. There was no way she could explain away Russian sable, although it had broken her heart to refuse.

On entering the box that evening she had been surprised and delighted to find a bottle of Bollinger's — 1904 vintage — on ice, an enormous box of De Bry's most expensive Continental chocolates and eight red roses. She knew that in Larry's eyes nothing was too good for her and she adored him for it. If ever they were man and wife, she would learn to love opera to please him. But she would ask Alex to buy a phonograph and a selection of operatic recordings; it would be a labour of love to study them for Larry's sake. For Larry she would learn Italian if necessary!

Now she watched as Violetta staggered, clutching at the bed-post for support. The atmosphere in the opera house was electric and Virginia felt a moment's regret that she alone of all the watching audience was untouched by the power of the acting and not stirred by the haunting music. Larry would teach her how to appreciate it, she reassured herself. Larry was an experienced, cultured, much-travelled man of the world, by comparison with whom poor Alex looked like a country bumpkin. She had loved him, and still did, but he could not hope to offer her the glittering existence which would be hers as Mrs Larry Scott. If *only* it were possible, she knew she could find fulfilment in the new life. She sighed deeply as the music swelled to a conclusion. Campanini laid down his baton, the audience leaped to its feet and the opera house reverberated to prolonged and rapturous applause. She had hidden reserves locked away within her, she told herself as she too rose to her feet, and Larry Scott was the key.

*

Fanny stood at the pump, raising and lowering the handle with a furious display of energy and thinking about John Martins who, since their ride together two months earlier, had made no move in her direction. Worse, he seemed to have forgotten the incident entirely and her many references to it had been rewarded with blank looks and vague nods of the head.

'There has to be a way!' she thought desperately as water gushed into the wooden tub full of wrung-out soapy linen which now needed rinsing. The woman who came to do the washing had not turned up and Fanny and Dot had been persuaded (by the promise of a florin apiece) to undertake the mammoth Monday wash. Fitting it in between their other duties was proving to be a work of art, but both were determined to complete the task: Dot because she wanted a new hat and Fanny because, determined to wed John, she was saving up for her bottom drawer and had already translated the florin into a pair of pillow-slips.

When the tub was full of water she bent over it and began to pummel and pull the sheets, scooping up handfuls of soapy scum as it formed on the surface and hurling it on to the cobbles with gay abandon. Working for her marriage to John made the effort worthwhile and Fanny's mood was cheerful as she splashed away. She took up each sheet and wrung out as much of the water as she could before transferring it to a second empty tub. When at last that was full, she upended the first tub and emptied the rinsing water down the drain. She then dragged the tub of clean washing over to the large mangle and was just watching the first sheet slide between its wooden rollers when a voice behind her made her jump.

'Excuse me, I'm looking for Miss Grace Martins.'

Fanny turned. 'Good Lord!' she cried. 'It's Alfred, isn't it? Alfred Harris?'

He nodded. 'You look busy,' he remarked.

She tossed her head. 'This isn't my job,' she said. 'I'm just helping out.'

'You're the parlourmaid, Fanny. I remember.'

'That's right. And you're the Post Office clerk,' she grinned. '*I* remember, too.'

'I won't be a clerk for much longer,' he told her. 'I'm due for promotion. *Senior* clerk. Should be some time in October.'

'Senior clerk! My, that sounds rather grand. I don't suppose I'll even be promoted to senior parlourmaid. No,' she laughed, 'doesn't sound right. I think I'm stuck with parlourmaid. But well done!'

'Thanks.'

'And you want to see Grace?'

'Yes, please. It *is* rather urgent, or I would have written – not that she ever answers.'

His shoulders still sagged and with his last remark his large eyes grew even more mournful. 'Like a dog pining for his master,' thought Fanny and felt sorry for him.

'Well,' she said carefully, 'she has told you "No" lots of times and she has asked you to stop writing. But there . . .' she lowered her voice, 'I know what it's like to love someone who doesn't love you back.'

'Do you?' He looked interested at once and she warmed to him.

She gave a deep sigh. 'Oh yes! I know what heartache's like, but I can't say who. I'll tell Grace you're here, but I won't promise she'll come down. Just say, it's urgent, shall I?'

'*Very* urgent,' he amended. 'It's my mother; she's desperately ill.'

'Oh dear, I am sorry. I'll do my best.'

The two children were in the garden with Kitty and Grace was alone in the nursery mending socks, her feet resting on a stool.

'Oh no!' she wailed as soon as Alfred's name was mentioned, but when Fanny elaborated she reluctantly agreed to go down and see him.

He was waiting on the far side of the courtyard, staring moodily at an overgrown lavender bush.

'Alfred. You wanted to see me.'

He swung round eagerly and began at once to stammer. 'Grace. You look so – oh, it's been so – so long. I –'

She allowed him to take her hands. 'Fanny tells me your mother is ill,' she said. 'I'm so sorry. Is it serious?'

He nodded. 'It's her lungs. Congestion, the doctor called it. She had a bad chest and then it turned into

258

pneumonia. Now it's congestion.' His eyes widened fearfully. 'Oh Grace, she thinks she's going to die!'

'Oh, poor Alfred. Do *you* think she is? What does the doctor think?'

'He won't commit himself. Afraid of being wrong, you know how doctors are. I think she might, Grace. She looks so pale. Grey, almost, and she is so thin. You know how . . . robust she was. Now she's almost skin and bones. It's terrible!'

'I'm so sorry,' said Grace. 'Do give her my best wishes.'

'No,' he said, 'you give them to her. I've come to ask you to come back with me. She wants to see you – to ask you something.'

Grace was startled and immediately apprehensive. 'Me?'

'Yes.' He took a deep breath. 'She wants to ask you to reconsider.'

Grace looked at him without comprehension and he ploughed on breathlessly, 'To reconsider your answer to me. To marry me, I mean. She hasn't got long to live and she wants to see me settled.'

Grace gasped. 'But Alfred, I've already told you that I can't. I don't love you; I never will.'

'But love can *grow*, Grace,' he insisted, 'and I love you enough for both of us. I always have. Mother thinks now that maybe you and I *could* make a good match. We'd have a home of our own – the house will be mine – and in the autumn I'm expecting promotion. *Senior clerk!*' His eyes shone as he rushed on. 'You'd never want for anything, Grace. We'd have a family. Mother says we could be "very snug". Those were her exact words.' He laughed excitedly. 'I promise you you'd never hear an unkind word from my lips, Grace. I'd – '

'Stop!' cried Grace. 'You mustn't go on like this. Your mother's health can't make me change my mind, Alfred. I like you. I respect you.' She searched for another compliment to help soften the blow. 'I admire you tremendously, but – '

'There you are then!' he cried. 'You're half-way to loving me. Mother said you were; she's very canny that

259

way. She said you don't know your own mind, Grace, and she so wants to see you. You must come – it might be her last wish.'

'Don't!' cried Grace. 'I'm sure it won't be. I thought the vicar was going to find you a suitable wife; your aunt was sure he would.'

His eyes darkened. 'He did suggest someone, but it didn't work out,' he said. 'She was a nice enough girl, but I couldn't love her.'

Grace could not resist a cry of triumph. 'There you are then! You couldn't love her and I can't love you.'

His expression changed and his eyes darkened.

'But Grace, if mother goes I'll have no one,' he whispered wretchedly. 'I only ask for a little love. You don't have to be madly in love with me. Couldn't we give it a try? Oh dear, my mother puts it so much better than I do. She may be *dying*, Grace. Won't you please just come and see her? Talk to her? She'll convince you. She doesn't want to leave me on my own; she needs to die happy.'

A few cutting remarks floated into Grace's mind, but resolutely she disregarded them. 'So,' she thought, 'the vicar's choice has not fallen for Alfred and now he is afraid of being left to fend for himself.' Poor Alfred. Would she have been tempted, she wondered, if she had never met Alexander Latimer? A home, a husband with a good job, an *adoring* husband – most girls would jump at the chance. Once she might *just* have considered it but now it was impossible. She must be firm but kind.

'Even if I wanted to marry you,' she said slowly, 'I could never leave George and Victoria. Never.'

For a long time they faced each other.

'I'm truly sorry,' she added lamely.

He was obviously wrestling inwardly and she watched anxiously as various expressions flitted across his face and she saw his throat contracting as he struggled for words.

Hoarsely he muttered, 'Perhaps *this* will change your mind!' And before she could guess what he intended, he had seized her in his arms and was kissing her passionately. The more she struggled to evade his grip, the tighter he held her.

'For heaven's sake!' she spluttered, as clumsily his lips covered hers. 'Let go of me, Alfred!'

'Perhaps you've never been kissed like this before!' he told her.

She tried to wriggle free, but his arms did not relax.

'Just say you'll marry me!' he cried. 'Say you'll be mine!'

'Alfred Harris, I will not say anything of the sort. This is so ridiculous. If you won't let me go, then – '

She kicked his shin as hard as she could and he yelled with pain . . . and at that precise moment she became aware of Virginia Latimer! There was an unmistakable air of triumph about her as she regarded them coldly.

'Miss Martins,' she said, 'I thought you understood that we do not encourage followers. This rather unpleasant scene is the reason why. We do like our servants to apply themselves to their work and not fritter their time away in these ridiculous relationships. This young man, whoever he is . . .'

Grace stared at her, white-faced, her hands clenched by her sides. 'It's Alfred Harris,' she told her. 'You met that day at Buckler's Hard.'

'Oh yes. I remember.'

Blushing furiously, Alfred said, 'It's not her fault, Mrs Latimer. It's mine. I – '

She turned on him swiftly. 'Please don't interrupt. I am speaking to a member of my staff.'

'But you're blaming her for encouraging me and – '

Hastily Grace put a hand on his arm. 'It's best you just go, Alfred,' she told him in a low but urgent voice. 'It won't do any good to argue with her. Please, Alfred. For my sake.'

'But you haven't given me an answer,' he protested.

'I have. I've said "No".'

Virginia snapped, 'Oh, for heaven's sake, young man, take yourself off.'

Alfred stood his ground, however. 'I want to marry

her,' he repeated. 'She deserves a home and a family of her own.'

At his words Virginia's gaze moved slowly from one to the other. 'What a good idea,' she said. 'Perhaps, Miss Martins, you would do well to reconsider the offer. Your time with us may be limited. Who knows?'

Alfred, surprised by this unlikely ally, looked at Grace but she shook her head.

'I'm sorry, Alfred. I don't want to marry you or anyone else.'

Virginia gave a snort of exasperation. 'You really are a most foolish young woman,' she said, 'and you may well live to regret your decision. As for you,' she turned to Alfred, 'you may as well get along home. And if you want my advice – forget her. Really she is not worth it.'

Grace gasped but Alfred stood his ground. 'That's for me to decide, ma'am, and I reckon she is. I shall never give up hope.'

'More fool you, then,' retorted Virginia. 'But I have better things to do with my time than waste it in this fashion.' She turned to Grace. 'I feel bound to report this incident to my husband. I shall add that your behaviour was most unseemly and that once more I am beginning to doubt whether you really are a fit person to be nanny to George and Victoria. Now Miss Martins, please get back to the nursery, *at once!*'

Grace realized that only her own departure would persuade Alfred to leave. 'Goodbye, Alfred,' she said. 'I'm sorry about everything.'

'Grace, please – ' he began, but she was already hurrying back across the courtyard. He watched her retreating figure with despair while Virginia regarded him with irritation.

After a moment or two she said, 'One day soon she might be heartily glad to *accept* your offer,' then she turned and followed Grace back into the house.

Alfred appeared to be rooted to the spot, but eventually he shook himself out of his stupor and put his cap back on his head. As he turned to go, Fanny ran out.

'Here,' she said, thrusting a package into his hand, 'a

slice of game pie from Cook and she says you're to cheer up.'

'You were listening!' he said.

'Sort of,' she confessed. 'We didn't mean any harm. If I was Grace, I'd say "Yes" like a shot.'

'Would you?' He unwrapped the pie and took a bite absent-mindedly. 'Do you think I dare come again?'

Fanny shrugged. 'I wouldn't if I was you.'

'You're very kind. I just feel so . . . so *worthless*. Why did *she* have to come along? Just my bad luck.'

'She's got her knife into Grace lately.' She shrugged again. 'Try not to take it so hard.'

He took another bite of pie and mumbled, 'My mother's ill and she's so afraid for me. Silly, I know, but . . .' He glanced at her. 'So you've got someone you care about. A man friend, I mean, who doesn't return your feelings?'

'Yes. He just doesn't seem to notice me. I'd do anything for him, but I can't tell you who it is. Only Grace knows that.'

'Well, at least you understand how I feel,' he said. 'It's awful, isn't it?'

'It is, but we have to keep cheerful and hope for the best. I reckon that if I look miserable he'll fancy me even less, so whenever I see him I make a big effort.'

Mrs Wade rapped on the kitchen window suddenly and Fanny said, 'Lordy, I must go! Bye, Alfred.'

'Bye, Fanny.'

'And Alfred – there's plenty more pebbles on the beach. That's what they say.'

'I'll remember that – thanks.'

*

Later that evening Virginia glanced at her husband across the dinner table.

'Really, Alex,' she said, 'I can't imagine what you see in that silly little thing. I am so tired of her and her sordid little intrigues. Oh, didn't you know? That gangly youth from her past showed up again: Alfred Harris. I caught them at it – grappling together like a couple of animals.

263

It really does revolt me, that kind of behaviour.' She waited for him to speak, but he said nothing so she continued, 'Have you nothing to say in her defence? That does surprise me. Most girls would have the decency to do their courting in private but she just doesn't care. Kissing and cuddling and trying to pretend not to like it. Quite disgusting, but what can you expect from a girl like that? They're all the same.' She paused to take a few mouthfuls of soup and then continued. 'I soon put a stop to it, of course. I won't allow that kind of thing. It sets such a bad example to the rest of the staff. I sent her up to the nursery with a few home truths ringing in her ears. At least she had the decency to blush. This soup's excellent; I think we might have it next Friday when the Hattons come to dinner.'

'It is good,' he said quietly. 'I'm sure they would enjoy it.'

'Oh! You've found your voice at last!'

He leaned back, but there was a hard glitter in his eyes and she knew she had disturbed him by her news about Grace.

'I told him to take himself off, too,' she said. 'What a pathetic specimen he is! Stuttering and stammering and twisting his cap in his hands for all the world like a lovesick schoolboy.' She assumed a whining voice and said, ' "I love her. I want her to marry me." Good heavens! What a clown he is. I wish she would marry him. I daresay they deserve each other and I'd be glad to see the back of her!'

Just then Fanny brought in the main course but she retired as quickly as she could, aware of the tension in the room.

'I sent him away with instructions never to come back,' ended Virginia. She sighed heavily. 'I suppose it's too much to hope you will admit your mistake and dismiss her. Then she could marry her oafish sweetheart and raise a brood of oafish children.'

'I hardly think so,' he said. 'And no, I won't admit to having made a mistake. Really, your frenzied efforts to

264

blacken her name do you no credit – quite the contrary, in fact. They make you sound spiteful and shrewish.'

Her mouth fell open with shock. 'How dare you speak to me like that?' she began.

Alex went on relentlessly, his face white with anger. 'I am well aware that for some obscure reason you have taken a dislike to Miss Martins, but you should be prepared to consider the children's welfare. I think their well-being is more important than your personal likes and dislikes. Victoria and George are now happy, normal children, thanks to Miss Martins, and in my opinion we owe her a great deal.'

Virginia found her voice at last. 'I admit she is an improvement on Nanny Webster, but – '

'An improvement! She's in a different category altogether, and if you weren't so prejudiced you would admit that we are lucky to have her.'

'But her personal life is hardly to be admired. Alfred Harris – '

'You can't blame Miss Martins for the fact that she has a persistent suitor,' he told her, 'nor can I blame Mr Harris for persevering. She will make someone a very good, very charming wife – and when she does, it will be our loss. I hope it's not too soon, that's all. I shall be sorry to see her go. Nothing you say will poison my mind against her because I see her as she really is – a thoroughly decent, warm-hearted, hard-working young woman – and I don't want to hear another word on the subject, Virginia. Miss Martins stays with us and there's an end of it!'

*

Later still, after the children were in bed, Alex made his way to the nursery. Grace was sitting by the remains of the fire, but she jumped to her feet when she saw who it was and two bright spots of colour burned in her cheeks.

'Mr Latimer! How nice to see you.' She held up a small piece of tangled knitting. 'Victoria is learning to knit,' she explained. 'I have to unravel it secretly and do a few rows so that it grows a little each day.'

'Do please sit down, Miss Martins. May I join you?'

'Of course.' Flustered, she indicated a chair opposite her and they both sat down.

'I'm sorry,' he said, 'that you were upset today. I do hope your friend was not too offended. My wife told me what happened.' He was hoping it would not be necessary to criticize Virginia's behaviour to a member of the staff, and waited to see how she would react.

As he had feared, her eyes flashed angrily. 'Alfred *was* very offended,' she said. 'He was offended and humiliated – and so was I. I know he was behaving stupidly in kissing me the way he did, but he was miserable and frightened. His mother's very ill and might die and he's scared of being alone. That's why he wanted me to marry him. I'm sure he'll find someone to take my place; he's really a nice person.'

Alex hid his relief at knowing that she had turned Alfred down. 'So you won't be leaving us,' he observed.

'No. Never,' she said forcibly and then, confused, added, 'That is, not as long as you want me to stay. Mr Latimer, I'm sorry it happened, but your wife . . . well, I don't know what she told you, but I expect she made it sound . . .' She stopped. 'It really wasn't anything terrible. Oh dear! This is so difficult.'

She wanted to say that Virginia had made an unfortunate situation worse, but she too was reluctant to criticize her employer's wife.

After a moment, Alex said carefully, 'I'm afraid my wife may have been a little tactless, so I came to apologize and to say that I hope you will try to put the matter out of your mind.'

'How can I?' Grace burst out. 'She said that she would tell you I'm not a fit person to – ' She swallowed hard. 'She made me feel so cheap! It's not my fault if Alfred loves me. I've told him "No" again and again and I *don't* encourage him, so if she told you I do it's not true. I know you saw Stanley kiss me, but that was just him being cheeky. I don't encourage anyone, and I don't want to be sent away from the children. They're all I want.' To her chagrin tears began to roll down her cheeks and she brushed them away furiously. 'I'm *not* crying,' she told him, reaching into her pocket for a handkerchief.

'I know you're not,' he said. 'Here, borrow mine.'

Looking up, she saw that he was smiling and tried to return the smile. She put down the knitting, wiped her eyes on the immaculate white square and then, after a moment's hesitation, blew her nose.

'Keep it,' he said. 'I've plenty more.'

'Keep it? Oh, *thank* you!'

He was touched by her obvious pleasure and suddenly longed to give her a box of the most expensive handkerchiefs money could buy.

Her smile faded and she gave a deep sigh.

'What is it?' he asked.

'There's something I want to say to you,' she began, then broke off.

'Then say it.'

'It will sound wrong; it will sound like "telling tales".'

He raised his eyebrows. 'Telling tales! What a heinous crime!'

'I wish it was a joking matter.'

'I'm sorry.' He was contrite. 'Please say whatever you wish and I promise not to regard it as tale-telling.'

She took a deep breath. 'Mrs Latimer wants to get rid of me because of what happened when George was taken ill – she blames me somehow for putting her in a bad light – and for other things that I'd rather not talk about. I'm so afraid that she will turn you against me and make you believe something bad about me so that you *will* agree to sack me. I'm just so afraid . . .' She faltered and stopped.

He stood up and leaned one elbow on the mantelpiece; as he looked down at her bowed head, there was a tightness in his throat.

'You have my promise that that won't happen, Miss Martins.'

Her head came up and he was startled by the intense look in her eyes. 'You promise? Oh, that's all I needed to hear. I mean, if I did anything terrible then I would deserve to be sent away, but I won't. I swear it! All I

267

want is to stay here with you and with the children.' She corrected herself hastily. 'I'll do my very best for you, always.'

Her hesitation had been so slight that he thought he must have imagined it.

'Miss Martins, let me put it this way,' he suggested. 'If I hear ill of you from any source, I will ask for your side of the story. Is that fair?'

She nodded.

'So you will stay at Berwick House – unless one day you change your mind and *do* decide to marry.'

'Oh, but I can't . . . I mean, I won't!' To hide her confusion, she rose to her feet and smoothed her skirt. Then, after an awkward silence, she said, 'Would you like to see the children, sir, while you're here? They look so angelic when they're asleep'.

'I would, yes.'

He followed her into the night nursery and together they looked at the sleeping children – Victoria clutching her favourite rag doll, George sprawled untidily with his arms thrown up around his head.

Alex glanced at Grace and saw the tenderness and pride in her eyes as she tucked the covers round George's shoulders, then stooped to drop a brief kiss on his tousled hair. He had never seen that look in Virginia's eyes although he knew that she loved her son and daughter in her own way. For Grace Martins it was obvious that expressing affection came as naturally as breathing.

'We are very fortunate to have found you,' he told her. 'I'm sorry my wife does not share my opinion.'

'It doesn't matter to me, sir, as long as you're satisifed.'

'I am indeed.'

As he reached the nursery door he turned back. 'I can't blame Alfred Harris for trying to steal you away,' he said, with a smile. 'In his shoes, I would do exactly the same. Oh – and we didn't do anything about the furniture for your room. Shall we have a look in the attic tomorrow? Before I go out – say eight-fifteen? Good. I'll see you then.'

*

23rd June. Today I spent almost half an hour alone with my dearest Alex. We went up to the attic and I now have a new bedside rug, an occasional table and a rocking-chair, which I have put near the window so if I am reading I will get the light. He even helped me to carry it all down; I got the feeling he did not want anyone else involved. He could easily have sent Sid up to help me instead. Virginia was with Cook doing the menus for when the Hattons come on Saturday, so I doubt if she even wondered where he was. The rocking-chair is rather old, but I shall polish it up and maybe find a piece of velvet to renew the back and seat. Alex said I could – in fact, he suggested it. There is also a picture of some cows wading in a stream – I have hung that on the far wall – and a fancy-looking clock that does not go but looks very nice on the mantelpiece.

It was such heaven to be pottering about up there, just the two of us, and Alex seemed very cheerful. I think he wanted to make up for yesterday's trouble with Virginia. If so, it was worth it and she can rant at me again! Poor Alfred was very upset, but it is his own fault. I do so wish he would give up and find someone else.

I wish I dare ask Alex to call me Grace, but I know I can't. It would be so wonderful, just once, to be called by my Christian name instead of 'Miss Martins' which puts such a distance between us.

Oh yes, and I also have a new jug for the washstand. It does not match the basin and soap-dish, but at least it is not chipped.

I wonder what Alex would say if he knew his handkerchief is now my most treasured possession. Laugh, I suppose, but in a kindly way. I feel sure he would never humiliate me the way Virginia does. How I hate that woman – partly because she hates me, and partly because we are all so sure she is deceiving Alex with that hateful Larry Scott. We don't even know if he is still in England because since Sid's nephew saw him in Lyndhurst no one has set eyes on him, but

Virginia now goes up to London much more than she used to. I think he is still here.

Tomorrow Alex is going down to Devon again to see old Mr Latimer's brother who is still very ill. I do hate it when he's not here. I miss him even though I don't see him very often. There was also a trunk full of clothes in the attic which belonged to Alex's mother, and he has given me a grey silk dress. It is too big, but I can alter it. He said it went with my eyes; he was being so kind. I tried to pretend he did not have a wife and was *my* husband, but the ghost of Virginia haunted me and I could not really believe it. I hate to think of them together, but Mrs Wade says a man has to have someone to satisfy his urges and so I don't want her to refuse him. It's very difficult to know what I do want. He would never take another woman. He is much too honourable.

Fanny was thrilled this morning because John winked at her. He seems to be taking notice of her at last. I wish he was not so bad-tempered, but Stanley will torment him – tooting the horn to frighten the horses and then pretending it was an accident. John hates him like poison. Dot has cut herself again; she is so clumsy. This time it is her left thumb and it did look bad, but Cook said it served her right for being careless. Her sister is having a baby and I think it has given Dot ideas! Fanny says she's always daydreaming.

I wish Lucien would come home on leave again. He cheers everybody up, but now he spends most of his time with his fiancée which is natural enough. I wish they were going to be married from Berwick House, but Cook says they won't.

Must get some sleep, but I hate to blow out the candle because then I won't see my lovely new furniture.

Bless you, my dearest, *dearest* Alex. Please God take care of him.

Chapter Fourteen

The time had come, Stanley Marcus told himself grimly. He had had enough of John Martins, whose sneering remarks, black looks and icy silences were beginning to wear him down. Baiting him was no longer sufficient; Stanley was no longer prepared to suffer in silence — it was time to show his claws. Of course he had done his own share, he didn't deny it, but that had merely been in retaliation for the groom's unrelenting disapproval. He had rejected Stanley's early attempts at friendship and had gone on to make derogatory remarks about the motor as well as its chauffeur. Remarks about himself he could bear, but the car was his pride and joy and he could not and would not tolerate John's unkind comments any longer. The man was an arrogant pig, Stanley told himself. After all, he had not started the hostilities — that had been John's doing. From the very start the older man had resented him as well as the motor-car; had annoyed him wherever possible; had triumphed over his mistakes and had tried to turn the rest of the staff against him. He had even — and here Stanley's eyes grew steely with anger — laid hands on the motor, leaning his dirty elbow on the newly-polished bonnet or leading the horses dangerously close to it in wet weather so that their hooves threw muddy splashes over the gleaming spokes of the newly-cleaned wheels. No, Stanley affirmed, he had put up with the insults for too long already and today the final reckoning was due.

He had been waiting to find a chink in John Martins' armour. He dared not meddle with the horses and the groom seemed to have no weaknesses he could exploit. Now, however, to everyone's amazement, he suddenly seemed to be taking an interest in Fanny, so Stanley had decided to use her in his grand revenge. He licked the pencil and re-read the first line of the note he was composing.

'Fanny. You must know that I care for you.'

Yes, he liked that word 'care'. Much more subtle than 'love' and, after all, she didn't know John loved her although she was hoping he would.

He thought deeply and wrote again: 'I must see you alone. Come to the stable at nine tonight –'

He paused again. Mustn't get too carried away in case he aroused her suspicions. What would John Martins say in such a note? Probably nothing too romantic. The man lacked imagination.

'I must talk to you,' he wrote.

Yes, that would do very well, but should he sign it? If he put John's name and Fanny ever showed him the note it might count as forgery, and Stanley was a little nervous about the implications of that. Was it a criminal offence if you weren't making money out of it? Could he claim it was just a bit of harmless fun? A new thought struck him. Suppose she showed the note to someone else? Women were silly creatures and Fanny might decide to confide in Grace and Grace might mention it to her brother . . . damnation!

He thought calmly for a moment and was rewarded by a flash of inspiration. So he licked the pencil again and added the words: 'Do not show this to *anyone*.'

Yes, that was brilliant – the work of a genius – but how best to sign it? 'Anonymous?' 'A well-wisher?' 'Guess who?' He rejected these as too frivolous and furrowed his brow again. Fanny must think it was John. If she suspected it was John's arch-enemy, she would never come to the stables. Ah! More inspiration.

He wrote: 'Signed by an admirer.'

That was true enough, for he, Stanley, did admire her. He admired all women. Well, nearly all. He stared at the letter feeling very pleased with himself and then suddenly a new doubt crept into his mind. Perhaps he should disguise his handwriting? Yes, of course! He must re-write it in capital letters.

He tore another page from the notebook and started

272

again. A few moments later he had finished writing and was pushing the letter into the envelope. He wrote her name and kissed it.

'That ought to bring her,' he said. 'Tonight, John Martins, you'll get your come-uppance!'

*

It was nearly ten minutes past nine when Fanny slipped into the stable-yard and Stanley, from his hiding place in the hay-loft, heard the tell-tale creak of the gate and grinned to himself in delighted anticipation. From what he had gleaned from general chit-chat, Fanny had never been 'walking out' and therefore, he reasoned, she must be longing to find out what 'canoodling' was all about. Since John Martins seemed unwilling to initiate her into its mysteries, he himself was prepared to do the honours. She would no doubt be grateful for his attention and he would thoroughly enjoy himself.

Tomorrow he would drop several large hints in John Martins' hearing to the effect that he had stolen a march on him, and if he ever did marry Fanny he would live with the knowledge that his hated rival had enjoyed her first. Stanley's only worry was that Fanny might give up her designs on John and transfer her affections to him, and that must never happen. Grace must not find out what had happened. Somehow he would have to swear Fanny to secrecy, but that shouldn't be too difficult because she wouldn't want John to hear about it.

He heard a click and, peering down, he saw the outer door of the stable open and a shadowy figure appeared silhouetted against what little was left of the daylight.

'John! Where are you?' hissed Fanny. 'It's me.'

Stanley hissed back, 'Up here!'

Fanny glanced upwards into the shadowy loft. 'Where? I can't see you. Is it you, John?'

He tried to disguise his voice by cupping his hands round his mouth. 'Come up the ladder.'

In the gloom the horses stirred restlessly, disturbed by the unfamiliar sounds and aware of intruders.

Fanny paused, trying to remember the whereabouts of

the ladder that led up into the hay-loft. Her heart was thudding and her throat was dry with excitement.

'Second to last stall,' hissed Stanley.

He was crouching in the darkest corner of the loft, willing her to hurry. His plan was to entice her into his arms before she realized that he was not John. Once he had his arms around her, he was sure he could arouse her interest and hopefully her passion.

He craned forward until Fanny's head appeared at the top of the ladder, then immediately he drew back into the shadows.

Fanny stepped off the ladder and said tremulously, 'John?'

'I'm here.'

Lifting her skirts free of the hay, Fanny took a few unsteady steps towards him then stopped uncertainly.

'I got your note,' she said unnecessarily. 'Oh John, I – ' She broke off and took another step forward until less than two yards separated them.

Stanley was terrified that at any moment she would recognize him and take fright. That would be the end of his grand scheme. Impulsively, he hurled himself forward and just managed to catch hold of her skirt. She gave a scream as he tugged her forward and at the same time she recognized him.

'Stanley Marcus! Oh, you . . . you wretch! What are you doing her and where's John?'

She was tugging at her skirt, trying to free it, but he now clasped one of her ankles and in an effort to kick him with the other leg, she overbalanced and fell on top of him, temporarily winding both of them.

When Stanley could speak again, he remembered his plan. 'Who said anything about John?' he asked, sounding suitably indignant. 'That letter was from me.'

She slapped at the hand that still held her ankle, but he told himself her heart was not in it.

'But you're not "an admirer",' she protested. 'Oh, for heaven's sake, let go my leg, you idiot! That hurts.'

'Stop fighting me then and I will.'

'You let go and then I'll stop.'

They regarded each other warily. He saw her eyes, wide and furious, while she saw the flash of his white teeth as he smiled.

'Let go my ankle, Stanley Marcus, or I'll scream,' she threatened.

'You wouldn't do that.'

'I would.'

'And let John find us together? Oh dear! Whatever would he think?'

It took a few seconds for the significance of his remark to dawn on her and then she gave a squeal of indignation.

'You hateful, rotten swine! Oh, I could kill you! I never would have come if I'd known. I thought – ' She stopped again, unwilling to admit her mistake.

He released her ankle and she sat up, picking hay from her hair. She smelt faintly of perfume, he noticed.

'You thought it was from John?' Stanley contrived to sound hurt. 'Why should you think that? Has he ever said he cared two hoots about you? It's me that cares, not him.'

Fanny tossed her head. 'A likely story. You're always making up to Grace. Oh, don't deny it. I've heard you many a time.' As his hand crept to her arm, she slapped him again and said, 'I hope there aren't fleas in this hay.'

'Course there aren't,' he assured her. 'Me and Grace? Is that what you thought? The truth is, I was trying to make you jealous.'

'You weren't; you're just saying that.'

'I was, I swear it. Grace is a bit too uppity for me.' He hoped none of his comments would ever reach Grace's ears.

'God's honour?'

'Cross my heart and hope to die!'

'Well, you could have fooled me, Stanley Marcus.'

She scratched at her leg and said, 'This hay's awfully itchy,' then suddenly began to giggle. 'If I thought you were lying, Stanley Marcus – if I thought you were up to something . . .'

'You'd what?' He tried to hide the triumph he felt. She believed him and she wasn't mad, only disappointed –

and maybe not even that. Perhaps secretly she was delighted.

The tantalizing perfume excited him. 'You smell nice,' he said.

'It's hers,' confided Fanny. 'Mrs Latimer's eau de cologne. I pinched some from the bottle on her dressing-stand. She'll never notice; she's got so many bottles and jars of stuff. No wonder she always looks so blooming perfect. If I had all that lot, *I'd* be beautiful.'

Stanley seized his chance. 'You look *very* beautiful to me right now,' he said. 'You're not sorry you came, are you?'

She hesitated. 'Yes and no,' she said honestly. 'I thought the note was from John but I should have known better. He's just not a romantic man. Anyway, how did you know I like John?'

'A little bird told me.' He laughed.

'Which little bird? Not Grace. She promised not to tell. If she told you — '

'Nobody told me, I just guessed.'

She began to get to her feet, but he caught hold of her wrist.

'Listen, Fanny,' he said, 'you might as well give up the idea of John Martins. There's a barmaid in the village — '

'No!' cried Fanny. 'I asked Grace about her and she says she's not his style at all.'

'Grace!' he scoffed. 'What does *she* know? She's never in the pub and I am. I see them together; I see the look in his eyes and the smirk on her face. There's something going on between them. Whisper, whisper, giggle, giggle! You know what I mean.'

'No, I don't,' she protested, but he could hear the doubt in her voice. 'I don't believe you.'

'Have you ever been kissed?' he asked suddenly. 'Like this!' He grabbed her, pulled her close and kissed her fiercely, then thrust the top of his tongue between her surprised lips.

'Ugh!' She struggled to free herself. 'That's horrible. I don't call that much of a kiss. Let go of me, Stanley. I must go.'

'You've only just got here.'

'I told you – I thought it would be John.'

'Oh, bugger John!'

'Stanley Marcus!' She was shocked and affronted. 'I'm not staying here to hear that sort of language.'

She jerked herself free and took a few steps, knee-deep in the yielding hay so that he easily caught her again.

'Have you ever been kissed before?' he demanded. 'Truthfully!'

'Mind your own business, Stanley Marcus, and let me go.'

'That means you haven't.'

'It does not.'

'Course it does. Look, Fanny, give me a chance. Let me show you how it's done. You've got to learn sometime – and how old are you?'

'That's none of your business.' She was getting cross. 'You got me here under false pretences.'

'How did I?' He was all injured innocence.

'By not putting your name on the letter. By signing it "An admirer". That's how, and you know it, so don't go on pretending. I'm going before someone misses me – and I shall tell Grace. See what she thinks of you when I tell her you only pretended to like her to make me jealous.'

'That was just talk –' he began and his own good humour started to fade. 'You keep your mouth shut, Fanny, or . . .' He tried to think of something that would keep her from confiding in Grace.

'Or you'll what?' she taunted.

'Or I'll tell John *you* sent *me* a note – asking me to meet you here.'

The impudence of this threat took Fanny's breath away, but not for long. 'You sneaky, spiteful, hateful pig!' she screamed. 'Don't you dare! If I thought you meant that –'

'Give me another kiss then and I won't.'

'No, I won't. You're – you're *despicable!*'

'Oh my! Big words!' he mocked. 'Swallowed a dictionary, have you?'

Furiously she turned to retrace her steps to the ladder, but Stanley made a last desperate grab at her. For a moment they struggled wildly, while Fanny cursed and Stanley jeered at her efforts. Suddenly she broke away, but as she stepped backwards she lost her footing and with a scream of fear plunged downwards off the hay-loft into the stall below, where Caradox had been increasingly alarmed by the unusual commotion. When Fanny tumbled down on to his broad back, he took fright and reared crazily.

Fanny slipped from his back to the floor, terrified but unhurt, but as his descending hooves narrowly missed her she screamed, 'Stanley! Oh God!'

Startled afresh by her voice, the horse kicked backwards and then sprang forward so violently that he snapped his halter and at the same time burst open the ancient lock on the stall door. Within seconds he was out of the stable door and heading away into the darkness in a clatter of frenzied hoofbeats.

All was quiet as Stanley peered fearfully over the edge of the loft, afraid of what he might see. To his great relief Fanny was pulling herself to her feet.

'Are you hurt?' he asked, jumping down beside her.

Fanny, one hand to her heart, leaned against the wall. Every nerve in her body shrieked, every muscle ached and she could hardly believe that no bones were broken. She burst into tears.

'Fanny!' he repeated. 'Are you all right?'

'I'm still alive, if that's what you mean,' she sobbed, 'but no thanks to you. I could have been killed, do you realize that? I could have broken my neck. I could have been trampled on.' She allowed him to pull her up to a standing position.

'I'm sorry, really I am. Are you sure you're not hurt?'

'I'll be black and blue tomorrow – and my head aches – and the horse has gone.' She dabbed ineffectively at her tears and Stanley offered his handkerchief.

'We'll have to get him back,' he said. 'John will slay us if he ever finds out.'

'Us?' Fanny's head snapped up and her tears stopped.

'He won't slay me because it wasn't my fault. He'll slay *you!*'

'Me, then.' Stanley, recovering from his fright, was still chastened. 'Look, Fanny, we'll have to go after him. We'll – '

'Don't keep saying "We", Stanley Marcus,' she told him angrily. '*You'll* have to go after him. Count me out. He could have killed me; I thought he was going to come down on top of me when he reared up like that. *You* go and look for him.'

'Fanny, *please!* For Pete's sake. I'll never catch him single-handed.'

'Ask Ben to help you, then. I'm not going near that animal again.'

'I can't ask Ben. He'll be sure to tell John and then I'll be for it.'

'Serves you right, then, for it's all your fault. I'm going back to my room and I'm staying there.'

'Fanny, *please*,' he begged, abandoning his pride. 'It was only a joke and I *do* like you and I need your help. I promise I won't – '

At that moment they heard footsteps clattering down from the room over the stables.

'Hell and damnation!' whispered Stanley, thinking it might be Martins, but it was Ben who appeared.

'What the heck's going on?' he demanded. 'I thought I heard a horse loose. Oh, crikey!' His gaze swept the empty stall. 'Not Caradox! How did he get out? I could have sworn I shut his door.'

He stared suspiciously at Stanley and Fanny, who could not think what to say. 'Did you see him go?'

Fanny nodded. 'He went that way,' she said, pointing. 'Honestly, Ben, we didn't mean it to happen. He just kicked open the door.'

'Strewth!' Ben looked scared. 'The master will go mad if anything happens to Caradox. He raised that horse from a foal; broke it in himself and schooled it – everything. His pride and joy, that horse.'

Fanny looked helplessly at Stanley, who said, 'Shouldn't we go and look for him?'

'I'd best tell Mr Martins – ' Ben began uncertainly, but Fanny grabbed his arm beseechingly.

'Don't tell him, Ben. Please don't! If you find him, there'll be no need to tell anyone.'

Ben was still hesitating when they heard footsteps approaching at a run and a tall figure loomed up out of the darkness. It was John Martins!

'What the hell's going on here?' he roared. 'Where's Ben? There's a horse loose. I heard it as I came up the lane. Ben!'

Stanley and Fanny looked at each other, speechless with dismay.

'Oh God!' muttered Stanley. 'That's torn it! Why did he have to come back early?'

John strode in through the open stable-door and caught sight of them. His eyes took in the empty stall.

'So, it was Caradox,' he said. 'What the hell's happening?'

Ben said, 'It wasn't me, Mr Martins. Honest it wasn't.'

Stanley, speechless, was searching his mind for a convincing lie, but before he could think of one Fanny had stepped forward.

'Oh John, I'm sorry,' she said. 'It was my fault. I fell into his stall and he was frightened and . . .' She swallowed and stopped.

'*Fell* into his stall?' John's tone was incredulous.

'Yes – I was in the hay-loft and I . . . sort of fell.'

'Sort of fell!' His voice was soft with suppressed anger. 'How did you come to be in the hay-loft, if it's not a rude question?'

Fanny tried again. 'Oh John, please don't be angry,' she whispered.

Stanley found his voice at last. 'We were together,' he said hoarsely.

'I see,' said John ominously.

He stepped forward and grasped Stanley's shoulder so hard that he winced.

'I'm going after Caradox,' he told him, 'and Ben's coming with me, but when I get back – God help you! If that horse has come to any harm – '

280

He strode away with Ben running beside him.

'Oh dear,' said Fanny helplessly. 'What will you do, Stanley?'

He drew a long breath. 'What can I do? Wait for him, I suppose. You'd better get going before he comes back.'

Fanny shook her head despairingly, shocked by the suddenness with which they had been plunged into disaster.

'Do you think he'll tell Mr Latimer?'

'Christ knows! He might. He's got it in for me.'

'About us being . . . you know?'

'I don't know.'

He clenched his right fist and swung it violently and uselessly into the air.

'Hell and damnation!' he muttered. 'Christ, what a mess! I've got you into this, Fanny, and I'm really sorry.'

At last she summoned up enough courage to ask the fateful question. 'Will we get the sack, do you think?'

He shrugged without answering and Fanny began to cry again.

'I'll never get another job,' she wailed. 'Not without a reference. My ma's going to wallop me. She got me this job.'

Her tears added to Stanley's guilt and in his distress he turned on her. 'I can't think with you bawling like that,' he told her brusquely. 'I told you – get out of here.'

'But Stanley – '

His patience snapped. 'Just go, stupid! And don't tell a soul. I'll try and think of something.'

She went.

*

Fanny fled upstairs to the attic and threw herself face downwards on her bed in a blind panic. Fortunately Dot, who shared the room, was still in the kitchen talking to Cook. Fanny groaned aloud. Sent home in disgrace! The prospect filled her with dread. Her mother had found her the job at Berwick House and had brought her to the interview at the tender age of twelve. She had primed her with suitable answers, for she had been in service herself before her marriage.

'Oh, Ma!' whispered Fanny. 'I never meant any harm. It was his fault.'

There were three sisters at home and one of them had a baby. The little cottage was already bulging at the seams and there would be no fatted calf for a penitent daughter who had been dismissed from a good position as a result of her own stupidity. She could imagine the reproaches and her father's baleful looks. No, she decided, she could never go home. Would Mr Latimer give her a reference? It seemed highly improbable.

She sobbed into the pillow, scalding tears of frustration and injured pride. How dare Stanley call her stupid? It was all his fault and she hadn't called him anything. Stanley Marcus was an ignorant, selfish lout – and who did he think he was, anyway, to go giving her orders? 'Don't tell a soul,' he had said. Well, she *would* tell someone; she would tell Grace. She sat up and blew her nose, then made her way along the passage and down the stairs to the nursery. Grace was ironing the children's clothes and she listened in dismay as Fanny poured out a garbled account of the events in the stable. As the sad tale unfolded, Grace was filled with a strange foreboding.

'Do you think, Grace, that you could ask John not to be too hard on me?' Fanny pleaded. 'If I hadn't thought it was John I never would have gone, but how could I tell him that? Oh, I *know* I'm going to get the sack. I just know it – and all over a silly prank. I could kill Stanley Marcus.'

Grace up-ended the flat-iron in front of the fire and filled the small kettle with water.

'A cup of tea,' she promised. 'Then you'll feel a bit better.'

'But will you go down? Will you talk to John? I keep thinking about Caradox; he may be lost and it was me that fell on him.'

'Do stop blaming yourself,' said Grace. 'Let's hope nothing worse happens. I'll go down and see John – I'll go while you're drinking your tea. I'm sure he'll understand, although I can't promise anything. Maybe he'll just give Stanley a rollicking and not take it further.'

But in her heart she did not believe these comforting words. She knew her brother and was aware of the passionate concern he felt for the animals in his care; she also understood better than most the hatred he felt for the young chauffeur and his 'mechanical monster'. If John had a chance to rid himself of the usurper, she felt certain he would exploit that chance to the full. When she had settled Fanny in a comfortable chair, she set off for the stable, hardly knowing what to expect when she got there. The stable-yard was deserted except for Stanley, who leaned dispiritedly against the stable wall. When she was near enough to be identified, he pulled himself upright and said, 'Hello there, Grace,' with an attempt at his normal voice.

'I know what's happened,' Grace told him. 'Fanny told me.'

'Trust her! I told her to keep it quiet. That's women for you.'

'What about men, then?' Grace demanded. 'Who was it who got her into this mess?'

He grunted by way of an answer and Grace went on, 'I'm here to try and soft-soap John, but I'm not very hopeful and I wouldn't like to be in your shoes when he gets back.'

'You think I don't know?'

He stared at her gloomily. The moon had risen and by the pale light he saw Grace's eyes, large and anxious, and thought how attractive she was and how foolish he had been to play such games with Fanny. Now he had almost certainly lost both women and would probably lose his job.

'If I was you,' said Grace, 'I'd make myself scarce.'

'Well, you're not me.'

'John will be in a towering rage –' she began.

He shrugged. 'If it's a choice between a good hiding and the sack, I'd sooner have the hiding,' he told her morosely. 'If he's set on clobbering me, he'll find me

283

sooner or later, so I may as well hang around and get it over.'

They stood together staring towards the gate that led out of the stable-yard. The silence lengthened and Grace shivered.

'Creepy, isn't it?' she suggested, but Stanley was too wrapped up in his own problems to bother with her remark. A bat fluttered erratically overhead before disappearing over the stable roof.

'They get their claws caught in your hair,' said Grace with a shudder.

'Course they don't.'

'Well, that's what they say.'

'They say wrong, then.'

Another silence.

'I can hear something – someone's coming,' said Grace and they both listened, straining their ears for the sound of hoofbeats which would indicate that Caradox was fit and well, but all they heard were footsteps as Ben came into the yard at a run, puffing and panting and holding his side.

Grace darted forward. 'Have you found him?'

Ben paused to catch his breath. 'We found him,' he said.

'And is he all right?'

Something in his expression frightened her.

'He's fallen,' he told them. 'Broken both his forelegs.'

Grace gasped. 'Oh, poor Caradox! Should we send for the vet? Is that why you've come back?'

'No,' said Ben. 'I've come for Mr Martins' pistol. He says Caradox is too far gone to save and all he can do is put him out of his misery.'

Stanley and Grace stared at Ben in horror.

'You mean you're going to shoot him?' cried Stanley.

'Oh, but you can't – ' Grace began. 'Surely if he's the master's favourite – '

'Mr Martins says it's the kindest thing.'

'Then shouldn't you at least tell Mr Latimer?'

Ben gave her a withering glance. 'Do you think he wants to shoot his own horse?'

'I don't know . . .' she began.

'Would *you*?'

Grace hesitated.

'I wouldn't,' said Ben, 'not if I loved the animal like he loves Caradox. Anyway, right or wrong, it's up to Mr Martins and he says he'll do it and tell the master afterwards. I wouldn't be in his shoes – but I can't hang about. Sooner the poor creature's out of its misery, the better!'

They watched in silence as the boy disappeared inside the tack-room and quickly reappeared holding the pistol in his right hand and carrying a lantern in the other.

He turned to them and shrugged helplessly; then he spoke to Stanley. 'I shouldn't be around when we get back, if I was you,' he advised. 'I've never seen Mr Martins in such a state.'

After he had gone Stanley remained where he was.

'You'd better go,' said Grace gently. 'I'll do what I can.'

'I'm stopping right here.'

'Oh please, Stanley! It's just asking for trouble.'

'He can only kill me,' said Stanley, but his voice shook.

'I do wish you'd go,' said Grace. 'He'll have cooled down by tomorrow and I'll put in a good word for you, the same as for Fanny. You didn't mean any harm; you couldn't have known where it would lead.'

'The horse will still be dead though.'

Grace could not think of any counter to that remark. She imagined the wounded animal lying on the dark grass with his broken legs sprawled unnaturally beneath him. She saw again the smooth neck and noble head, the way she had seen him that first day in the stable when she had fallen in love with Alex Latimer. A gentle giant – that was how he had described the horse. She recalled the soft feel of the horse's velvety muzzle as he scooped the sugar-lumps from her hand while the dark, liquid eyes regarded her anxiously. Tears came into her eyes, but she brushed them away.

Minutes passed, and they did not speak again until a sudden gun-shot shattered the still night air.

'That's it, then,' said Stanley. 'That's Caradox gone.'

'Poor thing,' said Grace. 'He was so beautiful.'

And poor you, she thought, astonished at Stanley's courage. In his place she felt sure she would have run.

There was nothing to do but wait. As the minutes ticked by, Grace wondered how Alex would take the news that his favourite horse had been destroyed – not by an unavoidable disease, but because of an accident brought about by a stupid prank. It was all so unnecessary; a dreadful twist of fate; an accumulation of unforeseeable circumstances.

Stanley broke the silence at last. 'I keep thinking of that horse,' he said, heavily, 'cantering along in the darkness . . . terrified.'

'Perhaps not,' said Grace, in an effort to console him. 'Maybe horses don't mind the dark. Maybe he enjoyed his last gallop. Wild horses wouldn't be afraid of the dark, would they?'

He shrugged. 'I suppose in the darkness he couldn't judge distances and thought he could jump whatever it was.'

'I suppose so. Well, whatever happened, he's at peace now.' She put a hand on his arm and pressed it briefly.

It was all so sad, she reflected. A fine animal dead and so much human misery. Sighing, she wished she need not be involved, but she had promised Fanny.

After what seemed an age, they heard John and Ben returning. They both entered the yard without speaking and went straight into the tack-room. When they came out, Grace took her courage in both hands and stepped forward.

'John, please may I say something – ' she began, but faltered in the coldness of her brother's stare.

'Stay out of this, Grace,' he told her.

'But I want to . . . oh John, I know how black it looks, but – '

'Would you like to go up to the house and tell the master what's happened?'

'No, but . . . John, I just want to explain *how* it happened. It was an accident, it was – '

286

'I know how it happened, Grace, and it had nothing to do with you, so I'll thank you to mind your own business!'

Stanley stepped forward. 'He's right, Grace. You get on out of it.'

She looked appealingly towards Ben. 'Ben, you tell John . . .'

Ben shook his head firmly. 'I'm keeping out of it,' he assured her. 'I'm not poking my nose in where it's not wanted and nor should you. Hop it while the going's good.'

She made a last appeal. 'John, Fanny wasn't to blame at all. She was tricked into coming down. Stanley sent her a note and she thought it was from you — '

'I don't give a damn!' said John. 'I know who's to blame and I'll deal with him.'

Grace looked at Stanley.

'I'm not denying it,' he said hoarsely. 'It was my fault. Fanny had nothing to do with it.' He turned to Grace. 'Get out of here, Grace, for God's sake.'

But Grace stood her ground stubbornly, hoping that somehow her presence would prevent the fight which seemed inevitable. Then an idea occurred to her and she said suddenly, 'I'm going to get Mr Latimer! He should deal with Stanley, not you.'

John stepped forward and grabbed her arm with fingers of steel. 'You'll regret it if you do!' he hissed. 'If you won't go, then I'll have to put you where you can't meddle any more!' and before she could protest, he had dragged her into the stable and locked her into an empty stall.

'No, John!' she screamed. 'Don't you dare!'

She hammered on the door with her fists and screamed to be released, but quickly realized that no one would open it. From outside she could hear scuffles and blows and her imagination did the rest. She looked round frantically as her eyes became accustomed to the gloom and saw that the hay-loft above her extended along over the next stall. But that stall would hold another horse and she did not fancy trying to find a way out through there.

Perhaps further along she would find an empty stall with an unfastened door. She climbed up into the hay-loft from which Fanny had so recently fallen and scrambled along above several stalls until she found what she was looking for: an empty stall, with only the lower half of the door fastened. It was the work of seconds to climb down and let herself out.

In the yard, by the light of the lantern, Stanley and John were struggling together while Ben looked on unashamedly enjoying the downfall of his enemy.

As Grace cried out in horror, Stanley was thrown backwards and fell dazedly against the whitewashed wall of the stable. One of his eyes was closed and blood trickled from his mouth. As he slid to the ground, barely conscious, John hurled himself at him and, yanking him back to his feet, gave him another vicious punch in the stomach.

'John, don't!' screamed Grace. 'Oh, please, John. No more!'

Her brother gave no sign of having heard and Grace turned frantically to Ben.

'For heaven's sake, stop them!' she cried. 'He'll kill Stanley.'

Ben's eyes did not leave the two combatants as he said, 'He had it coming to him, the cocky bastard.'

'But he's going too far. John! Stop it, for God's sake! You'll kill him.'

Stanley sagged, but John held him upright with one massive hand and continued to punch him with the other. On his face was a look of such malevolence that for the first time in her life Grace was frightened of him. 'He's going to kill him,' she told herself. 'He'll go too far and kill him and then he'll be hanged. Oh, my God. I *must* stop him.'

Running forward, she clutched desperately as her brother's arm.

'Let him go, John,' she panted. 'He's had enough, you've punished him enough. He's smaller than you, anyway. Oh, for God's sake, let him alone.'

John elbowed her roughly away, but she regained her

balance and tried frantically to halt the rain of blows which he was inflicting on his unconscious adversary.

'John! That's enough, I say,' she screamed and in desperation began to flail at his back with her fists. She glared at Ben and cried, 'Don't just stand there gawking. Help me to pull them apart, can't you?'

Ben shook his head. 'More'n my life's worth,' he told her. 'I've never seen Mr Martins like this before.'

'Oh, you coward!'

But John was tiring . . . suddenly his rage evaporated and to her intense relief he let Stanley slump to the ground where he lay sprawled on his back on the cobbles, his face bruised and bleeding, his eyes closed, his breathing stertorous.

At least he was breathing, thought Grace, as she knelt beside him. 'Bring that lantern, Ben,' she cried, 'and don't argue with me.'

By the glow of the lantern they examined Stanley fearfully, and Grace could see that now even Ben was alarmed at the extent of the damage John had inflicted.

When at last she rose to her feet she discovered that her legs were trembling. John was standing a few yards away, his back to them, wiping his face and hands on his handkerchief.

Grace looked into Ben's shocked face. 'We shan't be able to hide this,' she told him. 'Stanley's in a bad way. Go up to the house and fetch Mr Latimer. Tell him it's urgent. Just say there's been some trouble and we shall need the doctor.'

'Why me?' he protested, unwilling to be the bearer of such bad news.

Grace looked at John for support but he was sitting on the mounting block with his head in his hands and obviously was going to be no help.

'Then I'll have to go,' she declared and waited hopefully for either John or Ben to demur. When they did not, there was nothing else for her to do but set off towards the house, bitterly regretting that she had not taken John's earlier advice to 'Get on out of it'.

*

Alex was in the library reading a newspaper and he called her in cheerfully enough, but one look at her stricken face removed his smile.

'What is it, Grace? I hope the children are – '

She broke in clumsily. 'No sir, it's not the children, but it's bad news. About one of the horses ... there's been some terrible trouble.'

His eyes darkened with apprehension. 'Not Caradox?'

'Yes, sir. He broke loose and ran away – '

Alex jumped to his feet and threw down the newspaper. 'Then we must go after him at once! Does Martins know about it?'

He was half-way to the door, but Grace moved swiftly to block his path. 'I'm dreadfully sorry,' she stammered, 'but it's too late ... that is, the horse has had to be put down. No, wait. Please, sir, don't go yet. You can't undo what's happened – and there's more to it. If you would only listen to me ... it's not easy.'

Something in her manner made him pause. He looked into her face, read there the panic she felt inside and was touched by her vulnerability.

'Why are you telling me all this?' he asked. 'I would have thought it Martins' job if one of the horses is involved.'

Grace took a deep breath and tried to sound calmer than she felt. 'Caradox broke his forelegs,' she said quietly.

'Caradox!' he cried. 'Oh, *not* Caradox!'

'John didn't want you to be the one to shoot him, knowing how much he means ... meant ... to you.'

'Oh, my God!'

She could not bear to look at his stricken face, but went on hurriedly. 'He didn't suffer long, but I'm afraid that afterwards there was a fight, because in a way it was Stanley Marcus' fault and John gave him a hiding and – oh, Mr Latimer, he really lost his temper and Stanley's badly hurt.'

'A good hiding? Goddammit, who does John think is master here? Who is he to dispense justice?'

'Sir, I think we should call the doctor.'

'The doctor! He's that bad?'

'I think so; he's hardly conscious.'

Alex swore under his breath and strode past her without another word. She ran after him as he hurried downstairs to make the telephone call and hovered nervously nearby until he had finished, then said breathlessly, 'Please, sir, will you consider how upset John was? I'm sure he . . .' She swallowed. ' . . . It was because of Caradox and knowing how you'd feel about it.'

Before he could answer, Virginia came out of the drawing room and looked at them in surprise.

'What's the matter, dear?' she asked Alex. 'You look terribly pale.'

'I'll explain later,' he told her abruptly. 'There's been some trouble in the stable. When the doctor arrives, please send him down to the yard at once.' He turned to Grace. 'I think you should go back to the nursery now, Miss Martins. You've done all you can, I'm sure, and I don't want you to be away from the children longer than is necessary. If I need to talk to you again, it will not be until the morning.'

As she turned to go he added, 'I don't relish your news, Miss Martins, but I appreciate the way you told me. It was a thankless task.'

'Thank you, sir.'

As Grace moved away in the direction of the nursery stairs, Virginia – keen to know more about what had happened – put out a hand to delay her, but Alex said, 'Please, Virginia, don't bother Miss Martins now. She is rather shocked.' To Grace he added, 'Make yourself a cup of tea and try to keep calm.'

'I was only going to ask her . . .' Virginia protested. But as Alex repeated that he would explain later, Grace took her chance and escaped thankfully upstairs. Alex was right, she *was* badly shocked. Already she could feel herself trembling and was eager to return to the comparative peace of the nursery where Fanny still waited to learn the success or otherwise of Grace's intervention on her behalf.

*

Later the next morning Virginia and Alex faced each other across the breakfast table as Fanny, red-eyed, brought the kedgeree to the table with carefully averted glance. She had been severely reprimanded for her part in the disaster, but at least the job of parlourmaid was still hers although Virginia had docked some of her wages to 'bring home to you the seriousness of your behaviour'.

As she scuttled thankfully from the room, she knew that the fate of Stanley and John still hung in the balance, however.

Virginia helped herself to kedgeree, but Alex left his plate empty. He looked pale and strained and his eyes were dark with anger and loss.

'If you think,' he continued, 'that I shall allow Martins to remain here after that callous attack on young Marcus, you are sadly mistaken. The man went berserk – you heard what the doctor said. Marcus has massive bruises and he's going to be laid up for weeks with that leg.'

Virginia toyed with her food. 'Marcus deserved a whipping, Alex,' she said, 'and you know it. You are just using this as a way to get rid of the carriage because you know I prefer it to that awful motor. I can tell you this, Alex – if you get rid of the carriage, you will make me virtually a prisoner in my own house, because I will *not* set foot in that contraption. From what we heard from Fanny, Marcus was obviously the instigator of the whole senseless affair, and if I had been in Martins' shoes I would have done the same thing. I don't know how you can take Marcus' side against Martins' when your favourite horse lies dead. If you are going to punish Martins for his perfectly understandable treatment of Marcus, then Marcus should be punished for his part. He's cost you a valuable horse – '

'You know it's not the value of the horse. He was my favourite.'

'Then you should understand how Martins felt. He wanted to avenge his death. Marcus has been nothing but trouble ever since he arrived here with his trumped-up pretensions. He couldn't drive and you had to waste money on sending him to London . . .'

Alex nodded wearily. Everything she said was true, yet the thought of the beating Marcus had sustained sickened him and his heart rebelled against keeping a man who was capable of such violence. Yet he was forced to admit that his wife's argument was sound. Each of the two men had transgressed, and yet for each there were mitigating circumstances. Martins had been sorely provoked and Marcus had originally been guilty of nothing more than a foolish trick. Fate had intervened to magnify its significance in a way which could never have been anticipated. In the cool light of morning Alex was fair enough to acknowledge these facts, yet deep down he wanted to rid himself of both protagonists.

'And don't forget Fanny,' Virginia argued. 'You've forgiven her, although it might be argued that she is the real culprit because she was the one who fell. If she had had her wits about her, she need never have fallen and – '

'It's a mercy *she* wasn't injured.'

'Exactly. But who would you have blamed for that, Alex? Her own carelessness or Marcus for his foolishness? If he hadn't planned what one can only assume was a seduction – '

'It was a joke that misfired,' he broke in.

'Do you call the seduction of one of the maids a joke?'

'I didn't mean it in that way and well you know it.'

Virginia forced a smile. 'You're not eating anything, Alex.'

'I'm not very hungry.'

'Oh Alex, don't let us quarrel over this.'

She dare not push him too far, she reminded herself, but she must intervene on behalf of Martins. Were he dismissed, she would find it difficult to meet Larry Scott without arousing suspicion. She paid Martins handsomely for his discretion although no word on the subject had ever passed between them, but now she was forced to admit how vulnerable this made her. If Alex dismissed Martins, he might – just *might* – reveal her own various deceptions. She hoped he would be too chivalrous to betray her, but if sufficiently resentful he might prove less than loyal. She grew cold at the thought of it as her problems with Nanny Webster loomed large in her thoughts. Without Martins, her occasional trips to Challis Court would also be more difficult to arrange. No. Martins *must* remain at Berwick House; she needed him.

'It's all most unfortunate,' she said, 'but we must keep a sense of proportion. What will you do about poor Caradox? You can't let him go for – ' She did not finish the sentence.

'Of course not.'

'Why not bury him in the grounds – in the paddock, perhaps. We could put up a small stone. He wasn't just a horse – not to us, Alex.'

She saw with a thrill of hope that Alex's attention had been temporarily diverted. If only she could soften his anguish at the horse's death, she might defuse his anger towards those responsible.

'You must excuse me,' he said abruptly and he pushed aside his plate and stood up with a sigh. Impulsively, she stretched out a hand towards him.

'Poor Alex,' she said with a genuine rush of compassion. 'I know how much Caradox meant to you. I really am so sorry, my dear.'

He took her hand briefly in his and said, 'I'll postpone my decision until I can think more calmly about what's happened. But I have to go now – I've a meeting with Chambers in the Estate Office and I'm already late.'

'And you will keep Martins?' The words escaped her in spite of her intentions to say no more on the subject. 'He's been with us for such a long time.'

'Perhaps.'

It was Guy who finally persuaded his son to keep on both groom and chauffeur. At Virginia's request, the old man spoke up strongly in their defence and convinced Alex that circumstances really had played an inordinately large place in the affair and that what blame must be apportioned to the human element should be shared equally between the three participants. They had all three learned a hard lesson, he argued, and their relief at being allowed to remain at Berwick House would earn their undying gratitude and ensure their future loyalty. 'Let justice be tempered with mercy,' he added in a rare burst of eloquence, and Alex was finally won over.

Marcus and Martins both suffered similar deductions from their wages by way of punishment but there, to the intense relief of all concerned, the matter was allowed to rest.

Chapter Fifteen

Kitty, Grace's afternoon helper, decided to leave to get married and no one could be found to replace her, so Grace had her hands full during the next few months. Her diary was temporarily neglected, but in early September something happened which inspired her to bring it up to date.

1st September. Florrie died last week and was buried yesterday. I went to the funeral at Alfred's request, although I do hate them, and he asked me to marry him again. He looked so miserable that I almost took pity on him, but I know it would never do. I dropped a few hints about Fanny, though, for John has been so beastly to her since Caradox died that night and I don't think he will ever look at her in that way now. He is almost unapproachable and looks so unhappy.

Stanley told me on the QT that he is trying to find a new job, partly because he and John are at daggers drawn and partly because he wants to better himself. The trouble is that he will have to ask for a reference and then Alex will know he wants to leave. It's very awkward for him.

I feel so sorry for Alex with so many worries. Old Mr Latimer's brother is lingering on and the housekeeper keeps sending for him (Alex) to go to Devon. He's just gone away again for three days. I hate Berwick House when he's not here.

Lucien came home last month, but only for a long weekend. He's just the same as ever. The wedding is planned for 1st October and Virginia has offered to let them marry from Berwick House, because Eleanor's mother has been injured in a hunting accident and probably won't be well enough to organize it from their home. There is great excitement here. Cook is knocked all of a heap. After saying for so long that she wished it could be held here, she now says she doesn't know how she'll ever manage! But secretly I think she's pleased. There will be a marquee on the lawn and a small orchestra. Lucien kept joking about his 'big day' and pretending to fuss over what he would wear. He had us all in stitches. Only Virginia does not seem thrilled and we all know why. Her mind is on other things – or should I say another person.

They have put George's name down for Bramleigh Grange – a prep. school. I can't bear the thought of him going away in less than two years as he is still such a baby, but I suppose he must. If Alex thinks it best, then I expect he's right.

Certainly I shall have no say in the matter, and George seems quite happy at the prospect, but Victoria will miss him dreadfully and so will I.

Good night, Alex. Sleep well. (Fanny says they hardly ever sleep together now; she knows everything, that girl. She goes out late at night to see which windows are lit, but one of these days they'll catch her and then she'll be sorry.) Dear Alex, I love you. Come back soon.

Two days later Guy and Virginia were together in the morning room when he was surprised to receive a letter from his younger son which he opened with some misgivings. Lucien was not in the habit of putting pen to paper, finding it time-consuming and preferring to use the telephone.

As Guy had expected, the contents were unpalatable. He scanned the pages at a great pace and then reread the letter more slowly.

Dear Father,

This letter is not an easy one for me to write and I have deliberated whether or not I should write it at all, but maybe if you know the facts you will be able to deal with the situation constructively, although how I cannot imagine. Two weeks ago Eleanor was in London visiting her dressmaker, and after the fitting she went to the Dorchester where she had arranged to meet her sister for tea. Imagine her horror when who should she see at another table but Virginia and Larry Scott! She was doubly surprised and rather hurt, because Larry Scott had specifically told her family that he would not be visiting England until next year, when he plans to make the maiden crossing on the *Titanic*.

Eleanor says (and I believe her absolutely – why should she lie?) that Virginia and Mr Scott are obviously having an affair. They had eyes only for each other. Before she could think what to do, they left – fortunately without seeing her. The question is, should Alex be told or will that precipitate a crisis? Should we pretend ignorance and hope for the best? If I do not hear from you, I shall know you have decided to take no action and will never refer to the matter again. Eleanor says these passionate affairs often burn themselves out, but it is a risk. Suppose it continues?

Eleanor did not want me to write to you, but I thought it best. If you wish, you can tear up the letter and say nothing. The last thing I want to do is hurt either Alex or Virginia, but we might be saving them a worse hurt. Surely she would never be fool enough to leave Alex, but if he finds out will he divorce her? Eleanor has told *no one else* about this, so the secret is safe for the present, although it frightens me to imagine how many others will 'bump into them' if they continue to flaunt their relationship in so public a place as the Dorchester.

Your reluctant son, Lucien.

Guy glanced from the letter to Virginia's bent head and a great wave of shocked disenchantment engulfed him, followed immediately by one of fear. He loathed disruptions in his private life and if what Lucien told him was true – and it must be – then the tranquillity of his days might well be sadly interrupted. A selfish thought, but nonetheless valid for all that.

Autumn sunshine filled the room, which was heavy

298

with the scent of late roses. Virginia, looking very attractive in coffee-coloured lace, was reading a letter of her own. He frowned. Now that he came to think about it, she had received a great many letters lately — all allegedly from an old school-friend with whom she had recently made contact. His glance lingered on her slim neck where it curved delightfully into the dark hair which was drawn upward at the nape and flowered into curls on top of her well-shaped head. She was half turned away from him, but he saw that her lips framed the words she read. The affection he had always felt for her was suddenly replaced by anger which spurted through him. Was she daring to read a letter from a lover in front of her father-in-law? Had he been duped morning after morning by these innocent letters? What audacity! He felt as if he would choke, wanting to snatch the letter from her well-manicured hand and shout, 'It's my son you're deceiving, you wicked hussy!' Yet this was Virginia, the mother of his beloved grandchildren; Virginia who had always been such a credit to the family; Virginia whom he had admired for so many years and about whom he had often cherished such delightful fantasies. Virginia, his elder son's wife.

He said suddenly, 'You're smiling.'

Virginia glanced up and her dark eyes gleamed. 'She writes an amusing letter,' she said carelessly.

She followed the remark with a soft laugh and again Guy experienced an unpleasant feeling of betrayal. Now that he knew, it was all so damned obvious. She had been making a fool of him, reading the letters in front of him. Why on earth had he never thought it odd that the letters of a woman friend should be read so avidly — and reread so frequently? He cursed his blindness. He had been an insensitive fool . . . a stupid, blind old fool!

Virginia was suddenly a stranger to him. Her face and form were familiar, but her mind belonged to a different person; to a woman with a lover; to an unfaithful wife; to an erring mother. It was all so incredible. Unbelievable. Again he fought down the impulse to call her bluff, but if he challenged her he would see the truth in her eyes and he shrank from that.

As though aware of the coldness gathering within him, Virginia glanced up at him.

'Is anything the matter?' she asked, the offending letter held loosely in her hands. 'You sounded...' She shrugged. 'I don't know. Different.'

'There's nothing wrong with me,' he said, but even to his own ears his voice sounded unfamiliar. He knew he ought to smile at her, but his lips refused to form themselves into the required shape. His throat felt tight and dry and he could not swallow comfortably. He wanted a brandy, but if he asked for one at this time of day she would *know* there was something wrong. He was beginning to tremble and felt slightly nauseous.

'Guy?'

With a start, he realized that she was staring at him. He managed a brief nod.

'Aren't you well?' she asked.

'I'm fine. Never felt fitter.'

Her concern for his welfare – was all that a pretence also? Did she care a jot for him? How did she write about him to that scoundrel Scott? 'The silly old fool', maybe, or worse: 'the old buffer'. To his horror, tears sprang to his eyes and he felt helpless and confused – just as he had felt when his familiar and much-loved nanny had been sent off into a reluctant retirement. Nanny Cape – that small, stout, elderly soul who had loved him so wholeheartedly and who had taken the place of the mother who spent so much time abroad that he hardly knew her. He had felt safe with Nanny Cape. He remembered how he had sat at the nursery window with his eyes full of tears, watching for the new nanny to arrive. He had been six then and his mother had urged him not to cry. 'Pull yourself together,' she had told him. 'Be a little man.' He had felt lost and uncertain then and he felt the same way now. The unknown was always uncomfortable and he no longer knew or trusted Virginia.

She had returned to her letter, but now she folded it

carefully – *too* carefully, he realized, for a letter from a woman friend. He had intended to mull over the contents of Lucien's letter and only act upon it after long and serious consideration. That would certainly be the best course of action. He was shocked therefore to hear his own voice say suddenly, 'Someone saw you with Larry Scott!'

There was an electric silence as the accusing words rang out between them, stark and irretrievable.

He saw Virginia blanch and saw the shock that wiped the softness from her eyes.

As he waited for her answer he asked himself dazedly why he had uttered those terrible words. Why had he blurted it out like that? It was rash and he had not intended to do it, but the enormity of the knowledge and responsibility had somehow overwhelmed him. It seemed an eternity before Virginia spoke and then she merely shrugged.

'Who was it?' she asked.

'Eleanor Sharp.'

'The little cat!'

'No, no.' It seemed important for him to set the record straight. 'She didn't want to say anything. This letter is from Lucien.'

'Lucien!'

Now he saw that the knowledge wounded her.

'Where did she see us?'

'The Dorchester – but does that matter?' He drew a long, quavering breath and wished his heart would beat less loudly for fear she heard it and realized how afraid he was. He must try to keep his head, for Alex's sake, but he suspected he had already lost control of the situation. What was the phrase Lucien had used? Ah yes. 'Precipitate a crisis'. Yes, that is what he had done. He had made a bad mistake, but unintentionally. The words had just slipped out – had somehow spoken themselves. Now that it was too late, he knew he should have confided in Alex. Or maybe written to that blackguard, Scott, demanding that he end the liaison. Or perhaps . . .

There was a strange buzzing in his head and he put a

301

hand to his forehead where beads of sweat were beginning to form.

Virginia's jaw tightened as she stood up. 'And what do you intend to do about it?' she demanded.

Guy looked at her with unwilling admiration. Dammit all! She was a cool customer. He thought of his own wife and knew that in the same circumstances she would have given in under the strain.

He shook his head, finding it hard to breathe.

'I don't know,' he mumbled. 'The letter – it's only just arrived. I have to think . . .'

'You'll tell Alex I suppose,' she said, her expression grim. 'Well, Guy, if you do, I think you should know that I shall leave him!'

'Leave him?' He looked up at her, but there was a rushing sound inside his head and his eyes were so blurred that he could not see her clearly. '*Leave* Alex?' he whispered. 'Leave the children? You'd leave the *children*?'

'Larry Scott wants me to marry him. So far I have refused, but if Alex knows then it will all be impossible and I shall have to go.'

Vaguely he realized that she was challenging him – but was she bluffing? Was she . . .

An agonizing pain materialized suddenly inside his chest. He groaned aloud and the sound frightened him. Then he cried, 'Nanny Cape!' and toppled slowly forward on to the floor . . .

Virginia telephoned for Doctor Collett and then she read and destroyed Lucien's letter. When the doctor arrived Guy was still unconscious and a heart attack was diagnosed, but he was hopeful that the patient might make a reasonable recovery. Six days later, however, Guy had another attack. Although less severe than the first, the old man had already been seriously weakened and the doctor warned the family to expect the worst. Somehow Guy clung to life, but no one could pretend that he had a very long future.

The old man could remember little of the events leading up to his first heart attack, so Virginia knew that her secret was safe — at least for the time being. When Lucien received no answer he would presume his father had decided not to act on the information in his letter. If ever he discovered that the letter had been the cause of the attack, he would have to live with the guilt. Virginia had no sympathy for him. Furious with Eleanor and Lucien for their betrayal, she used the gravity of Guy's health as a reason for withdrawing her offer to hold the wedding in Berwick House. She would never tell them she had seen the letter, so they would never know that her change of heart had been prompted by pure malice. For Virginia, however, the last-minute disruption of their wedding was her revenge and the proverbial claims for its sweetness were not exaggerated.

*

It was early in October. Alex was in the library supposedly working on his accounts, but in reality he was standing at the window staring out over the lawn with unseeing eyes. He was depressed by his father's unhappy state and by the realization that his death could not be far distant. His mother's death had shaken him badly, but he had never been as close to her as he was to his father. A quiet, gentle woman, his mother had always seemed beautiful but remote, and even as a child he had been overawed by her apparent fragility. His father had made an effort to offer him companionship, had taken him fishing and taught him to ride and shoot. Guy had treated him with the respect due between two adults, whereas his mother had always called him 'my darling boy'. He could not imagine Berwick House without his father, and now that Guy was confined to bed the house was already much quieter and emptier. When the old man's bedroom was also empty . . . Alex could not bear to think about that.

He was glad that Virginia had insisted on cancelling the plans for Lucien's wedding, for Alex's heart was heavy with dread and he did not feel like playing host at so festive an occasion. Now he tried to recall his father in his prime — a bluff, dashing, figure with a boisterous voice. He could fill a room with his personality, and as a boy Alex had longed to emulate him, but it was Lucien who would finally step into the old man's shoes for Alex was made from a different mould, taking after the gentle mother he had never really known. With a deep sigh, he turned back to his desk and his thoughts returned to a day many years earlier when, in this room, he had told his father that he wanted to marry Virginia.

'A penniless widow?' Guy had roared. 'Are you out of your mind? You've the country's wealthiest virgins to choose from! I won't allow it, Alex, I simply won't allow it.'

But at last he had agreed to meet Virginia and his defences had crumbled. The dark-haired beauty, tragically widowed, had stolen his heart and he had welcomed her into the family.

Alex sat down at his desk, trying to push the thought of Virginia to the back of his mind. He was losing his wife's love and he was losing his father. He felt alone, adrift in unchartered waters.

As he picked up his pen, there was a knock at the door. 'Come in.'

His heart sank as the chauffeur came into the room, resplendent in his uniform, his peaked hat clutched in his hands. More trouble, thought Alex wearily, and could guess what was coming.

'Yes, Marcus, what is it?'

Stanley approached the desk. He was still very pale and moved with a slight limp from the damage his knee had received during his fight with the groom.

'It's like this, Mr Latimer,' he began. 'I'm sure you'll understand if I say that things between me and Mr Martins are not very good now and never will be.'

He waited for Alex to comment, but when his employer did not do so he went on. 'I know you said let bygones be bygones, but it doesn't work like that in real life, sir. To tell you the truth, I still hate him and he hates me, so I've been thinking I'd like to apply elsewhere, and I have, but if you won't see fit to give me a reference, I don't stand an earthly.'

'Hmm. I see.' Alex ran a hand distractedly through his hair. 'I should hate to lose you, Marcus. You're a good chauffeur.'

Stanley shrugged. 'It's him or me, and he won't budge. No, it's me that's got to move on – and I have taken the liberty of writing to someone else. I saw an advertisement in *The Motor* a few weeks ago for a second chauffeur. They've got *two* cars, so there's a chance for promotion later on – leastways, that is what it says. A chance of promotion. So then I'd be first chauffeur with another bloke under me, so to speak.'

'Where is this, Marcus? And who is it?'

'Sir Dudley Bray in Frome in Somerset.' He could not resist adding, 'He's got a Rolls and a Bentley.'

'And the wages?' asked Alex, ignoring the boast.

'A bit better. Not much – but there's this chance of promotion. It's not marvellous or anything, but the truth is that I can't stand much more of John Martins and I'm afraid we'll come to blows again. I can't hold my tongue indefinitely and he tries my patience that much I – '

Alex nodded. 'Yes, I can imagine it's very awkward. Will there be a period of probation?'

'Three months, and then a small rise. The way I see it, the first chauffeur might be elderly and due to retire – or he might be moving on up the ladder, so to speak. If you *could* see your way to giving me a reference . . .'

'I will, Marcus, and I won't refer to the . . . the trouble you've had with Martins. I don't want to give the wrong impression. Purely from a work point of view, you deserve a decent reference.'

He saw the relief in Marcus' eyes as he began to stammer his thanks.

'Collect it in the morning then. But a word of advice, Marcus. Keep your head, or you'll ruin your chances. You've still got some growing up to do and the sooner you do it, the better. So no more silly pranks. I'm telling you this for your own good.'

Stanley had the grace to look chastened. 'I know. And I'm very grateful.'

Alex nodded. 'Off you go, then.'

305

'Thank you . . . sir.'

As the door closed, Alex sighed. More changes! How he hated them. Two years ago, if he had thought about it he would have considered himself a fortunate man in a settled and secure world. Now it was slowly but surely falling apart.

My sweet Larry, [wrote Virginia on the tenth of October]

I hardly know how to write the next few lines. I cannot judge how you will react to the news. Indeed I hardly know how *I* feel about it myself but, dearest, I am with child and it is yours. Those last few hours we spent together have given us a child. Can you imagine how confused I feel? Delight and joy that I am bearing your first child; shock and fear that you will be angry.

My precious Larry, I pray that you do not feel anything but pleasure at the knowledge that our love has borne fruit. You must believe me when I tell you that I did not expect such a thing to happen, for the doctor told me it was most unlikely that I should ever conceive again – but you have made it possible. Of course, I will not tell Alex that the child is not his. That will be our secret, my darling. Please, *please* write to tell me you are happy. I shall cherish our child while it lies within me, and when it is born it will be treated equally with George and Victoria. I promise you that.

I am unwell, suffering this beastly sickness, but I suffer it gladly for your sake.

We can never marry, but if – as you so often assure me – you remain single, at least you will know you have a child.

Lucien's wedding is on the twenty-first and we have all been invited to stay with the Sharps for a long weekend. I shall not be able to go, as I could not stand the journey, and will therefore be alone at Berwick House while they are all away and will telephone you then. Do not worry about me, darling. I am well cared for. Just remember that if I cannot be with you in body, I am with you in spirit and that you have my heart. You are my husband in all but name.

Very soon I shall have to tell Alex I am with child, but have no fear he will accept it as his. I promise you there will be no problem.

As soon as I am well enough, I will find an excuse to come to London. It will be such bliss to be in your arms again.

My thoughts and love are with you always,
                                      Your own Virginia

*

The morning before the family was due to leave for Berkshire, Virginia broke the news to her husband that the indisposition from which she had been suffering was in fact a fourth pregnancy. His delight at the unexpected news made her feel guilty and that in turn made her irritable, but she managed to subdue her feelings and smiled bravely up at him as she begged to be excused the long journey to Berkshire.

'But of course you mustn't travel,' Alex told her. 'Has the doctor given you any indication of when the child is due? George and Victoria will be so thrilled. Oh, Virginia, this is the best news you could have given me. I've been feeling so low – so uneasy – but now . . .' He smiled broadly, took hold of her hand and kissed it. 'Tell me you're pleased too, Virginia. You haven't said you are.'

'Of course I am, Alex. I couldn't be happier. It's just this wretched sickness – '

'But that will pass; it did before. After all these years of thinking we'd never have another child! It's marvellous news. May I tell Father? It will give him something cheerful to think about.'

'Break it to him gently then, Alex. You know he mustn't be excited.'

'But *happy* excitement can't hurt him, surely? As for the wedding, we shall have to go of course, although Lucien will no doubt be bitterly disappointed that his favourite sister-in-law is absent!'

Virginia thought otherwise. Lucien and Eleanor might

307

well have found her presence embarrassing in view of what they knew about her, and would probably be relieved that she was to stay at home. They would also be intrigued to know whose child it was she was carrying, but could hardly expect to satisfy their curiosity on that point. No one knew the answer to that question, but Virginia was certain in her own mind that Larry Scott was the father. At his insistence, she had promised not to share her husband's bed too frequently, but in fact she had continued to do so purely as an insurance against just such a predicament. Legally it *might* be Alex's child, but she was sure it was Larry's. In one way she was glad that Lucien knew about her relationship with Larry Scott, for now he also knew that *he* was no longer the centre of her universe. Their relationship would never be the same again, so he would not be too disappointed in her failure to be at the wedding. Eleanor would probably be *pleased*. Virginia gave an imperceptible shrug of her elegant shoulders. She would not be missed, but Alex was going to be Lucien's best man and George and Victoria were to grace the occasion as page-boy and bridesmaid respectively.

'*You* tell the children, Alex,' she said. 'About the baby, I mean. It is due around the end of May, so perhaps it is a little early to tell them. They will get so impatient. You know how children are. Do let's wait a month or two.'

'Just as you like.' He hid his disappointment. 'Yes, of course, I suppose that's sensible. I ought to have a talk with the doctor; we mustn't have you taking any risks.'

'Oh, don't fuss so, Alex. Doctor Collett will keep an eye on me. We'll keep the news to ourselves for the time being; it's early days yet.'

They talked for a while longer, but as he left to go down to breakfast she shook her head at his retreating back and snuggled down into the bedclothes whispering Larry Scott's name to herself.

*

Guy was propped up in bed looking very pale and thin.

His eyelids drooped over his eyes and his bony fingers on the counterpane were grey and still, like the hands of a man already dead. As always, Alex experienced a pang at the sight of him and marvelled that he had survived another night.

'Good morning, Father, I have some good news for you,' Alex told him. 'News to bring the colour back into your cheeks. Guess what it is?'

'Guess?' The old man's voice was scarcely more than a whisper.

'Yes.' He pulled up the bedside chair and leaned his elbows on the bed. 'What could happen at Berwick House which would make *everyone* happy? Even the servants!'

The bony fingers plucked erratically at the counterpane. 'A guess?' he repeated. 'Something here at Berwick.'

'That's right.'

'Oh dear. Let me see.'

The old man's hair was much whiter than it had been before the attacks and there were unhealthy blotches on his face, pale but distinct splashes of brown pigment. Alex felt a rush of pity for the once proud man.

'I give up,' whispered Guy. 'Tell me.'

'We're going to have another child! *You're* going to have a new grandchild! In May, probably.'

'But I thought the doctor . . .' Guy shook his head in confusion. 'Another child? Oh, but . . .' He stared at Alex with an unfathomable expression in his eyes. 'Virginia is expecting a child, you say?'

'Yes. I thought you would be thrilled.' Alex was puzzled by his father's lack of enthusiasm. 'Don't you want another grandchild?'

The old man seemed uncertain. He shook his head and repeated, 'Virginia's with child?'

'Yes, she is. It's due next May.'

Guy turned his head slightly so that he was not looking at his son directly. 'That's splendid,' he said at last, his voice flat. 'I expect you're pleased.'

'Naturally I am. You know I have always wanted a big family and three is bigger than two!' He laughed.

'We'll tell the children nearer the time. I'm longing to see their faces. Do you remember when we told George about Victoria? He was only a baby himself really and couldn't understand. Suddenly there was a crying baby in the house – and Victoria *did* cry for the first few months! He was so jealous, poor little lad. It's a wonder they get on so well together now. They do seem very fond of each other . . . Father?'

The old man did not appear to be listening and Alex wondered again at his surprising lack of interest. It occurred to him suddenly that perhaps his father did not expect to be still alive in May and that might account for his attitude.

'You have something to live for now,' he said with determined cheerfulness. 'You've got to fight back, Father. None of this leaving your food. Mrs Wade says you never finish up anything she sends you, no matter how small the portion. No wonder you're fading away.' He leaned forward and his tone changed. 'You mustn't let go, Father. The doctor says it's a matter of will-power. Now you must work hard to build up your strength so that by the time the new baby arrives you're fit enough to dandle him – or her – on your knee. We can't have a new baby with no grandfather and babies have to be dandled. We're relying on you!'

Guy nodded vaguely and his lips moved.

'Are you tired, Father? Is that it?'

'Yes, that's it. I'm tired. I don't feel so well. It's my head.'

'Your head aches?'

'Yes . . . I mean "No".' He lifted a trembling hand and pointed towards the window. 'The light.'

'Is the sunshine too bright? Is that it? I'll close the curtains a little.' He got up and pulled them across so as to cut out some of the light. 'How's that?'

Guy nodded and closed his eyes as Fanny bustled into the room with a tray. She beamed at them both and said cheerfully, 'Cook's sent you a glass of warm milk and honey, Mr Latimer. She says you're to drink it all up.'

310

She laughed. 'I think she wants to fatten you up for Christmas!'

Alex left them, but as he closed the bedroom door behind him he made up his mind to consult the doctor again on the question of a resident nurse. Virginia was now in no fit state to look after an invalid. He went downstairs still puzzling over his father's disappointing reaction to the news but then, with an effort, pushed the matter to the back of his mind and began to think about the most pressing problems which would need his attention during the coming day.

*

Later that night Fanny and Dot sat up in their respective beds. Only an inch of candle remained and that was spluttering. Dot screwed up her eyes as she struggled by the dim light to pick up a fallen stitch.

'I wish I'd never started this,' she grumbled. 'I should have chosen something a bit easier, like a blanket for the pram.'

'That's not easier,' said Fanny. 'It would take you ages.'

'Yes, but it's all straight knitting; just one big square. This bonnet is going to get really tricky because it has to be shaped.'

'You can always undo it and start again — tell your sister you couldn't manage the bonnet. She'll understand.'

'But I *want* to do a bonnet.'

Fanny grinned. 'But will you get it done by the time the baby arrives? You started weeks ago and all you do is unravel it.'

Dot pulled a face. 'I can't help it. I'm doing my best. I never could knit; my grandmother used to say I was too impatient. She tried to teach me but — ' She shrugged, then muttered, 'Oh, blow it!' and threw it petulantly on to the bed. 'I'll finish it later.' Drawing up her knees, she clasped her arms around them and looked across at Fanny. 'So,' she said, 'are you going to tell Grace?'

Fanny was leaning back against the pillow, but now she blew out the candle stub and snuggled down under the blankets. 'I suppose I'll have to,' she said, 'in case she finds out and gets mad because I didn't. I hope she's not upset.'

'Why should she be? She doesn't want him, so why should she object? I wish he wanted to take me to the Social. I like him.'

Fanny considered. 'He has got rather big ears,' she admitted. 'Big ears and big hands, but – '

'Big anything else?' asked Dot innocently.

Fanny gave a scream of laughter and then said, 'Dot! You're dreadful, you really are.'

'You are a lucky beggar, Fanny.'

'I nearly *died* when he asked me,' said Fanny. ' "May I have the pleasure of your company at the Post Office Social?" Just like that. All formal and as if he thought I might say "No". I tried to look as if I wasn't sure. I was going to say, "Can I think about it?" or something like that, but then I thought he might lose interest and ask someone else.'

'Like *me!*'

'Well, maybe,' said Fanny, although in fact she did not think this very likely.

Alfred Harris, having finally given up on Grace, had turned his attentions towards Fanny who was secretly glad that his mother was not alive to disapprove. A children's nanny had been bad enough, but a parloumaid as a daughter-in-law would be unthinkable! Fanny knew that Alfred was an only child, so she assumed Florrie had left all her worldly goods to her son.

Her sudden interest in Alfred Harris had followed much heart-searching on her part. Sadly John Martins had ceased to feature in her plans for the future since the débâcle in the stables in which she had featured so disastrously. He had refused to discuss her part in the incident and Fanny finally and reluctantly admitted to herself that any chance she might have had of a romantic attachment in that direction had been irretrievably lost. She had shed many bitter tears before coming to terms with her loss, but now Alfred had suddenly turned to her and she was wise enough to see that although physically he was not in the same class as John Martins, he *was* what Cook called 'a good catch' and she was trying hard to see him in a more glamorous light.

She said, 'His eyes are sort of soulful, don't you think?'

'You used to say he had fish eyes,' Dot reminded her rather unkindly. 'A big sad fish – that's how you described him once.'

'I did *not!*'

'You *did*. Cook heard you. So did Sid and me. That's three witnesses.'

'Well, *I* don't remember saying any such thing.'

'Because Cook said you were jealous because he fancied Grace and not you. So you see, you *did* say it.'

'So what if I did! I've changed my mind.'

'Whatever will you wear to the Social?'

'My blue sprigged, I suppose; it's the only one I've got, more's the pity. Do you think they'll all be very grand? I do hope not.'

'Sure to be.' Aggrieved because she alone lacked a beau, Dot refused to be sympathetic. 'You'll be like Cinderella – after midnight, I mean, not before.'

'Meow! Meow!' Fanny sighed deeply. 'I might ask Grace if she'd lend me her new silk, the one Mr Latimer gave her.'

'So you can spill lemonade down it? I bet she won't; I wouldn't if I was her.'

'I wish he'd give me a silk dress.'

'If wishes were horses . . .' It was Dot's turn to sigh. 'I wish Stanley wasn't leaving. It's all going sour, d'you know that. Everyone falling out or wanting to leave. I like Stanley. Now he really *is* good-looking.'

'Meaning?' Fanny rose to the bait.

'Nothing,' said Dot.

'Meaning Alfred isn't? Is that what you mean?'

'You said it. I didn't.'

'You just jealous, Dot. So I'll forgive you.'

Dot searched for a smart reply and, unable to find one, slid further under the bedclothes with a loud sniff. 'Who cares about a stupid Social?' she muttered. 'I just want to get some sleep.'

Chapter Sixteen

Virginia was in the garden half-heartedly pruning roses when Fanny appeared to inform her that she was wanted on the telephone.

'Well, who is it?' she asked. 'I've told you repeatedly to ask the caller's name. Did you do that?'

'Yes, ma'am.'

'And – ?'

'He wouldn't give it, ma'am,' said Fanny.

'He?' Virginia nearly dropped the pruning shears and her left hand went to her throat in a gesture of agitation. Fanny looked her straight in the eyes and said, 'It sounded like Mr Scott, ma'am – and he sounded rather upset.'

Virginia's eyes had widened with shock, but after a few seconds she managed to control her features and said unconvincingly, 'Mr Scott? But he's in America. You must be mistaken.'

'It wasn't a transatlantic call or anything like that. He sounded ever so near . . . just down the road, almost.'

Virginia felt the colour drain from her face as she fumbled with her gardening gloves and handed them to Fanny with hands that shook slightly.

'Well,' she said brightly, 'maybe he's come to England again – if it is him, that is.' She took a few steps towards the French windows and then stopped. 'Upset, did you say?'

'Yes, ma'am. Sort of cross.'

'Oh.' Virginia thought frantically. 'I'm sure it *can't* be Mr Scott,' she said, 'but whoever it is, you had better say that I'm not available. He probably wants to speak to my husband – whoever he is.' She now felt the colour flood back into her face and was angry with herself for allowing the parlourmaid to witness her confusion.

'He asked for *you*, ma'am,' Fanny persisted. ' "Tell

314

your *mistress* someone wants to talk to her." They were his words. He rang yesterday too, but he asked if Mr Latimer was home and then when I said "Yes" he rang off. It was the same voice. He asked the same question today and when I said Mr Latimer was out, he said – '

'Yes, yes. I see,' said Virginia, putting a hand to her head. 'You can go, Fanny. Thank you.' Still she remained irresolute.

'Shall I tell Mr Scott you're coming to the telephone?'

'Oh . . .' She nodded. 'Yes, tell whoever it is that I shall come in – no, I'll go now. You go back to the kitchen.' She quickened her pace.

'I was laying up lunch, ma'am, in the dining room,' Fanny corrected her.

'Go to the kitchen, I say – and shut the door.' Virginia's voice was shrill with nervous excitement.

Fanny allowed a knowing look to settle on her face. 'Oh yes, I see, ma'am,' she added innocently. 'Shall I lay an extra place for Mr Scott?'

Virginia stopped so suddenly that Fanny, hurrying behind her, nearly bumped into her.

'Certainly not. Whoever it is will not be coming here.'

She went through the drawing room and out into the hall and, picking up the receiver and rest, waited until Fanny had obediently disappeared.

'Larry? My God, have you gone out of your mind?' she cried. 'How *dare* you ring me here, after all I've said. That wretched girl recognized your voice! She *knows* who you are.'

His voice crackled down the line, sharp and clear. 'Cut that out, Virginia. Who the hell cares what she knows? I have to talk to you. We have to meet. You can't expect – '

'Larry, she knows it's you. She said so. Suppose she – '

'For God's sake, Virginia, forget the girl. When can I see you?'

'Where are you?'

'At the Dorchester, of course. Where did you think I was?'

'Fanny said you were so near. I thought maybe you'd

315

come down to Beaulieu or Lyndhurst. Oh, Larry, you sound so *angry*. Please don't be like this; I can't bear it.'

'*You* can't bear it? What about me? I'm supposed to hang about month after month waiting for you to make up your damned mind – '

'Larry!' she gasped.

'Oh hell! I'm sorry. I didn't mean to shout at you, but what kind of man do you think I am? I'm not made of wood. I love you and I want to marry you. I offer you the whole world and you turn me down. Then you write and say you're having our child! Jesus, Virginia! You'll *have* to marry me now. Alex is going to know; it will be out in the open – and you write me a letter like that. Don't you *know* what's happened? I don't think you quite realize the significance of the baby. You're going to have to tell him and you're going to have to leave him. He'll throw you out anyway. My God, Virginia, when I think of those few brief hours we had together. Can't you imagine how I feel. I want to throw my hat in the air and shout it to the world. Do you know how many times I've read your letter?'

'Larry, please darling. Let me get a word in edgeways.'

'No, I won't, Virginia! You'll hear me out. You say the child is ours and yet you daren't tell Alex it's not his. How the hell could it possibly be his? You told me – you *promised* me – you weren't sleeping with him. Either he's very slow on the uptake – and I don't think he is – or you lied to me. What the hell's going on down there, Virginia?'

'Darling, I can't discuss this over the telephone. I meant to telephone you while they were all away – '

'I want to know *now*, dammit. I love you, don't you understand? Is this my child or isn't it?'

'Of course it is – oh, please Larry, don't speak to me like that. If you knew how it hurts me – it's your child, Larry. A woman can tell – at least, I can. I can't talk over the telephone; the servants – '

'Damn the servants! Listen to me. You tell me this is my child. Now prove it to me.'

'Larry . . .' She stopped and swallowed, her throat dry

316

with fright. If she did not convince him, he would go back to America and she would never see him again. Irresolutely she began, 'When I fell for George, I knew the next morning. Some women are like that but others go for weeks, months even, without knowing. You must believe me.'

'How can you be so sure?'

'I felt different — there were changes.'

His voice was relentless. 'What sort of changes?'

She hesitated, then whispered, 'In my breasts.'

'I can't hear you.'

'In my breasts and . . . and elsewhere. I waited a few weeks and then went to the doctor, but I already knew. It was the same with Victoria — I just knew. It happened and I knew the very next day. You must believe me, Larry. I thought, suppose Larry doesn't want a child and suppose Alex leaves me? I panicked. I thought, Alex will know it's not his child unless — so the next night I slept with him.'

'Just that one night? You swear it?'

'I swear it. Darling, I was so thrilled I wanted you to know. I need not have told you yet.'

'You've got to marry me, Virginia. If you won't tell him, I will.'

'No, Larry! Please don't threaten me. Don't rush me. I need time to think; this changes things.'

'Too right it does!'

There was a long silence and then Larry said, 'I'm sorry I bawled you out. I don't know if I'm coming or going! Me, a father!'

'If I left Alex — '

He gave a war-whoop of triumph. 'That's what I like to hear! That's a big improvement on "I can't leave Alex!" ' His laughter rang in her ear.

'I only said "if",' she amended.

'Virginia, listen to me carefully. We've got to make plans for our future, ours and the child.'

'Larry, I have two other children, remember?'

'Them, too.'

317

'They're Alex's children. He won't part with them. Oh, it's all so terribly difficult.'

'You've never asked him to part with them. Nothing is certain. Listen, I have to go home to the States – '

'Oh no, Larry!'

He hastened to reassure her. 'Not for long, just a few months. Then I'll be back to make the maiden voyage on our latest beauty.'

'The *Titanic*? But when will that be?'

'March or April of next year. When is the child due?'

'Next May.'

'Would you be able to travel as late as April? It would be no hardship physically, I mean. She's like a floating hotel. A luxury hotel. Not the fastest ship in the world, but certainly the most luxurious. You'll come with me on the maiden voyage and we'll travel to New York together. What do you say? What a way to start a new life.'

'Larry! There's so much to be considered. I can't just drag the children away from their father. I can't – '

'I've told you. Either you're going to tell him, or I am. He's got to know, Virginia.'

'You mustn't say a word, Larry. Promise me you won't! If he has to be told, I'll do it in my own way and in my own time. And I won't do anything until the New Year at the earliest. I simply don't feel well enough to cope with all the worry and rows.'

'But you do agree to leave him?'

'Not exactly.'

There was a long silence before he spoke again.

'Look, darling, I'm going back to the States in late November, but before I go a colleague has offered me the use of a small lodge in Scotland. Why don't I go up there and wait for you? When Alex goes away for Lucien's wedding, you could join me there. Use that old school-friend as an excuse.'

'If I was well enough to say I was going to Penelope's, I'd be well enough to go to Berkshire – and anyway, aren't you invited to the wedding? They must have sent you an invitation, unless . . .' She broke off, wondering whether to confide in him. Then taking a deep breath, she said, 'They know about us, Larry. Eleanor saw us together at the Dorchester.'

Briefly she told him about the letter she had seen.

'Damnation!' he muttered. 'Who says "All the world loves a lover!" What damnable bad luck!'

'I wasn't going to tell you.'

'Hell! I don't have to answer to them,' he told her. 'I'd rather be in Scotland with you. Say you'll come.'

'I'll try, but I don't feel very fit at present. It's only the normal nausea — they call it morning sickness — but Scotland. It's such a long journey.'

'I'd make you forget the sickness. We could have two whole days together. We have so much to talk about. I'll convince you. I've got to hold you in my arms again, Virginia; you owe me that.'

'I'll try, Larry. I'll come if I'm well enough. Now I must go — it's nearly lunchtime and I've banished Fanny to the kitchen. Alex said he would try to get home for lunch — he's being so sweet,' she added tactlessly.

After an awkward silence Larry said, 'My darling girl, I'd be so much sweeter.'

'Oh, I didn't mean — '

'I know. I'm just so impatient where you're concerned. Once I know you're going to be my wife, I shan't begrudge Alex his last few months.'

There was a sudden crunch of wheels on gravel and Virginia cried, 'Speak of the devil! He's here now — I must go. I love you, Larry, I really do!'

'But darling — '

'Goodbye, Larry.'

She replaced the receiver on its rest and flew down the hall to the kitchen.

'Fanny — lay the table at once! Dot, run and open the front door.'

Mrs Wade maintained an icy silence, but Virginia was in no mood to soothe ruffled feathers.

'Serve luncheon in ten minutes,' she told her and then hurried back along the passage to greet her husband, a

319

smile of welcome on her beautiful face but panic in her heart.

*

Fanny knocked at the door of Guy's bedroom and it was opened by Nurse Binns, a stout middle-aged woman in a grey dress and white apron who had recently joined the household and was proving herself invaluable. Guy, after protesting against her employment, discovered to his surprise that he quite enjoyed the attentions of the garrulous but kind-hearted woman. He felt reassured by her presence and she had suggested that a temporary bed be put in one corner of the bedroom (tactfully hidden by screens) in case his health should ever require round-the-clock supervision. His fears that another heart attack might find him alone receded and he quickly surrendered himself to her brisk ministrations with a docility that astonished the entire household.

Fanny smiled up into the homely features.

'The children are dressed in their wedding clothes,' she said, 'and want to show off to their grandfather. Can they come up?'

Nurse Binns turned to Guy, beaming. 'Do you hear that, sir? Your little grandchildren want to show you their finery. Yes, of course they can come up. You go and fetch them, Fanny, and I'll prop Mr Latimer up on his pillows so he can see better.'

A few moments later Grace appeared with George and Victoria and with an excited Fanny in tow. George, resplendent in a dark blue sailor suit, marched up to the bed and crooked his arm in a stiff salute.

'Reporting for duty, captain!' he declared and then, forgetting his words, looked at Grace.

'Aye, aye, sir,' she prompted.

'Aye, aye, sir,' he said. 'Permission to come aboard.'

Guy reached out a shaky hand and patted his shoulder. 'Quite the little sailor boy,' he whispered. 'Quite the little sailor.'

'These are bell-bottoms, Grandfather,' George told him earnestly, 'not trousers. Because they flare out at the bottom – see?' He held up one leg for inspection. The tunic top was short and straight and the collar, pinned at the front with a bunch of black ribbons, was piped with two rows of white braid. He wore a round sailor's hat with a dark blue band and flat white top.

'And look at my new shoes, Grandfather,' he went on. 'Black leather – and Nanny has polished and polished them so they shine fit to dazzle the King.'

Greatly daring, he laid one shoe on the coverlet so that his Grandfather could inspect it more easily.

'George!' cried Grace. 'What are you thinking of!'

But Guy was running his fingers over the gleaming shoe with a nod of approval. 'Now stand back and let me see you,' he whispered. 'My goodness, you *do* look grand. Every inch a sailor!'

George treated him to a broad grin and saluted with such vigour that he knocked his hat off, but only Victoria laughed as he hastily retrieved it. As he put it on again Grace prompted, 'Tell your grandfather what's written round the band, George.'

'Oh yes,' cried George. He snatched it off and held it closer to the old man's eyes. 'HMS *Berwick*. That's us; this is our ship. Nanny stitched it for me in yellow silk because real sailors always have the name of the –'

At this moment, however, Victoria decided she could wait no longer for her share of the limelight and, bursting with excitement, she ran forward and spun round so that her new dress swung out in a mass of frothy white frills. It was made of white lace and reached to her calves. Pink ribbon was threaded through each white frill, while a wide pink satin sash was tied around her waist and fastened in a huge bow at the back. She wore white shoes and socks and a huge white hat with pink roses that balanced precariously on her tiny head.

'What do you think of me, Grandfather?' she asked.

Guy peered at her. 'Now, who is this young lady?' he enquired. 'It can't be little Victoria.'

'It *is* me, Grandfather.'

'But you look so grown-up!'

Victoria gave him one of her sweetest smiles. 'And I'm

to carry a posy, Grandfather. Pink flowers with white ribbons.'

'You will outshine the bride!' he told her. 'Won't she, Nanny?'

'Yes, indeed.'

Grace was so proud of her two young charges that she was finding it hard to hide her own delight. Virginia was not going to the wedding 'because of ill-health', and Alex had told her *she* would accompany him in order to look after the children. The prospect of a long weekend with the man she loved, miles away from Virginia, filled her with rapturous anticipation. As if this was not promise enough, Alex had insisted that she must have two new outfits – one to travel in and one for the occasion itself. In spite of Virginia's protests, a dressmaker in Southampton had made a grey jacket and skirt (so that she need not wear the customary 'nanny's cloak') and a day dress in a light blue with deep lace collar and cuffs. Although the material suggested a uniform, the clothes had been cut with a reasonable regard for current fashion and flattered her figure.

'And now look at Nanny!' cried George generously. 'She's wearing *her* new dress. Do say she looks nice, Grandfather.'

'Of course she looks nice. You all look utterly splendid. I envy Alex, travelling in such handsome company.'

Victoria's eyes widened suddenly as an alarming thought occurred to her and she drew George aside with a whispered, 'Do you think Papa has a smart new suit to wear?'

George consulted Grace, who in turn consulted Guy. He did not know and it was left to Fanny to finally reassure them that she had seen a large box arriving from the tailor several days earlier with Mr Latimer's name on it.

Nurse Binns was watching the old man carefully and now she saw that the effort of responding so well to the children had exhausted him. He was very tired and breathing with difficulty. A few quick words to Grace brought the visit to an end and as the old man slipped

322

thankfully down on his pillows, Grace took the children back to the nursery.

*

The days immediately prior to Lucien's wedding were cold, with a heavy overcast sky which constantly threatened rain, but to everyone's relief the weather showed a marked improvement on the actual day. It was still cool, but most of the clouds had dispersed allowing the sun to shine fitfully on the numerous equipages which drew up outside the church to deposit their occupants. A large crowd of villagers had gathered to watch the event, some of the children sitting along the church wall while others clustered round the gate or stood on the opposite side of the road holding bags of rice or rose-petals and murmuring excitedly among themselves.

The adults, mostly women, exclaimed over each new arrival and marvelled at the beautiful clothes.

The Sharps had lived in the village for several generations and were well-known and generally liked; so the villagers had been delighted to learn that, after many rumours to the contrary, the wedding would take place in Eleanor's home church after all. The vicar arrived on foot from the nearby vicarage and, greeted by a ragged cheer from the children, waved a hand graciously in acknowledgement as he made his way up the brick path to the church porch.

His arrival apparently signalled the start of the musical accompaniment, for the organ began to swell and the waiting crowd grew restless, craning hopeful necks in the direction of the Sharps' residence.

The last visitors were deposited on to the cobbles and made their way into the church; then after a short lull a carriage brought Eleanor's mother and two of her sisters who were also bridesmaids. Dressed in pale blue, they hovered ineffectually as their mother, still suffering the effects of her fall, was helped down from the carriage by the groom and a footman. Her brother then descended and they made their way along the path, Mrs Sharp leaning heavily on his arm. The two bridesmaids followed their mother and brother after allowing the crowd ample time to admire their outfits, then almost immediately a Daimler drove up bringing Lucien – resplendent in his uniform – and Alex, suitably attired as best man.

Cheers and more applause and cries of 'Good Luck!' followed them into the church as Grace and the children arrived. The two young children at once drew forth admiring comments from the bystanders, and Grace reflected with secret satisfaction that they did her great credit. George held Victoria's hand as they made their way to the church door, where they joined the two older bridesmaids and waited for the bride to arrive. This she did with one minute to spare, and as she floated into the porch the vicar appeared for a few hasty words.

Grace slipped into a pew at the rear of the packed church and the music changed abruptly as the bride and her retinue moved slowly down the aisle towards the chancel steps. As heads turned towards them there were admiring gasps, for Eleanor Sharp – soon to be Mrs Lucien Latimer – looked wonderful in a very full gown of heavy figured satin with a circlet of white orange blossom supporting her long veil. Grace watched as Alex and Lucien moved into the aisle and then George and Victoria came into view and she forgot everything else while she crossed her fingers surreptitiously and prayed that they would behave themselves properly. George was looking straight ahead, his back straight, every inch the sailor on parade, but as he drew level with Grace he caught her eye and his stern expression melted into a dazzling and conspiratorial smile. Victoria walked beside him, holding her posy close to her heart with both hands, her face composed and serene. For a moment Grace was overwhelmed with emotion but almost at once she rebuked herself sharply, remembering Mrs Wade's warning. They were not hers and never would be and she must never invest all her love in somebody else's children. She *must* be able to distance herself from them against the time when circumstances would take them from her care and she would no longer have any claim on either their time or affections. The discarded and ageing nanny was an unhappy but all too common sight; only the exceptional parents made provision for their children's nanny when she had outlived her usefulness.

Today Grace acknowledged the truth of that and had made a real effort to accept it. If Virginia had not been unwell, *she* would have been watching the children on their big day instead of Grace. God moves in a mysterious way, she thought, and was truly grateful.

The ceremony proceeded without a hitch, and when it was over the register was duly signed and the happy bride and groom emerged into the churchyard to the joyful clamour of bells. There the photographer – a small, wiry man – was waiting behind his tripod, his head buried beneath a black cloth; however, seeing the bride and groom he at once emerged, flushed with importance, and began to flutter about like an officious hen.

By the time Grace came out of the church he had arranged the main participants into a large group and was urging everyone to 'Smile please and keep *absolutely* still'. She wondered how much each photograph would cost, and decided to ask Alex if he would order one for her as a memento.

When the group photographs had been taken, a smaller family group was arranged and then a smaller one still. Eventually the bride and groom were posing together in the porch and Grace found Alex beside her.

'You made a splendid best man,' she told him with a smile, 'and weren't the children wonderful?'

'It went very well,' he agreed. 'I'm so pleased for Lucien and Eleanor. She looks radiant – but then all brides do. I thought perhaps you would like a photograph taken with the children?'

Grace gasped with pleasure. 'I'd *love* it,' she cried. 'Oh, how very kind you are!'

'They've almost finished,' he said, 'so you go and find George and Victoria and I'll have a word with the photographer.'

Five minutes later Grace found herself on the porch steps with George and Victoria on either side while the photographer fussed over them, tweaking their clothes into suitable folds and making minor adjustments to their hair.

Victoria said, 'I'm hungry,' in a loud stage whisper and Grace saw Alex smile and smiled back.

George said suddenly, 'Why can't Papa be in the picture?' and Grace felt her heart beat faster at the heady prospect. A photograph with the children was an unexpected bonus, but to be photographed with Alex also . . . her senses swam. She dared not look at him in case she saw reluctance in his eyes, but she sensed his hesitation.

Victoria cried, 'Oh yes, Papa. You too!'

The photographer seemed unhappy at the prospect and murmured, 'Perhaps the children's mother also?' as though he doubted the propriety of such a picture.

Grace resisted the temptation to add her own plea but simply waited, hoping against hope, her eyes fixed firmly on the ground. She was aware of curious faces turned their way and was forcibly reminded of the huge gulf that existed between herself and Alex. As the children's nanny she was simply a servant, while he was a member of what her father had often referred to as 'the ruling classes'. 'There's them and us,' he had said on one occasion, thumping the table with his large fist, 'and there's no gainsaying it. Folks can pretend all they like, but they won't make us equal. Nothing will.' At the time, he had been commenting on the latest scandal — the elopement of a peer's son with a ballet dancer.

To Grace's amazement she heard Alex say, 'Of course I'll join you, George — if Miss Martins has no objection, that is.' He smiled at the photographer and added, 'My wife is unable to be here.'

Grace looked up, startled, and met his eyes. There was no hint of mockery in his expression and the children turned eagerly towards her, waiting for her answer. In confusion, she could only think of three words and they were, 'I love you'. Unable to trust herself to say anything less dramatic, she merely nodded.

'Come on then, Papa,' cried George, and Victoria said, 'Hold *my* hand, Papa. Stand next to *me*.'

Grace saw George hesitating. He was thinking that if

326

he, too, opted to hold his father's hand, Grace would feel hurt. However, Alex resolved the dilemma.

'Suppose I stand next to Nanny,' he suggested, 'with Victoria next to me. Then if George stands beside Nanny, both ladies have an "escort".'

The prospect of being an 'escort' appealed to George and he quickly took his allotted place.

One of the guests said, 'Oh, don't they look adorable!' referring to the children.

The photographer adjusted his lens and said, 'Move in a little, please. Closer – that's the way.'

Unbelievably, Alex's arm went round Grace's waist as obediently he pulled her closer to him. Then the photographer darted forward again.

'Don't hold your posy so high, little miss,' he told Victoria. 'You're hiding your face ... and you, young man, tuck your chin in and stand up very straight. That's the way!' He knelt to straighten the hem of Grace's skirt and still Alex had not taken his hand away from her waist. She could feel the warmth of his fingers through the stuff of her gown and felt breathless with joy. When at last the photographer was satisfied, he retired under his black cloth, there was a flash and it was all over.

*

23rd October. Came back yesterday from Berkshire after four blissful days. It was wonderful to have Alex and the children all to myself and Alex was *so* kind to me. I don't know what I expected but he made me feel like a real person – asking my opinion and listening to my answers. I was so happy. I tried not to think about coming back to Berwick House and Virginia and all the nastiness that's happening. Why, oh why, doesn't Virginia see that Alex and Mr Scott are simply not in the same class. How dare she be unfaithful to him! I shall never forgive her. Still, at least we have had four days together and I shall have my precious photograph to prove that once he put his arm round me. I shall never forget how good it felt. Afterwards I had a terrible fright imagining that his fingers might show in the photograph and Virginia might see that his arm was round me and be angry. I imagined her tearing up the photograph in a temper and I finally plucked up courage to tell Alex, but he just laughed and told me not to worry so much.

The food was marvellous and everyone ate too much and I had two glasses of champagne! Alex insisted I must try it, but I was rather disappointed. A lot of fizz but not much taste, to my way of thinking. I also tried smoked salmon, which was nice, and caviare which was too salty. The cake was enormous and I have brought my piece home. They gave me a tiny silver box to put it in. The reception was in a marquee in the garden and there must have been about two hundred guests including children (and nannies!) Some of the children were very badly behaved but nobody took much notice of them except the other nannies who made rude comments. There was a treasure hunt for the children, and a magician, but some of the older boys were very scornful and called out, 'You've got it up your sleeve!' I felt quite embarrassed for the poor man.

Lucien and Eleanor have gone to Italy for their honeymoon – to Venice, where the streets are all rivers and everyone goes about in gondolas. It sounds very romantic and they did look so happy. I shall look in the library for a book about Italy.

Now we're back and it's back to normal with a bump, but I don't care. I've got so many memories and when the photograph comes, I shall sit and look at it and eat the wedding cake and pretend it's happening all over again.

*

Guy's condition was causing concern and at Christmas the celebrations were kept to a minimum. In the New Year he suffered another severe attack from which the doctor did not expect him to recover, but he surprised everyone by surviving. Gradually his memory began to improve and this brought back to him the knowledge of Virginia's duplicity and the burden of his responsibility.

The news that Virginia was expecting a child was an extra complication. The letter from Lucien had disappeared and he suspected that Virginia had destroyed it so that he now had no evidence to show Alex should he decide to tell him what was happening. He felt that Alex should be told; the problem was that he could not screw up his courage to tell his son because he was haunted by the thought that the ensuing, inevitable commotion would bring on another heart attack which might prove fatal. The prospect of Alex's grief and Virginia's anger was more than he could bear, so day after day passed and he did nothing at all.

The possession of such highly charged information, however, preyed on his mind until one day in a fit of weakness, he poured out the whole story to Nurse Binns after first extracting a vow of secrecy from her. He had expected her to be shocked but to his surprise, she listened in silence without any hint of emotion.

When he had finished, she said, 'I wondered what was bothering you, Mr Latimer. So that's it.' Her tone was matter-of-fact, which Guy found reassuring. 'Now you listen to me, sir,' she told him, folding her arms. 'These things happen in the best families – oh yes, you'd be surprised what I've heard over the years. People go on carrying guilty secrets for ages, but when they're ill they want to get it off their consciences so they tell Nurse Binns, who's as close as an oyster! Now my advice to you is to say nothing, do nothing and put the whole matter out of your mind. It's not your problem, and I won't have you ruining your health over it. You're not up to carrying a burden like that, but my shoulders are broad. I shall say nothing to anyone and neither will you. Time has a funny way of dealing with these matters – something that seems insoluble one year solves itself the next. I've seen it all before – you can take my word for it. Forget it, Mr Latimer. You never received that letter. See what I mean? "Let sleeping dogs lie" is not a bad motto. You hear me?'

'I hear you.' The old man smiled weakly. 'I don't know what I'd do without you,' he said huskily. 'I wake up in the morning and straight away I remember you are sleeping there behind the screens. Sometimes I wake up in the night and hear you snoring.'

'I do snore,' she agreed complacently. 'I always have.'

'And I know you're near and I don't feel so – '

'So afraid? I know how it is. Now you mark my words, forget the letter and its contents. Don't think about it again. Worry shortens your life and that worry belongs to someone else. Think happy thoughts. Now then, shall I read to you for half an hour?' She reached for the book at his bedside and Guy closed his eyes gratefully. He would leave her something in his will, he thought, to show just how much he appreciated her.

*

Berwick House was never at its best in the winter, but at last the seasonal discomforts of its burst pipes, draughty passages and smoking chimneys gave way to the occasional clear sky and a hopeful optimism that spring was just about to perform its annual miracle. Chilblains were forgotten as the last of the snow melted in February, and cold March winds blew themselves out over Easter. April was not as showery as might have been expected.

One evening early in April, the children were painting and Grace was ironing when Fanny came to the nursery bubbling over with excitement. She drew Grace to one side and with the air of a conjuror, produced a crumpled piece of paper from the pocket of her apron.

'Take a look at this,' she told Grace. 'I found it when I was helping Dot make the beds. I didn't show it to her because . . .'

'Where was it?'

'Oh, just somewhere!' Fanny told her and smiled disarmingly. She tapped the side of her nose. 'I didn't show it to Dot because she's such a chatterbox, but I can't make head or tail or it.'

Wonderingly, Grace smoothed out the paper and read:

'I need more. You know what I mean. You and M.L. And soon. N.W.'

Fanny said, 'It was in *her* bedroom. Someone must have brought it to her, because I take the post up and I'd recognize that scrawly writing. I wonder if it was that boy Sid was going on about the other day – the one he found snooping round the garden?'

Grace frowned. 'But what does it mean? It doesn't make much sense to me. More what? And who are M.L. and N.W.?'

Fanny shrugged. 'That's what I'd like to know.'

Grace handed back the note. 'Are you going to put it back?'

Fanny looked chastened. 'I was, but now I can't because she asked me if I'd found a note and I said "No". She must have had a good look for it, so if I suddenly put it back under the bed she'll guess I was lying. Or that somebody was. At the very least, she'll know someone else has read it.'

'M.L.' repeated Grace. 'Who do we know with those initials? Or N.W.?'

'But what does it mean?' Fanny insisted. ' "I need more." That could mean more money.'

Grace gasped. 'You mean blackmail? Somebody's blackmailing her?'

'Why not? If that was L.S. instead of M.L. . . . wait, that could be Mr Scott; his first name's Lawrence. Maybe it's M.L. for Mr Lawrence. N.W. doesn't ring a bell either. I reckon it's something to do with her and Mr Scott because of what she was saying on the telephone that day.'

'Which day?'

'Oh, I forget you're marooned up here. Everyone else knows. She was talking to Mr Scott ages ago about the baby and – '

Quickly she told Grace about the conversation she had overheard and was pleased to see that her news had had the desired effect.

Grace sat down slowly in a chair. 'So, she's having Mr

Scott's child. Oh, that's terrible. How could she do such a thing?'

'I know,' said Fanny. 'You should have heard what Cook had to say about it – a hussy, that's what she called her.' She glanced down at the letter. 'So could someone be blackmailing her? Threatening to tell Mr Latimer the child's not his?'

'Who could possibly know that except Mrs Latimer and Mr Scott?'

'The doctor?'

Grace thought about it. 'He wouldn't know that unless Mrs Latimer told him – and she never would, surely. Anyway, doctors don't usually go round blackmailing people. It didn't look like a doctor's handwriting, either. Let me see the letter again . . . No, it looks somehow ignorant, don't you think? All those short sentences and the writing all higgledy-piggledy.'

George appeared suddenly at her elbow. 'My light green's all used up and Toria won't let me have any of hers and I'm doing some grass.'

Victoria protested, 'I haven't got much light green either. He could use dark green.'

Her brother scowled. 'I don't want dark green grass.'

Grace crossed to the table and examined the two paintboxes. 'Look, Victoria,' she pointed to the tub of blue. 'You'll soon be out of blue and then how will you do the sky?'

'George will let me use some of his blue.'

'Then you should let him use your green. But look here, George – I'll show you how to mix blue and yellow and *make* light green!'

A few minutes later she returned to Fanny and the mystery letter. 'So, if we know any man with the initial N.W., do we assume he's the blackmailer?' she asked.

'Don't ask me,' said Fanny. 'I thought you might know.'

Grace snapped her fingers suddenly. 'What about that man you had to go to in Lyndhurst, when I refused to take the letter? Who was that – d'you remember?'

332

'That was supposed to be a Mr Bell, but it *could* have been N.W. Oh, blow it! We're getting nowhere.'

Grace shrugged. 'Maybe it's better for us if we don't know too much. It could land us in trouble. Maybe you should just burn the letter and forget it.'

'Burn it? I certainly won't. I shall keep it somewhere safe in case I ever need it. I'd like to see her face if she knew I'd got it. Perhaps one day I'll simply put it on her dressing-table; that would throw her into a panic!'

'She might guess it was you.'

But Fanny was not listening, she was thinking. 'I bet your brother knows what's going on,' she said. 'If Mrs Latimer goes anywhere, she uses the brougham. Can't you ask him?'

'No, I can't,' said Grace. 'I can't get near him these days – since you-know-when. And I don't think you should ask him. Stirring up trouble could lose you your job. My advice is to leave well alone – and stop listening at keyholes.'

Fanny giggled. 'We'd never know anything then. My father used to say, "Forewarned is forearmed".'

'And mine used to say, "People who play with fire always get burnt". Just be careful, Fanny and don't do anything reckless. And if you're determined to keep that letter, for heaven's sake put it somewhere *safe*.'

Fanny promised and departed and Grace was left to her decidedly uncomfortable thoughts.

Chapter Seventeen

Pat Casey lolled back on the hard wooden seat that ran the length of the Baltic's public bar. It was too narrow and hard ever to be really comfortable, but he was not yet past caring – though with a few more pints he wouldn't feel it. He raised his glass and eyed his fellow drinkers. His brother Harry sat on his right and Sam Harbutt sat next to him . . . or rather sprawled, for he had been in the pub longer than the rest of them and with blurred speech and a vacant expression, was already well on the way to oblivion. Robbie Potts sat opposite them, his elbows on the table.

'Oh, she's a beauty!' Pat repeated. 'You've never seen anything like that ship! Never.'

'Course they haven't,' said Harry. 'Nobody has. The *Titanic*'s – what's the word? – unique. You're a lucky sod, Pat, you really are.'

'How come you got to see over her then?' Robbie asked him, 'and Sam here didn't?'

Pat tapped his forehead. 'I get to use this, don't I?' he said. 'I'm down on the quayside and I see this chap in a fancy overcoat – you know, fur collar and all that – and he's struggling with a couple of files and a big box. "Can I give you a hand with that lot?" I says and he jumps at the chance. So once on the ship I goes all humble like, and say as how I'm signed on in the stokehold and never likely to see the rest of the ship. He can't say much else, can he, but, "Do you want to have a quick look round?" Think he said he was to do with the furniture, from Maples or somewhere; I'm not sure. Anyway, off I go and see it all – well, not all, but enough for me to see she's a floating palace!'

'Trust you,' said Robbie enviously.

'You lucky old sod!' Harry repeated wistfully. 'Always falls on his feet, does our Pat.'

'Why not? Best place to fall,' said Pat. 'Who wants to fall on his backside?'

Robbie drained his glass and said, 'Drink up, you lot! Can't you see I'm dying of thirst here? All this yapping. We're here to do some serious drinking.' He glanced at Sam and then turned to Harry. 'Is he all right?'

Harry looked down at his semi-conscious friend. 'Eh, Sam? Are you still with us, lad?' Sam groaned weakly. 'He's OK,' said Harry. He held up his glass and looked at it carefully, then set it down on the table again. 'So, tell us about the ship, then.'

Pat's eyes positively glowed with enthusiasm. 'Well, she's that big and –'

'*How* big?'

'Big enough – and like I said, she's a bloody palace. I'm telling you. All polished wooden stairways and carving and glass domes to let in the light. Oak panelling everywhere – they must have used a forest full of trees; cut-glass chandeliers good enough for Buckingham Palace; mirrors all over the place and all that, like. There's everything to do, too. You can play squash – whatever that is – swim in the pools, keep fit in the gymnasium.' He whistled. 'That gymnasium! It's got everything – bicycle machines, rowing machines – and then there's this Turkish bath, like, where you go to sweat and lose weight.'

'You can sweat in the stokehold,' grinned Robbie, 'and it don't cost anything. Who needs a Turkish bath?'

They all laughed and Pat continued, '*And* there's a smoking-room *and* a library, not to mention the decks all marked out for games.'

He paused for breath and Harry said, 'The *Mauretania*'s got a lot of that gear, as you well know.'

'Not as much, though,' Pat insisted, 'and not so new. Not so . . .' he searched for the right word. 'Not so *lavish*. There's no other word for it. It's all the very, very best. I wish Ma could see it all. I'd like to see her face; her eyes'd be out on stalks. I'd like to say, "Here's a ticket, Ma, you're going to America on the *Titanic!*" ' He shook his head wistfully at this wonderful fantasy. '*And* the dining rooms! Talk about posh! In first class it's all what they call Jacobean – in the Jacobean style, like – and it seats five hundred. It's so big, it goes on and on. I tell you, when that room's laid up with all the silver and glass and them napkins in fancy shapes, the way they do it, well, it will look like something out of a fairy tale. It will, honest.'

Robbie grinned. 'You'll have to hope for some rough weather, then they won't be able to eat all the food. You remember your rights, lad – the "black gang" always gets what's left over from dinner. You'll just have to work your shifts right and maybe you'll get to try caviar and such like.'

Sam groaned again, but no one took any notice and Pat went on doggedly, determined not to be robbed of his moment of glory.

'There's a suite on the starboard side that's got its own private promenade. I'm not kidding. Course, only a millionaire could afford a suite like that – '

'There'll be plenty of *them* on the ship,' put in Robbie. 'You can bet your life they'll all be making the trip. A maiden and all that, they can't resist it. Come over specially, some of them. Just so they can go back on the maiden.'

Harry nodded. 'Just so's they can boast about it afterwards.' He screwed an imaginery monocle into his left eye and adopted an exaggerated upper-class accent. 'Oh yes, one crossed on the maiden voyage. The *Titanic*, don'tcher know! Awfully good fun. One wouldn't miss it for the world!'

'Fun for them,' said Pat. 'Not so bloody funny when you're sweating your guts out in the stokehold! Still, we can't all be millionaires and most of us aren't. Mind you, that suite was really something with its own bit of deck.' He sighed. 'Just imagine getting up in the morning, breakfast in your stateroom, then strolling outside to sit in a steamer chair on your own bit of deck. Bloody marvellous!' He shook his head in wonder. 'I also had a quick look at the menus when no one was about. Grub you've never even *heard* of, yet alone tasted. The really big nobs get breakfast, luncheon *and* dinner, but the third class get breakfast, dinner and tea.' He sighed again, 'I'd just like to say to Ma, "Here's your ticket" and see her face. If only she could travel on a big ship, she'd most likely stop worrying. Put her mind at ease, like.'

Robbie stood up. 'It's my shout,' he said. 'Same again?'

They nodded and handed over their glasses. When he had gone, Pat said reverently, 'Twenty-nine engines and each one forty feet high. Reciprocating, they are, and all been checked and double-checked. Surveyors crawling all over it like flies yesterday. Or was it the day before? What day is it today?'

Sam suddenly raised his head. 'Twenty-sixth of March 1912,' he mumbled.

Harry and Pat looked at him in surprise. He was very pale, almost green, and holding his stomach.

'You still alive then, mate?' asked Harry.

But Sam's only answer was to throw up the contents of his stomach all over the floor.

'Jesus Christ!' exclaimed Pat, inspecting his boots to see if they were badly splashed.

'He'll never learn,' said Harry.

*

Two days later Virginia sat up in bed in a state of deep depression. She felt ill and out of her depth, weighed down with problems for which she could see no solution. After months of silence, she had received another demand from Nanny Webster and to make matters worse, she had mislaid it. Her beloved Larry was back in England, but so far she had been unable to see him because Alex had been at home. Now that he had gone to see his uncle, Virginia's health had deteriorated so that she felt too unwell to travel. On the tenth of April, in three more days, when the *Titanic* left Southampton, Larry would be on board, threatening never to return. She wanted to be with him for the rest of her life, but how could he expect her to part with George and Victoria? It was all so hopeless!

In another month, the child would be born and Alex

would claim that as his too. If only Larry would settle
for an occasional meeting and an exchange of letters . . .
would let things go on as they were, instead of demanding
all of her. Yet even as she regretted his insistence on
marriage, it thrilled her to know the extent of his passion,
the depth of his love for her. Any woman would glory
in such devotion. If only she did not feel so
overwhelmed . . . if only she could see a way out of the
labyrinth of lies, deceits and desires in which she now
wandered, confused and frightened.

Looking at the clock, she said to herself: 'I should have
been with him now, lying in his arms' – and yet the
unwelcome thought nagged at the back of her mind that
Larry Scott had never seen her looking anything but slim,
well-groomed and beautiful. Alex had already shared two
pregnancies with her, but he had seen a gradual change
in her appearance. She thought wistfully that he had
always claimed she was just as beautiful when she was
with child, and although she recognized it as a kindly lie
she found it comforting. Would Larry be as considerate?
What would he think if he could see her now? Would he
be shocked? Would his devotion falter just a little? She
could not bear to imagine the disillusionment in his eyes.
Or worse, pity! She had telephoned to tell him she would
not be able to meet him in London, but he had not been
in his room so she had had to leave a message with the
reception desk.

With an effort, she turned her thoughts to the problem
of Nanny Webster. As soon as she felt well enough to
travel, Martins must take her to Challis Court. Perhaps
tomorrow . . . Ten minutes later she dragged herself out
of bed and rang for Fanny. While she waited, she looked
at herself in the mirror and hated what she saw. In her
eighth month of pregnancy, she was overweight in spite
of the doctor's admonitions. She had developed a craving
for sweetmeats and had indulged herself too often with
fancy cakes and chocolate. The delicate outlines of her
cheeks and jaw had disappeared under a layer of fat and
a problem with her bladder made her prone to puffiness
around the eyes. In spite of all her efforts, her dark hair

338

had lost its lustre and her face had assumed a harshness that had never been there before.

'Oh God!' she whispered. 'I'm ugly. Horrible.'

There was a knock at the door and Fanny came into the room. To Virginia she looked bright and carefree and her face still wore the bloom of youth. The contrast was unbearable and Virginia felt tears spring to her eyes.

Quickly she turned away, picked up the silver-backed hairbrush and began to pull the bristles through her hair as she fought for control of her emotions. Suddenly she hated Fanny and wanted to hurt her. When at last she could speak, she said, 'Mrs Wade tells me you want to change your night off. I can't see any reason why you should.'

Fanny's disbelief gave way to dismay and her face fell. 'Oh, but ma'am – I've been invited to a special supper. A *charity* supper run by the Post Office, and it's in a very good cause – '

'Invited by Alfred Harris, I hear.'

'Yes, ma'am.'

'The young man who, if my memory serves me correctly, made himself such a nuisance over Grace Martins.'

'Oh, but I don't think – '

Virginia regarded the nails of her left hand with a slight frown. 'That's your trouble, Fanny,' she said. 'You don't think. You don't think of the trouble you're causing to other people. Mrs Wade, Dorothy – '

'Dot doesn't mind changing days,' Fanny protested. 'She's not going anywhere.'

'And neither are you, Fanny.'

Fanny swallowed hard and counted to ten. 'But please, ma'am, I don't often ask to change my hours and Alfred and I . . . well, I suppose we're stepping out together – and I wouldn't be late home or anything.'

'Stepping out?' Virginia repeated, her eyebrows raised. 'A Post Office clerk and a parlourmaid?'

She made it sound incongruous and Fanny flushed. 'He's not a clerk any more,' she said. 'He's just been promoted and now he's an assistant superintendent.'

'Is he really? How fascinating. And do you see yourself leaving Berwick House to marry an assistant superintendent?'

Fanny hesitated, fearing a trap. 'I'd consider it if he asked me,' she said at last.

'And he wants to take you to a charity supper?'

'Yes, ma'am. I swear I won't be late home or make a noise or anything.'

'You won't, Fanny, because you will not be going.'

'But – '

'If you are preparing to argue with me, Fanny, let me advise you against it. I won't have the household disrupted simply to satisfy a whim on your part. If the assistant superintendent wants to take you out, he must do so on your night off.'

Fanny gazed at her, speechless with disappointment, while Virginia put down the hairbrush and picked up a nail-file. 'You can go now,' she said. And Fanny went with tears in her eyes and rage in her heart.

'Miserable old cow!' she exploded when she reached the safety of the kitchen. 'I hate her! Oh, I could kill her!' And she burst into tears, unable to believe that all her plans for Saturday evening were coming to naught. Grace had offered her silk dress, Dot had promised two tortoise-shell combs and Mrs Wade had agreed to do her hair up for her. Alfred had been so attentive lately, and so insistent that she should attend the supper; Fanny was sure he was intending to declare his intentions. He had kissed her several times and had talked about his home incessantly, and even Grace had agreed that he would make a good husband and provider. The Post Office was a secure job, with good prospects of promotion.

Fanny had convinced herself that Alfred would propose during or after the charity supper, and now she would not be able to attend.

Dot put an arm round her quivering shoulders. 'Don't cry, Fanny. If he loves you, he'll ask you some other time. He's sure to.'

'Course he will,' Mrs Wade agreed. 'I just can't see, though, why she won't let you go. It's nothing to her.'

340

'Just being bitchy,' declared Dot. 'She's jealous because she looks fat and horrible and you don't.'

But Fanny would not be comforted. 'I *hate* her!' she sobbed and fled upstairs to the attic where she could give vent to her feelings in private. There she threw herself face-down on the bed and kicked her heels in a paroxysm of frustration . . . but when, a quarter of an hour later, her tears ceased and she could think clearly, she set about planning her revenge.

*

Next morning Fanny retrieved the mystery letter from its hiding-place and waited for Virginia to go down to breakfast and then – telling no one what she was about – she went into her bedroom and left the crumpled note on the chest of drawers in front of the mirror. She expected that when her mistress found it she would send for each member of staff separately to question them. When it was her turn she would deny all knowledge of the letter and so, obviously, would everyone else, for no one knew about it except Grace and she would have enough sense to pretend ignorance. That would leave Virginia wondering if perhaps *her husband* had put it there and she might even break down and confess. Virginia could hardly ignore such a blatantly provocative act, Fanny thought. The question was, what exactly would she do? Whatever she did she would be sick with worry – or Fanny hoped she would – and would learn what it was to feel helpless and afraid. She would understand how it felt when someone else held the whip-hand. Yes, Fanny was looking forward to an interesting morning.

What she did not know was that Guy's brother had died the previous day and that Alex was making a quick return trip to Berwick House to see Virginia and break the news to his father, before returning to Exeter to see to the funeral arrangements. Therefore it was Alex and not Virginia who discovered the note. For a long time he stood with the letter in his hand, his eyes bleak with anger and misery, for he recognized it for what it was –

a blackmail note — and guessed that Virginia was the intended victim. He struggled against the nightmare, his thoughts chaotic, his peace of mind shattered. The death of his uncle paled into insignificance as he considered the unpleasant ramifications of his discovery. He felt betrayed, defiled even, as though he and not Virginia was guilty of whatever the blackmailer knew; but slowly, he began to rally his senses. He could not stand there for ever with the letter in his hand. He must decide what was to be done; he must discount his own emotions and think only of what was best for the family. Whatever Virginia had done . . . 'Oh God! What *has* she done?' he groaned and he crumpled the offending letter in a furious fist. But whatever it was, he must try to forgive her, he told himself. There was so much at stake. His family, of which he had always been so proud, must stay together. His wife must learn to love him again. And he must love her. His third child deserved a home that was full of love. Gradually his anger began to fade, to be replaced by a fierce determination to put matters right.

'Think carefully,' he told himself as he smoothed the letter and reread it. 'Don't do anything rash. Don't do anything to make matters worse. Oh, Virginia! My poor, foolish girl. How has all this come about?'

Studying the wording again, he decided that it was not the first demand for money and came to the conclusion, erroneously, that these demands were the reason for Virginia's changed behaviour over the past year. After more thought, it seemed to him that two courses of action were open to him. The obvious one was to confront Virginia and ask for an explanation, but that would distress her — she was eight months pregnant now and the shock might harm the unborn child. The alternative was somehow to confront the blackmailer and put an end to the situation. That way Virginia need not know of his intervention in the matter until some time in the future — if at all. Part of him wanted to know what indiscretion she had committed which had given rise to the blackmail, but another part longed to remain in ignorance. Whatever she had done, hopefully it was over.

He stood a while longer, irresolute, then an idea came to him. He put the letter in his pocket and went down to the stables to find Martins.

'I don't know what you mean, sir,' said John when Alex demanded to know where he had been taking his mistress. 'I've only taken her – '

'Don't lie to me,' said Alex with a rare show of impatience. 'Mrs Latimer has had to make more than one visit to someone who is causing her a lot of unpleasantness. I don't think I need to say more than that. She never uses the motor, so she must have used the brougham or the dog-cart, and it's more than likely she asked you – or possibly paid you – not to mention her outings.'

John was beginning to sweat. He had only once seen his guv'nor with that look on his face, and that was over the fight with Marcus. John knew he had come within an ace of losing his job then, and had a nasty feeling he was now facing a similar crisis. Yet Mrs Latimer *had* supported him over the fight, but it was *Mr* Latimer who paid his wages. However, if he betrayed Mrs Latimer, she could then deliberately switch her allegiance to the motor in order to put him out of a job.

'Outings, sir?' he mumbled, running his fingers through his hair and trying to collect his wits.

'I'm not stupid, Martins,' said Alex. 'I can imagine how awkward this is for you, so I'll put it to you plainly. Mrs Latimer desperately needs my help and I need yours. I want to know where you've taken her on the occasions when she requested great secrecy. If you aren't prepared to tell me, you're sacked.'

John almost reeled under the attack. 'Mr Latimer,' he stammered, 'I admit there was somewhere that I wasn't supposed to know exactly where ... or who ...' He faltered.

'Go on, man, for God's sake! I haven't much time.'

'But I did find out – I couldn't help noticing ...'

'And who was it and where?' snapped Alex. 'Get to the point if you value your job.'

'Sir, I hope you won't tell Mrs Latimer that it was *me* that – '

'I hope I shan't have to tell her anything at all. But that's rather up to you.'

John hesitated, inwardly cursing all women and Virginia Latimer in particular.

'I couldn't very well refuse . . .' he began again.

Alex stepped forward and his eyes were cold. 'I said *tell* me,' he repeated. 'Tell me or get out *now!*'

'It's Nanny Webster, sir,' cried John, 'No. 11 Challis Court.'

'Never heard of it.'

'It's in Southampton – in the back streets. The poorest area.'

'Take me there.'

*

When Alex strode into Nanny Webster's shabby front room, he found her relatively sober. Too sober, she thought when she saw him, wishing she had something left to drink so as to steady her nerves.

'This is a surprise,' she said, deciding that attack was the best form of defence. 'Am I supposed to feel honoured? If so, I don't. You've no right to come barging in like that.'

Her words were slightly slurred, but she was reasonably alert, he noticed with relief. He had neither the time nor the inclination to come back and he hoped to get his message across today. His gaze went round the room, taking in the empty grate, the dirty windows, the unswept floor.

'Nice little place, isn't it?' she said bitterly. 'You see, this is all I can afford or *can't* afford, and I owe six weeks rent and they're going to throw me out into the street if I don't pay up.'

Alex held out the letter. 'So you wrote *this* to my wife?'

Her mouth tightened. 'What if I did? I've got to live. I've got to eat and have a bit of a fire in the winter. No one will give me work.'

'You admit you wrote this? And others like it?'

'Maybe.'

He drew a deep breath and returned the letter to his jacket pocket. 'You're despicable. Utterly despicable!'

'*I'm* despicable? What about *her*? What about what she did? That was . . .' She narrowed her eyes and gave a crafty smile that was almost a leer. 'I bet you'd like to know what she did? You would, wouldn't you? That's why you've come here, isn't it – to find out what filthy – '

Alex cut in, 'Hold your tongue, you wicked woman! I have *not* come to ask you anything. Just to tell you something. Blackmail is a criminal offence and this letter is evidence that could be used in court. Do you understand what I'm saying? You could end your days in a prison cell.'

'I saw her with Master Lucien,' she said suddenly. 'I only said what was true; I didn't tell any lies.'

He stared at her, stunned, hypnotized by her words.

She nodded grimly. 'Ah, that took the wind out of your sails. Her and Master Lucien in the summer-house. The things they were doing – at least, *he* was doing it and she letting him – '

'Shut up! I don't want to hear – '

'Oh yes, she was letting him, too. She was *enjoying* it all. If you don't believe me, ask her. Ask him, too.'

'I don't believe you!' Shocked and sickened, he was trying to regain his composure but she went on relentlessly, 'Oh yes, your fine wife was *half-naked*. How d'you like that, Mr Latimer? Now who's despicable, eh? If it wasn't true, then why did she pay up? Think about it, Mr Latimer. Take your time.'

Alex reeled inwardly from the revelation. His wife and *his own brother*! And half-naked! It was not possible – and yet Virginia had paid up! His mind fought to reject the idea, but intuition told him Nanny Webster was speaking the truth.

'That's enough,' he told her. 'One more word and I shall haul you off to the Police Station and lay charges against you. I mean that.'

A sulky look settled on Nanny Webster's features. 'You get out of my house,' she muttered. 'You and your sort . . . look here, ten pounds and I'll never bother her again. How's that?'

Alex looked at her with a terrible loathing that was laced with fear. He knew this hateful creature could bring about the ruin of all he held dear.

'You won't get a penny out of me,' he told her, 'but I will give you some advice. Find yourself a job, however humble, and earn your keep like everyone else. Work in a shop, a factory, do housework, take in washing. If you write to my wife or to me again, the letter will go straight to the police and I shall see to it that you *rot* in jail. Am I making myself clear? Your days as a blackmailer are over. You can't threaten to tell me because I know, so my wife will not give you another farthing and neither will I. Get some work and stand on your own two feet. It's either that or prison – or the workhouse.'

'You hard-hearted – ' Words failed her.

Alex shook his head wearily. 'You've brought all this on your own head.'

She gave him a long, unfathomable look and then her gaze faltered and she lowered her eyes. Neither spoke until, without warning, two tears slid down her cheeks and fell on to her clasped hands. Alex fought against a wave of pity.

'I've nothing left,' she whispered. 'Nothing to eat or drink, no firewood, no coal. I'm finished.'

Alex hardened his heart. 'Nonsense. I've told you to get a job. There's no shortage of work and you're perfectly fit and capable.'

She shook her head. 'I'm finished. Done for. Brought it on my own head, d'you say?' She shrugged. 'Well, that's as may be, but I worked with children all my life and no one else thought I was too strict. No one else sacked me, so how d'you account for that, eh?'

'Probably they didn't know as much as we did.'

'You did me a great wrong.'

Alex regarded her irresolutely. He knew he had acted in the children's best interests, but he had never imagined the once proud woman would allow herself to be reduced to these straits. Impulsively he took a guinea from his pocket and tossed it into her lap.

'Get food and fuel,' he said, his tone brusque, 'but that really is the last of it. Make no mistake – I meant every word I said,' he told her. 'I shall tell my wife that I know all about it. If you contact her again, you'll go to prison.'

'She's a trollop!' muttered Nanny Webster. 'A nasty trollop! You'd be better off without her!'

But Alex, broken-hearted, was already stumbling towards the door.

*

During the long night, as the church clock struck three Alex lay wide awake and alone, thankful that tonight Virginia had chosen to sleep in her own bedroom. Without her presence he could more easily concentrate on the problem in hand, and to this end he was wrestling with his thoughts which were sombre in the extreme. In spite of his declaration to Nanny Webster that he would tell Virginia of his visit to Challis Court, he had not done so. His reasons for the omission were confused, and he was trying desperately to create some semblance of order from the chaos of his emotions. Time and again he attempted to rationalize his feelings, an attempt rendered more urgent by his departure next morning to Exeter. He would have preferred time – even a day or two – to let his immediate anger subside, and to allow his own resilience to render his misery a little more bearable.

How, he wondered despairingly, had all his hopes come to so little? Searching his conscience, he tried to confess his own faults so that he could find extenuating circumstances for Virginia's betrayal. Perhaps he had allowed estate business to dominate his life? Perhaps he had taken his wife for granted? Alex wanted an excuse to blame himself so that he could forgive her more easily. If he had been a poor husband . . . but no, in all honesty he thought he had done all that a husband could. He had loved her and had cared for her and the children. Had he loved her too well? Had he turned a blind eye to her growing disenchantment? Staring up into the darkness, he thought that was possible. Honesty was of vital importance if he was to save the marriage, he told himself, and since that were so he must be scrupulously fair. He had been aware for some years now that her attitude towards him was changing in subtle ways, but he had been unwilling to face it for the simple reason that he did not know how to deal with it and had hoped matters would improve with patience and understanding. Virginia was not an easy person to talk to; she hated being questioned about her moods, would lose her temper at the slightest provocation and could not bear to be criticized. Not that these were unusual traits, but they made any attempt to discuss the relationship more difficult than it need have been.

'Oh, Virginia!' he whispered into the darkness. 'Why have you done this to me?'

With a deep sigh, he rolled over on to his side, but unwelcome thoughts and images haunted him still. Virginia and Lucien together in the summer-house! How on earth had she allowed such a thing to happen? Had she encouraged Lucien or had he led her into temptation? He was reluctantly forced to admit that as the older and more experienced of the two Virginia must at least have been willing, even if she had not actually initiated the affair. And what of Eleanor? Did she mean so little to Lucien? Alex found it all quite incomprehensible. He knew he should tell Virginia what he had learned at Challis Court, but feared that once the matter was aired between them it would never go away and would linger to sour and finally poison any love they still had for each other. Now that Lucien was married, he argued, hopefully the affair was at an end. Lucien would be unlikely to visit Berwick House without his new wife and Virginia must surely see that the madness was over. Better, maybe, to pretend ignorance, to show her as much affection as he could and trust to the advent of the new baby. . . . Suddenly a new and terrible thought struck him. Was the child Lucien's? Frantically he calculated the dates and was filled with an overpowering feeling of relief. Lucien had not been at Berwick House during

August, and if the baby was due in May there could be no doubt that it was his own. But from what Nanny Webster had told him, it sounded as though there might well have been a child and the thought sent shivers down his spine. What would he have done if the interlude in the summer-house, which might have been one of many, had resulted in a child?

With a supreme effort, Alex made yet another attempt to identify the priorities amongst the welter of conflicting thoughts and fears with which he was beset. Firstly, he wanted to save his marriage and to do that, he knew he could forgive Virginia and hopefully, eventually forget. Secondly, rightly or wrongly, he did not wish to force a confrontation with her. As far as he was concerned, the matter was closed. He sighed again. Easy to say but less easy to put into practice, though he would try and somehow he would succeed. There was too much at stake to think of failure.

*

The following day, on April 9th, Alex left to catch the train to Exeter – grateful that, for a few days at least, the arrangements for his uncle's funeral would require all his attention and would distract him from his own problems. He believed that he had arrived at the right conclusions with regard to his wife, and was therefore a little happier, but he had in fact made two fundamental errors that were to have far-reaching repercussions for everyone concerned. He believed that he had solved the problem of Nanny Webster, but this was far from being the case and even as he stepped on to the train, Virginia was preparing for a visit to Challis Court. He also assumed, with no evidence to the contrary, that Lucien had been his wife's only lover. Only much later would he appreciate the significance of his failure to see the picture in its entirety, and by then it would be too late.

When John received a message to prepare the brougham, he was distinctly uneasy. Mr Latimer had led him to believe that there would be no more visits to Challis Court and Mrs Latimer was hardly in a fit state, in his opinion, to go shopping or visiting. A lady 'in a certain condition' should rest quietly in the privacy of her own home and not order the carriage the moment her husband's back was turned. He waited outside the front door with a harassed expression on his face, and Fanny did nothing to improve matters by remarking that he looked as miserable as a wet week. She, too, was brooding over the most recent instance of Virginia's autocratic behaviour, and was illogically determined that if she could not be happy then no one else should be. She had already been rude to Mrs Wade and had received a severe dressing-down; she had snapped at Dot and had knocked the spout off the best white china teapot, thus forfeiting a large part of her next week's wages.

In a fine drizzle John, marvelling at man's inhumanity to man, waited morosely beside the horses with a growing apprehension somewhere deep inside him.

Virginia came down the steps looking distraught and ill and he helped her into the carriage.

'To Challis Court,' she said as he tucked the rug solicitously over her knees.

He nearly choked. 'Challis Court? Oh, but – ' He broke off, reddening with dismay at his stupidity.

Virginia looked at him sharply. 'Oh do stop fussing,' she told him, interpreting his protest as concern for her state of health. 'It won't take long and you must drive with extra care.'

'Yes, ma'am.' Thankful that his indiscretion had not landed him in trouble, he closed the door and swung himself up into the driver's seat.

'Keep your own counsel, John,' he told himself sternly. 'You're not supposed to know anything, so remember that and act dumb!'

If she wanted to go to Challis Court, that was her business. He would take her there; he would take her to Timbuctoo if she so required; he was only the groom, so he would do as he was told without question and hope to retain his position for a little longer. Since the advent of the motor-car, that was the most for which he could hope, and John knew better than many others how to protect his own interests.

'Challis Court it is, then,' he muttered and with a jerk of the reins, urged the impatient horses into a trot.

*

Virginia made her way gingerly along the rain-soaked pavement of Challis Court, uttering up heartfelt thanks that so few people were about. As she knocked on the door an old man peered out from the doorway of a house a few yards further along, but apart from him the street was deserted. When the door failed to open to her knocking, Virginia's spirits rose fractionally, for that meant Nanny Webster was too drunk to answer and Virginia had found this to be a distinct advantage. Nanny Webster sober could be argumentative and insulting in the extreme, but under the influence of alcohol she was less aware and therefore less truculent.

She pushed open the door and went inside. Nanny Webster was sprawled in a chair with her legs apart, her head thrown back. She was drinking from a bottle of gin, but she paused as she heard the door open and gazed stupidly at Virginia. For her part, Virginia's surprised gaze took in the fire in the grate and the full coal-scuttle.

'You've got money,' she said with an accusing wave of her hand. 'How else did you buy all this? Why did you write to me?'

Nanny Webster peered at the bottle in her hand and then at the fire and shook her head, perplexed.

'Why did I write?' she repeated with an effort. 'Why did I write what?'

'To me. You're not in need; you've got coal and you've got money to waste on gin. Yet you dragged me down here – '

Nanny Webster frowned, trying to understand what was happening. Vaguely she remembered that Mr Latimer had called. Hadn't he told her it was all over? Yes, that was it.

'It's all over,' she said. 'All . . . all over.'

Virginia eyed her furiously. 'What's all over? What are you talking about?'

She thought: 'Tomorrow Larry is leaving me. I should be with him today.' Then taking a pearl brooch from her purse, she held it out.

'Take this. It's worth a few pounds but I warn you, there is very little more that I can give you without my husband – '

She broke off as the old woman suddenly pointed a wavering finger in her direction. 'Hullo?' Nanny Webster gave a crooked grin. 'What's all this? Expecting a happy event, are you?'

'That's no concern of yours.'

Nanny Webster began to laugh and the sound grated on Virginia's already jangled nerves.

'Stop it!' she shouted. 'Stop it, do you hear me!' But the old woman was laughing helplessly, her face distorted by drink, her mouth twisted.

'That's rich, that is!' she crowed. 'That's priceless. And the old man doesn't know! Oh, dearie me! That's really rich!'

Her eyes narrowed suddenly as a thought struggled to surface in her bemused brain. Leaning forward, she wagged a finger in Virginia's face, making her recoil with disgust.

'Suppose I was to tell him whose it is . . . next time he comes! How would you like that, eh? Oh, I'd love to see – ' She broke off and began to giggle childishly.

Virginia's face had lost its colour at the old woman's heedless words. '*Next time* he comes?' she repeated. 'Next time? You mean Alex has . . . but that's impossible. Alex has never been here. He doesn't know anything about it. He hasn't . . . oh God! Tell me he hasn't been here. You stupid old fool!'

Seizing the old woman by the shoulders, she shook her violently. 'Tell me he hasn't been here,' she repeated desperately. 'You're making it up to frighten me. You are, aren't you?'

Nanny Webster struggled to control her hysterics. 'Oh, but I'm not,' she assured Virginia, wiping tears from her eyes with the back of her hand. 'It's the truth. God's truth. God's – Ask him if you don't . . . if you . . .'

She took another drink from the bottle. 'He came here. Oh yes, he did. I told him a thing or – '

Virginia looked at her in horror. 'He came here? But why? How? How did he know?' Her thoughts flew and she suddenly groaned. 'Oh God! That letter! The missing letter! So that's where it went! Oh my God!'

With her fists clenched, she took a few steps backwards. So Alex knew! And yet he had said nothing to her. How long had he known? How long had he allowed her to go on suffering at the hands of Nanny Webster? An illogical bitterness filled her. Her husband had known and he had not lifted a finger to help her.

'When was this?' she asked. 'When did he come here?' But now the old woman's hilarity had deserted her, to be replaced by a hazy animal cunning.

'Wouldn't you like to know?' she taunted. 'Wouldn't you like – ' She frowned in sudden perplexity as she lost the drift of her sentence. 'What was I saying?' she demanded blearily. 'What was I telling you? What was it?' She drank again and then inspected the bottle which by now was half-empty.

Virginia had put as great a distance as possible between herself and her tormentor, but now her back was to the wall and she felt like a cornered animal as Nanny Webster swayed unsteadily towards her.

'Nanny Webster! You're to tell me what he knows!' she cried.

The old woman's face creased into a knowing smile. 'Oh he knows about that!' she answered, pointing once more to Virginia's swollen body. 'He's not daft, your husband. He can put two and two together. Two and two . . . he can . . .' Her eyes closed and she put a hand to her stomach. 'I feel sick,' she moaned. 'I feel – '

As though to prove her point, she retched violently several times and threw up the contents of her stomach. Immediately the sour smell filled the tiny room and Virginia resisted the urge to run from the ugliness of the whole situation. If Larry could see her like this! Whatever would he think? She felt a fierce hatred building up inside her for the old woman who had made her life such a misery. Bitterness flared within her. She ought to be in Larry's loving arms, she told herself, instead of in this disgusting room with an evil-minded old witch.

Struggling to maintain the last remnants of self-control, Virginia once more offered the pearl brooch and this time the old woman accepted it, peering at it short-sightedly with the usual look of greed on her face.

Virginia was trying to understand the implications of Nanny Webster's revelation about Alex. If he knew about the incident in the summer-house, then surely Nanny Webster's blackmail was no longer valid? Did that mean that the months of fear were over? That the old woman no longer had any power over her? Shock and fear had slowed down her thoughts and she was still wrestling with the puzzle when Nanny Webster spoke again.

'Very surprised he was, to hear about you and Master Lucien. Very surprised indeed. Very – ' She clutched her stomach again and retched, but brought nothing up.

'What did you tell him?' Virginia demanded.

'What did I tell him? What did I . . .' She closed her eyes and groaned. 'I told him what I saw. You and that brother of his, rolling about together like two animals. Two nasty, dirty animals! Oh yes, I told him everything! You should have seen his face!' She laughed briefly, then abruptly frowned with the effort of concentration. 'That took the smile off his face, that did. The thought of his wife and his . . . the thought of – ' She put her free hand up to her head with a faint moan. 'A cuckoo in the nest!' she muttered. 'A cuckoo in the nest! That's what that is.' She pointed again in the direction of the unborn child and Virginia was swept with black despair. Was this horrible creature going to sully everything? Larry's child was innocent of any wrongdoing, but the old woman had the power to defile everything she held most dear.

'A happy event!' muttered Nanny Webster. 'A cuckoo in – ' She returned the bottle to her lips and at that moment Virginia's brittle self-control snapped. Stepping forward, she tried to snatch the bottle from the old

354

woman's hand, but Nanny Webster clung on to it with unexpected ferocity, allowing Virginia to pull her to her feet rather than relinquish her hold on the precious liquid. Clutching it with two hands, she held on tenaciously as Virginia, maddened by her temerity, redoubled her efforts to take it. They wrestled incongruously for almost a minute, but then the old woman caught her heel in the frayed carpet and stumbled. As she did so, Virginia took advantage of her momentary loss of concentration and wrested the bottle from her. Nanny Webster staggered, righted herself and swore under her breath.

'Give me that, you whore!' she muttered.

Virginia was overwhelmed by a blinding surge of fury against the Fates who were conspiring against her. Hardly aware of what she was doing, she swung the bottle of gin upwards and then brought it down heavily on her opponent's defenceless head. There was a frightening sound as bottle hit skull and a gasp of pain was torn from the old woman. For a moment their eyes met in horrified disbelief, then slowly Nanny Webster crumpled and fell backwards towards the open grate. As Virginia watched, frozen into immobility, her head struck the lower part of the iron fireplace and her eyes closed.

'Oh God!' breathed Virginia. 'Oh, my God!'

Panic flared instantly. The sight of her hated enemy now huddled on the hearth stirred no compassion within her; her only emotion was one of fear for herself. Had she *killed* her? She took a step forward, then could go no further. Becoming aware of the bottle she still held in her right hand, she stared at it in terror as her heart began to beat a fierce tattoo. Then with an instinctive gesture, she hurled the bottle into the fire where it shattered on impact. The alcohol exploded with a dull roar and for what seemed an eternity flames leaped outward, singeing the grey cloth of Nanny Webster's grimy skirt.

'What have I done? Dear God, whatever have I done?' Virginia backed away, one hand to her heart, her eyes wide with terror.

Flames licked upwards from the singed skirt, taking a rapid hold, but still Nanny Webster made no move nor did she utter the slightest sound. Was she dead? No, that was impossible. Virginia had no intention of finding out. All she could think of was escape and the idea of helping the old woman did not enter her head. Had it done so she would have rejected it, for if she called for help how could she satisfactorily explain her own presence there?

Acrid smoke swirled upwards as the fire took a firmer hold on the skirt and Virginia began to cough. Striving desperately to hold down a growing hysteria, she groped blindly for the door that led back into the street. Try as she could, she could not tear her horrified gaze from the crumpled figure of the erstwhile nanny. For a moment her resolution wavered and she hesitated. She ought to drag the old woman away from the fire . . . it would only take a moment. Then she would roll her in a blanket and smother the flames. *Then* this sordid little drama would be at an end and she could escape into the outside world. Yes, she could save her enemy from certain death; she *ought* to do it, although deep down she wanted her to die. Yet death by burning was a terrible fate. Did Nanny Webster deserve it? Virginia thought of Larry's child curled trustingly within her womb and she hardened her heart. 'A cuckoo in the nest!' Those words had cheapened her love for Larry and she would not forgive.

Opening the door, she glanced fearfully into the street. Only the old man remained in his doorway, surveying the bleak surroundings with a cheerless expression. Virginia almost envied him, for he was not a murderer! As she closed the door on the burning woman, Virginia heard the words again and again. Murderer! She had killed Nanny Webster! She closed the shabby door and leaned against it.

'Oh God! What am I to do?' she whispered.

A terrible weariness enveloped her as she began to walk and it became an effort to put one foot in front of another. The rain had developed from a drizzle to a downpour and as she stumbled along, picking her way between the puddles, she suddenly saw how ludicrous it was – she had *murdered* Nanny Webster and she was worried about wetting the hem of her skirt! She began to laugh hysterically, then clasped a hand guiltily over her mouth to silence herself. No one must notice her. She must not draw attention to herself, or someone would connect her with the murder. How much did the neighbours know about Nanny Webster's background? Had she told any of them the name of her mysterious visitor?

A nightmare vision of arrest and subsequent imprisonment closed in inexorably on Virginia as she saw herself led away to the police station, charged with the most serious of all criminal offences and incarcerated with the dregs of humanity. She imagined her trial and saw her photograph in the newspapers. Her good looks and wealth would not serve her in that situation. The best lawyer in the land would not be able to save her, even assuming that Alex was prepared to try. Perhaps he would abandon her. Perhaps for his own sake and that of the children, he would throw her to the wolves! As these grim visions closed in, Virginia felt faint and ill. If only she could reach the brougham . . . Martins would help her.

She tried to call him as she turned the corner and the brougham came into view, but no sound emerged from her stiff lips. Fortunately for her, he turned at that moment and noticed her shuffling gait as she stretched out a hand appealingly towards him. He jumped down in alarm and began to run towards her. As he reached her, she cried out and then collapsed like a broken doll into his waiting arms.

'Christ!' he muttered as he struggled to prevent her from slipping to the ground. His immediate fear was that she was going to have the baby; he had heard of women nearing their time who went into labour prematurely and was appalled at the prospect on several counts. Mrs Latimer giving birth to a child at the entrance to Challis Court would take a hell of a lot of explanation, and he was pretty sure that Mr Latimer would not approve of his own part in the event.

'Ma'am, are you all right? Christ Almighty! Can you hear me, ma'am? Can you open your eyes?'

After what seemed an age, her eyelids fluttered and she stared up helplessly into his face.

'I think I fainted,' she whispered.

'You certainly did, ma'am. Scared the life out of me! Are you better? Is it the baby?'

She shook her head and he breathed a deep sigh of relief.

'Do you think you can get into the brougham with a bit of help?' he asked.

'I think so.'

But with the return of consciousness came the memory of what she had done and she was jolted rudely back into the most painful awareness. In her mind's eye she saw the flames consuming the body of Nanny Webster. There would be a lot of smoke ... were the windows open, she wondered frantically? How long would it be before someone noticed the fire and discovered the body? And suppose – another dreadful thought occurred to her – suppose Nanny Webster was *not* dead, only stunned. Suppose she woke up and called for help? The neighbours would most certainly hear. The old man would hear. She might be rescued and then, although Virginia would no longer be a murderer, Nanny Webster would be able to identify her as the attacker and everyone would know that she had hit a defenceless old woman with a bottle and left her to burn to death. There would be headlines in the papers and she would be branded for ever as a wicked, callous woman. She had lived down the scandal of her first husband's suicide, but she would never live down a second scandal, certainly not one of such magnitude. At the very least she was ruined. At the worst, she could be hanged for murder. Her senses swam and she almost fell again.

'Please take me home,' she begged and somehow John managed single-handed to pull her up into the carriage. After what seemed an eternity, they were finally on their way home.

Chapter Eighteen

The next few hours passed for Virginia in a haze of terror. Somehow she went through the motions of everyday life, but inwardly she churned with fear, expecting that at any moment the forces of justice would reach out for her. Back at Berwick House in a familiar environment, she could scarcely believe that the events at Challis Court really had happened. It seemed impossible that she, Virginia Latimer, had brought about someone's death, yet the memories remained and from time to time she recalled with terrible clarity the crumpled, lifeless figure in the burning dress. One thought dominated all others – she *must* get away before the law caught up with her. She knew that she could never submit to the humiliations of a public trial or the prison sentence that would most certainly follow. Was blackmail an extenuating circumstance, she wondered – and if so, would it reduce her sentence? But if she ever survived the rigours of incarceration, she would then have to live with the stigma of her experience and she would be shunned by everyone. The children would be branded with her shame! The prospect was impossible. She had tried so hard to prevent Alex from discovering about Lucien or Larry Scott, but now she had committed a much more serious crime. If only she could turn back the clock . . . but that was out of the question.

At last her thoughts turned towards Lucien. He had shared the initial experience, so why should he not share the present anxiety with her? Yes, he must advise her, and yet . . . the idea of sharing her guilty secret appalled her. The prospect of putting all that horror into words was so daunting that for a while she convinced herself that to confide in Lucien would be to court certain disaster. But if not Lucien, then who else would help her? Larry must *never* know. Alex just *might* denounce her.

Guy? He was too old and frail to be forced to share such frightful revelations. Lucien was the only one ... but would he too reject her? Humiliation turned inside her like a knife. Once so proud and beautiful, she was now alone, defenceless, without a soul to turn to. Tears of self-pity threatened but she blinked them back. It would have to be Lucien. After further agonized deliberations, she eventually went to the telephone and asked the operator to connect them. It seemed an eternity before she heard his voice. Thank goodness he was at home!

'Two seven two.'

Her fingers held the apparatus so tightly that her knuckles showed white.

'Lucien! Oh, thank God. Listen, you've got to help me! I've no one else to – '

'Is that you, Virginia?'

'Of course it is,' she replied illogically. 'For God's sake, don't talk, Lucien. Just listen!'

'Are you all right? You sound rather agitated.'

'Agitated! Lucien, you don't understand. I'm in terrible trouble. I'm in danger of my life. You've got to help me!'

'In danger of your life? What on earth are you talking about?'

Frantically she burst out, 'Lucien! For the love of God keep quiet and *listen* to me. You remember that day when we were together in the summer-house? You must remember. Well, someone saw us together ...' She heard him swear under his breath, but rushed on without giving him time to interrupt. 'Lucien, it was Nanny Webster and she's been blackmailing me. For months. Threatening to tell Alex – '

'Christ Almighty!'

She took a savage pleasure in his shocked tone. She had suffered alone for their joint misdeeds and now it was his turn.

'Alex knows,' she went on. 'He found one of her notes. At least, I imagine it was – '

'Did he tackle you?'

'No. Not a word.'

'Then how do you know for sure?'

'Because she told me – ' Her voice faltered. 'And Lucien – there's been an accident. A terrible accident . . .'

'He knows? But he's never said a word to me about it. Hell and damnation! If this gets back to Eleanor – ! God, this is so unfair! She'll never understand how little it meant! She'll be so – '

'So little!' Virginia's voice was shrill. 'How dare you say it meant "so little". You insensitive – ' Words failed her.

'Virginia, I didn't mean it like that,' he protested. 'But we both knew it was just a bit of harmless philandering, while Eleanor will think the worst.'

'Damn Eleanor?' Virginia cried furiously. 'And damn you, you selfish brute! All you can think of is precious Eleanor while I'm in the most terrible trouble. There's been an accident – '

'Oh God! Not Alex! He hasn't – '

Virginia took a deep breath and then another. She was not doing this at all well. She had planned just how she would break the news, but now she was making a mess of it.

'Lucien, please listen,' she begged. 'It was not Alex. He's quite all right. It was Nanny Webster. She . . . she fell and hit her head. Oh, Lucien. It was so dreadful! She just lay there, not moving.'

'Is she all right now?'

Virginia wanted to throttle him! How could he be so dense?

'No, of course she's not all right,' she told him angrily. 'She's dead!'

There was a long silence and then he said cautiously, 'Well, doesn't that solve the problem? If she's dead, she can't do you any more harm.'

'No,' she said, 'except that *I* killed her!'

She could imagine his face, his expression changing from incredulity to understanding and then to horror. When he did speak, she detected a note of disbelief.

'You *killed* Nanny Webster?'

'Yes.'

'I thought you said it was an accident.'

She hesitated, afraid now that the moment had come to trust him. 'It wasn't . . . not exactly.'

There was another longish silence and then he said, 'You'd better tell me the whole story. All of it – and for your sake I hope to God you're wrong.'

'I'll tell you, Lucien, but you must swear on your honour that you won't repeat it. Not to anyone! Certainly not to Eleanor. Is she there?'

'Not at the moment. The sergeant-major's wife is giving a small reception for the wives of the – '

'Good. Then listen carefully. I can't raise my voice in case the servants hear me and if I suddenly break off it's because one of them is nearby. Oh, Lucien – ' she faltered.

'I'm so terribly afraid. You must help me, you must tell me what to do. There's no one else I can turn to. I daren't tell Larry.'

At once she bit her lip, cursing the slip. Lucien did not know she had seen his letter to Guy.

There was a strained silence, then Lucien said, 'How did you know I know about Larry? Did Guy tell you?'

'No, I saw the letter. I tore it up. But Lucien, that doesn't matter now. You know and that's the end of it. Just listen to me, for God's sake.'

She explained it as well as she could, but although her voice was steady the knot of panic inside her grew steadily. She felt as though the very substance of her being was being eroded by an excess of emotions. She was being eaten away from within by a voracious fear.

When she had finished he said, 'Christ, Virginia! What a mess!' and at once she felt that confiding in him had been a mistake. He was too young and too inexperienced. He had no worldly wisdom and could never help her. Maybe no one could help her. She saw herself as she must appear to him – as an unfortunate incident from his past, an awkward encumbrance, someone he would rather forget. Yet he had been as much to blame, she reminded herself, and a spark of anger burned momentarily only to be consumed in its turn by the all-powerful sensation of looming disaster. This was the worst moment in her whole life and she must face it alone.

'It doesn't matter,' she said, her voice flat. 'I'll think of something.'

At once his voice rose. 'You'll *think* of something! Such as what, Virginia?'

'I don't know yet.'

'Look, Virginia,' he said firmly. 'I think you'd better disappear.'

'How can I? Where could I go?'

'Go to your precious Larry!'

'Oh no! I couldn't tell him. Larry mustn't know.'

'I didn't say *tell* him, Virginia. I said *go* to him. You've no need to tell him anything.'

'But the police – '

He broke in, 'What date is it today? He's going back to America on the *Titanic*, isn't he? Then go with him.'

'Just like that? It's not so easy. What would I tell him?'

'Say you want to be with him. Say you've wanted to leave Alex all along and have only just plucked up courage. You'll think how to explain it.'

'And you'll be well rid of me!' she answered bitterly. 'It would be so convenient for you, wouldn't it.'

'It would be a damn sight more convenient for *you!*'

'You're a – '

With a despairing shake of her head, she bit back the word and began at once to consider his suggestion. After a moment he asked, 'What exactly does Alex know about us?'

She did not answer and he said, 'Virginia! What does he know? Has he said *nothing?*'

Virginia tried to swallow, but there was a bitter taste in her mouth and she felt weak and ill. How could she ever have imagined that she loved Lucien, she wondered. He was so shallow. Thinking only of himself. Disillusionment added to her other emotions tipped the scales against her and she felt hot tears well up in her eyes.

'Just go to Hell!' she said. 'I'm already there, and we'll be company for each other.'

She was on the point of hanging up when she heard

Eleanor say, 'Who is it, darling? What's the matter? You look terrible.'

So now *he* was in an awkward spot, she reflected with savage satisfaction. Young Eleanor was no fool. Perhaps she would find out about the scene in the summer-house and Lucien would have a lot of explaining to do. She was glad. Serve him right! She hated him. But if he told Eleanor about the summer-house, would he also tell her about Nanny Webster's death? Immediately her mood swung again. Too many people knew. Too many people could betray her to the authorities. Lucien was right after all. Larry had wanted her to run away with him to America and there was still time; she would get in touch with him. But she could not leave George and Victoria. She must accept Larry's plea to run away and the children must go with her. At least she could try to lose herself and them in the vast continent. She would telephone Larry and tell him she was accepting his offer but dare she tell him of her reason for the change of heart? The question loomed large. If he truly loved her as much as he professed, then what she had done would make no difference to his feelings, but suppose he did baulk at the prospect of marrying a murderer. No, she would never tell him. She would spare him the terrible truth and maybe someday she would learn to forget. She had *allowed* Nanny Webster to die, but she had not *intended* her death; she would cling to that small shred of comfort.

By four-fifteen that afternoon she was sufficiently composed to make a telephone call to Larry Scott. Before she could change her mind or lose her courage, she launched into the speech she had prepared.

'Larry – this is Virginia. Darling, I'm coming with you. I must. I can't let you go away again! Please, let me finish. I'm going to bring the children with me. You did say I could and I can't leave them. Larry, say you love me. Say you're pleased?'

His voice came to her – infinitely dear, warm and reassuring.

'Virginia, I'm delighted! Of course I am. It's just so

sudden. Quite frankly, I'd given up all hope. Are you quite sure it's what you want?'

'Yes, yes! Quite sure. Oh Larry, I just want to be with you; to make a new life; to forget England and everything in it . . . but – oh Larry, I'm not looking my best. Promise you won't be disappointed.'

'My darling girl,' he protested. 'It's my *child* you're carrying. To me you'll look beautiful.'

Virginia breathed a heartfelt sigh of relief. 'I just want us to be together,' she told him. 'And Larry, you will love me, won't you, whatever happens? I mean for better, for worse – whatever it is.'

'I'll always love you, Virginia. Always.'

'But say it, Larry.'

'Say what?'

'For better, for worse.' Her voice trembled.

'For better, for worse,' he repeated. 'Honey, you sound kind of strange. Somehow strained. Is anything wrong?'

'No!' she snapped, then amended hastily, 'No, of course not, darling. I'm about to walk out on my husband and abduct his children! Doesn't that give me the right to sound a *little* strained?'

'Of course it does,' he said soothingly. 'I'm sorry, sweetheart. I just can't grasp that this is actually happening. I can't believe it.'

'You said you had reserved tickets for us in case I changed my mind. Have you still got them?'

'No problem. I have them safe and sound. Five first-class tickets to New York.'

'Five? But who is the fifth?'

'You'll need your nanny, won't you?'

Virginia put a hand to her head. She had not given the problem a thought.

'Virginia?' he said.

'Yes, Larry.' The prospect of taking Grace Martins did not appeal, but she was too distraught to argue. 'I suppose I will need her,' she agreed. 'I just don't like her very much. In fact, I don't like her at all, but you're right – I'll never manage the children on my own. Yes, she'll have to come.'

'You can get rid of her later on. Send her back to England and find someone else.'

'Yes. I could do that.' Suddenly she burst out, 'Oh, Larry, I'm so terribly frightened!'

Misunderstanding the cause of her fears, he said soothingly, 'There's no need, Virginia. My folks will love you and my friends will be tickled pink. There's nothing to be scared of, believe me. Everything's going to be great.' He paused. 'Darling, you *will* get a divorce, won't you? I want you to be my wife. I shall be so *proud* of you.'

Virginia wanted to scream at him, to silence his unbearable enthusiasm. If ever he learned the truth about her, he might sing a very different tune.

'Yes,' she said, 'of course I will get a divorce. Larry, what time do we sail? Where shall I meet you? Alex is away; I daren't tell him, I'm such a coward.'

'Let me tell him, then. Someone must.'

'No! For God's sake!' She had visions of Alex returning home intent on dissuasion. 'He mustn't know, Larry, or he'll stop me, I know he will. If you want me to join you, he mustn't find out until we're safely at sea. His uncle has died and he'll be away for several days arranging the funeral. I shan't tell anyone, not even Guy.'

'But someone will have to know, surely?' he protested incredulously.

'No, Larry. No one must know where I am, or what I intend to do.'

'But he can find out. He only has to question the groom.'

'Martins? He is much too loyal; he wouldn't tell him.'

'Money buys information and you can't expect a man to refuse to say where he drove you especially if you're no longer there to champion him. If he says he took you to the docks, Alex can put two and two together and send a wire to the ship.'

His words provoked a new rush of fear in her. 'I shan't answer it,' she told him. 'Oh Larry, please believe me. No one must know. *No one*. I don't care what Alex thinks or feels, I have to look out for myself. My own safety is – '

'Your *safety?* Darling, he's hardly going to do you any physical harm. Calm down, sweetheart. You are getting things a little out of proportion.'

'No, I'm not!' she cried. 'Oh Larry, I don't expect you to understand – but I'm not. My mind is made up, so don't try to alter it. I want to just *go*, like that. A clean break.'

After a moment's silence, he asked, 'There *is* something wrong. Virginia. You must tell me – let me deal with it.'

'No! There's nothing.'

'You would tell me?'

'Of course.'

'OK, then. We'll play it your way. We sail at noon – where will I meet you?'

'On board?'

He thought for a moment. 'That won't work because they'll want to know your cabin numbers first. Better if I meet you on the quayside at noon and we'll go on board together – start as we mean to go on. And just pack enough for the voyage; I'll buy you everything you need when we get home.'

'Oh, thank you, Larry. You're so good to me! At noon, then.'

She heard him laugh suddenly with joy. 'Virginia, I still can't believe all this,' he told her. 'You've made me the happiest man alive. My own precious girl, I – '

Virginia could bear it no longer and she cut him short. 'I've got to go. We've plenty of time to talk . . . all our lives.'

'My darling Virginia! You promise you will be there? You won't change your mind, will you? I couldn't bear that. Not now. If you don't turn up, I won't sail. I'll cancel the trip. I'll come to Berwick House. Virginia, I couldn't bear it if you disappoint me now. I love you so – '

'Tomorrow at noon,' said Virginia. 'And don't worry, Larry. Believe me, I'll be there!'

*

The next morning Grace was surprised by several urgent

367

knocks on the nursery door. A quick look at the clock showed her that it was only a quarter-past seven.

George sat up in bed, his hair tousled. 'What is it, Nanny? What's the matter?'

'I don't know, dear, but I'll soon find out.'

As she spoke the door opened and Virginia Latimer came into the room. She looked flustered and ill at ease and her first words immediately explained the reason for her agitation.

'We're sailing on the *Titanic!*' she announced. 'Today. Mr Scott has managed to get five tickets. It will be such a thrill. Can you imagine? Her maiden voyage.'

Grace looked at her without a glimmer of comprehension. 'The *Titanic?*' she echoed. 'Going on the *Titanic?* But – doesn't that go to America?'

'Of course it does. Now I want you to hurry. Get the children dressed at once – '

'But why – I mean . . .' Grace tried to think clearly. Surely if they were going to America Alex should be going with them, but he was in Exeter.

'Five tickets,' she repeated. 'But who's going?'

Virginia's expression was hard to read. 'All of us except Mr Latimer. Unfortunately, he can't be away from the estate too long.'

Grace's apprehension was increasing to the point where it bordered on alarm, but when she tried to catch Virginia's eyes, the latter averted them and quickly went on talking.

'Please don't just stand there staring, Miss Martins. I hope I've made myself clear. Get the children up at once; there's no time to waste.'

'But what is it?' cried George. 'What are we going on, Mama?'

'The *Titanic*, Georgie dear,' Virginia told him. 'It's a big ship.' She turned briefly to Grace. 'And it's today, Nanny. It sails at midday, so we've got to hurry. No time to lose.' She hurried across to Victoria, who was still asleep, and shook her arm. 'Wake up, darling,' she said. 'It's Mama. We're going on a big ship for a lovely holiday. So wake up and let Nanny get you ready.'

368

Victoria opened her eyes drowsily and seeing her mother, said promptly, 'Where's Nanny?'

'She's here,' answered Virginia. 'Now children, listen carefully to Mama. You have to get up quickly and be as good and as quiet as you can. We're going to have a grand adventure and when we come back you can tell Papa all about it.'

By now the children and Grace were giving her their full attention. Grace stammered, 'This is all very unexpected, ma'am. Perhaps you could give me a few more details?'

Virginia took a deep breath and at last managed to meet Grace's eyes.

'We've been hoping since last summer to arrange a visit to the States,' she invented. 'We had been invited to stay in New York with Mr Scott's mother – perhaps you remember him – but no date had been fixed. Now suddenly it has, because Mr Scott's family has some influence with Harland and Wolff who are . . . oh, this is such a waste of time and you wouldn't understand all the background.' She took another deep breath. 'The point is that it's a most splendid opportunity and we'd be fools to refuse such a marvellous offer. When he knows, Mr Latimer will understand that we must take it.'

Grace stared at her. 'It's a speech,' she thought, and her alarm deepened into suspicion. 'She hasn't told Alex; it's some kind of plot and I'm to be part of it.'

George asked, 'Is Grandpapa coming?'

'No, dear. He isn't well enough and in any case there aren't enough tickets,' Virginia told him.

Grace tried to speak normally but her voice sounded husky. 'And you have told your husband we're going?'

Virginia's eyes hardened. 'That's no concern of yours, Nanny. Please remember your place. We are going on the *Titanic* with Mr Scott – it's her maiden voyage – and your job is to look after the children. You are paid to be their nanny whether they are here or in New York. Is that quite clear?'

'Yes, ma'am, but I would feel a lot happier if Mr Latimer was informed – '

'Of course Mr Latimer will be informed,' Virginia cried angrily. 'You really are a stupid, ungrateful girl. The chance of sailing on the *Titanic*'s maiden voyage is not to be missed and you should realize how lucky you are. Thousands of people would give anything for an opportunity like this and Mr Latimer would be most unreasonable if he expected me to turn it down.'

Grace's thoughts were chaotic and there was a hard knot of fear forming within her. Intuition told her that this trip was more than a holiday. The servants had been hinting at an affair between Virginia and Mr Scott . . . and there were the letters – those letters she had been collecting for Mrs Forster! Grace knew suddenly with a sickening certainty that those letters had been from Mr Scott to Mrs Latimer. Now they were running away to America together! And taking George and Victoria.

Her throat was dry as she stammered, 'Then I'd like to speak to Mr Latimer before I go. I'd like to telephone him in Exeter. Please.'

To her surprise, Virginia looked almost frightened. 'You will do no such thing!' she cried. 'I absolutely forbid it.'

Somehow Grace persisted in spite of her employer's obvious anger. 'I think I should.'

'And I say you shan't!' cried Virginia. 'How dare you even suggest such a thing, you impudent little nobody. He has better things to do with his time than listen to whining, ungrateful servants who can't see further than their own noses.'

Every nerve in Grace's body cried out as she imagined a future without Alex. They would never come back from America, she was convinced of it. She would never see him again.

'I still want to speak to him,' said Grace, 'before I decide whether I shall come or not.'

Virginia's cheeks flamed with colour as she stepped forward and slapped Grace across the face. 'That's enough impudence from you, you little fool! Who do you

370

think you are? I won't put up with another word. Your choice is clear: either you come or you don't. For my part, I have never liked you and should be heartily glad to see the back of you. You have five seconds to give me your answer. If you don't come, you will be dismissed on the spot, and without a reference, and I shall find a new nanny for the children as soon as we reach New York. Don't flatter yourself that you are indispensable.'

Grace stared into Virginia's furious face. Her own was pale and there was an agonized expression in her eyes. A long silence followed as she tried to decide between Alex and the children. The choice was unbearable.

'Well? Are you coming? Or do we go without you?'

Victoria began to cry and George looked horrified, for they had understood enough of the exchange to know that their beloved Nanny might disappear from their lives.

Virginia snapped, 'Oh stop that noise, Victoria. You're not a baby now.'

But the little girl slid out of bed, ran to Grace and clung to her. 'Don't go away, Nanny. Please stay with us,' she begged.

Enraged by this display of affection, Virginia grabbed the child by the arm, pulled her away and began to smack wildly at her bare legs.

'Don't, Mama!' cried George, distressed. 'Leave her alone!' White-faced, he hurled himself towards his mother, his fists clenched, but Grace caught him round the waist before he could deliver the first of his intended blows. He was tense and trembling and the tears were not far away.

Virginia released Victoria and the child ran screaming back to Grace, who put her arm round both children.

'It's all right,' she told them. 'I'm not going to leave you. Of course I'm not.' She looked at Virginia, whose face was distorted by ugly emotions. 'You win,' she said. 'I'll come.'

Without another word Virginia turned on her heels and swept out of the room, leaving Grace and the children staring at one another, shaken and dismayed.

Grace comforted the children and wiped away Victoria's tears. 'What is it, Nanny?' asked the little girl, still puzzled by the speed of events. 'Where are we going? Why is Mama so angry?'

'We're going on a ship,' said George. He looked uncertainly at Grace. 'Do we want to?' he asked her. 'Will we like it?'

Grace drew a deep breath in an attempt to calm her shattered nerves. She knew she must make an effort for their sakes. 'Yes,' she said. 'I think it will be fun. I'm glad I decided to come with you.'

'Are you?' asked George, not entirely deceived by this about-turn on her part.

'Yes, I am,' said Grace. She hugged them reassuringly. 'At first I thought I didn't want to, and then I changed my mind. I think a trip on a big ship and a holiday in America will be great fun – a real adventure! So we've got to get you ready and packed by midday. There really isn't much time so let's get started, shall we?'

As George rushed to the washstand, Grace thought about her brother John and decided she must talk to him.

'Listen,' she told the children, 'I'm just going downstairs to ask Dot to bring the water up early. You be tidying your beds while I'm gone.'

Victoria's lip trembled. She was still not happy about the idea. 'I don't want to go on a ship,' she began. 'I want to stay here with you.'

'But I'm not staying here,' Grace told her. 'I'm coming with you to America.' She thought how patently absurd it sounded. She, Grace Martins, on her way to America? It was a crazy idea. It couldn't be true. She felt desperate to see John – perhaps the sight of him would bring a little sanity back into her life. She smiled at Victoria. 'Now we're going to have lots of fun. You heard what your Mama said? And I am coming with you, so there's nothing at all to worry about.'

George looked at his sister. 'We're going to have a real adventure – you and me and Nanny.'

'And Mama,' Victoria amended.

'And Mama.'

'And Mr Scott.'

For a moment no one spoke, while each of them considered the implications of Mr Scott's presence in the adventure.

'I like him,' said Victoria. 'He tickles me and makes me laugh, even when I don't want to. He's funny.'

George looked at Grace for guidance. 'Do *you* like him, Nanny?'

'Of course I do,' she said promptly, hoping God would overlook the lie. 'Now, I'm off to see about the water-jugs. When you've tidied your beds, you can each choose your favourite toy to take with you. Just one each.'

Downstairs in the kitchen she found Dot and Fanny. Cook was still in bed, awaiting her breakfast tray. Grace's news provoked cries of disbelief, followed by suspicions.

'I told you so!' cried Fanny in triumph. 'I told you time and time again and you wouldn't have it. They've been carrying on, those two – all this time. Now you can see for yourselves. Was I imagining things?'

'Doesn't look like it,' said Dot. 'Whatever will Cook say? She's got the menus done and the food ordered for the whole week. She won't half carry on if there's nobody here to eat it!'

'Going on the *Titanic!*' said Fanny. 'You are lucky, Grace. I wish I was a nanny instead of a parlourmaid; you get all the fun!'

Grace sighed. 'I wish I *wasn't* going,' she said. 'I suppose I ought to be jumping for joy, but I'm not. It's so sudden and it feels all wrong – but I must have a word with John.'

She ran down to the stables where John was preparing the brougham, having already heard the news. He greeted her rather coldly, for he was still unable to accept her friendship with Stanley Marcus.

'John, did you know Mrs Latimer is going to America with Mr Scott?' Grace asked.

'Yes, I knew,' he said, his tone guarded. 'Bit sudden, but there you are.'

'And me and the children?'

'Yes. Some people have all the luck.'

'But John, I don't know when we're coming back; she won't say. I've said I'll go, but I do wish Mr Latimer knew what was going on and he doesn't. Oh, I know you'll take her side, but at a moment's notice it's a bit difficult to get used to the idea.'

John was torn. He did think it very short notice, but he didn't want to be disloyal to Virginia Latimer, since without her to champion the brougham he would probably find himself out of a job, and he had never forgiven Alex Latimer for patronizing the horseless carriage and planting Stanley Marcus in their midst to aggravate and cause trouble.

'You'll manage,' he said. 'You ought to think yourself lucky. The holiday of a lifetime and it's not costing you a penny!'

'It's not that, John,' she protested, 'it's just . . . well, I know this sounds silly, but I don't think we'll ever come back. It's Mr Scott that worries me. I'm sure he and Mrs Latimer have some sort of . . . well, you know what I mean. Fanny reckons they're as thick as thieves, she's thought so for ages.'

John removed his cap, ran his fingers through his hair and set the cap on his head again. Her words had disturbed him more than he would admit, for if Mrs Latimer did not return then he would be out of a job. He knew also that the sudden change of plan was due to whatever had happened the previous day at Challis Court, but he did not know what that was. When he next went to the pub he would pick up a local paper and see if there was any clue in that. However, he did not see fit to share what information he did have with his sister.

'You'd best keep those ideas to yourself,' he advised her. 'Too much thinking will get you into trouble. You stick to your job and never mind what other folks are doing. Mrs Latimer's too much of a lady to do anything like that, and you'd better not repeat that nonsense to anyone else. You get too big for your boots, Grace, and you'll come a cropper!'

Of course he *had* wondered on several occasions. All

those secret trips into Southampton — was everything somehow connected? And as for Mrs Latimer . . . if she stayed in America for good . . . he went hot and cold at the thought of all the changes that would follow.

'No,' he repeated. 'You forget such ideas and just stick to your nannying. Now I must get on.'

Grace glared at his back as he bent to the wheels to apply fresh polish, but she bit back a sharp retort for she understood where his loyalties must lie.

As she turned away she saw a familiar jaunty figure approaching and recognized the chauffeur. She hurried to give him a garbled account of events and was gratified to meet with a more solicitous reaction.

'Going to America *today!*' he gasped. 'But who? How? And for how long? When will I see you again? Oh Grace, I've been wanting to talk to you again, about us. Look, you can't be forced to "go to America" just like that. Stand up to them. I do.' He lowered his voice. 'I didn't get that second chauffeur's job, but I've applied for another one. Mr Latimer's not too pleased, but I'm my own man and —'

Grace shook her head. 'I'm sorry, Stanley. I daren't stop and talk. She'll *kill* me if I don't get the children ready on time; she's already had a go at me. But Stanley, if you get the chance, will you drop a hint to Mr Latimer that I didn't want to go to America and I don't want to stay there. He might —'

'*Stay* there? You mean you're not coming back? Not ever?'

'I can't explain now, Stanley. You'd best ask Fanny — she knows what's going on. Oh, Stanley!' Impulsively, she leaned forward and kissed him. 'I shall miss you,' she said. 'Good luck if I don't see you again.' She turned away and began to run back to the house.

'Grace!' he shouted. 'You can't just dash off like that. Dammit all! Grace!'

But she had gone. Moodily he began his early-morning inspection of the motor, but found no comfort in its gleaming chrome and shining paintwork. Grace Martins

375

was off to pastures new and he was still stuck at Berwick House.

'Damn and blast!' he muttered, thoroughly disgruntled and upset by the news. He stared down at the front near-side tyre for a long time and then kicked it.

Before she left the nursery, Grace managed to scribble a hasty note to Alex Latimer which was entrusted to Fanny who promised to deliver it as soon as he returned.

*

Ellen stood beside her son – one hand on the pram handle, the other shading her eyes from the early morning sun as she stared up at the White Star's newest liner. Unable to hold back a gasp of incredulity, she continued to stare wordlessly at the steep, black side that towered above them and the crisp white superstructure that could be glimpsed above it.

'It's more like a mountain than a blooming ship,' she said at last.

Pat laughed proudly. 'I told you you'd like it,' he crowed.

Ellen glanced at his eager face, then back to the ship. 'I never said I liked it,' she corrected him. 'It's big, that's all I said.'

'But you do like it, don't you?' he persisted. 'You've *got* to like her, Ma. She's such a beauty. How could anyone *not* like her!'

Ellen shook her head without answering. She had been persuaded (reluctantly and after much heart-searching) to break with tradition and see for herself the glorious ship which everyone praised so highly. To please her son, she had finally given in and now stood on the quayside at five minutes to seven in the morning. Pat stood beside her, very much alive – his feet planted on either side of his sea-bag, the gusting wind ruffling his hair. The excitement had brought extra colour to his face and a gleam to his eyes; there was an almost arrogant tilt to his head as he surveyed the ship with a proprietary air, and she thought wistfully that for a plain lad he looked almost handsome.

The crew's muster was at eight o'clock, but after that the 'black gang' would be free to go ashore for a last drink in the pub of their choice or to exchange a final word with wives and sweethearts.

'So what do you really think of her, then?' Pat persisted.

Ellen hesitated. She knew that he longed for her approval and she wanted to please him, but to her the ship – *any* ship – was the enemy and she was unwilling to confer any praise.

'She's certainly bonny,' she said at last.

He laughed. 'Oh dear!' he said in mock dismay. 'I've clean forgotten to buy you a ticket. Never mind, Ma. Next trip, perhaps?'

She smiled faintly and, encouraged, he rushed on, 'You shall have the best stateroom, the millionaire's suite. How'd that do you, eh?'

'When pigs fly,' she said. 'And you watch yourself, young Pat. No fighting!'

'Do I ever?' He gazed at her, the picture of injured innocence.

'How would I know? Your brother did – came home with a black eye and a tooth broke clean in half.'

'He had to stick up for himself, Ma. Would you rather he got minced up? He never started it.'

'That's what you all say. It's always someone else . . . always.'

'It's true. You wasn't there, Ma, so you don't know.'

'*And* it wasn't the first time,' she said. 'I tried to bring you lads up respectable.'

Pat shuffled his feet, a scowl darkening his face briefly. 'Well, I'm not him, Ma.'

'I know you're not. I'm just saying, watch yourself.'

They were silent for a moment and then suddenly he pointed. 'See that fellow in the bowler hat and long coat? That's Captain Smith. Captain Edward John Smith, to be exact. Best captain in the whole of the White Star Line. Best in the whole world, most likely. You won't see many of the officers, though. They slept aboard last night.'

'Who are all that lot, then?' She waved a hand to indicate the dozens of men converging on the liner.

'The other ranks,' he told her.

Pat watched them and was suddenly keen to be free of his mother and join his mates, finding his quarters and stowing his gear. But he tried not to show his impatience, for he had talked her into coming and he did want to put her mind at ease, so he chattered on – pointing out people or things of interest, trying to put an end once and for all to her doubts and fears on his behalf. At eight o'clock the Blue Ensign was run up at the stern of the ship and fluttered fiercely in the rising wind.

'Ah, now, not every ship can fly that flag,' he told her. 'You have to be very special to fly the Blue Ensign and Captain Smith *is* special. He's very *senior*. Your son, Ma, is sailing under a very important man – you tell the neighbours that. There's men would give their right arms to be in my shoes.' He pointed again. 'And there goes the company's own flag up the main-mast. See it? The red one?'

Ellen shivered suddenly and stopped rocking the pram to pull her shawl closer to her with both hands.

'You cold, Ma? Perhaps you'd best get on home.'

'I'm not cold, son. I'm – '

At that moment a gust of wind snatched her hat and, tugging it loose, sent it bowling along the quay. She sent Pat after it and he brought it back, crumpled and dusty.

'Someone trod on it,' he said. 'Never looked where he was going. Stupid bas – ' He corrected himself hastily. 'Stupid idiot.'

She took the hat and tutted over its condition, and he said quickly, 'First thing when I get back, I'll buy you a new hat; that's a promise!'

She jammed it back on to her hair and pushed in a hat-pin. The baby began to cry, a thin half-hearted whine, and she jiggled the pram absent-mindedly.

'A promise, is it?' she repeated. 'A new hat?'

He nodded. 'Soon as I get back. A real smart hat with flowers and a bit of a feather. How's that? A *red* hat maybe, with little flowers and all stuff like that.'

'I'd like that, son. That'd be grand.'

'Oh, Ma!'

Suddenly they looked into each other's eyes for a long, wordless minute, then he said, 'I must go,' and bent his head to kiss her briefly on the side of her face.

'God bless,' she said. 'And Pat – '

'What then?' He hid his impatience; he hated 'goodbyes'.

Ellen swallowed back the last desperate plea and repeated, 'God bless!'

He picked up his sea-bag, put it down, hugged her fiercely and picked it up again. Then he was gone, his steps jaunty, the sea-bag perched on his shoulder, every inch a seaman.

Ellan wanted to watch him go, but her sight was blurred with the tears she had sworn not to shed. Blinking rapidly, she sniffed hard and wiped her eyes and when she opened them again he was already lost among the crowd.

For a long time she stood there alone, looking up at the vast side of the ship, watching the hundreds of men who climbed the gangways like so many ants. High above her more men stood silhouetted against the ship's rail, dwarfed by their surroundings. Some of them waved and she waved back, just in case one of them was her son.

At last, with a deep sigh, she turned the pram and made her way back along Ocean Road, bumping noisily over the railway tracks, down Central Road and back through Gate Four. As soon as she got home she closed the front door and leaned back against it, then pushed the sleeping baby into the kitchen and went upstairs. Slowly, she unpinned her hat and brushed it half-heartedly with her hand, trying to remember exactly how Pat had looked as he walked away from her, or stood beside her, or ran after the hat. Try as she would, she could not see him; his image refused to materialize – as though, she thought, he had already gone.

'Patrick John Casey,' she whispered, as she put the hat away in the wardrobe. 'You come back! Never mind the new hat. Just come back, that's all I ask.'

His photograph stood on the chest of drawers and she picked it up. Patrick John Casey, aged eleven, stared back at her with his shy smile. Could he possibly *not* come back, she wondered? The icy fear clutched at her again? *Could* he drown? Could that huge ship – that 'blooming mountain' – possibly sink?

'No!' she cried. 'That's nonsense! It never could.' She had seen it for herself and it was too big, too beautiful, too *solid* ever to sink. So many rich people, passengers and crew . . . no! it was impossible, she told herself. She was being foolish; a foolish morbid woman. How long was it since she had last dreamed the dream? Several months now. Four, or maybe five. So maybe the danger was past. Maybe she had kept him from the sea long enough and now the danger period was over. If the dream had stopped, then the danger was over and he was safe. Yes, that was the only way to look at it. No dream, no danger. She willed herself to relax, repeating the words like a charm until she felt a little better.

But that night she had the dream again.

Chapter Nineteen

Pat hurried on board and was soon part of the noisy crowd below decks. He found himself a bunk, greeted his friends and together they inspected their new quarters. Then it was time to go up top for the muster. They assembled on deck, were given a cursory inspection by the medical officer and then their names were put on the roll, which meant they had 'signed on' for the voyage. When that was over, Pat and a few friends watched two of the ship's starboard lifeboats being lowered under the watchful eye of two of the officers. The boats reached the water, were rowed around for a few minutes, and were then hoisted up again.

By the time this brief drill was at an end, it was time for breakfast in the new dining room – porridge, bacon, eggs and toast and plenty of cocoa to wash it down.

'We'll go home pounds heavier!' laughed Sam Harbutt. 'But who's complaining? Hey, Casey! You like toast with your marmalade, do you? Leave some for the rest of us.'

Pat grinned, his mouth too full to answer back. If there was one thing he liked about life at sea it was the food, and if the first breakfast was anything to go by, the *Titanic* promised that in plenty.

The main topic of conversation during the meal was of a small fire that was burning in one of the coal bunkers and the news was not welcome. After breakfast, while the passengers boarded, the 'black gang' were supposed to be free to go ashore again for a last drink in their favourite pub.

'It'll be just my luck,' groaned Sam. 'You just see! They'll want a crew to douse the fire and it'll be "You, you and you" – and I'm supposed to be meeting Annie in the Red Lion.'

Half an hour later he was proved right.

'Hell and damnation!' he cried as his mates enjoyed

his discomfiture. 'She'll be that mad if I don't show up. I don't suppose one of you lot would swap with me, would you?'

There was a chorus of 'No', and he swore under his breath.

'There'll be hell to pay,' he grumbled disconsolately. 'You don't know what she's like, that one.'

'We do,' said a wiry Scot who went by the name of Jock. 'We've got women of our own – all except young Casey.'

All eyes turned on Pat. 'How do *you* know?' he blustered. 'I might have a girl; I might not be letting on.'

'You'd let on, mate,' cried Jock. 'It'd be written all over your face. Course you haven't!'

Sam Harbutt seized on the information eagerly. 'I'd make it worth your while, Casey,' he urged.

'Such as?' Pat was intrigued.

'Three bob!'

'You must be kidding. Three measly bob!'

'Four then.'

Patrick thought of the new hat he had promised to buy for his mother. He had promised feathers and flowers.

'Make it four and six,' he said, 'and it's a deal.'

It was agreed and Sam wrote an IOU for the money and departed at a run for the Red Lion and a last kiss from Annie.

Pat changed into his working clothes and went below to No. 6 boiler room where the fire burned in one of the starboard bunkers. There he joined the other men who were pouring water on to damp it down, while others shovelled into the pile to reach the source of the blaze. The Chief Engineer was there, supervising their efforts and assessing the extent of the danger, if any. If the fire went on record, the ship might well be delayed by Board of Trade regulations, but he had decided that they could get it out before it did any damage and he made his report to that effect. Pat toiled away for two hours before he was relieved and allowed to clean up and go back on deck, grinning with satisfaction. A quick way to earn four and six! He must put the money on one side or else he would spend it when they reached New York.

He was leaning on the ship's rail looking down at the gangway. The boat-train stood alongside the dock, and the first class passengers alighting from it made their way towards the gangway which led to the main entrance on B-deck.

Pat watched without much interest, for the majority of passengers were unfamiliar to him. Even if he had recognized the names of the rich and famous, he would not have recognized their faces. Suddenly, however, he leaned forward for a better view, his brows drawn together in concentration. For a moment he peered down at a group of people near the top of the gangway. Two children, two women and a man – and he could have sworn the woman was Mrs Latimer of Berwick House! She did have two children, and there was a nanny who might be travelling with them. The man, however, was *not* Mr Latimer, and that was what puzzled him. He leaned further over the rail and suddenly recognized the other woman as the young nurserymaid who had given him a florin.

A broad smile spread over his face as he straightened up. How astonished they would be to know that he was part of the ship's crew – well, the nurserymaid and the children would be, though Mrs Latimer probably would not care one way or the other. He began to wonder if he would be able to alert them to the fact that he was on board, but almost certainly the first class area of the ship would be out of bounds to the 'black gang'. Perhaps he could persuade one of the stewards to take a message to the nurserymaid? It occurred to him that he didn't know her name, but then a new idea struck him.

'The passenger list!' he cried and rushed away in search of a copy. As he had expected, he saw the familiar names – three Latimers and a Miss Grace Martins. No 'Mr Latimer' – so who on earth was the man who was obviously accompanying them? Or had he simply escorted them to the ship? Could it have been Martins, the groom? Pat didn't think so. Too tall and thin. He shrugged; it wasn't important. What mattered was that he, Pat Casey, actually *knew* some of the first class passengers. None of the rest of the gang could make such a claim. *Knew* them, not just by sight, but to *speak* to! He imagined himself meeting Mrs Latimer on deck. He would smile, give a polite nod and say, 'I do hope you are enjoying your trip.' Yes, that would be quite enough. None of this, 'Hullo, Mrs Latimer, do you remember me?' Of course she would remember him. He would say, 'Hullo, Master George and Miss Victoria' and he might even wink at the nurserymaid. They would doubtless be impressed.

He waited eagerly for the return of his mates so that he could tell them his news, but when at last they did come back they were without Sam. Having misjudged the time he was too late to get back aboard, and was one of several men who stood helplessly on the dockside as the liner prepared to move out. Pat Casey cursed. So much for his IOU. His four and six was gone for ever!

*

Later the same morning Grace stood at the ship's rail with the two children one on either side of her. George's two small hands were firmly clamped to the lower rail.

'Now you are *both* to hold my hand,' she told them sternly, 'otherwise we shall have to go inside.'

'I don't want to hold hands,' George repeated. 'I can hold the rail by myself. I'm eight now. I can – '

'George Latimer!' Grace told him. 'If you fall over the side it's a long way down – much, much further than falling off the roof at home – and then it's splash! Into the sea you'll go, and I shan't be able to rescue you because I can't swim.'

George scowled at this awful picture, but continued to hold firmly to the rail while Victoria looked on anxiously.

'Do be good, Georgie,' she pleaded, but George replied with a stubborn shake of his head.

Virginia and Larry Scott stood close together on the other side of George, and now Virginia turned her head.

'If you can't keep proper control of them,' she said to Grace, 'you'd better take them inside.'

'Right then,' said Grace. 'You heard your Mama? We must go back inside and then we won't be able to wave goodbye to England. Never mind. Come along.'

Immediately George made a grab for her hand and gave her a sweet smile. 'All right then, Nanny, I'll be good,' he said and the brief mutiny was at an end.

Grace thought, not for the first time, that one day George would break a lot of hearts, for although he could be wilful his nature was basically sunny and his charm intense, and she was sure he would never lack friends. She gave the hand a little squeeze and returned his smile, then together they all looked down on to the quay below them.

'Everyone's so tiny,' marvelled George. 'They look like toy people. The band look like toy men with toy trumpets.'

'And toy drums,' said Victoria. 'Don't forget the drums, Georgie.'

She had hardly finished speaking when, as though inspired by their interest, the band sprang into action once more with a selection of suitably nautical music.

Grace watched them for a moment, then let her gaze wander beyond Ocean Dock to the view of Southampton beyond. To the left she saw the large and unlovely buildings that made up the dockyard and behind them row upon row of houses crowned with a pall of smoke from countless kitchen ranges. Slightly to the right lay another stretch of water on which hundreds of small boats moved erratically, and further back there were still more houses backed by an area of dark trees which extended to the horizon. Further to the right, Grace saw several more boats, all of which were keeping a respectful distance from their towering new cousin. Beyond them lay the open sea.

Surrounded by excited and enthusiastic passengers, Grace felt isolated by her feeling of reluctance. If only she had run back down the gangway while there was still time – back to John and the brougham, back to Berwick House and Alex Latimer. She glanced sideways and saw Virginia smile up into Larry Scott's face – an unguarded

385

smile which revealed only too well the true extent of her feelings for him. In a strange way Grace sympathized, because she recognized love and knew that, had circumstances been different, she might have looked at Alex in just the same way. Glancing down, she saw that they held hands and her heart contracted with envy, for she would never hold Alex's hand that way and might never even see him again. Larry Scott was obviously in love with Virginia and Grace felt more certain than ever that the child Virginia was carrying must be his. As she thought of the heartache ahead for Alex, her brief sympathy for Virginia vanished. While they had all been at Berwick House none of the staff had dared to do anything about contacting Alex, but it seemed probable that Mrs Wade might feel it necessary to inform him. Guy Latimer would have been the obvious person to confide in if his health had been better, but as it was this was out of the question. If no one telephoned Alex, then he would not know until he returned home after the funeral – by which time his family would be well on the way to America and out of reach.

At first Grace had been hoping for a miracle – half expecting to see Alex hurrying up the gangway to rescue them – but as time passed she knew it was most improbable and had resigned herself to the journey at least. What lay ahead on the other side of the Atlantic was another matter. She must take each day as it came, for there was nothing else she could do, but she was not able to share in the general enthusiasm for the ship or the voyage. The *Titanic* was taking her away from Alex and no amount of luxury could compensate for that loss.

With a conscious effort, she forced herself to concentrate on her present surroundings. The boat-deck on which they stood was a place of bustle and excitement as passengers scurried to and fro, seeking the best vantage point from which to observe the ship's departure from Southampton and eager not to miss anything. Nearby a group of young people waved frantically to friends on shore, while next to them a young man popped the cork from a bottle of champagne and, with a shout of triumph, held it up at arm's length and poured the frothing liquid straight into his mouth.

The ship's whistle sounded a single mournful blast, and almost at once her hawsers were released. The gangway swung away from the ship, back to shore, and the huge vessel — guided by several small tugs — began almost imperceptibly to move away from the quayside. While Grace watched, a narrow band of jade water appeared far below as a roar went up from the crowds on both ship and shore and whistles and rattles accompanied the strident sirens and hooters of small boats. The *Titanic*'s maiden voyage had finally begun and everyone wanted to share in the celebration. Myriad coloured streamers were hurled from the ship and fell curling into the water or drifted further to festoon the crowd on the quayside. At the same time the *Titanic*'s own orchestra took over from the band on shore and popular tunes from *The Chocolate Soldier* set people singing and toes tapping.

'We're off,' said Grace as cheerfully as she could. 'Wave goodbye to Southampton, both of you. Say, "See you again soon".'

'See you again soon!' they chorused dutifully.

Please God we will, thought Grace. Please let my fears be groundless. I don't want to stay in America; I want to come back to Alex.

'What are those puffs of smoke?' asked George, pointing to the rapidly receding quayside.

'Newspaper men taking photographs of the ship,' Grace told him.

'Where's Mama gone?' Victoria asked suddenly, for Virginia and Mr Scott were nowhere to be seen.

'Perhaps they've gone for a stroll,' Grace suggested. 'Or maybe your Mama has gone to lie down in her stateroom. I expect she's tired, or perhaps she has a headache.'

'Has Mr Scott got a headache too?' asked Victoria artlessly.

'It's possible, with all this excitement and the band playing so loudly.'

'Doesn't Mama want to wave goodbye to

Southampton?' demanded George indignantly. 'I would if I was her, even if I felt *very* tired. I'd want to wave goodbye to England.'

'Well, obviously she doesn't,' said Grace, 'so that's all there is to it, though I daresay she'll be well enough to wave "hullo" to America.'

Fortunately her sarcasm was lost on the children.

'Perhaps she's tired because of the new baby,' George suggested. 'Will the new baby be born in America?'

'I don't know, dear.'

'If it is, then Papa won't be able to see him.' George looked up anxiously.

'He'll see the baby when we go home,' Grace told him.

'When *are* we going home?' asked Victoria.

'I don't know. Not for a few weeks at least.'

Grace imagined that Virginia and Mr Scott were together in either his room or hers. No doubt Mr Scott was delighted to see the last of England, for now he had Virginia all to himself. If only she knew for certain what plans they had made. Surely, *surely* they could not hope to stay together in America, for the scandal would certainly ruin them – unless things were very different over there? Grace knew that people's manners were more relaxed in the United States, but were their conventions less strict also? Could they possibly hope to get away with it? It would mean a divorce, presumably, and would Alex agree to that? She wished she knew how much Alex understood of what was happening – if, indeed, he understood anything. If there *was* a divorce, what would happen to George and Victoria? 'Oh, Alex,' she cried silently. 'I may never see you again, and I can't bear it.'

She sighed deeply as she watched the gap between ship and quay continue to widen inexorably, parting her from the man she loved. Now white gulls swooped over the intervening water and mud swirled among the green wavelets. The buildings on shore dwindled minute by minute and the band began to play 'A Life on the Ocean Wave', all around her people laughed, sang and hugged each other in an exuberance of high spirits. Far below them a small piece of wood drifted into sight in the muddied water, bobbing drunkenly among the spreading ripples.

Victoria pointed. 'Some of the birds are sitting in the water,' she said. 'Why are they, Nanny?'

'I suppose they're resting their wings,' said Grace.

'Can they swim, then?'

'No, but they can float.'

She kept her voice steady with an effort as her eyes blurred suddenly with tears. If only Alex could reach out and pluck her from the midst of this cheerful, cheering crowd. 'I want to come home,' she told him in her heart. 'I don't want to leave you!' But what could she do? Perhaps tonight she would write to him and tell him of her suspicions. She considered this idea hopefully for a moment or two, then shook her head. No, that would not do. Once Alex *knew* of the affair, he might refuse to take Virginia back into his life. If he remained in ignorance, there was a chance – albeit a very slim chance – that the affair might run its course and then Virginia would return to her husband. Grace decided that this might be the very best she could hope for. By now the strains of the shore band had faded altogether and the ship's own orchestra, looking very grand in their blue jackets, came at last into their own.

Grace shaded her eyes and searched the thin ribbon of road for a glimpse of John and the brougham, but the highway was so congested and the vehicles so small that she could not distinguish one from another.

'I want to go right round the ship,' declared George. 'I want to see the other side.'

'Later on,' said Grace.

'I want to go *now*.'

Victoria put in, 'We'll go later, Georgie.'

'*Now*,' he repeated, with a little stamp of his foot.

'Later,' said Grace. 'I promise.'

'Cross your heart and hope to die?' he demanded.

Victoria gasped. 'Georgie! How could you?'

Again the boy's sweet smile flashed into action as he said quickly, 'I was only joking, Nanny.'

'I know you were,' said Grace, smiling back at him.

389

'I love you,' he said suddenly.

'Oh Georgie, I love you – and Victoria. I love you both. You're my two best darlings.' She bent to hug them both, a lump in her throat. Whatever happened, she could not leave them while they needed her. Later, maybe, she would make her own way back to England, but in the meantime nothing would part her from her two young charges. Their father was in England; their mother had eyes only for her lover and would soon have a new baby to think about. Without Grace, George and Victoria had nobody.

Her thoughts were interrupted by a sudden cry of alarm from some of the nearby passengers and she turned to see what was happening. The *Titanic* was passing another liner, the *New York*, which was moored alongside the quay. It seemed that the *Titanic*'s draught was beginning to affect the smaller ship and as the crowd watched in horror, the *New York* began to swing outwards as though drawn towards the *Titanic* by a magnet.

Cries of panic arose on all sides as a collision became a frightening possibility.

'She's going to ram us!'

'Her mooring ropes have snapped!'

'Why don't they *do* something?'

'Mother of God!'

Some people crossed themselves, others averted their eyes, but just as disaster seemed inevitable the miracle happened. Tugs got hold of the *New York*'s hawsers and somehow held her steady, so that the *Titanic* passed safely with no more than four feet between her and the smaller vessel.

'Jesus Christ! That was close!'

'Did you ever see anything like it!'

'That tug-boat captain deserves a medal!'

George gazed up at Grace. 'What was it?' he asked. 'What happened, Nanny?'

'We nearly bumped into that other ship,' she told him, 'but luckily we didn't, so there's nothing to worry about.'

'Are we going to crash? Are we going to sink?' he insisted.

'Of course not. Don't talk that way. You'll frighten Victoria.'

'I'm frightened,' she said obligingly.

Grace laughed. 'You fibber! You're not a bit scared. Now, how about that walk round the ship? Let's see what we can see.'

They set off in high spirits to explore the boat-deck, admiring the four tall cream and black funnels that soared overhead, the gleaming white lifeboats and the dozens of steamer chairs stacked in readiness for the first sunny day. The two children asked innumerable questions which Grace answered as best she could, but eventually they moved inside to continue their exploration of the ship and to discover yet more wonders – the huge Aeolian organ, revolving doors, a beautiful clock above an elegantly curving stairway and above that a soaring dome of glass and elaborately wrought iron. Grace and the children marvelled over everything, but for George and Victoria the greatest thrill was a ride in one of the lifts.

Grace was pleased to find a well-stocked library and on the same deck the Verandah Café and Palm Court. Lower down on F-deck they discovered Turkish baths and a gymnasium (although the kindly attendant told them that it could only be used by children between one and three o'clock). There was a swimming-pool, however, which was duly admired before they set off again to find the special children's room which contained a selection of toys and games beyond their wildest dreams. The rocking-horse caught Victoria's eye and she had a quick ride while George examined the extensive train set.

'Now,' said Grace, 'we must try to find our stateroom and you must wash your hands for luncheon.'

George frowned. 'What is luncheon?'

'Dinner to you,' Grace told him, 'but grown-ups call it luncheon and they eat again in the evening after you've gone to bed – and they call *that* meal dinner.'

'So they have two dinners!' he said. 'That's not fair.'

'It's not fair,' echoed Victoria. '*I* want two dinners.'

'So do I,' said George.

Grace laughed. 'Well, you'll have to wait until you're grown-up.'

'It's not *fair*,' George persisted.

'*Life's* not fair,' Grace told him, 'so don't go thinking it is and then you won't be disappointed. You'll have dinner and tea the way you do back home in the nursery.'

Finally, after a hilarious search, they found their stateroom on C-deck and went inside. Compared with the nursery at Berwick House, the room was very sumptuous and there was much opening of drawers and peering into cupboards before the children were satisfied that they had seen everything. It was surprisingly spacious, with ample storage space, and contained three beds with flounced bedspreads, a dressing-table, a writing desk, chairs, cupboards and a wall mirror. A small vase of flowers stood on the dressing-table. Their own bathroom and toilet led off the main room.

Grace opened the desk drawer. 'Look, here's some special stationery,' she told George, 'with the White Star Line crest on it. Now you'll be able to write letters to your Papa to tell him all about the trip.'

Victoria called excitedly from the bathroom, 'There's teeny, tiny bars of soap. Can I wash my hands, Nanny?'

Grace laughed. 'Now I've heard everything! Of course you can.'

George looked up at Grace, his eyes shining. 'Are we having the adventure?' he asked earnestly. 'Like Mama promised?'

She smiled. 'Yes, George,' she said, 'I think we are.'

*

The *Titanic*'s schedule did not take them directly to America, for she was due to make two stops. The first was at Cherbourg in France, where she was to pick up a further 274 passengers, many of them wealthy Americans who had been touring Europe. These started to come aboard at six-thirty that evening after the few cross-

Channel passengers had disembarked. The sun was dropping fast below the horizon and the beautiful ship, silhouetted against the dark backcloth of the sky, already sparkled with a thousand lights.

By eight o'clock they were ready to put to sea once more and, with the children safely tucked up in their beds, Grace stood alone at the rail. In spite of her personal misgivings about her presence on the liner, she was impressed as she listened to the sound of the anchors being winched up once more. There was a prolonged ringing of bells, a powerful rush of steam and then the ship was on its way to the second port of call.

She was up again at dawn the next morning to see the coastline of Ireland, but it was not until eleven-thirty that the ship finally dropped anchor off Roche's Point, two miles out from the shore. There Grace and the children watched as 120 passengers were ferried out to the *Titanic* in tenders and hundreds of bags of mail destined for the United States was also brought out to the ship. Two hours later, she again weighed anchor. Three soulful farewell blasts on the ship's whistles mingled with the plaintive sounds of 'Erin's Lament' which was being piped by someone on a lower deck, and suddenly Grace felt a shiver of apprehension. Instinctively she put an arm round each of the children as the ship turned its bows towards the American continent. At last they were on their way, Queenstown would be their last glimpse of 'home' and Grace felt a rush of tenderness and longing for the land of her birth. By the time the ship was butting her way through the first Atlantic rollers she was already homesick, and she went to bed that night in a state of deep depression which bordered on despair.

The following morning Grace and the children were in their stateroom when Virginia made an unexpected appearance. She was looking less strained than of late and wore a skirt and jacket of deep red which helped to disguise her shape. Her eyes were brighter and her face slightly flushed.

'My dears!' she exclaimed. 'It is really too blowy to walk the deck, but Mr Scott is so ridiculous about fresh air. We have walked for the best part of a mile and I am quite breathless.'

She had spoken very little to Grace the previous day, after their initial exchange, but now she was apparently trying to put that behind her.

George raised his head from his writing and, ignoring her, asked, 'Nanny, how do you spell "camel"?'

'Really, Georgie!' cried Virginia, 'where are your manners? What about "Good morning, Mama, did you sleep well?" '

Victoria put down her pencil and slid to the floor. 'Good morning, Mama. Did you sleep well?' she asked.

'Yes, thank you dear. I did.' Virginia bent down to kiss the top of her head.

Grace nudged George, who repeated the greeting his mother had requested and then spoilt it by adding, 'Is it e-l or l-e?'

Virginia looked baffled.

'Camel,' Grace explained. 'It's e-l.'

Virginia frowned. 'There are no camels here in mid-Atlantic. Whatever are you writing about, George?'

'They're writing letters to their Papa,' Grace told her, with a slight but unmistakable emphasis on the word 'Papa'. 'There's an electric camel in the gymnasium, and they both had a turn on it yesterday afternoon. They're telling him about it.'

'Oh, *that* sort of camel,' Virginia ignored Grace's reference to the children's father. 'I see it now. So, you're managing to amuse yourselves. That's good. I did mean to pop in yesterday afternoon to see how you had settled in, but the time went so quickly. We met some friends of Mr Scott's, and you know what it's like when you get into conversation. Still, I can see you are all managing very well without me.'

She gave George's unfinished letter a cursory glance and then consulted the small gold watch which was pinned to her jacket.

'Good gracious, is that the time? I mustn't stay any longer – we're meeting for coffee in the Parisienne. Have you seen it — the coffee lounge on B-deck? All in green and white — so pretty and airy, so relaxing.'

Seeing that her visit was to be a brief one, Grace said firmly, 'I thought I'd enclose a covering letter with George and Victoria's — unless you prefer to do so yourself.'

Virginia's pleasant mask slipped a little and she gave Grace a warning look. 'I don't think that's at all necessary,' she told her. 'I shall write later. The letters won't be sent, of course, until we reach New York, so there's plenty of time. Well — say goodbye to your Mama, children, and be good children for Nanny.'

Suddenly Victoria said, 'Will you tell us a bedtime story, Mama?'

'A bedtime story? Whatever next? No dear, I shall be at dinner when you are put to bed.'

'Will you after dinner then? *Please*, Mama.'

Virginia hesitated, aware of Grace's hard stare. 'I don't think I can, Victoria,' she replied. 'Mama gets very tired in the evenings because of the new baby and I shall probably go straight to bed.'

Grace said artlessly, 'Mama will only be *next door*, Victoria. She won't be far away.'

Victoria pushed out her lower lip and gazed up beseechingly at her mother. 'I *want* you to come,' she insisted.

George smiled disarmingly. 'I don't,' he said. 'I like Nanny's stories. I like the one about the thirsty elephant who sucked up all the water in the pool and then squirted it over the other animals and they ran away and he laughed and — '

'Oh, don't go on so, Georgie,' Virginia said. 'You make my head spin. I really must go.'

'Goodbye, Mama,' said Victoria.

George, deep in thought, was licking the point of his pencil and said nothing.

Virginia turned to Grace. 'Don't let him do that,' she said sharply, just as Grace herself said, 'Don't lick the pencil, please, George, and say "Goodbye" to your Mama.'

George said 'Goodbye' and Virginia kissed both children absentmindedly. Then he glanced up. 'Can we come with you?' he asked suddenly.

Virginia frowned. 'Come where?' she asked.

'To the place on B-deck that's all white and green. Can we come with you and Mr Scott?'

'No, dear ... I don't think so. You must stay with Nanny.'

'But why, Mama?'

'Why?' Virginia looked at Grace, who stared back, refusing to help her. 'Because that's what Nanny is here for,' Virginia said at last. 'She is paid to look after you. If I looked after you all day, what would Nanny do?'

However, George refused to be side-tracked and stared up at her wide-eyed. 'Doesn't Mr Scott like children?' he asked.

'Why, of *course* he does.'

'Would *he* like us to come to the place on B-deck? Can I ask him if Toria and me can come too?'

'Victoria and I,' Virginia corrected him. 'And no, you can't ask him, George. You have a nanny and you must stay with her.' She managed to make it sound like a penance.

'I love Nanny,' said Victoria. 'I want to stay with Nanny, but I do like Mr Scott.'

'I don't,' said George, wanting to be different.

Virginia's earlier good-humour had by now vanished completely. 'That's not a nice thing to say, George!' she snapped. 'Don't you ever let me hear you talk like that again.' She glanced at Grace. 'I'm beginning to think their behaviour was a lot better under Nanny Webster's rule!' she said. 'I suggest you give them a talk about manners before the day is out. I shall call in tomorrow and I shall expect a more courteous welcome.'

Before Grace could answer, she turned angrily on her heel and left the room.

'Oh dear,' said Grace.

'I don't care,' muttered George. 'I hate Mama and I hate Mr Scott.'

'No, you don't,' said Grace. 'So stop behaving like a

baby and get on with your letter. And when Mama comes again, you must say you're sorry.'

George's mouth tightened. 'Won't!' he said.

'Oh, Georgie,' said Victoria. 'Do please be good,' but eliciting no answer to this plea, she lost interest in her brother's behaviour and applied herself once more to her letter to her father. Earlier she had dictated what she wanted to say and Grace had written it down for her to copy.

It said: 'Dear Papa. We like the ship and we like the sea and we like the four big funnels. Love from Victoria.'

'I've finished my letter,' she said at last. 'I beat you, Georgie.'

George said, 'I've nearly finished, but my letter's longer than yours.'

'It is not.'

'It is so!'

Grace counted to ten. 'When you've both finished,' she said, 'we could go for a walk on the boat-deck to get some fresh air. What do you say to that idea?'

George's smile reappeared. 'I'd like that,' he said.

*

On Sunday, their fourth day at sea, the evening was calm and clear and much colder than anyone had expected. At five minutes to nine Grace was sitting up with Victoria, who had earache and was tearful, but George was already asleep in his bed with his arms thrown up over his head, his mouth open.

'My ear hurts,' Victoria mumbled for what might have been the hundredth time.

'Still?' Grace's eyebrows rose in polite disbelief.

The purser had brought warm olive oil and this had been dripped into the troublesome ear, then her ear and head had been bound round with a length of red flannel. Victoria was well aware of the pathetic picture she made – 'like a wounded solider', Grace had said – and, secretly enjoying the attention, she was in no hurry to relinquish the limelight. Her ear had long since ceased to ache, but

Nanny was reading her a story and she resisted the onset of sleep as hard as she could.

'It *does* hurt,' she insisted. 'Go on with the story, Nanny, please.'

Grace turned the page. 'So the ugly sisters went off to the ball and poor Cinderella was left alone,' she read. 'Two big tears slid down her cheeks. "I do wish *I* could go to the ball," sighed Cinderella – '

'She can,' said Victoria, 'because the fairy godmother comes.'

Grace nodded and continued, 'Suddenly there was a knock at the back door and when Cinderella opened it, there stood an old woman.'

'An *ugly* old woman,' Victoria corrected her sleepily.

Grace hid a smile. 'Sorry. There stood an *ugly* old woman in a faded gown and tattered shawl. "Spare me a glass of water and a crust of bread," she begged, so Cinderella invited the old woman into the kitchen.'

Victoria looked up at Grace. 'You've missed another bit,' she said crossly. 'You've missed "who had a very kind heart".'

'Oh dear, so I have,' said Grace. 'So Cinderella, who *had a very kind heart*, invited the old woman into the kitchen . . .'

*

High above them, in the ship's crow's-nest, the two lookouts were half-way through their watch. At ten o'clock they would be relieved and could look forward to a comforting cup of hot cocoa. It was cramped in the crow's-nest, with just enough room for two to stand, and they chatted desultorily to pass the time. They stamped their feet and slapped their hands against their sides trying to keep warm, for the temperature had dived steeply during the evening due to the unseasonal presence in the area of pack-ice and a few icebergs. They scanned the darkness around them with the naked eye and not a little ill-feeling. The binoculars that had been used during the ship's trials had mysteriously disappeared from the

398

locker before they sailed from Southampton, and had not been replaced.

On the bridge somewhere below the crow's-nest, Captain Smith was talking to the Officer of the Watch, commenting on the clear sky. He was going to bed, but asked to be advised if the weather deteriorated in any way.

Far below the bridge in the bowels of the ship, Pat Casey and the rest of the 'black gang' were hard at work, stoking the many furnaces that heated the twenty-nine boilers which combined to power the ship's propellers. In the boiler-room itself, the air was foul with the acrid smell of the men's sweat mixed with the hot sulphurous fumes given off by the burning coal. In his bunker, Pat was shovelling coal into a wheelbarrow as if his life depended on it – his back aching, his throat and lungs full of the ever-present coal-dust, his eyes smarting from the smoke of the fire in the bunkers which still resisted all efforts to put it out. When the wheelbarrow was full, he pushed it to the top of a shute, below which Jock, a coal 'passer', waited with his barrow. When this was filled with coal, Jock wheeled it to the fireman and tipped it immediately to one side of the furnace door. The fireman, whose name was Eddy, was stripped to the waist and worked methodically with ferocious energy, his feet protected by heavy wooden clogs, his hands encased in thick canvas mittens. From time to time he thrust a ten-foot 'slice bar' into the glowing furnace to rake out the ash and separate the clinker. Eddy had worked as a stoker for seven years and knew a thing or two. In bad weather he would wait for the ship's bows to go down before throwing the coal into the furnace, and he would slam the door shut fast before the bows could rise and throw it all out again. Tonight, however, the sea was very calm and easier working and he was thankful for small mercies. Whistling tunelessly, he covered the layer of glowing fire bed with a further four inches of coal. Outside it was bitterly cold – or so he was told – but in the stokehold the temperature was a hundred degrees and still climbing.

*

The watch on the bridge changed at ten o'clock and fifty feet above them the two shivering lookouts were also relieved. The *Titanic* steamed on majestically at just over twenty-one knots, but by now a slight haze was developing directly ahead of the ship and in the crow's-nest Fred Fleet and Reg Lee leaned on the rail, staring out intently into the darkness. Time passed slowly until without warning an eerie shape loomed up out of the mist and Fred, seeing it, leaped into action. He rang the warning bell three times to signify 'Object directly ahead' and then snatched up the telephone that linked the crow's-nest with the bridge. Meanwhile, he had identified the dark mass which was drawing closer with every second that passed.

'Are you there?' he shouted.

From the bridge came the answer. 'Yes. What do you see?'

'Iceberg right ahead!'

'Thank you.'

Below, the order rang out. 'Hard-a-starboard' and seconds later, 'Stop. Full-speed astern.'

The two lookouts knew the emergency drill and could imagine the flurry of activity far below them while they stared down on to the snowy top of the enormous iceberg that was now gliding past the ship on the starboard side like a darkly glowing wall. They heard lumps of ice breaking from the berg and falling on to the ship's deck.

Below them in the starboard boiler-room there was a sudden rumbling noise and even as someone shouted, 'Shut down the dampers', water began to rush in. As the watertight doors began to descend, the incredulous men made a frenzied dash to escape. Some got under the doors in time, others were forced to climb the escape ladders to the comparative safety of the deck above.

It took Captain Smith ten grim minutes to discover that the ship's evasive action had proved unsuccessful and to realize the full extent of the damage. As the iceberg passed, a jagged outcrop of rock-hard ice had sliced open the *Titanic*'s hull; sea water was already pouring into No.6 boiler-room and the bow of the ship was being tilted by the massive weight of water. The watertight doors extended upwards only as far as E-deck, so that when the ship's angle was steep enough the water would spill over the top of the watertight door and into the next boiler-room. Then that, too, would fill up. The Captain was joined by one of the managing directors of Harland and Wolff and together they faced the terrible truth. The *Titanic*, the world's largest and most luxurious liner afloat, had suffered a mortal blow. She was fatally stricken and would not stay afloat. She had an hour left, perhaps two. The two men regarded each other with dawning horror. It was twenty minutes to midnight, the night was bitterly cold and there were insufficient life-boats to hold all the passengers and crew. Nevertheless the order must be given to abandon ship.

Chapter Twenty

Victoria was fast asleep and Grace was writing a letter to Alex when she felt the ship shudder. She glanced up, pen poised momentarily above the notepaper; then, when nothing else happened, she resumed her writing. Around her were the crumpled remains of several earlier attempts.

My dear Mr Latimer, [she had finally written]

I am so sorry for that scribbled note I left you, but I was in such a rush to get the children ready but could not bear the thought that we would all disappear, and you might think I had gone willingly or were part of the plot. I hate to write again and add to your troubles, but I feel it my duty to tell you I do not believe this trip is just a holiday. I understand we will be staying with Mr Scott's mother, but I don't know where that will be so cannot help you.

I have tried not to upset the children; they think it is a holiday. I am so afraid we will never come back or that Mrs Latimer will sack me and I will have to return to England without the children.

I am desperately worried, as you must be, and do wish I could be more help. I will post this letter directly we reach New York and will write to you and let you know as soon as I have more information.

Do please forgive me if I have let you down. It was all so hurried I could not think straight and did not want to be parted from Victoria and George at such . . .

She stopped again and frowned as the familiar vibration of the ship faltered and in the bathroom the tooth mugs ceased to rattle. The ship had stopped. Almost at once there was a deafening roar of escaping steam that drowned out all other sounds. Grace laid down her pen, crossed to the door and looked out into the passage. She was relieved to see that the steward, walking towards her, appeared quite unconcerned.

'What's happened?' she asked. 'Have we stopped?'

'It'll be nothing to worry about, madam,' he assured her cheerfully. 'Rest easy.'

Reassured, she closed the door, glanced at the two sleeping children and returned to her letter.

*

Larry Scott and Virginia were together in the casino. Virginia sat on a stool brought in from the bar while Larry stood beside her, his hand resting on her shoulder. The air was hazy with the cigar smoke and spiced with expensive perfumes as discreetly whispered comments rose above the chink of ice in glasses. The slap of cards on baize at the blackjack tables vied with the rattle of the ball against the polished wood of the roulette wheel. The lights were low and thick carpet muffled footsteps and helped to minimize any distractions which might spoil the gamblers' concentration. Larry and Virginia were watching a short, balding man who sat alone at the roulette table. A small crowd had gathered to watch him – not because he was winning, but because he was losing and seemed determined to go on doing so. He was playing with a reckless abandon that was proving quite magnetic. His wife stood beside him, her face impassive while her eyes followed every movement of her husband's plump hands as he laid out his stake money. Once he whispered something to her, but she shook her head and resumed her vigil. In twenty-five minutes he had lost over six hundred dollars by the simple method of placing his chips on every possible combination of numbers.

'He can't hope to make any money like that,' Larry repeated in whispered disbelief. 'Doesn't he know that?'

'But why not?' Virginia had no real desire to understand the intricacies of the game, but she enjoyed Larry's nearness as he leaned towards her. She was still suffering deeply from the trauma of Challis Court, but the suddenness of her removal from England, the novelty of her surroundings and the presence of the man she loved made it possible for her to keep at bay the twin hounds of guilt and fear. The sordid scene had lost the sharpness of reality and she could pretend to herself that it had never happened. It seemed so very unlikely that it *had*. Larry Scott's adoration, the strength of his personality – *that* was real. An old woman engulfed by flames was surely no more than a horrid illusion. As long as she was with Larry she felt safe, and hour by hour her terror receded to be replaced by a growing sense of security. Cocooned in luxury, it was impossible to believe that any harm could come to her. Larry was with her, a tower of strength, a rock to which she could cling. When she *did* allow her mind to dwell on the tragedy, she was able to convince herself that no one would be able to connect her with what had happened. It would be considered an accident. The old woman was drunk, she fell into the fire, broke the bottle of gin in her fall and was thus responsible for her own death.

Looking up at Larry now, she felt a surge of confidence in the future as his wife. Anyone would think they were already man and wife, she thought, and the idea gave her a thrill of satisfaction. A man, his wife and their unborn child. One day, somehow, she *must* be free of Alex. Larry was her reason to live; he was her whole world, now and for ever. She regretted the heartache her desertion would cause to her husband, but she knew now that their marriage had been a mistake. Alex had never been the right man for her. There was a price to pay for all happiness, that much she had learned, but whatever it was she would pay it gladly for the chance to spend the rest of her life with her lover.

'There are thirty-six possible bets,' Larry was explaining in a low voice, 'so if he bets on each one as he *is* doing, one of them is bound to win, but the highest odds are thirty-four to one!'

She looked at him blankly. 'Is that bad?' she asked. 'Thirty-four times the original bet – '

'But if he puts ten dollars on each number or group of numbers, then he stands to *lose* thirty-five times ten. He can only *win* thirty-*four* times ten.'

He kissed her lightly as he straightened up and turned once more to the table.

'I see,' said Virginia. 'Yes, it does sound a little crazy – but sometimes he puts more than ten dollars on some of the numbers. So he could win more.'

'He could also lose more . . . which is what he is doing!'

'Oh yes. I see.'

The man at the table raised his right hand briefly and a bar steward materialized beside him with the inevitable whisky topped up with crushed ice.

The wheel turned, slowed and stopped.

'Number thirty-eight!'

With a deft movement, the croupier set a white marker on the winning number and removed all losing bets from the table with a practised sweep of his hands.

At that moment there was an unfamiliar sound – like tearing calico – and the room shook slightly.

The gambler looked up. 'I guess we ran aground,' he quipped and there was a murmur of amused appreciation, even admiration for a man who – losing so relentlessly – could still retain his sense of humour.

Virginia looked at Larry. 'What was that?' she asked.

He shrugged. 'Maybe something wrong in the engine-room,' he suggested. 'Teething troubles; they'll soon put it right.'

'What sort of something?' she persisted.

'I don't know. Do you want me to go and find out?'

'No, it doesn't matter. Stay here with me.'

One or two of the other passengers, however, decided to investigate further and five minutes later one of them returned to the casino bearing a jagged piece of ice the size of a football.

'Seems we shook hands with an iceberg!' he announced. 'This stuff's all over the boat-deck.'

'Ice?'

He held his chunk aloft as proof. 'We must have passed pretty close. A near miss, I should say.'

Larry looked at Virginia. 'What do you say we go up top and take a look?'

She hesitated. 'It's too cold,' she demurred. 'Let's stay

405

here.' Lowering her voice, she added, 'I want to see him lose some more money. I should think he'll be bankrupt by the time we reach New York.'

'More than likely, I'd say.'

The bar steward asked, 'Can I get you anything, sir? Madam?'

'Would you like another drink?' Larry asked her.

'No, thank you,' she said. 'I think I'll go to bed soon. I'm terribly weary.'

When the steward had moved on Larry whispered, 'You said we would spend the night together.'

'Did I?'

'You did. I hope you haven't changed your mind?'

'Oh Larry, do we dare?'

'Why not? The stewards are paid to be discreet. Nothing will be said, I promise you.'

'I do want to,' she told him.

'Then we will.'

Gently, he took her hands and pulled her to her feet. 'My room or yours?' he whispered.

'Yours, I think. Nanny and the children are next to mine. Oh, darling – '

Their arms tightened round each other.

'Shall we go, then?'

She nodded and they murmured their excuses and edged a way through the crowd towards the door.

*

Pat Casey's eyes widened with shock. His mother's premonition leaped to mind with a terrible clarity as he stared at the bearer of the terrible news.

'What d'you mean, holed?' he cried. 'We can't be holed.'

'We bloody well are, I tell you. See for yourself. There's water everywhere – we'll be next.'

'Holy Mother of God!' Pat swallowed, but his throat was suddenly painfully dry and panic flared within him. Suppose, just suppose . . . controlling his fears with an effort, he said, 'It can't be that bad. It *can't*. Not the *Titanic*.'

'It bloody is, mate, I'm telling you. An iceberg – bigger than a house – and it's done for us.'

They glanced round fearfully. The engines had been closed down and the noise of escaping steam shrilled overhead.

'How do you know so much then?' Pat demanded.

'From Billy. He got it from Albert. The mail-room's flooded.'

'Holy Mother!'

They stared at each other.

'My Ma – ' Pat began hoarsely. 'She had this dream, like, afore I was born.'

'Dream? Who the hell cares about dreams?'

Pat could not bring himself to put it into words, it was too awful. He shook his head. 'Forget it,' he muttered. 'What'll we do? We can't stay here.'

'They're pumping out.'

Suddenly Pat thought of Mrs Latimer, of the nanny and her young charges.

'She's got to stay afloat,' he said. 'She can't *sink!*'

He wanted to look down the coal-shute into the stoke-hold, but was afraid of what he might see.

Albert, a short stocky man, put his head round the door.

'Captain's ordered lower the lifeboats,' he told them, then disappeared again.

'Christ Almighty!'

'I've got to go somewhere,' said Pat. 'I've got to warn someone up top.'

'Someone?'

'Those people I know – I told you.'

'You'll cop it if you're seen.'

'We're all going to cop it, so what difference?' Ignoring protests from the others, Pat began to run.

*

As the knock sounded at the door, Grace looked up from her letter. 'Who is it?'

'Me. Pat Casey.'

She opened the door and, startled, looked into Pat's grimy face.

'It's me, Pat Casey, the gardener's boy,' he told her breathlessly. 'Don't you recognize me, miss? I'm a bit grimy. I'm sorry, but they say the ship's going down. You must take the kids and go up top right away. Get into a lifeboat. All of you.'

He saw her expression change. 'But why – whatever . . .' She stared at him. 'Going *down*? You can't mean it. Not sinking?'

He nodded. 'We hit an iceberg. They'll be sending the stewards round to tell everyone, but I must get back below.'

Grace stood in a state of acute shock as he turned to go. 'Going down,' she repeated incredulously. 'The *Titanic*?' She called after his retreating figure. 'Please wait!' and he hesitated briefly.

'Must you go back below?' she asked. 'Isn't it dangerous, I mean – and if there's nothing to be done?'

'There's pumping to be done,' he told her. 'They'll keep the water-level as low as possible, but they can't do miracles.'

'But will you – ' She tried to pick her words. 'Will *you* be safe? Oh, Pat . . .'

She regretted her question as she saw his mouth tremble. He's so young, she thought wretchedly, and so frightened. Impulsively, she held out her hands and, after a moment's surprise, he grasped them with his own.

'Good luck then, Pat,' she whispered, 'and thank you.'

'You could pray for us,' he said and then ran back along the passageway.

For a moment Grace's mind would not fully accept what he had told her. It was impossible . . . out of the question. How could the biggest and best ship in the world go down? It couldn't happen – and yet she had seen it in Pat Casey's eyes. It *must* be true. Slowly she closed the door and leaned back against it, her eyes roaming the room until they reached the children's beds. Then her frozen thoughts melted into an acute awareness of what was happening and the terrible threat it posed to George and Victoria – and, of course, their mother. Where was Mrs Latimer, she wondered, and did she know what was happening?

Grace ran into the passageway and banged on the next door.

'Mrs Latimer! Ma'am!' she shouted. 'Please open the door. Quickly! Something has happened.'

There was no reply. So Mrs Latimer wasn't there. Grace's mind began to work at top speed. If she went in search of her mistress, precious time would be lost. If Mrs Latimer was not here to tell her what to do, she must think for herself. Yet she had seen no one else in the passageway, which was odd. Did no one else know the extent of the damage? Pat Casey's words echoed in her head: 'She's hit an iceberg. She's going down.' Grace willed herself to stay calm: first things first. The children must be roused, then dressed. *Then* she would go in search of their mother, taking them with her – but not for one moment would she let them out of her sight. She crossed to their beds and reaching out, gently shook both children.

'Wake up, George. Wake up, Victoria,' she said as cheerfully as she could. 'Time to wake up.'

Victoria murmured sleepily and Grace had to shake her again and again before she finally opened her eyes. George had opened his eyes and was instantly wide awake and looking round.

'Is it morning?' he asked doubtfully seeing that no light showed at the window.

'No, George, it's not morning, but we're going to get dressed just the same.'

'Why are we, Nanny?'

Already Victoria's eyes were closing again.

Grace hesitated, reluctant to tell them a lie but equally unwilling to frighten them with the truth.

'We're going to find your Mama and Mr Scott, and then we'll all have an adventure,' she said. She shook Victoria again and began to reach for their clothes. 'First, we'll have a race,' she told them. 'We'll all get dressed and see who wins.'

George hurled himself enthusiastically towards his pile of clothes. 'I'll win!' he shouted. 'I can beat you and Toria. I can beat anyone. I'm the fastest dresser. I *am*, Nanny!'

'Let's see it,' said Grace. 'Come on, Victoria, you can't go back to sleep in the middle of an adventure.'

The little girl pouted. 'I don't want to race,' she grumbled. 'I don't want an adventure. I don't want – '

'It's not a case of what you want,' Grace told her, her tone sharper than she intended. 'Just start to dress yourself and I'll help you as soon as I've put my own clothes on.'

George protested. 'That's not fair, Nanny. You mustn't help her to win.'

The next few minutes seemed to Grace like an eternity, but at last she and the children were dressed. There was another knock on the door and this time it was the steward, his face concerned and anxious.

'Oh, you're dressed,' he said. 'Good! Best to go up on deck, miss, right away. You'll be well looked after.'

'It's true, then?'

'We've had a bit of bother, yes, miss.'

'Mrs Latimer? Have you seen her?' Grace asked. 'I must find her, but she's not in her room.'

'I wouldn't wait for her, miss, if I was you.'

'But we must stay together. She'll be terribly worried if we don't find her – and she's expecting a child in May.'

'It's up to you, miss, but I'd get those kiddies to safety. Their mother's most likely up on deck right now.'

'Oh, but she wouldn't. She'd come here first, looking for them, I'm sure she would.'

With no time to spare, he could only shrug and hurry on, banging doors as he went along the passage, leaving Grace in an agony of indecision.

'I want to find your Mama,' she told the children.

'Is she lost?' asked Victoria.

'Not exactly lost, no, but I don't know where she is.' Still she hesitated. 'It *can't* go down,' she said in an effort to reassure herself.

However, a moment or two later the steward reappeared and one look at his face told Grace that, as Pat Casey had indicated, the situation was more serious than 'the bit of bother' he had mentioned earlier.

'You must put on your life-jackets at once,' he told them. 'I'll give you a hand. Then you must go directly to the boats as fast as you can. Directly, mind! And don't take any luggage.'

Grace felt a great coldness in the pit of her stomach. 'The boats?' she cried. 'You mean the lifeboats?'

He nodded.

'Is someone taking us off then?' she asked. 'Another ship? Is another ship standing by?'

'Not yet, miss, but one will be along soon,' he told her. 'They're putting out a distress call at this very moment. You're going to be fine, so don't worry.'

While he talked he was pulling down life-jackets from the top of the cupboard and between them they put one on to each of the children and fastened them securely. When Grace's had also been fastened on, the steward advised, 'Go up to the boat-deck. There'll be someone there to tell you what to do next.'

Grace glanced at the vase of flowers. The water was no longer level and the knot of fear hardened within her. 'Is the ship tilting?' she asked.

He nodded. 'A bit of a list to starboard, I'm afraid.'

Grace nodded as though in comprehension but port, starboard, aft and 'for'ard' were still mysteries to her.

Seizing her purse and abandoning the rest of their belongings, she took the children along the passage and up the stairs to the boat-deck in the company of several other worried passengers who also wore life-jackets. On deck more people were gathered in small groups, talking anxiously in low tones, and an elderly woman clutched Grace's arm. She wore an expensive fur coat under her life-jacket and fear was etched deeply into her face.

'Is it really true?' she demanded. 'I mean, Jesus Christ! Is the ship really going to sink? Do you believe that?'

Grace recognized the American accent.

'I don't know,' Grace confessed. 'I don't think they would pretend about a thing like this.'

'My neighbour thinks it's a boat drill,' the woman insisted. 'She wouldn't even leave her bed. Do *you* think it's a drill?'

'No,' said Grace. 'I wish I did.'

More people were appearing on deck – some fully dressed, others in their night-clothes with top-coats over them. A few carried their life-jackets over their arms, while others were struggling into them. Everyone looked apprehensive and no one knew what to do. There was a lot of discussion about the number of lifeboats compared with the number of passengers and crew, but Grace tried not to understand the significance of the figures. She and the children had counted the lifeboats. She *knew*. There was talk, too, of a ship coming to their aid, but no one knew the name of the ship or when it might reach them.

George tugged at her hand. 'Where's Mama?' he asked.

'I don't know,' said Grace, 'but we'll find her soon. Or she'll find us. You'll see.'

They waited for perhaps ten minutes and then a new and more terrifying message was given.

'Everyone down to A-deck, please.' And then the chilling words: 'Women and children first.'

Grace closed her eyes briefly to hide her dismay. Where on earth was Mrs Latimer? Surely she would come to find them?

'Well then,' she said briskly, 'we have to go to A-deck now – '

'Why do we?' demanded Victoria.

'Because we do,' Grace hedged.

Beside them a plump middle-aged woman was holding tightly to her husband's arm, repeating that she would not go without him.

'But Clarrie, it's always women and children first. You know that.'

'If you stay, I stay,' she insisted.

'But Clarrie – '

'I won't go, Herbert, so don't "But Clarrie" me,' she told him. 'We'll stay together until the rescue ship comes.'

Grace turned to her eagerly. 'Is there definitely a ship coming to help us?' she asked.

412

'Oh yes, dear. They're sending out distress calls – the steward just told us.'

'So why do we have to get into the lifeboats?'

Herbert shrugged. 'It might not come in time. You should go. Take your children and get into one of the boats – just in case.' He turned to his wife. 'You go with these people, Clarrie. Help the young woman with her children.'

'I won't leave you, Herbert,' Clarrie repeated. 'I know what you're up to, but it won't work. I'm too old to be caught that way.'

Grace caught the man's eye and he shrugged.

'I must go,' she said. 'Come along, children.'

'Are we sinking?' George asked.

The directness of his question shocked her. She tried to swallow, but her throat was dry.

'Maybe,' she told him. 'They're not quite sure. We're going to get into the lifeboats just in case. I told you we would have an adventure.'

She hurried them back inside and down the stairs to A-deck and as they reached it, a rocket shot into the starry sky overhead and burst into a white flare which briefly lit up the icy sea. Grace shuddered involuntarily.

'Fireworks!' cried Victoria, with a little skip of excitement. 'George, did you see the lovely firework?'

Everywhere passengers clustered in horrified or disbelieving groups. One of the lifeboats had been lowered from the boat-deck above them and now it hung outside the A-deck window parallel to the ship's rail, but because of the ever-increasing angle of the ship, there was a gap between the ship's side and the lifeboat and it was decided to lash two steamer chairs across the gap to form a makeshift bridge. Grace stood back with the children as the officer in charge began to call for women and children to get into the boat. A woman next to them, with tears in her eyes, was pushed forward by her husband who promised faithfully to join her later.

Overhead another rocket burst brilliantly against the black sky and fell into the water. Should she take the children into the lifeboat, or should she wait for their mother to appear? Grace longed to relinquish the fearful responsibility of the children's safety, but it was becoming increasingly obvious that she might be unable to do that. If Mrs Latimer did not come to find them then she, Grace, would have to decide whether to take a chance in the icy darkness of an open boat in mid-Atlantic, or to wait in the comparative security of the *Titanic*. If she made the wrong decision, it might cost them all their lives. On the other hand, there were not enough lifeboats and if another ship did *not* arrive to take them off, hundreds of people would have to die.

'Missus! Bring your kids and get into the boat.' She became aware that one of the crewmen was addressing her.

'I'm their nanny . . .' she began. 'I'm waiting for their mother.'

'She's probably in another boat. Come on, get in.' He held out a large hand and then, seeing her unwillingness, he snapped, 'For God's sake, woman! Do you want to drown?'

In that second the decision was made. She shook her head and, still holding the children by the hand, led them forward to the open window, trying not to look down at the dark void between ship and boat. If they slipped . . .

'Come on, kiddies!' cried the crewman and before Grace could protest, he had snatched Victoria into his arms and passed her out through the window to his colleague in the waiting lifeboat. As she disappeared from sight, Grace knew a moment's terror. Whatever happened, she must not be separated from the children. As George followed his sister, Grace heard a wail from Victoria.

'Nanny! I want my Nanny!'

'I'm coming, Victoria! I'm right behind you.'

She scrambled across the bridge of chairs but, at the last moment, caught her foot and tumbled headlong into the lifeboat.

Victoria was sobbing, 'Nanny! Nanny!'

Willing hands reached down to help as Grace, half dazed by her fall, struggled to get up. She had struck her

414

head a nasty blow against one of the thwarts, but she was too preoccupied to pay the pain too much attention.

'Take it easy, missus,' someone told her. 'Your children are here, safe and sound.'

She was guided to a place on the seat which ran along the inner edge of the lifeboat, and there she was reunited with George and Victoria who clung to her frantically.

'I'm not hurt,' she told them. 'We're all together again. Don't cry, Victoria.'

She sat holding the children tightly against her as more women were helped into the boat. Some were dazed and silent, others noisily tearful. Many waved to beloved husbands still on the ship, who waved back from the windows or called down into the darkness with words of encouragement, their voices thin in the cold air.

At last those in charge of the lifeboat decided it was time to lower it and they began an apparently endless and erratic descent. First one end of the boat fell a short way, then the other, so that their progress was painfully slow down the steep black side of the stricken ship. At last, however, they hit the water with a sickening jolt and for the first time the full enormity of their plight was brought home to everyone. The sea was mercifully calm but, dwarfed by the towering *Titanic* beside them, the lifeboat felt horribly insubstantial by comparison and Grace fought down an urge to scream in sheer terror. As her eyes became gradually accustomed to the darkness, she could distinguish the mass of small broken ice-floes that bobbed and jostled in the sea around them. She shivered in the cold air. There was no moon, but the sky was full of brilliant stars. Far above them another lifeboat was beginning its harrowing descent and Grace imagined the terrible heartaches as loved ones were forced to part with no guarantee that they would ever be reunited.

The crewmen in their boat began to row, and each sweep of the oars carried them further from the *Titanic*. Grace watched in fearful fascination as slowly but inexorably they drew away from the big ship which had been home to them for the past four days – providing for their every need, wrapping them in every conceivable luxury.

Now they were suddenly helpless, cast adrift in a vast uncaring blackness, cold, frightened, stripped of everything – except life and the hope of rescue.

From the far end of the boat, an elderly woman cried querulously, 'There will be a ship, won't there? They will be saved. My husband is seventy-nine – '

'Don't worry, ma'am. There'll be a ship along soon. It's on its way.'

Even to Grace's ears the man's voice sounded insincere.

'You're sure of that?' the woman persisted. 'My husband is not a well man. It's his heart, he has a problem with his heart.'

'There'll be a ship, ma'am.'

They all fell silent, lulled into a precarious hopefulness by his words.

'Nanny, where's Mama?' asked Victoria. 'Why isn't she in the boat? You said she would find us.'

'I expect she's in one of the other boats,' Grace told her. 'The sailors will look after her. See, up there?' She pointed to the next boat being lowered. 'She's probably in that boat.'

The rhythmic creak and splash of oars was strangely comforting as she strained her eyes, trying to penetrate the darkness that surrounded them, listening to the voices that carried across the water from other boats. As the lifeboat pulled further away from the ship, they could see for the first time that the *Titanic* lay low in the water with a decided list, although all her lights were blazing and incongruously the ship's orchestra was playing ragtime music, superimposing a veneer of normality on the extraordinary events which were taking place all around them.

A woman muttered, 'I don't believe this is happening. Not any of it. Oh God, someone tell me it's not happening? Just tell me it's all a bad dream.'

Next to Grace another woman struggled to stand up, holding out her arms imploringly towards the ship. 'Harry! Oh Harry, my love. I want to come back. I want to stay with you.'

Grace, choking with grief for her, tightened her grip

on the children and thanked God that she had not had to leave a beloved husband, brother or son. At least the children were safe, for the present at any rate, though she had no way of knowing what the future might hold. She was thankful when the woman was persuaded to sit down again.

The two lowest rows of portholes were now below the water but the lights glowed on, green and eerie. The nightmare continued; another boat was being lowered; orders were shouted and countermanded; a woman sobbed hysterically and the desolate wail of a baby quavered in the still air. One of the crewmen cursed; water lapped hungrily at the sides of the lifeboat and the women whispered brokenly to one another, desperately seeking the comfort that none of them could give.

George raised his head. 'I don't like it here,' he announced in a voice that trembled. 'I want to go back. Nanny, I want to go back to the ship.'

'We can't go back, George,' Grace told him as steadily as she could. 'The *Titanic* has got a big hole in it. We're much safer here; this is a nice little boat.'

'It's not nice, it's dark. I hate it and I want to go back.'

'We have to stay here,' she told him. 'I'm sorry, but we do.'

'But why? I don't like it here. I'm cold.'

Victoria leaned across Grace and pleaded, 'Please be good, Georgie. We must stay here.'

Harry's wife was sobbing again. 'Harry! Oh God, Harry, please forgive me. I ought to be with you. I'm so sorry.'

George forgot his ill-temper. 'Who's Harry? he asked Grace.

She could not bring herself to tell him that Harry was a frightened man who had been separated from his wife, and who was probably going to drown in a freezing black sea if the *Titanic* sank before a ship came to her rescue. She left the question unanswered and turned her head, searching the blackness around her for a glimpse of distant light which might herald the arrival of another ship. She thought of Pat Casey and wondered where he was. If rescue did not reach them in time, could any of the crew hope to be saved? On their first day aboard the children had counted sixteen boats on the boat-deck, and she had seen four others of a different design stowed in various places. It flashed through her mind that they had had no boat drill, and she thought bitterly that if they *had*, it would have been patently obvious that the provision of lifeboats was woefully inadequate.

'How could they?' she whispered, holding the shivering children to her. 'How could they do such a thing?' If the ship went down, hundreds of people would drown or would freeze to death in the icy water. Then a fresh thought struck her. Suppose Alex Latimer had been travelling with them? He would have been one of those men stranded on the *Titanic*, facing the loss of their loved ones as well as the prospect of almost certain death. If Alex had been on that ship, she knew her heart would break. She would feel like Harry's wife, that she would rather die with him than live on alone. The thought of it brought tears to her eyes and suddenly she was crying silently. Some of her tears fell on to George's upturned face.

'Are you crying, Nanny?' he asked.

Grace could only shake her aching head while the crew rowed steadily and their little craft drew further and further away from the big ship which was settling even lower in the waves. Ominously another row of submerged portholes showed greenly through the water, but in the velvety darkness the music played on.

Chapter Twenty-One

Virginia lay in bed, warm and sleepy, but somewhere in the recesses of her mind warning bells rang insistently.

'Larry,' she murmured, 'there's something going on.' She sat up and the vague anxiety crystallized uncomfortably into a certainty that all was not well.

'We've stopped, Larry. The ship's stopped.'

'So what? We're in no hurry,' he joked, propping himself up on an elbow and smiling at her.

'Who was that knocking at the door just now – when you didn't answer?' she asked him.

'How do I know, honey? It doesn't matter. We're together. That's all I – '

'Hush, Larry. Listen for a moment.'

They became aware of hurrying footsteps in the passageway, raised voices and the slam of more than one door.

'Something *is* happening,' she said.

He shrugged. 'It can't be anything serious. Forget it. Think about us.' His fingers moved gently around her neck and ears and up into her hair. 'You're all that matters to me, Virginia. You and me, together for always and a day. That's what – Virginia!'

She had slipped out of bed and now moved heavily to the stateroom door. She put her ear to it, listening, then re-crossed the room to lift the curtain and stare out into the night.

'There's something not quite right,' she insisted. 'I don't like it.'

Ignoring his protests, she went to fetch her clothes, then suddenly she stared down at the richly-carpeted floor. 'My God! We're not level!' she cried. 'The ship's at an angle. It *is*, Larry! Don't laugh at me.' She began to hurry into her clothes, tugging at sleeves and fumbling with buttons. He shook his head, but her unease was

419

infectious and with a smothered curse he too began to dress.

Virginia was ready first and without waiting for him, she went to the door and looked out into the passage. 'There's no one about,' she said and called, 'Steward!'

There was no answer and she half ran back into the room to press the bell that would summon him. They both waited in vain.

'Something *has* happened,' cried Virginia. Her voice rose. 'Quickly, we must find someone. Oh Larry, the children!'

'Take it easy,' he urged. 'They'll be fine. Wait for me. There, I'm ready now. You'd better go out first, alone, then I'll follow, just in case anyone – '

But Virginia had already gone and after a moment he followed and caught up with her where she stood transfixed with horror as she gazed round at the deserted reading-room. A couple of overturned chairs spoke of a hurried departure.

'Where is everyone?' she stammered. 'Something terrible has happened. I can feel it.'

As she spoke, a large group of men and women, obviously steerage passengers, pushed into the room from the far end, talking rapidly in Italian. A few wore life-jackets.

'What is it?' Virginia demanded, but they ran past her and disappeared in the direction of the boat-deck.

Virginia whirled to face Larry. 'They were wearing life-jackets. Oh God, I've got to find the children!'

'We'll look together,' said Larry, 'but maybe we should go back for our life-jackets. It won't take a – '

'There's no time,' she cried and he was forced to follow her as she hurried out of the room and up the stairway to the boat-deck.

There a terrifying sight met their eyes. All the lifeboats had gone and in their place hundreds of men lined the rails, staring desperately across the water to where a few dim lights could be seen bobbing on the water.

'Jesus!' cried Larry. 'They've launched the lifeboats!' He grabbed the arm of one of the men. 'What the hell's going on?' he demanded.

The man turned haggard eyes towards them. 'Don't you *know?*' he asked, his voice hoarse with emotion. 'We're going down – that's what's going on. They've taken off the women and children. They're out there – ' He pointed towards the lights.

'What?' screamed Virginia. 'Oh, my God! My children! I want my children. And my baby! Oh God, help me, someone.'

The man looked at her incredulously. 'You two didn't *know?*' he asked. 'Where have you been? We struck an iceberg.' For the first time he seemed to notice that she was pregnant. 'You should have gone into one of the boats, a lady in your condition.'

Virginia felt sick. While she and Larry had been making love disaster had overtaken the ship. Her stomach churned and she clutched at Larry's arm as the enormity of her knowledge overwhelmed her and a terrible thought struck her. This was retribution; this was God's punishment for Nanny Webster's death. He had been swift to judge and sentence. An eye for an eye . . . tonight her own life was to be forfeited, and that of her unborn child. She began to tremble uncontrollably and tried to speak, but before she could utter a word she felt herself losing consciousness and slid almost gratefully into temporary oblivion. The next thing she knew, she was on the floor with a group of anxious faces peering down at her. Weakly she struggled to get up.

Larry said, 'Virginia, are you OK?'

She nodded and willing hands helped her to her feet. As she stood up, she remembered what had happened and clutched Larry's arm.

'We must find Miss Martins and the children,' she begged.

The man said, 'They've all been taken off. There's nothing we can do now except wait and pray. There's supposed to be a rescue ship coming, but if it doesn't hurry it'll be too late for the likes of us.'

'Where are your life-jackets?' another man asked. 'You're going to need them.'

'We didn't have time to get them,' said Larry. He

looked at Virginia. 'The children will be safe,' he assured her. 'Miss Martins will be with them.'

There was a sudden gurgling sound as the ship shuddered and the bows settled deeper into the sea. People began to scramble aft as water followed them, rolling up the sloping deck as though in pursuit. Virginia screamed as Larry pulled her away from it.

'We're going to drown!' she screamed. 'We're going to die! Oh no, Larry, no! I don't want to die.'

Heads turned in her direction and she saw as though in a nightmare rows of pale faces, etched with a horror and grief that mirrored her own feelings. She began to scream repeatedly until Larry suddenly slapped her hard across the side of her face.

'Stop that!' he told her fiercely. 'Do you hear me, Virginia? Take a hold of yourself. We're not alone here, there are hundreds of people.'

She began to whimper. 'I don't want to die, Larry. I can't swim. And the baby – our beautiful baby. Please don't let us drown!'

'We won't drown,' he told her, but he looked round desperately as the deck under their feet continued to tilt crazily and it was no longer easy to remain upright. Dozens of people began to jump overboard.

'Look, people are jumping off the ship. We'll jump together,' he suggested. 'Then we'll be picked up by the lifeboats.'

Some of the remaining crew began to throw steamer chairs overboard for the swimmers to cling to.

'We'll stay together,' he promised her. 'And we'll hold on to the chairs; they'll keep us afloat.'

'No!' she screamed. 'I can't jump all that way – I'll never manage it – and it's so dark down there.' She began to sob hysterically. 'Oh, Alex! Alex! Forgive me. Oh God! I want my husband and my children. That's all I ask. I want to go home to my husband, I want Georgie and Victoria.'

'The children are safe,' he told her roughly. 'You heard what the man said. Look, we're going to have to jump,

Virginia, before it's too late. Trust me. I'll look after you – I swear I won't let you drown.'

But she struggled frantically with him as he tried to pull her towards the rails.

'If you won't come, I'll jump without you,' he threatened. 'If we go down with the ship we shall be dragged down by the suction. Jumping is our only chance.'

Terrified of being left on her own, she allowed him to help her to climb on to the rail and then, precariously, over it. Below, the distance to the water grew as the stern of the ship rose and a dizzying blackness yawned below them.

'Jump!' he cried and they plunged together into the dark air, arms and legs sprawling. As they did so, there was the sound of tearing metal and a huge black shape plunged down after them. It was one of the ship's funnels which had broken away under the strain put upon it by the *Titanic*'s list. It landed among the struggling swimmers, killing many but washing others away from the doomed ship. Then, without warning, the vessel's stern lifted right out of the water. People in the lifeboats watched in fascinated horror as the great liner hung, poised, perpendicular against the starlit sky. Inside the hull her giant boilers broke free from their mountings and crashed downwards through the ship towards the already submerged bow, accompanied by the sound of splintering wood. For a long time the ship seemed to hang in the dark air ... then all the lights went out at once and the great liner was nothing more than a slender shape outlined against the stars. There was a moment's terrible silence and then, with a dull roar, the huge ship slid into the sea with hardly a splash to mark her passing.

*

The woman beside Grace cried, 'She's gone! Oh my poor dear Harry!' and broke into uncontrollable weeping but Grace, dazed with shock, could make no effort to console her. Instead, she hugged the children to her and stared speechlessly across the smooth water which had closed so inexorably, so finally, over the *Titanic*. For a few seconds there was a breathless silence and then the air was clamorous with a new horror – the sounds of the survivors struggling in the icy waters; despairing voices which echoed in the darkness like the cries of souls in torment.

'We must go back,' cried Harry's wife. 'We must go back! We can pick some of them up – we must find Harry.'

Grace waited for the chorus of approval for this suggestion, but instead an argument developed between those people who thought they should go back and others who thought they should not do so.

'There'll be so many,' one woman argued. 'There are hundreds of people in the water and they'll swamp us. We shall overturn and then we'll all be drowned.'

'Oh, we must go back!' cried Grace. 'We've got room to pick up some people. The water will be freezing.'

'No!' It was a different voice. 'We can't save them all. We must save ourselves.'

'Go back, I say!'

'No!'

The two crew members were undecided.

'Please save my husband,' cried Harry's wife. 'Please go back before it's too late. He's an old man – he won't be able to swim for long.' She was wringing her hands.

'I agree,' said Grace. 'We're not much more than half full. We must go back.'

A voice from the darkness cried, 'Shut up, you stupid woman! You should have more sense. What about your children? Do you want to see them drowned? Poor little souls – you should be ashamed of yourself!'

While Grace hesitated, Victoria said shakily, 'Are we going to drown, Nanny? I don't want to.'

'No, dear, of course you're not going to drown.'

'Why are we poor little souls?' asked George.

'She's just being silly,' said Grace. 'You're quite safe. Now hush.'

Those against returning won the argument and the boat did not turn back. Harry's wife sat with her hands over her ears so that she could not hear the anguished cries as slowly those struggling in the water were frozen into silence. Grace, with an arm round each of her charges, could not shut out the dreadful sounds and knew that they would haunt her for the rest of her days.

Time passed and eventually the last pitiful pleas for help were silenced and all was quiet. Those in the lifeboats, stunned and disbelieving, stared back to where the ship had last been seen as though by a conscious act of will they could bring her back.

The enormity of the tragedy was more than anyone could appreciate, and most of the survivors had all they could do to cope with their individual griefs. Grace prayed that Mrs Latimer had somehow survived even if Mr Scott had died. Surely she must be in one of the other boats, Grace told herself, for there had been plenty of time. The children would be reunited with their mother on the rescue ship which must certainly reach them in an hour or two.

An hour passed; there was no wind, and the sea remained calm. Sound travelled on the still air and Grace could clearly hear fragments of conversation as well as weeping from other boats in the vicinity, some of which had lights so that it was possible to see that the lifeboats were scattered over a comparatively large area. For a while they had rowed towards what seemed a line of lights on the horizon, believing it to be a rescue ship, but after a while the lights had disappeared and now various people took a turn at the oars simply to keep warm and with no real destination in view.

Grace offered to take her turn at the oars, but the offer was rejected because she had the children to look after. Overhead she was surprised by the number of shooting stars that flashed across the dark heavens. The air, although still, was bitterly cold and there was water in the bottom of the boat, so that even the stoutest leather boots were soon saturated. One of the crewmen had wrapped a blanket around Grace and the children, but she still shivered violently and marvelled that, thankfully, the children had fallen asleep. She was not affected by the boat's movement, but Harry's wife was and her anguished cries for her husband were eventually superseded by the wretched sounds of sickness as she hung over the boat's side. In the unfriendly darkness their prospects of survival seemed very small and Grace longed for the dawn.

The night wore on, but so slowly. Some of her fellow survivors dozed, snoring stertorously or crying out in their sleep; others talked in subdued whispers; still more, like Grace, stared into the gloom – reliving the horror of the past hours and trying to come to terms with the harsh realities of their predicament. There was isolated activity on the seas around them. From the boat nearest to them they heard a man muttering deliriously. From another came the sudden burst of whistling, then the first bars of 'John Brown's Body' but it was just as suddenly hushed.

Grace imagined the hundreds of frozen bodies that must now be floating in the sea and began to dread the light of day. Suppose one of them was Mrs Latimer . . . but no, she told herself sternly, she mustn't allow such morbid thoughts. Whatever the next day had in store for them, she must bear it as well as she could for the children's sake and be grateful that the three of them were still alive. Three of the lucky ones. For a moment a faint smile touched her frozen lips. They were hungry, cold and frightened, floating in the middle of the Atlantic with no sign of rescue, yet they were 'the lucky ones'! She tried to imagine Alex when the news reached him that the *Titanic* was sunk. He would fear the worst – that they were all lost – but at least he would eventually hear some good news. Some unfortunates would learn that all their loved ones had gone – parents, children, brothers, sisters – all gone for ever. At least Alex would have his children.

'Oh, please God,' she whispered, 'send a ship to pick us up.'

She looked around her. The boats were drifting and bobbing, sometimes drifting towards and sometimes away from each other. If the sea rose, they would soon be parted. And what had happened to the rescue ship they had expected earlier?

'Oh please God, let them find us,' she begged silently. 'If you love us at all, just help them to find us.'

For perhaps half an hour she dozed uncomfortably, but then she was awoken by shouts from another lifeboat. The night was giving way to dawn and George raised his head.

'What is it, Nanny? What's happening?' he asked querulously. 'Are we being rescued?'

Harry's wife leaned towards them. 'We're being tied to another lifeboat,' she told him, her voice expressionless. 'One of the officers is trying to get all the boats together in a line because the sea's rising a bit.'

Now wide awake, George sat up. 'I'm stiff,' he said, 'and I'm starving!'

'You had your supper last night,' Grace reminded him.

Someone sitting on the other side of Harry's wife passed him a small bar of Nestlé's chocolate. 'Share it with your sister,' she told him, her voice dull with pain.

Grace said, 'Thank you very much. His sister's still asleep, but I'll save half for her to have when she wakes up.'

She turned back to Harry's wife and asked, 'Are you feeling less sick? Did you manage to sleep?'

'A little, thank you. I slept a little. I dreamed I was with my husband at Cherbourg, before we boarded the ship. They told us there was a delay of at least an hour and poor Harry was so cross – he hates delays.' She paused and said, 'I should say "hated" delays. I keep forgetting that he's gone.'

'Please don't give up hope,' said Grace. 'He may be in another lifeboat.'

The woman gave a shuddering sigh. 'No, he's gone, I know it. He couldn't swim . . . An hour's delay, they told us in Cherbourg, so we walked up and down along the Grande Jettée because there was nothing else to do. Harry wanted to give up the trip when it was delayed; he was so cross about it – he's very hot tempered.' This time she did not correct her use of the present tense. ' "Let her go without us," he said. "If she can't even get to Cherbourg on time, how long will it take her to get to New York?"

I calmed him down, the way I always do. But when she came, she was so beautiful. If I'd only known . . . if I'd only listened to Harry – just this once.'

Searching for a few words of comfort, Grace said, 'If he is . . . gone, you'll meet again in heaven. The parting's not for ever.'

'Do you believe in life after death?'

'Of course.'

She sighed. 'Harry didn't. He always said this was all we got, but I used to try to believe. Now I shall try harder than ever.'

'Do you have any family?' asked Grace. 'Children, I mean.'

'No, we only had each other. Oh, my darling Harry!' Her voice broke.

Grace reached out and took her hand. 'I understand,' she said. 'Cry if you want to.'

Harry's wife shook her head helplessly. 'We were so close . . .' she began.

George asked, 'Why is the boat going up and down?'

'The waves are getting bigger,' Grace told him, 'but we're quite safe.'

'Where's Mama?' he asked next. 'Is she in another boat?'

'I'm sure she is,' she assured him.

Victoria raised her head sleepily and rubbed her eyes. 'I don't like it here. I want to go home. Please can we go home, Nanny? I don't like the adventure any more.'

'Nanny?' echoed Harry's wife. 'Aren't you their mother?'

'No.'

'But their mother *was* with you on the *Titanic*?'

'Yes.'

Grace injected a warning tone into the word and hoped she would not say anything to alarm the children. She was relieved when the woman said, 'Ah!' and fell silent.

George piped up, 'Her real name's Virginia Dorothea Latimer, but we just call her Mama. She's going to give us a baby brother.'

Victoria, not to be outdone, confided, 'Mr Scott's on

428

the ship, too. We can call him Uncle Larry if we want to, but he's really Mr Scott. Only we don't know where they are. Mr Scott is Mama's friend and – '

'Hush now!' Grace broke in hastily. 'That's enough. It's still night-time and you two must try to go back to sleep.'

'I don't feel sleepy,' George protested. 'I can see a bit of light in the sky.' He pointed. 'Is that morning?'

'The dawn,' whispered Harry's wife. 'I wish I needn't see it.'

'My feet are cold,' grumbled Victoria, 'and so is my nose.'

'Rub your hands like this,' Grace suggested. 'Both of you. That will warm you up.'

'Mama won't be cold,' said George, 'because her coat's got a lovely fur collar.'

Suddenly one of the crewmen pointed. 'Look! The lights of a ship! I swear it! See over there?'

All heads swivelled and all agreed eagerly that it did look like a ship. Some agreed with wholehearted optimism, but others, afraid of further disappointment, were more cautious.

'I can definitely see *something*,' Grace said, 'but is it a ship?'

Snippets of information were passed from the other end of the lifeboat.

'They say it might be the *Carpathia* or the *Virginian*,' said Harry's wife. 'Apparently they sent out distress signals and messages – from the *Titanic* I mean – and they were two of the ships that answered the calls. So it could be either of them.'

Somewhere on one of the other lifeboats the order was given to move towards the lights and hope flared at once amongst the survivors.

As the sky grew lighter, they drew nearer to what proved to be another liner, but now their own progress through the water seemed agonizingly slow for the wind had freshened and the calm sea had given way to sizeable waves. In the pale light of dawn they could make out the rest of the lifeboats and could see for the first time the

429

extent of the disaster, for the fragile boats held so pitifully few survivors. Many people, visualizing the tremendous loss of life, broke down and sobbed despairingly and Grace was among them. The children watched anxiously as the tears she could no longer hold back rolled down her face.

'Don't cry, Nanny,' begged George. 'We're going to be saved. Please don't cry.'

'I'm sorry . . .' she sobbed. 'Take no notice of me, I'll be all right in a minute.' But the tears continued, hot against her frozen cheeks.

Harry's wife said suddenly, 'Come and sit by me, children, and we'll play a game, just until Nanny is herself again. We'll play "I have a basket". Do you know that game? I used to play it when I was a girl.'

'No,' chorused the children and they hurried to move along beside her.

'Well, it's very simple,' she explained. 'I say to you "I have a basket" and you ask "What have you in it?" and I say "Something that begins with 'A' " – like apple. Then it's your turn, George. You say you have a basket and we ask what's in it, and you say an apple and something that begins with "B".'

'A ball!' cried George, grasping the idea at once. 'I know. And then Toria says cabbage.'

'I don't,' said Victoria. 'I don't say cabbage. I don't like cabbage.'

'You don't have to *like* it, silly,' he told her. 'You only have to have it in your basket. It must start with "C".'

'Then I'll have a kangaroo in my basket.'

George hesitated, looking at Harry's wife. 'Does that start with "C"?'

'No,' she said, 'but cat does,' and so the game progressed while Grace cried out some of her misery, grateful for a few moments to come to terms with her emotions.

In the growing light she saw Harry's wife for the first time and realized with surprise that she was older than she had imagined – a small, frail woman probably well over seventy. She imagined Harry being drawn down into the icy water by the ship's final plunge. Perhaps, she thought wearily, those who could not swim were better off than those who could, for the end of their agony would come that much sooner. She shuddered. Poor 'Harry's wife', she thought, and made a mental note to ask her proper name.

A cry went up from one of the leading lifeboats.

'It *is* a ship!'

'A ship!'

'Oh, sweet God! It's a ship and she's heading this way!'

'She's coming towards us! Heaven be praised.'

Grace uttered her own prayer of thanks, and the sight of the distant liner was one she would never forget as the vessel sailed towards them with rockets bursting overhead and all her lights blazing.

'She's coming,' whispered Grace. 'Thank God, she's coming for us!'

*

It seemed an eternity before the ship reached them. Slowly she steamed towards them – a four-masted vessel with one tall slender funnel amidships – unbelievably beautiful to the shocked survivors who, even as the ship loomed nearer, hardly dared to believe that their ordeal was almost at an end. It was the *Carpathia*, diverted from her normal route, under the direction of Captain Rostron. Cheer upon cheer went up from the lifeboats as the rescue ship drew alongside and cut her engines. Then began the slow and dangerous business of transferring the survivors from the lifeboats to the liner, while the steadily mounting waves threatened disaster at the very moment of rescue. The greatest care was taken over this manoeuvre as one by one the lifeboats went alongside and the exhausted survivors were taken on board.

George and Victoria were hoisted aboard in large mailbags and then it was Grace's turn. Supported by an underarm sling, she was hauled up the side of the ship and helped over the rail to safety. As she knelt to hug the children to her, she could hardly believe that they were safe at last.

'Come along, my dears,' said a kind and welcoming voice. 'I'm sure you could all do with a nip of brandy and a nice hot drink.' Grace looked up into the sympathetic face of a motherly-looking woman and could only nod her thanks.

'We've coffee and cocoa, but first let me help you off with your life-jackets. You won't be needing those any longer, thank goodness!'

Five minutes later as they sipped their cocoa, Grace found time to look around her. The *Carpathia*'s lounge had been turned into a temporary dormitory and blankets, steamer rugs and toilet articles were being distributed to the *Titanic*'s passengers. Most of the survivors had lost everything and Grace was no exception. Her only thought had been for the children's safety and apart from her purse, she had brought none of her personal belongings.

'I'm not the children's mother,' she explained to one of the *Carpathia*'s stewardesses. 'I'm only their nanny. I must find their mother; her name's Latimer. She'll be frantic with worry. I haven't seen her since early yesterday evening.'

'Don't you worry, my dear,' the woman told her. 'One of the officers is compiling a list of survivors and you should be able to find her if she's here. Have a look round when you're feeling rested.'

Grace finished her cocoa and settled the children into a makeshift bed of cushions and blankets, but then waited until they had both fallen asleep before she slipped away in search of her employer. Eagerly she made her way among the survivors, peering into the hundreds of shocked faces for the only one she would recognize. Among the crewmen she found a grimy-faced stoker and paused to ask after Pat Casey.

'Haven't seen him,' was the dazed reply. 'I don't reckon the poor kid made it. Most of 'em down there didn't.'

There was still no sign of Mrs Latimer and Grace fought back a mounting panic. Some people, she knew, had been taken to the ship's hospital and it was possible that Mrs Latimer was among them. At last, after an exhaustive search, she was directed to the officer who was listing survivors and waited impatiently in line with the rest of the desperate relatives.

'Virginia Latimer,' she told him when at last her turn came. 'Mrs Virginia Latimer, from Beaulieu near Southampton, Hampshire, in England.'

He ran his finger down the list, turned a page and tried again.

'I'm sorry, miss,' he said. 'There's no one of that name.'

Grace stared at him, numb with horror. No one of that name? But Mrs Latimer couldn't be dead, she *couldn't*. He was wrong.

'Are you sure?' she whispered. '*Really* sure? It's Latimer with only one "t".'

'I'm sure, miss,' he told her. 'There is no Virginia Latimer. I'm truly sorry, believe me.'

Still she could not accept what he told her. 'But are *all* the survivors on board this ship?'

'They are.'

There was one more possibility. 'What about the hospital?' she asked.

He tapped the second sheet with another shake of his head. 'This is the hospital list. I've been through them both. I'm afraid your friend must be considered amongst the missing.'

'Scott, then?' she asked desperately, her voice hoarse. 'Larry Scott from America. I suppose that's Lawrence Scott. I think he's from New York.'

His finger retraced the two lists and then he shook his head again. 'I'm sorry. He's not here either.'

Blindly she turned away, but then on an afterthought tried a final name.

'Pat Casey,' she said. 'He worked in the stokehold.'

'Different list, ma'am. You'll have to see Second Officer Lightoller. I've just got the passengers.'

The woman behind her pushed forward. 'Look,' she said to Grace, 'he's told you. There's others waiting.' She turned to the officer. 'Do you have a man name of Schultz? Johann Frederick Schultz? Tall and thin. Dark hair.'

Grace stumbled away, her thoughts chaotic. Virginia Latimer and Larry Scott *missing*.

'No,' she whispered. 'Not missing. *Dead*. Both dead.'

She returned to the children and sat beside them, her eyes dark with the unimaginable, her throat aching. She longed for a familiar face in the surrounding chaos; she wanted a pair of strong arms to hold her close; she yearned suddenly for Alex Latimer. But when she did see him again it would be to shatter his world with the terrible knowledge that his wife was lost for ever. His adored Virginia had been drowned at sea. Grace hoped desperately that *she* would not have to be the bearer of that bad news.

*

The shocked survivors mostly rested for the remainder of the day while their names were transmitted to the *Olympic* and from there to Cape Race. Dimly Grace became aware that eventually the terrible news would reach England and plunge Berwick House into mourning. All around the world hopeful relatives would be receiving confirmation of their worst fears, for the true extent of the disaster was now apparent and rumour had it that out of more than two thousand people aboard the *Titanic* two-thirds of them had been lost.

Grace curled up on a mattress beside the children and tried to sleep, but her mind was too active and at last she gave up the attempt and, leaving the children in the care of 'Harry's wife', went to enquire after Pat Casey. He, too, had been drowned, and the news added intolerably to her burden of despair. She made her way on deck where a chill wind was blowing, but she stood alone at the rail staring out over the choppy sea.

The *Carpathia* had turned round and was now on its way back to New York; from there, Grace assumed they would be sent back to England. The prospect of another voyage through those cold, hostile seas terrified her, but if the children were ever to be reunited with their father it was inevitable.

She was wearing dry clothes which the *Carpathia's*

passengers had given her. They had been altered to fit, but she felt strange in them and hoped to get her own clothes back some time. George and Victoria slept in borrowed nightwear, but Harry's wife had stubbornly refused to change out of her wet clothes, confiding in Grace that if there was an afterlife Harry's ghost would seek her out and she wanted him to recognize her.

Leaning back against the ship's rails, Grace looked up at the *Carpathia*'s single smoke-stack and recalled how welcome a sight that had been. Now the ship's flag flew at half-mast, fluttering strongly, a small flash of bright colour against the sombre grey skies above it. Like a flicker of hope in the midst of despair, thought Grace, and felt some of her courage returning. She must not be so crushed by the tragedy of Virginia's death that she overlooked the miracle of their own survival. If the *Carpathia* had not come to their aid, the rising seas might have claimed them all. It was a sobering thought and Grace was overcome by guilt. In the confusion she had not properly thanked Him for their safe deliverance and now she sank to her knees on the deck and, resting her clasped hands on the bottom rail, she began to pray.

Almost at once a voice interrupted her prayer. 'You all right, miss?'

A burly crewman from the *Carpathia* was regarding her with a mixture of sympathy and suspicion. 'You'd be better off down below with the rest of the passengers,' he told her. 'The wind's getting up and we don't want you falling overboard now that we've rescued you!'

Or throwing myself into the sea to join a lost loved one, Grace thought, correctly interpreting his anxiety. Yes, that must be a temptation to a bereaved relative. She wanted to stay where she was, away from her grieving fellow survivors, but she understood that alone on deck she might be considered a risk to the already over-burdened rescuers so she rose obediently to her feet.

'I'm fine,' she said, 'but I'll go below. Please don't worry about me.'

But he took her arm and guided her to the doorway,

and did not release her until she was safely inside once more.

'Try and get some sleep,' he advised and she nodded, and made her way back to the children. George was still asleep, but Victoria was sitting beside Harry's wife who was singing nursery rhymes to her.

'You sleep,' she told Grace. 'I'm better with something useful to do. I don't want time to think.'

'You're very kind.'

'Nonsense! Victoria and I are great buddies, aren't we?'

Victoria nodded, then asked Grace, 'Where is my night-gown? I don't like this one. Mine's got lace on it and ribbons and – '

Grace hesitated then said firmly, 'We left it behind on the *Titanic* and it's gone down with the ship, but when we get home we'll buy you another one.'

Victoria pouted a little and over her head Harry's wife mouthed the words, 'When are you going to tell them?'

Grace knew what she meant. 'I thought their father, perhaps . . .' she stammered, aware that she had in fact been unwilling to accept responsibility. 'I don't think I should – at least, I don't think I *could*. Oh dear!'

She looked appealingly at the older woman and Harry's wife took her hand.

'I was just nine years old when my beloved elder brother died,' she told Grace. 'I've always remembered how it was. They tried to keep it from me – kept his bedroom door locked; spoke in hushed voices; smiled artificial smiles. I suspected the truth long before they finally told me, and that meant I had to bear the grief and fright all alone. How could I ask for comfort when no one would admit that anything was wrong? It was such a relief when my father said "Sam is dead".'

Grace nodded slowly without comment.

'The point I'm making is that if they had told me right out, there would have been none of that waiting and wondering. Children are very sharp, honey, they don't miss a trick. I'd guess that these two . . . you see, I'm doing it too. I'm disguising things, talking in a kind of code.'

'What is a code?' asked Victoria.

'I see what you mean,' said Grace. 'I just felt that maybe it wasn't my place. Suppose their father wants to break it to them in his own . . .'

'Break what, Nanny?'

Harry's wife shook her head. 'I guess I should have kept my mouth shut. Harry always said I – ' She broke off. 'I'm sorry if I did wrong,' she said. 'I wanted to save them from what I went through.'

'You're right,' said Grace, but her heart still shrank from the prospect. 'Maybe tonight – or tomorrow morning . . .'

Harry's wife squeezed her hand and then let it go. 'It's hard for you, but for their sakes the sooner they know the sooner the healing can start. So . . . why not now?' she said softly and, struggling to her feet, added, 'I'm getting the cramp in my legs. I'll take a bit of a walk.'

When she had gone, Grace steeled herself to look at Victoria.

'Tell us what?' Victoria was all eyes.

Grace thought frantically. Was this the right time? Should a nanny be the one to break the news? Suppose Harry's wife was wrong and Alex was angry with her? Yet the older woman's words made sense; there was a kind of logic to them.

At that moment, as if roused by some sixth sense, George stirred, rubbed his eyes and sat up. He looked into their faces and, instantly alerted by Grace's tension, asked, 'Are we sinking again?'

'No, no,' said Grace and as he sat up she pulled both children closer to her and put an arm round each. 'We're not sinking but . . .' – she lowered her voice – 'but I do have some bad news. Bad and sad, too, and I want you both to listen very carefully while I tell you.'

Two pairs of anxious eyes stared trustingly up into hers and she almost changed her mind. Then she thought about Alex and how distressed he would be by his wife's death. If he also had to break that news to his children . . . No! Grace told herself. This is your chance to do something for him. Do it!

'Is it about Mama and Mr Scott?' asked George.

'Yes,' she told them. 'Poor Mama and Mr Scott were still on the ship when she sank; they weren't in a boat like us. So . . .' she swallowed hard, 'so I'm afraid they are both drowned.'

There was a moment's silence as the children digested the information.

'How do you mean?' asked George, his lower lip beginning to tremble. 'Drowned dead? In the water?'

Grace could only nod.

Victoria slid a finger into her rosebud mouth, then took it out again and said, 'Like Harry, do you mean?'

'Yes, dear.'

George was trying to take in the enormity of what Grace was telling him. '*And* the baby brother?' he asked.

'He's gone too, George.'

'Won't we see Mama again?' he asked. 'Not ever?'

'No, George. We won't – and that's very sad,' Grace told him. 'It makes me want to cry when I think about it and I expect you'll want to cry, too. I think we'll all be very sad for a while – Papa, too.'

'Papa isn't drowned, is he?' asked Victoria quickly.

'No. Papa is safe and sound at home and soon we'll all go back there – '

'Except Mama,' said George. 'Has she gone to heaven like Charlie Abrahams?'

'Yes, she has.'

Victoria said, 'There are angels in heaven?'

'Yes.'

George frowned. 'And we're all going home to Papa?'

'Yes – and one day we'll stop feeling sad and be happy again.' Grace wanted to give them a little hope.

Suddenly two large tears rolled down George's face and he put out his tongue and licked them away. Two more tears followed and wordlessly Grace bent her head to kiss him.

'Kiss me, too, Nanny,' begged Victoria and Grace complied as the little girl, finally moved by her brother's stricken expression, dissolved into tears.

George reached out and took hold of his sister's hand

and through his own tears said, 'Don't cry, Toria. We've still got Nanny. Nanny's not drowned.'

'Certainly not,' said Grace. 'You'll always have me and Papa to look after you.'

George struggled to hold back the tears, but Grace said shakily, 'I think we're so sad that we'll have to cry,' and then he allowed himself to give way to his grief and they clung together for a long time while the storm of sorrow broke over them all. When eventually it rolled on it left them dazed and exhausted, but Grace knew intuitively that, thanks to 'Harry's wife', the worst was probably already over.

*

They woke next day, on the 18th April, to find the *Carpathia* making slow progress in thick fog. They had passed the Ambrose Lightship earlier in the morning, but the passengers who crowded to the rails later in the day could see very little and when rain added to their discomfort many gave up and went below again.

Later, as the *Carpathia* steamed towards New York harbour, the passengers and crew were startled to find the ship surrounded by a mass of small boats which had been hired by members of the press who – with the help of countless megaphones – bombarded them with unintelligible questions which most people made no attempt to answer.

George asked Grace, 'What are they shouting for, Nanny?'

'They want to know what happened to the *Titanic*,' she explained.

Both children were pale and subdued, but Grace was pleased to see that they were taking an interest in what was happening. The *Carpathia* stopped at Piers 59 and 60 and the *Titanic*'s lifeboats, which had been taken aboard, were swung over the side and lowered into the water to be rounded up by a single waiting tug and towed away to a temporary berth.

But for those lifeboats, thought Grace, we would all have shared Virginia's untimely end.

A little further on, the ship passed Staten Island and took on board a doctor to deal with the procedures of quarantine; then later still they passed the Statue of Liberty, which showed up in eerie flashes of lightning accompanied by menacing rolls of thunder. New York Harbour, though a welcome sight, was hardly welcoming as Pier 54, hushed and silent, appeared through the darkness. Police barriers kept the crowds at bay as at half-past nine the liner berthed. As the gangways were lowered, ambulances waited below for the injured and motor-cars and taxis were there for those fortunate enough to live in the City. Passengers with nowhere to go would be accommodated in hotels until further arrangements could be made for them. It was nearly ten o'clock when Grace and the two children set foot on American soil.

Chapter Twenty-Two

On the morning of the sixteenth, in an upstairs room in Millbank Street, Ellen sat in front of the chest of drawers and stared at her own reflection in the tarnished glass of the swing-mirror. Her eyes were wide and frightened and all the colour had left her cheeks. She lifted the hairbrush with mechanical movements of her right arm, but she did not feel the bristles as they slid through her lank brown hair, not did she hear the fretful wail of the baby in the cot beside the bed. Her ears were deaf to the subdued chatter from the street below the window, although she knew what they were talking about. They were discussing the terrible rumours that had reached the town just after nine o'clock that morning; discussing the message which had been posted up in the window of the *Southampton Times* and round which a shocked crowd still waited for news that the *Titanic* had somehow survived. Only Ellen knew for sure that it had gone down, taking Pat with it. She could have told them not to expect good news. The news would be bad . . . very bad. She had seen it so many times in the dream, and now she sat brushing her hair and her son was drowned as she had always known he would be.

Her two sisters and her mother were waiting outside the *Southampton Times* office, but she had refused to go with them. The dream had been very specific – she had heard the hiss of steam escaping and had never forgotten the fear on the men's faces as the water engulfed them. Oh no, she did not need to stand outside in the street parading her fear. She had lived with it for nearly seventeen years and now the nightmare had become reality. She would not pretend to be surprised, nor did she intend to wait on a busy corner for the list of survivors to be posted up. Her son's name would not be there. He was dead. She had *seen* him die many times, his arms waving helplessly, his eyes bulging, his fingers clawing desperately as the rushing, foaming water tumbled him around, tossing him and his fellows like corks, carrying them all down into the depths of the sea, and she had seen the ship lying on the seabed, hidden from the curious eyes of men.

A white face with red-rimmed eyes stared back at her from the mirror and she thought sadly that there would be many more faces like that before the week was out. Women without husbands, children without fathers, mothers without sons. With a sigh she put down the brush and thought, 'Did I ever tell him that I loved him? Did I need to? Did he guess?' He'd been such a skinny little kid. In her mind's eye she saw him now on his first day at school. She had sent him off with his brothers, but at playtime she had walked past the school on her way to the baker's to catch a glimpse of him in the playground, although she had never done that for any of the others. So why had she needed reassurance about Pat? She had waited outside the railings, not letting herself be seen, just to make sure no one was bullying him, but he looked so small and helpless that she had gone to the baker's in tears. Still, St Mary's was as good a school as any – not that he was bright, but he'd never been caned. Not once. At least, not once that she knew of. And he would always run errands, whether he got a halfpenny or not. Off down St Mary's Street to fetch a bit of fish, and sometimes they'd let him wash down the slab and sweep the floor and then they'd give him the herrings for nothing. He was a bit of a charmer in his own way, was Pat. Everyone liked him. And how often had he run down Chapel Road with his father's best suit? First thing of a Monday morning before school to take it in, and last thing of a Friday night to redeem it. He hated going to the pawnbrokers, but he never grumbled.

Slowly she opened the top drawer and took out a folded scrap of paper. She read it carefully, although she knew it by heart: 'Dear ma, I can swim, I dun it for you.' He was nine when he had written that. Tears blurred her eyes, but she forced them back. He'd been going to

Northam Baths without telling her, and someone had taught him to swim. Not that swimming could save him now. When he was eleven he got diphtheria with the rest of the kids at the school, and the doctor blew sulphur or some such down their throats. Pat didn't die. She had known he wouldn't because he wasn't meant to go that way, but one of his brothers had gone. Now it was Pat's turn.

*

The city of Southampton was plunged into gloom by the disastrous news and, as well as the newspaper office, the White Star Lines Office in Canute Street was besieged with women clamouring for news of beloved fathers, brothers, husbands and sons. They stood for hours with babies in their arms and toddlers clinging to their skirts, talking in low voices, trying to reassure one another that the worst had not happened; vainly hoping against hope.

Alex and Guy, at home in Berwick House, were also waiting for news. By the evening of the same day several rumours were circulating in the town. The first was that *all* the crew and passengers had been taken off the ship by the *Carpathia*, the *Virginian* and the *Parisian*. The second was that the *Titanic*, despite being badly holed, was still afloat and making her own way to Halifax, Nova Scotia. These rumours gave them hope, but on the next day a contact in Southampton rang Berwick House with bad news.

'No truth in them, then?' said Alex. 'What's that? The *Carpathia* has some of them? Not all? They weren't picked up until the next *morning*? Why not, in God's name? She must have put out a distress call . . . oh God, that's unbelievable. I *won't* believe it . . . What about the White Star offices in London – in Cockspur Street? I can't get through, I've tried again and again . . . Oh, you have. And no luck? I suppose the lines are jammed. It's pretty hopeless . . . How could such a thing happen? It's incredible. Yes, I'll keep hoping, but – Oh, Hugh! My wife and my two little ones . . . President Taft has done

443

what? The line's very bad, I'm afraid. Oh, a *statement*. Yes, I see.'

After what seemed an age, he replaced the receiver, rubbed his eyes tiredly with the back of his hand and went back upstairs to his father's bedroom.

'For God's sake tell me,' begged Guy, his face haggard.

'It's not so good,' Alex said quietly. 'There's been some loss of life. The only ship to pick up survivors was the *Carpathia* and . . .' he drew a deep breath ' . . . she has fewer than half the passengers. Most of the men and the crew have almost certainly been lost.'

Guy looked at him dully. 'Have they saved all the women and children?'

Reluctantly, Alex shook his head. 'It seems that after the *Carpathia* left, the *Virginian* went to the area of the sinking but found no one alive. Only bodies frozen to death. The *Parisian* reports the same story.'

The old man put a shaking hand to his head and Nurse Binns hovered anxiously beside him.

'President Taft has sent two fast cruisers to meet the *Carpathia*, but so far there's no list of survivors.'

They looked at each other, hardly daring to hope.

'It would be women and children first, you know,' said Guy. 'There's every chance.'

Just then there was a tap at the door and Fanny came into the room. Her face was pale and she had obviously been crying.

'Is there any news, sir?' she asked. 'We was all wondering . . .'

Alex turned to her. 'Nothing definite, I'm afraid, Fanny. There are some survivors, but hundreds have perished.'

'Oh, sir!' she said. 'Cook says to tell you we're all praying hard and she says God will provide.'

He smiled briefly. 'Thank you. Please tell the staff that I appreciate their concern. We mustn't give up hope.'

Fanny gave a nod and turned to go but suddenly she turned back, her eyes glittering with fresh tears. 'Oh sir, those two lovely children! It's too terrible!' She burst into tears and ran out of the room, leaving the door open behind her.

'She's overwrought,' said Alex. 'She meant well.' He sank down into a chair and covered his face with his hands.

He had been unable to keep the news of Virginia's desertion from his father. John Martins, increasingly uneasy about his own role in the affair, had confided in Mrs Wade who had immediately decided that Alex should be told, but had had to ask Guy for the number of his brother's telephone. The old man, contrary to his nurse's ominous predictions, had survived the shock without another heart attack and had rallied surprisingly to offer Alex moral support and to rail against Virginia.

'If only she hadn't met that damned Scott fellow!' he now burst out. 'I'm surprised at her . . . letting him talk her into this trip. I thought she had more sense. I blame myself; I should have stopped them, Alex.'

'How could you?' Alex glanced up at him. 'It was all so sudden – at least, I assume it was. Maybe it wasn't; maybe they'd been planning it for some time.'

Guy shook his head. 'Going off like that – and taking the children too, not to mention Grace Martins. Risking their lives. She's behaved abominably.'

Exhausted with worry and lack of sleep, Alex found himself defending her, trying to play down the probability of infidelity.

'It's easy to talk like that with hindsight,' he said, 'but no one could have foreseen such a monstrous tragedy. How often does the impossible happen? She suddenly decided to take the children for a holiday to New York. It was damned thoughtless and impetuous, I grant you, but not exactly a crime.'

'Holiday be damned!' cried Guy. 'Let's not pretend we don't know what's going on. She didn't even leave a note, for God's sake. Half-way across the world with a man she hardly knows . . . or maybe she knows him better than we thought. I *knew* he was no good the moment I set eyes on him. Money, but no morals. That's the Larry

445

Scotts of this world. You should never have trusted the fellow!'

'*You* spoke very highly of him at the beginning,' Alex protested. 'We all liked him.'

'Virginia liked him a sight too much! That's obvious!'

Alex shook his head wearily. 'These things happen – ' he began.

'Only if you *let* them happen. Women are weak and Virginia was no exception . . . weak and foolish – and men like Scott prey on them.' The old man shook his head wearily. 'I'd like to get my hands on that scoundrel. I'd tell him a thing or two. If anything's happened to those children . . .' With a choked cry he began to sob, an ugly breathless sound and the nurse gave him a large handkerchief. Alex envied the old man his tears for his own eyes were dry, his heart was constricted and his body felt cold with dread. He blamed himself for what had happened. He had sensed that something was wrong and now he knew he should have forced the matter into the open months ago. But he had been so sure that the blackmail was the reason for her coldness; had thought himself so clever in dealing with Nanny Webster; had been so confident that with Lucien married to Eleanor, his relationship with Virginia would be finished. And all the time she had been having an affair with Larry Scott and now he was tortured by the suspicion that the child was not his. He had been so terribly blind.

So many revelations in so short a time, followed by the news of the *Titanic* disaster, had left him too confused to think clearly. His earlier bitter thoughts on divorce had been totally swamped by the fear that he might have no wife to forgive or divorce; that he might have no children either. The prospect was too terrible for comprehension and Alex found himself living a nightmare, prey to conflicting fears and nameless horrors that hovered like wraiths around the edges of his consciousness, threatening to materialize into even more dreadful realities. He covered his face with his hands, imagining them still and lifeless, trapped in the gigantic hulk of the sunken ship. George and Victoria, his beloved little ones, might already be dead, gone from him for ever. 'No!' he whispered. 'No! She would never let them die.'

With a start, he realized that he meant Grace Martins. The nanny was devoted to them and she would never have allowed them to drown. Slowly the notion grew in his mind, strong and comforting. Whatever had happened, Grace Martins would have been with them and she would have found a way into one of the lifeboats. But what of Virginia? How much *did* she feel for Scott? If the women had to leave the men behind, would she have left him? Abruptly, he stood up and, moving to his father, patted his shoulder and said, 'Grace Martins wouldn't let them die.'

Guy, wiping his eyes, glanced up in surprise. 'Nanny?'

The nurse spoke up suddenly, 'She has a good head on her shoulders, sir.'

'She loved them,' said Alex. 'She lived for them. I think she'd save them somehow, I feel it.'

'My God, Alex, I certainly hope so.' Guy drew a long, trembling breath. 'It's this waiting. I know now how they feel . . . the wives and mothers in a mine disaster, waiting for hours at the pit-head for news. Perhaps you should go into town?'

Alex shook his head. 'Hugh says you can't get near the White Star office. We're fortunate that he knows someone on the inside. I don't think I could bear the sight of all those women, most of them soon to be widowed. There couldn't be many crew saved; it would be passengers before crew.' He frowned suddenly. 'That gardener's lad we had – wasn't he going to sea? Let's hope he wasn't on it. He should have listened to his mother. Southampton's going to be hard-hit; half the crew must have been local men . . . maybe more.' He slammed his right fist into his left palm and cried, 'Oh, Christ, what a mess!'

The old man sighed again, but the tears had released his tension and brought a little colour back to his face.

'How could she sink?' he asked Alex. 'Surely ships have hit icebergs before now. How could a lump of floating ice – that's all they are – sink the *Titanic*? It's

crazy. Oh, Alex, those little ones; they'd be so frightened.'
His lips trembled again.

'Not with Miss Martins,' Nurse Binns reminded him
quickly. 'Like Mr Latimer says, she'd look after them.'

'Poor girl. Dragged off like that at a moment's notice,
maybe to her death, and all because of – '

He broke off and began to cough and then to gasp for
air. Alex watched anxiously as the old man struggled to
master the paroxysm and Nurse Binns darted forward
once more.

'Are you all right, sir?'

'Of course I'm not all right, dammit,' he spluttered.
'Get me a brandy.'

She was shocked. 'No alcohol, sir. You know what the
doctor said.'

'Damn the doctor! I want a brandy, I tell you!'

Alex glanced at the nurse. 'A small *medicinal* brandy?'

She hesitated. 'A *very* small one, then,' she conceded,
and they watched the old man toss it down in one rebellious gulp.

'Virginia was never right for you, Alex,' he burst out.
'Never! I've always said so.'

'You've never said so,' Alex contradicted. 'You've
always had a soft spot for her, and you know it.'

'She was too old for you and she was never good
enough.'

'Please, Father! This won't solve anything. All we can
do now is wait and pray.'

They sat in silence for a while, listening to the clock's
relentless tick, then Alex started suddenly.

'Poor Martins,' he said. 'I haven't given him a thought.
I suppose I should have a word with him – he'll be so
anxious about his sister.'

'What can you say?' asked Guy.

Alex shrugged. 'I don't know,' he admitted, 'but I must
let him know that I care. I'll go now; it will give me
something to do.'

He got up heavily. 'This waiting is bad for all of us.
Then I must ring Lucien. He'll be wondering why I

haven't been in touch again, but I was hoping for some good news.'

As the door closed behind him, Guy sighed deeply. 'You were always too good for her,' he growled. 'Always too good for all of them!'

After his talk with Grace's brother, Alex returned to the house and had just made his way into the library when his ears caught the sound of a carriage and wheels on the gravel drive. He was waiting for Fanny to appear with the caller's name when the door burst open and Lucien stood in the doorway.

'I had to come!' he burst out before Alex could greet him.

'There's still no news, I'm afraid,' Alex told him, keeping his voice as normal as possible. According to Nanny Webster this man – his own brother – had been his wife's lover. The thought still sickened him, but he had vowed never to speak of it to anyone else for in that way he imagined he could minimize the damage. He did not know that Lucien was aware he knew about the affair.

'It's not that.' Lucien closed the library door, but did not approach Alex. 'I've come about something else. About . . .' He hesitated. It was hardly the time to discuss his entanglement with Virginia, but his conscience would not let him rest. Also he was afraid that Alex would imagine the affair to be more serious that it had been. 'It's about Virginia and me.'

'I don't want to talk about it,' Alex said coldly. 'I simply assume it's over.'

'Of course it is,' Lucien told him eagerly. 'Long since, actually, but the fact is that it was never on. Not really. What I'm trying to say is that it never went . . . very far. I thought you might have the wrong idea.'

Alex could not look at him, although his heart leaped with sudden hope. He pointed to an armchair. 'Hadn't you better sit down,' he suggested. 'You look as though you are going to bolt at any moment.'

He was surprised and secretly impressed that his younger brother had had the courage to face him. He watched impassively as Lucien crossed to the chair and sat down, while he himself remained standing.

'I never would have believed it of you,' he said. 'I always imagined I could trust you with Virginia, even though I knew you found her attractive.'

Lucien could not meet his eyes. 'It started when I was a young lad,' he admitted. 'Puppy love, I suppose. Nothing more than that. Virginia was the first attractive woman I had ever known and she was so kind to me. She never made me feel gauche or insignificant.'

'I know. She had a knack – *has* a knack . . .' Alex corrected himself hastily and then fell silent.

'They'll come through, Alex,' said Lucien. 'I'm certain of it, I feel it in my bones. You mustn't give up hope.'

Alex shook his head. 'I thought that way at first, but now, as time goes on, I find it harder to be hopeful. In a way I don't want to hope. If the worst happens, the disappointment will seem so much greater.'

Lucien took a deep breath. 'Whether she survives or not, Alex, I want you to know that nothing serious happened between us, whatever Nanny Webster may have told you. Truly, it was . . . that is, we didn't . . . oh hell, Alex, it was just a final fling, if you like. Because Virginia knew about Eleanor and I suppose we both felt – dammit! I'm making things worse; I'm sorry.'

After a moment Alex asked, 'How did you learn about Nanny Webster? Was she blackmailing you, too?'

'Good Lord, no! And I had no idea she was blackmailing anyone until Virginia told me.'

'And when was that?'

Lucien realized suddenly that the conversation was leading him into forbidden waters, for he had promised Virginia not to tell anyone about the fatal accident.

'The day before she left,' he said cautiously.

Alex stared at him. 'Why didn't you tell me, for God's sake? Maybe I could have stopped her.'

'She made me promise, Alex, and she sounded so desperate. She said she had to confide in someone, but first she made me promise.'

'And you were so honourable that you felt you could

not break that promise!' Alex's tone was heavy with sarcasm and Lucien felt himself stammering a defence. 'I didn't know what she had done . . .'

Alex seized upon the word immediately. '*Done*? She hadn't *done* anything. It was what she was going to do!'

Lucien was beginning to regret coming to Berwick House. The confession was a mistake, he thought, but it was too late now. He must simply extricate himself as quickly as possible.

'Look,' he said as firmly as he could, 'I bitterly regret what happened between me and Virginia, and if you can find it in your heart to forgive me – '

'But you've just explained that there was virtually nothing to forgive!' Alex snapped. 'If that's the truth, then I wonder how Nanny Webster managed to extort money from Virginia? Don't treat me like a child, Lucien. I may have been too gullible, thinking I could trust my wife with my brother, but I'm not a complete fool.'

They glared at each other and as they did so for a brief moment the years slipped away and they were the two boys they had once been – quarrelling over a beloved toy, a missing rabbit, a childish lie or a petty jealousy. Always Lucien had won over his older brother with tears, guile or threats. Today both men knew that the issue involved could not so easily be resolved.

Lucien broke the silence. 'It was no more than a few passionate kisses,' he said, 'and a few caresses. Nothing more, Alex, I *swear* it. Oh yes, more than enough, I admit it. I'm not trying to excuse my part in it. I simply wanted to reassure you that we hadn't ever . . .'

'You needn't elaborate,' Alex said quickly.

There was a prolonged silence, broken by Alex who said, 'It all seems slightly academic now with this dreadful tragedy hanging over us.' He sighed deeply. 'If only I knew something! It's this uncertainty.'

'And I didn't know she meant to take the children, Alex,' Lucien told him. 'If I had known that, I would have told you, but she didn't mention them.'

'What exactly did she say?' Alex asked.

Lucien drew a deep breath and prayed for guidance.

'She told me that she was having an affair with Larry Scott and that she was going to join him on the *Titanic*. I urged her to talk to you first, but she was afraid to in case you persuaded her not to go. She thought she could do it if she had to go suddenly, but if she stopped to think about it she would change her mind.'

Alex turned towards the window so that his face was hidden from his brother. 'Did she say whose child it was?'

Lucien tossed up feverishly, knowing that whichever way he answered, there would be heartbreak. 'Virginia thought it was his,' he said slowly. 'She said she could always tell. She was afraid that if she stayed and you ever found out, you wouldn't love the child.'

'Poor Virginia,' Alex said softly.

Lucien decided suddenly that perhaps he should show Virginia in as good a light as possible, in case she was rescued and decided to return to England. It seemed likely that Larry Scott would be among those drowned – so many men had lost their lives. In that case, she would have nowhere to run to in America and if the murder was ever laid at her door, she would need all the love and support Alex could give her.

Lucien watched his brother hopefully. If Larry Scott were to emerge as the real villain of the piece, his own indiscretions would appear less odious by comparison.

'I think Larry Scott was putting pressure on her,' he ventured. 'I don't think she would have left you of her own accord; it was because of the child.'

Alex shook his head wearily. 'And how much does Eleanor know about all this?' he asked.

'Nothing!' cried Lucien. 'I don't want her to know anything.'

'No, you wouldn't, would you?' said Alex. 'You've treated us both very shabbily. I wouldn't like to be in your shoes, Lucien.'

Another silence followed, longer than the earlier one, then Alex said, 'The trouble is that I don't know whether or not I want her back. Isn't that terrible? First you and then Larry Scott. I'm beginning to think I never knew

Virginia. I seem to have been living with a stranger all these years. But I want my children back; I want Georgie and little Victoria. They've done nothing to deserve such a fate. And poor Miss Martins – she didn't want to go, but she wouldn't abandon the children. That's loyalty, Lucien, but you might not understand the word.'

He threw himself into the chair opposite his brother and closed his eyes.

Lucien swallowed. 'I deserved that,' he said. 'I'm not proud of my part in all this and I'd like you to forgive me, but I don't expect you can and that's understandable. I wouldn't in your shoes. I'll catch a train back; I won't stay.'

He stood up, feeling utterly worthless and thoroughly ashamed for the first time in his life. The sensation was not pleasant and he felt genuine remorse for the anguish he had caused his brother. At that moment he would have given anything to undo the mischief, but he was unable to do that and the knowledge hung heavily on his soul. Whether or not Virginia survived, Alex had already lost her. The wife he had loved for so many years had become someone else and that someone had betrayed him. Looking at Alex, Lucien was shocked by the haggard expression in the grey eyes. Once he had envied his brother his calm temperament. Now he understood that looks can be misleading and that beneath the quiet exterior Alex was suffering deeply. Lucien longed to take him in his arms but he knew he would be repulsed, and deservedly so.

'I wish you would hit me,' he said suddenly and to his horror he felt his lips tremble. 'Hit me!' he repeated desperately. 'Hurt me! For God's sake, Alex!'

Alex stood up and the two men looked long and painfully into each other's eyes – eyes full of grief and disillusionment. Then Alex said shakily, 'It's not easy, is it, being grown up? I used to think it would be.'

Tears brimmed in his eyes, then slipped down his face. He held out his arms, Lucien stumbled forward and they clung together trying to comfort each other.

When finally they drew apart, Alex said, 'Don't go.' And Lucien could only nod his gratitude.

*

Dinner in the kitchen that evening was a subdued meal. John Martins ate in silence, chewing the cold meat and cold potatoes without tasting them. His conscience pricked him, for he had snapped at Grace on that last occasion – too concerned with his own worries to pay any attention to hers – and now she might be drowned. He should have talked her out of the trip. Fanny sat next to him, her meal half-eaten, her eyes on the table, seeing nothing.

Mrs Wade cut a few more slices of bread and sent it round the table, but only Dot took one. She, too, was cast down by the general gloom, but her appetite was unimpaired.

'If you don't want your meat – ' she suggested to Fanny.

Without a word Fanny passed her plate and Dot helped herself to the last slice of pork.

'I don't know how you can sit there filling your face,' said Mrs Wade, 'with half the family maybe gone to their deaths.'

Dot scowled. 'Me starving myself won't bring them back,' she said. 'If it would, I'd willingly starve, but it won't and I'm hungry.' She glanced at John. 'No offence meant, but you know what I mean. Grace wouldn't want me to go hungry just because – '

'All right, Dot. That will do,' said Mrs Wade. 'Just eat it and keep quiet.'

Dot's temper flared. 'Anyone would think I'd committed a crime. All I said was, "If you don't want your meat." No point in wasting it. John doesn't mind, do you, John? The way you go on!'

John pushed back his plate, got up abruptly and walked out of the kitchen, slamming the door behind him.

Mrs Wade glared. 'Now look what you've done, you

454

silly girl. He's gone without his pudding and he loves apple pie.'

'Don't blame me. All I said – '

Fanny found her tongue. 'Shut up, can't you, Dot?'

'Oh, that's right! Now *you* start on me!'

Just then the back door opened and Stanley came in. He was waving the local newspaper and there was a gleam of excitement in his eyes.

'You'll never guess!' he told them. 'Not in a thousand years.'

'What?' cried Dot.

'They're safe!' cried Fanny. 'Oh, Stanley! They're safe! They are, aren't they?'

All eyes turned hopefully towards him.

'Hold on, Fanny,' he said. 'It's not about them; it's about someone else we know.'

The hope faded.

'I thought you'd seen the list of survivors,' said Mrs Wade.

'Well, what is it, then?' asked Dot.

Satisifed that he now had their undivided attention, he opened up the paper and began to read.

' "A fire broke out in number 11, Challis Court last Wednesday and severely damaged the house and those adjoining. The charred remains of a woman's body was found in a downstairs room and is believed to be that of the occupant . . . " ' He glanced up to see three faces staring at him blankly.

Mrs Wade frowned. 'Challis Court? We don't know anyone who lives in Challis Court, do we?'

Stanley went on, ' "who has been identified as . . . " ' He paused again.

'Stanley!' shouted Dot. 'Get on with it.'

' " . . . as Mary Agatha *Webster* who, neighbours say, was a retired nanny!" ' There was a stunned silence, then after a moment he read on. ' "A fire-engine was called and eventually the fire was controlled. Albert Stebbings, who lived next door but one to the deceased, told our reporter: 'She was a bit of a mystery and she drank a sight too much. She had no job that I could see, but never seemed short of cash for long.' The police have been unable to trace any next of kin. Foul play is not suspected." '

'Nanny Webster!' gasped Dot. 'So that's where she went.'

Fanny shuddered. 'Burned to death! What a terrible way to go.'

'Poor woman,' said Mrs Wade. 'You wouldn't wish that on your worst enemy. Here, Stanley, give us that paper. I want to read it again.'

He handed it over. 'There wouldn't be two retired nannies called Webster,' he said. 'It must be her.'

'Honestly,' said Fanny. 'It seems like it's nothing but disaster this week. Two in a row. They say troubles never come singly.'

'I hope they don't come in threes!' said Dot.

'Nanny Webster,' mused Mrs Wade. 'Well, maybe that's God paying his debts. She was a wicked woman, the way she treated those children. Perhaps she's got what she deserved.'

Mention of the children reminded everyone that they still did not know if they were alive or dead.

'If those kiddies have gone,' said Fanny, 'this house will never be the same again. My heart bleeds for poor Mr Latimer. First his wife runs away with another man – '

'We don't know that for sure.' Mrs Wade's tone was sharp.

'It's pretty obvious, though. Then their ship sinks. What's he ever done to deserve such rotten luck.'

'Nothing,' said Mrs Wade. 'Mr Latimer is a real gentleman and he deserves better luck.' She handed the newspaper back to Stanley. 'I'd keep that out of sight,' she told him. 'Don't want Mr Latimer to see it – He's got enough to worry about without that.' She went to the oven and brought out the pie.

Stanley said, 'Apple pie! My favourite.'

Mrs Wade grinned. 'I suppose you want a bit?'

'I wouldn't say "No".'

'Fetch up a chair then.'

She cut the pie into generous portions. 'And I don't want it wasted,' she told them. 'Dot's right; we can't help anyone and we've all got a long day ahead of us tomorrow.'

Stanley received his helping and said hopefully, 'Is there any custard?'

Dot got up sulkily. '*I* made it and I *know* it's a bit burnt, so don't all go moaning about it.'

'A bit of burnt custard never hurt anyone,' he assured her. 'Worse things happen at sea.'

There was a dismayed chorus of '*Stanley!*'

'What's up?' he asked but then immediately muttered 'Oh, sorry!'

*

The following day the first lists of survivors went up outside the office in Canute Street and Alex received the news that his wife and Larry Scott were among the dead. His children and their nanny were safe and well and would travel home on the Red Star liner *Lapland* with the surviving members of the crew. They would leave New York in three days' time on the 20th, and would dock at Plymouth nine days later.

That evening, after a few enquiries, he went to Millbank Street and asked for the Caseys. His first knock at the door went unanswered, but the second was answered by a woman with a baby in her arms. She looked deathly pale and there were circles under her eyes which were dark with misery. The baby stared up at her, a finger in its mouth.

'Yes?'

'Mrs Casey?'

'Who are you? If you're from the newspaper, you can hop it. I've nothing to say to – '

'I'm not from the newspapers,' he told her. 'I'm from Berwick House in Beaulieu – where your son once worked. I'm Alex Latimer.' He hesitated. 'I saw that your son . . . that young Pat – '

'That he drowned, you mean? Oh, you can say that

457

word to me, Mr Latimer. I've lived with it for years, ever since he was born.'

She became aware of curious neighbours. 'Will you come in?' she asked him. 'I've nothing much to offer you. A cup of tea maybe?'

'Thank you.' He stepped inside and followed her into the small kitchen where baby clothes hung on a line across the centre of the room.

Alex faced her awkwardly. 'I won't stay,' he told her. 'I can imagine what a bad time this is for me to call, but I had to come. I had to tell you how sorry I am. Patrick was a fine boy.'

'Yes, Mr Latimer, he was. One of the best.' Her voice was reasonably steady, he noticed, but a tell-tale muscle twitched below her left eye.

'Are you alone here?'

'My husband's at sea. So's my other boy. I've just got this one.'

'My wife . . .' Alex began. 'She was on the ship, too. She . . . she wasn't among the survivors.'

Ellen's expression changed. 'Your *wife's* gone? She was on the *Titanic*?'

He nodded. 'I heard this morning – so you see, I do know how you feel.'

'I'm sorry,' she said, 'about your wife. Got two kiddies, haven't you? Pat used to talk about them.'

'They were on the ship, but they were saved . . . and their nanny. I have to be thankful.'

Ellen shook her head. 'Poor kids. There's plenty round here lost their fathers, but a mother!' She sighed deeply. 'It's a very bad business, Mr Latimer, and someone's to blame. I'd like to know who it is. It won't bring folks back, I know, but someone's got to be responsible. Ships don't sink when they hit a bit of ice – specially *that* ship. I saw it with my own eyes. He wanted me to see her, like, before he sailed in her, so I went down to the docks. Did you see her, Mr Latimer? Did you *see* the *Titanic*?'

'No, but I've seen photographs.'

'Someone's slipped up somewhere. Someone's responsible for all those deaths. Question is, who is it? My guess is we'll never know. They hush these things up, Mr Latimer. The likes of us never get to know what's going on.'

'There'll be an enquiry,' he told her, 'both here and in New York.'

The baby whimpered and Ellen rocked it absent-mindedly while they both thought their own thoughts.

Then Alex said, 'I wanted to help you if I could. Times are hard and — '

He broke off and waved his hands in a gesture of futility. 'But what can I do? I can't bring your boy back. I'm so desperately sorry.'

She said suddenly, 'The trouble is there's nowhere to put a few flowers, that's what bothers me. I know it's silly, but I keep thinking . . . there'll be no *grave*. Nowhere I can maybe stand and look down at his name. At least with my other boy — I lost one with diphtheria — he's *somewhere*. He's got a bit of earth in the churchyard and a few words on a bit of a cross. Poor Pat's got nothing; he's just gone. Vanished. Same with your wife. See what I mean?'

'Yes, I do. I've thought of that and I thought I'd talk to the vicar. Maybe put up a small stone in the churchyard, or perhaps a plaque in the wall.' He looked at her eagerly. 'I could do the same for your boy. I'd be pleased to do it — if you like, that is?'

'A stone? Well, yes, if the parson would be agreeable. It would be something, wouldn't it?' Her lips quivered, but she took a long deep breath and blinked back the tears that glistened in her eyes. 'He would go to sea,' she said. 'I just couldn't stop him.'

'Do you think it was *meant* to happen,' he ventured, 'in some mysterious way that we can't begin to understand? I've thought about it and I still don't know, but it might be comforting to believe. Maybe people we love are given to us for a certain time, and we should be thankful for the time we have them with us. My cook believes that but I don't know if I do. If there was a plan, then it might not seem so terrible. If it is just sheer bad luck — a series of unfortunate circumstances — then it's harder to bear. My wife . . .' He stopped. 'All those poor souls – just because an iceberg happened to be in the wrong spot at the wrong time. It's almost *absurd*.'

Ellen shrugged. The baby whimpered and she moved it, bringing it to rest against her shoulder. 'To tell you the truth, Mr Latimer, I don't believe in much at all,' she said. 'Wish I did, but I don't. As far as I can see, you get up in the morning and work yourself to the bone just to keep body and soul together. Then something like this happens and it makes you wonder what it's all about.'

She glanced down at the baby. 'This one's hungry,' she said and Alex took the hint.

'Can I help you financially?' he asked. 'I'd be – '

'No, thank you, sir.' She gave him a straight look. 'We've enough coming in like, to see us comfortable, though it's more than some folks round here can say, with husbands gone – like her over the way, with five kiddies not started school yet. Twins she had last time. He was a trimmer, same as our Pat. And her cousin, Dora, further down, with an invalid mother to look after and another on the way. Her Albert was a fireman. Course, he was a bit older; he'd worked his way up, like. She went out like a light when she saw his name on the list. So they say; I wasn't there. Fainted clean away, she did and got trampled in the crush. Someone trod on her hand and tore all the skin off her fingers. They had to carry her home.' She sighed heavily. 'And then there's May in York Street – eight kiddies, she's got, and lost her husband *and* her father. Lord Mayor of London's starting up a fund, seemingly. If you've got a bit to spare, Mr Latimer, send it to him. There's plenty worse off than me. Knocked Southampton bad, this has. I don't reckon it'll ever be the same again.'

She followed him to the front door and as he replaced his hat she said, 'But that stone you mentioned – I'd be right pleased. Patrick John Casey. Born on – '

'I'll come back later for the details when I've spoken to the vicar.'

'Oh. All right. And Mr Latimer – '

'Yes.'

'When the grieving's done, you have to let them go. I learnt that when I lost my other boy. Somehow you have to let them go and get on with living. Your own turn'll come soon enough. A few flowers on a birthday – to remember them. That's all.'

He nodded, searched for suitable words and failed to find any. Their eyes met wordlessly and then he nodded again and turned away. For a moment or two Ellen watched him walk away, a slight figure with head bent, his shoulders hunched with defeat.

'You do your grieving,' she repeated softly, 'and then you let them go. That's the way, Mr Latimer. You'll learn.'

And she closed the door carefully and returned to her own grief.

*

The steamship *Lapland* arrived in Cowsend Bay in the early morning sunshine and Grace and the children were put on the first tender which went out to meet her. Members of the *Titanic*'s crew were being detained on board, partly to prevent them from talking to the waiting press and partly to allow them to give statements to officials of the White Star Line. With the rest of the *Lapland*'s passengers, Grace, George and Victoria were deposited on Millbay Docks where they expected to be met by Alex Latimer. To Grace, the knowledge that she was once more standing on British soil gave the moment an added glory and for the first time she allowed herself to believe they *were* safely home and that she *would* see Alex again.

She shaded her eyes with her hand and searched the waiting crowd.

'Nanny, is this England?' Victoria asked. 'Are you certain sure?'

'Certain, Victoria. It's Plymouth.'

'Then where's Papa? You said he'd be here to meet us and he *isn't* here.'

George said, 'He'll come, Toria. If he says something,

461

he does it. You know that time he said he'd take us to the fair? Well, he *did* take us.'

The children had to a large extent recovered from their ordeal, although Grace thought their father would detect a difference in them. George looked more serious, less of a child and more of a boy. They had both lost a little weight, but were otherwise in good health.

Suddenly George cried, 'There he is!' and raced forward as Alex pushed his way through the milling crowd and began to run towards them.

'Papa! Papa!' shrieked Victoria and not to be outdone she slipped her hand from Grace's and skipped forward.

Grace, a lump in her throat, watched as Alex knelt to put an arm round each of them. They have lost their mother, she reflected, but their father would see that they suffered as little as possible. Hopefully, they would grow up unscathed by the tragedy, because he was by far the most caring of the parents and she knew he would do his best to be both mother and father to them until such time as he remarried. She had thought about the situation very carefully and had come to terms with the idea that a man in Alex's position would be expected to take a second wife after a decent interval had elapsed. Now she waited for him to notice her.

Alex, holding George and Victoria by the hands, walked slowly towards her and thought how vulnerable she looked, a slim figure against the backdrop of water and sky. Various words of greeting flashed through his mind, but when at last he reached her he could only stare at her, choked by a rush of unexpected tenderness and overwhelmed with a burning sense of gratitude.

'You brought them back,' he said at last.

'Yes.' Her voice was low and husky.

'Oh, God!' he whispered and then, stepping forward, he pulled her into his arms.

Grace, taken by surprise, wished the moment could last for ever.

'Papa!' cried Victoria. She was shocked to see her father embracing Nanny and turned to George. 'He's *kissing* her now!'

George was equally stunned by the extraordinary sight, but he said, 'Yes, I know.'

Alex hastily released Grace, but he still held her hands, admiring her at arm's length.

'If you only knew . . .' he began. 'When I heard the news – '

Grace simply nodded, unable to tear her gaze away. If I have to die, she thought irreverently, let it be now while I am so happy, because nothing will ever be as good again as that moment when Alex's arms were around me and his mouth was pressed against mine.

'I thought I should never see any of you again,' he said. 'I thought . . . oh, God! I thought you had all gone.'

'I'm sorry about Mrs Latimer,' said Grace.

A little of the animation left his face. 'Yes,' he said. 'What a terrible death . . . and the baby, too.'

'I looked for her,' Grace assured him. 'I couldn't find her and the steward said we must go up to the boat-deck and Pat Casey – do you remember him – he came to tell me it was very serious. But I did look for her.'

'Good heavens, I'm not blaming you, Miss Martins, not for a moment. Please don't think that. You have saved my little ones. If anything had happened to George and Victoria . . . I had such terrible nightmares.'

He became aware of a continuing bustle of people around them and realized suddenly that he was still holding her hands and disengaged them.

'Where's your luggage?' he asked.

Grace managed a faint smile. 'We have nothing in the world except what we stand up in.' She thought incredulously, 'I don't have to make another decision. Not one. Alex is here and he'll look after us.'

As they walked towards the dock gates he asked, 'Where did you stay in New York?'

'With Harry's wife. I'll tell you about her some time.'

'Harry's wife?'

George said, 'Her husband was drowned. Poor Harry, he couldn't swim.'

'We played games with Harry's wife,' said Victoria.

We played "What have you got in your basket?" I said kangaroo, but George said – '

George interrupted her. 'Mama is drowned – and Mr Scott. Nanny says they've gone to heaven.'

Startled, Alex looked at Grace. 'They know?' he gasped.

'I thought it best.'

'But – '

'There was so much talk of death,' she told him. 'They accepted it; they cried, but they came to terms with it. Children are surprisingly tough, Mr Latimer. I really had no idea.'

He shook his head. 'My head's in such a whirl. I thought I would have to tell them and I was dreading it. Have I thanked you yet for bringing them back to me?'

'You don't have to thank me. We were just three of the lucky ones.'

'When I think what you've all been through – '

'It's over now,' she said. 'I want to forget it as quickly as I can.'

'I'm afraid the newspapers are full of it, and will be so for weeks to come. Oh, Grace! I mean Miss Martins . . .' He stopped.

Grace dared not meet his eyes. 'It doesn't matter,' she said and then to change the subject, asked, 'How is your father? I was afraid the shock might kill him.'

'He rallied marvellously after the initial despair, but he can't wait to see the children – and you, too, of course. Miss Martins, if you hadn't been on the ship with the children, I shudder to think what might have happened. It was so good of you to write me that note and I'm so grateful that you stayed with the children in spite of your doubts. It was all such a shock, but at least I knew you weren't involved willingly. It was a great comfort – I don't know why, but it was. By the way, I am increasing your salary – '

'Oh, that's not necessary. Please, Mr Latimer – '

He held up his hand to cut short her objections and went on, 'I shall also engage a nursery-maid. You will have sole charge of the children now and you must have help. You shall choose the girl and we'll do the interviews together. . . . oh, I do hope you don't mind, but Lucien and Eleanor are at home. Lucien came over to – to be with me, and then when we heard the good news Eleanor insisted on joining us. I may tell you, you are very high on their list of nice people!'

Grace laughed, a little embarrassed by the compliment, but he went on, 'Everyone is shouting your praises. You've brought back the little ones, you see, and they're so grateful. I'm afraid all the attention will swell your head!'

'I hope not,' she told him but then, confused by the look in his eyes, fell silent.

By this time they had reached the street and Stanley leaped down from the motor and greeted them rapturously. The children chattered endlessly on the way back, except when they passed through Southampton itself where the all-pervading sense of depression affected even their spirits and they watched in comparative silence as the sorrowing town revealed its heartache. Many of her citizens were in black, her flags were at half-mast. The imprint of disaster was stamped on every face and misery was obvious in every eye. In meeting such adversity, the inhabitants grieved as one while the town mourned its dead and struggled to adapt itself to the cruel vagaries of fortune.

Chapter Twenty-Three

15th April 1914. I can hardly believe, [Grace wrote] that two years have passed to this day since the *Titanic* went down – 'to her doom', as Dot will have it. This morning the entire household went to the Memorial Service and George and Victoria were very well behaved, I'm pleased to say. Afterwards, I met Pat Casey's mother and I told her all over again what I had told her last time, about Pat coming to our state-room to warn us. It always pleases her. George and Victoria laid flowers against Virginia's headstone and there were some on Pat's, too.

It seems strange at Berwick House without John and the brougham, but the job at the Hattons was very timely. Mr Hatton will soon be one of the few people round here who has gone back to horses, but it was understandable after his accident.

The new motor, a Talbot, arrived a fortnight ago (a week late – Alex was rather cross) and has been much admired. Stanley of course is like a dog with two tails. I'm glad he didn't leave us; he is his old cheerful self again without John.

Victoria still talks about her grandfather. She has taken his death very hard, but they had become very close with George away at school most of the time. I will talk to Alex about the possibility of finding a village girl to share her lessons. Maybe just the mornings.

Fanny looks very tired these last few weeks, but she will be leaving in a month's time to have the baby and devote herself to Alfred. They do seem quite well-suited, although Florrie would never have approved. In her estimation a housemaid for a daughter-in-law would be even worse than me! I'm to be a godmother, and Fanny is trying to screw up her courage to ask Alex to be godfather. I do so hope he says 'Yes' . . .

There was a tap at the door and Lucy's cheerful head appeared.

'I've bathed them and they're ready for their story,' she told Grace.

As Grace followed her into the children's bedroom, she thought how lucky they had been in their choice of nursery-maid. Lucy, sixteen, was slightly built with bright red hair and a personality to match. She was full of fun, but stood no nonsense from the children and Grace had every confidence in her.

The two children were sitting up in bed. Victoria clutched a new rag doll but George, now nine and a half, scorned such childish comforts. He had recently started at his prep. school, but was home for the Easter holidays.

He said crossly, 'I keep telling you I don't need Lucy to help me bath. I wish you'd tell her, Nanny. Matron doesn't help us at school. Lucy seems to think I'm still a baby, and I'm not.'

Secretly, Grace had been startled at the change in him. In two terms he had turned from a child to a schoolboy.

'Neither am I,' said Victoria, 'but I *like* Lucy to help me. She always says funny things – she says I'm a mermaid.'

George ignored his sister's interruption and went on earnestly, 'Will you tell her, Nanny, please? I am big enough and I don't want anyone to make me laugh. Nobody makes us laugh at school; we just have a bath and that's it.'

'I'll have a word with her,' she promised him, 'only you must wash behind your ears and in all the corners.'

He grinned suddenly. 'Now you sound like Matron.'

'I thought you said Matron doesn't help you bath?'

'She doesn't but she gives us a talk on the first day of term. It's awful! We all know it by heart.' He groaned and Victoria giggled.

Grace smiled. 'Well, just see that you do what Matron tells you and you won't go far wrong.'

467

'Stephen says – ' he began, but Victoria gave a shrill scream of amusement and clapped a hand over her mouth. Stephen was George's school-friend and he talked about him incessantly, quoting him as an irrefutable source on any and every subject.

'Stephen says! Stephen says!' she chanted.

'That will do,' said Grace, seeing George's expression change. 'If you waste any more time, there'll be no story.'

'We've got to choose a new one,' Victoria reminded her. 'We've finished *Coral Island*. It's my turn to choose and I want *The Weathercock*.'

George screwed his face into an expression of deep revulsion.

'That's girlish!' he cried. 'Horribly, utterly girlish, Nanny – and it's so long, it goes on for ever. I won't listen to it.'

To prove his point, he put a finger into each ear and glared defiantly at Grace.

'It is rather sugary,' Grace agreed. 'What about *The Secret Garden*, then – or Mrs Ewing's *Jackanapes?*'

Victoria cried, 'Don't say "what", say "pardon".'

Ignoring her, Grace repeated her suggestions and after a brief argument they finally agreed on the former. She took the book down from the shelf and began to read.

After about five minutes, Lucy looked in and said, 'I've tidied up. Shall I start the ironing?' and Grace nodded. 'Oh, and the master wants to see you,' Lucy added. 'As soon as you've a moment, he says. In the library.'

Ten minutes later Grace tucked the children up in bed, pleased that so far the new grown-up version of her beloved George had not resisted her 'Good night' kiss. No doubt if the worldly Stephen got to hear of it, he would prescribe firmly against such 'soppiness'. She smiled as she made her way along the passage and down the stairs to the library.

Alex stood up as she entered and she sat down in the chair he indicated. He smiled, but she sensed a certain reserve in his manner and wondered if she had done anything to displease him. Mentally, she checked through

468

the day's activities, but could think of nothing which might not have met with his approval.

He sat down in the chair opposite hers. 'I've been thinking . . .' he said, then stopped and stood up again.

He crossed to one of the windows, stood there in silence for a while and then swung round to face her. She was surprised to see how obviously ill at ease he was, and her heart sank. There was bad news coming, she felt sure.

'What is it?' she asked, unable to bear the suspense.

'Miss Martins,' he began. 'I've decided to make some changes. It's two years now since my wife died . . .' There was another silence.

Grace nodded encouragement, thinking that he never referred to Virginia by name. She was always 'my wife'.

'I'm thinking of the children,' he told her. 'They need a mother.'

She felt the colour drain from her face and hastily stared down at her hands which lay clasped in her lap. He was going to marry again! A dozen thoughts spun through her mind as she tried to hide her disappointment. She had enjoyed the past two years so much, and now everything would change. A new mother would come between her and the children. A new wife would be jealous of her relationship with them – might persuade Alex to remove her!

Bitterly Grace cursed her own stupidity. She had fallen into the very trap against which Mrs Wade had warned her so long ago, and had allowed herself to look upon the children as her own. Now they would have a new mother who would demand – and deserve – their undivided affection. Also, during the past two years Grace had become used to being consulted by Alex on matters concerning the children's welfare. She had accompanied him on his initial visit to Charters Close, George's prep. school. She had been given a free hand to choose their clothes, plan their meals, dream up their outings. She and Alex had taken them to the Zoo, and to Alexandra Park to see the balloons. She had thrived on the close relationship which had developed between herself and Alex, and

469

intuitively felt that he had enjoyed her company. He had even asked her advice on the redecoration of the morning room!

She shook her head. Not only had she allowed herself to grow too fond of the children; she had made the fatal mistake of attaching too much significance to the relationship that existed between herself and her employer. His gratitude for her care of the children during the *Titanic* disaster had created a strong bond and her subsequent role had changed in subtle ways. She had taken too much for granted . . .

Becoming aware that Alex was standing in front of her and composing her features as best she could, Grace looked up into his face and tried to prepare herself for the worst.

'I mean to marry again,' he said.

The words she had dreaded to hear echoed and re-echoed inside her head. The strange part was that she could not imagine who he intended to marry. There had been no rumours. Not even Fanny, with her habit of eavesdropping, had suggested a possible romance.

She heard her own voice: 'I'm sure I wish you every happiness.'

'She hasn't accepted me yet,' he told her, 'so your good wishes are a little premature.'

'No one could refuse you!' she blurted out and then, realizing how clumsy the words sounded, she felt herself blush. 'I didn't mean – ' she stammered.

'Miss Martins – oh, this is ridiculous! May I call you Grace?'

'Grace?' She was startled out of her embarrassment as he sat down abruptly.

'Grace, I'm making a mess of this,' he said. 'It's *you* I want to marry.'

Her eyes widened with disbelief.

'You want to marry *me?*' she repeated, stunned and incredulous.

'Yes. *You.* Oh, my poor Grace, don't look at me like that! I thought you must have guessed how I felt about you. Surely you could tell that – '

'No,' whispered Grace, still unwilling to trust her own ears. 'I couldn't. I thought we were good friends, that's all.' She looked at him pleadingly. 'Do you *mean* it?'

He gave a shaky smile. 'Of course I mean it. I know it's terribly sudden, but I hardly knew myself until a few days ago. I suddenly wondered why I felt so contented and I realized it was because of you. I realized that the happiest times of my life were when we were all together, and I thought that one day you might go off and marry someone . . . and leave us.' He took both her hands and pulled her to her feet. 'I wish you wouldn't look so shocked!'

'I'm sorry,' she said faintly. 'I just find it so hard to believe – '

'Grace, I *love* you. Maybe I always have. Oh please, just *say* you love me.'

'Of course I *love* you,' she said. 'I always have – from the first moment we met.'

He frowned.

'I was with John in the stables,' she reminded him.

'Oh yes.' Her words of acceptance were slowly registering in his brain and all at once a broad smile illuminated his face. 'So you *do* love me. Then you're going to say "Yes".'

But Grace still hung back, almost afraid to grasp the chance of happiness he was offering.

'Mr Latimer – '

'*Alex.*'

'Alex, then.' She took a deep breath. 'Alex, I *do* love you and I appreciate what you're offering, but couldn't I just stay on as I am? I'd hate to cause you embarrassment and . . . well, a man in your position marrying the nanny! It's just not done, is it, to marry your servant, I mean? I think it would cause a scandal, and I shouldn't like to think I had brought you down in any way. People would talk.'

'Let them. I don't care.'

'But I care, for *you*,' she cried. 'I'm never going to be a lady, Alex. Not in the way Virginia was a lady. No, please let me finish. I know I can learn how to use the

471

cutlery and I can dress in expensive clothes and wear perfume. But running the house, being a good hostess, knowing how things are *done* — even knowing what things to talk about. Alex, I would try my best, but trying won't make me a lady. Couldn't we stay as we are? You don't need to marry me. I could be your mistress in secret. No one need know and we'd be just as happy. If you married me and everyone was against us, you might grow to . . .' her voice dropped,' . . . to blame me. You might stop loving me. But if we stay as we are — '

'No, Grace.' He took hold of both her hands. 'It's all or nothing. I won't take you as my mistress, although I'll admit the thought crossed my mind.'

'There you are then,' she cried. 'We could do it!'

'The thought crossed my mind,' he repeated, 'and I at once rejected it and was ashamed of myself. You are the woman *I* love. You are the woman the *children* love. I want you to be my wife, Grace, and their mother. Nothing else is good enough for you. You may not be a lady by birth, but in every other respect you are a lady, Grace. You *think* like a lady and I love you.'

'Oh, Alex, I want so much to say "Yes" but — '

'Then say it, Grace, and we'll face the world together. I don't pretend there won't be talk. There might even be a scandal, but I'm prepared to face that if you are.'

'Oh, Alex, I'd face anything for myself, but it's you I fear for.'

He gave her a thoughtful look. 'Think about it this way,' he suggested with a faint smile. 'If I don't marry Grace Martins, I shall never take her as my mistress and I shall never marry anyone else. I'll grow older and lonelier and more frustrated until I'm just a nasty embittered old man. Everyone will hate me. Only you can save me from that terrible fate!'

Grace smiled, but she hesitated. 'What about the children?' she asked.

'They'll be delighted, I'm sure.'

'No, I mean the scandal. Will it hurt them?'

'Not if you and I are united. Anyway, these things die a natural death eventually.'

472

The words 'I will' hovered on her lips, but still she could not bring herself to utter them. She freed herself from his hands and walked away a few paces to stand beside the mantelpiece, one hand grasping it as though for support.

'If the scandal didn't die,' she said, turning towards him. 'If we have underestimated the way people will react . . . if the children were going to be affected as they grow older – could we move away somewhere?'

It was Alex's turn to hesitate. 'Leave Berwick House?'

'Yes. If it became necessary, could you do that? Could we leave it to Lucien and Eleanor and make a fresh start somewhere else? Another country, perhaps?'

He moved to stand beside her and his eyes were very serious.

'I could do it, Grace, and I would if it became necessary. I would go anywhere in the world with you. Please say you'll marry me. I know we could be happy. I would consider myself the most fortunate man to have you beside me always, and I'll make you happy in any and every way I can. I swear that none of us will ever regret it. I don't think anyone will begrudge us our chance of happiness.'

At last she was looking at him with shining eyes, her remaining doubts driven away by the logic of his arguments.

'I could give you a child,' she said softly. 'Maybe more than one.'

'That would be wonderful. Oh Grace, I love you! You do believe me, don't you?'

'I believe you.'

'And you will marry me? You haven't said you will.'

'I will marry you, Alex,' she told him. 'I *have* to. If I don't I shall stay an old maid because there will never be another man in my life.'

Gently, he pulled her closer and his arms went round her. His lips sought hers, but as Grace surrendered to his kiss she had no illusions about the future despite his reassurances. There would be problems and difficulties, she knew, even heartaches, but she felt a new strength

473

sweep through her and knew they would survive. She could face the whole world with a cheerful heart at the side of the man she loved. When he finally released her, he said, 'Tomorrow we'll buy you a ring, but now let's tell the children.'

GOLDEN TALLY

Pamela Oldfield

The triumphant conclusion of her epic saga of rural life

Vinnie Lawrence, the East End girl who married the Colonel's son, has been tragically widowed. Single-handed, and with immense courage, she has carried on running her beloved estate in the 'Garden of England'. But now there is family pressure for her to marry again . . .

Foxearth, they say, needs a new master. True, she is engaged to William le Brun, but she has been wearing his ring for two years now. She ought to be more grateful, says Cook, and hurry up and name the day. For old snobberies die hard at Foxearth, and neither servants nor villagers can forget Vinnie's humble origins in the hopfields she now owns.

But all their schemes and speculations are thrown to the winds when Vinnie is swept off her feet by a dashing French aviator, one of the first to fly the Channel. Handsome he certainly is, and devilishly charming. But is he the right sort of man for Vinnie . . . and, more importantly, for Foxearth?

FICTION
0 7515 0375 4

THE STATIONMASTER'S DAUGHTER

Pamela Oldfield

Tom Turner could have hoped for a better position than stationmaster of Gazedown, a small village in the heart of Kent. But a long-buried scandal had blighted his career – and dashed the hopes of his only daughter Amy. Instead of going to London to become a teacher, she has to look after the three menfolk in her family.

But previously unknown emotions erupt with the arrival of a fascinating stranger, the writer Ralph Allen – though there are rival contenders for his attention.

And Ralph provides the mysterious lure that sparks off events leading to final tragedy . . .

FICTION
0 7515 0132 8

LILY GOLIGHTLY

Pamela Oldfield

Lily Golightly has been married for just seven days – and
now she is alone. Her newly married husband, Patrick,
has set sail for New York to take up a position in his
uncle's firm, and she is eagerly awaiting a summons to
join him.

But Patrick has succumbed to gold fever and the
California Gold-rush, and Lily doesn't figure in his plans.

But she is determined to share his adventure and, together
with her housemaid, Lily embarks on a perilous journey
of hardship and deprivation, of pain, and love and loss,
and the bitterness of betrayal . . . The price of her
eventual happiness proves very high indeed.

FICTION
0 7515 0869 1

LONG DARK SUMMER

Pamela Oldfield

Life seems full of promise for Sophie Devine, young wife
and mother of two. But it is 1665 and, as spring gives
way to summer, the shadow of plague hangs over
London.

When the city is finally stricken, Sophie is offered a safe
haven for herself and the children on her brother's farm
in Woolwich. Fanny, their maid, is left behind in London
to care for her master, but discovers that Matthew is in
love with someone else.

Stunned by the knowledge of his infidelity, Sophie is
forced to return to a London now ravaged by sickness
and death to try to win back his love – and finds herself
also fighting for his health, and her own feelings for Luke
Meredith, one of the few dedicated doctors to remain in
the beleaguered city . . .

FICTION
0 7515 0137 9